DMETRI KAKMI is the author of *The Dictionary of a Gadfly* (as The Sozzled Scribbler), *The Door and Other Uncanny Tales, Mother Land* and *When We Were Young* (as editor). For 15 years he worked as a senior editor at Penguin Books. He was also fiction/non-fiction co-editor for the online literary journal *Kalliope X*. His essays and short stories appear in various anthologies. *Mother Land* was shortlisted for the NSW Premier's Literary Awards in 2008. *Haunting Matilda* was shortlisted for Best Fantasy Novella for the Aurealis Awards in 2013.

THE WOMAN IN THE WELL

DMETRI KAKMI

The Woman in the Well

ISBN-13: 978-1-923382-11-4

IFWG Publishing International
Gold Coast

www.ifwgpublishing.com

For Effie and Leigh.

"Earth and Ocean seem
  To sleep in one another's arms, and dream
  Of waves, flowers, clouds, woods, rocks, and all that we
  Read in their smiles and call reality."

  P. B. Shelley

CHAPTER 1

Once there was and once there wasn't.

Caught in a moment between being and non-being, the irretrievable yesterday, the malleable today, and the ill-defined tomorrow, I opened my eyes and told myself I must be dreaming. I had emerged from one dream to fall into another, without realising it. This could not be real. None of it could be happening. It had nothing to do with who I was and the safe, predictable life I led. Yet there I was, in a tent, in the desert south of Kulgera, near the South Australian border.

What was I doing there? What had I been thinking when I left my comfortable existence in Alice Springs for this? Silently cursing myself, I lay still and pricked up my ears.

A sound had woken me up.

It couldn't be the silence. I was used to that. All the same, the quiet in that lonely place was in a league of its own. I hadn't heard anything quite like it. It was oppressive, as if I was underwater with my ears blocked.

There it was again. Singing. Or was it chanting?

Whatever it was, it lodged an unsettling sensation in my bones.

For a moment, I thought that we were near an Aboriginal encampment. Maybe what I heard was a ceremonial song? But, no, this struck a different note from the haunting, rhythmic wailing Aborigines produce when they sing. This was more ominous and European.

I sat up. In the half-light I noticed Harun's sleeping bag was empty, a cast-off skin beside me. Alarm swept through me as I opened the tent door, the zipper making an excessive noise as I pulled it down. I was a light sleeper. I ought to have heard the boy open it. As the plastic flap peeled back, I saw Dom a few feet away. She sat with her back to me, staring at the campfire.

The flames flickered inside the ring of stones, intensified until they were almost blinding, a startling luminescence in the surrounding gloom. Too bright, too painful, to look at. They guttered, sputtered, making a gusting sound, as of many wings flapping, and froze.

Static, as though the gods had pressed pause on existence.

Nothing moved. Everything stood still.

Shielding my eyes, I rose to my feet. I was the only moving figure in a motionless world. A river of stars poured overhead, some large as diamonds, others tiny as dust motes, distant and remote. Galaxies, the sweep of the cosmos, making me feel as if I was falling up into the firmament. It was bitter cold. I trembled, stamped my feet and hugged myself to keep warm. Breath came in puffs of smoke that froze in front of my face, speech bubbles with nothing to say.

I stood in front of Dom and uttered her name.

No response. Wrapped in a black fleece hoodie and a blue blanket, she was still as a statue, her right arm outstretched in the act of throwing kindling on the fire.

"Are you alright?"

Still nothing. Not even a blink when I passed my hand in front of her face.

"I'm definitely dreaming," I told myself. Dom would have slapped my hand away and told me to get lost.

My attention was drawn away by something else. A smell. I straightened, sniffed like a dog, and screwed up my nose. Attar of roses, sweet and cloying. Revolting. How I hated that fragrance. What was it doing out here, in the desert? It wasn't coming from Dom, that's for sure. Going by the way she looked and smelled, I doubt she showered often, let alone dabbed perfume behind her ears.

I followed the aroma in the direction of the trees. When we arrived the previous day, I'd parked the van in a clearing, between the cemetery and a well surrounded by she-oaks. The smell was coming from there. So was the singing. I turned in that direction and did a double-take.

Seven naked boys stood around the well, holding hands and intoning in high, flutey voices the oddest lyric.

> *I am dying, looking to survive.*
> *My pleas roil fields, woods and plains.*
> *Without you, O Mother, no destiny is known aright,*
> *No deliverance be gained…*

Harun's reedy pitch climbed above Adam's deeper tones, only to be matched by Rashid's robust inflection. The curious gathering was cast in the brightness that shone on them from the fire and the starlight, tossing distorted shadows of bare branches and moving human forms on the ground.

To turn a man into woman and woman into man are yours, Alila.
Fecundity, replenishment, to grow, to spread are yours, Alila…

I approached on stealthy legs. Too afraid to make a sound in case they were sleepwalking and I startled them. I needn't have worried. They were oblivious to my presence, moving slowly in an anticlockwise direction around the well, from which, I swear, an eerie song emerged. No words. Only a curious string instrument from bygone times, lilting, swaying, answering as they sang.

To raise greenwoods are yours, Alila.
To be black, to be white are yours, Alila.

The chanting reached a vibrant, trilling pitch, building in cadence and tonality, rising and falling, simultaneously melancholy, ineffably beautiful and frightening. It was difficult to tell if it was a musical instrument or a human voice; it sounded like both. Glass on glass, music of the spheres. The smell of attar was strongest among the trees. Almost suffocating. I gagged, coughed. My head reeled. I clamped a hand over my mouth to stop from vomiting. It brought back a smothering avalanche of memories. Things I would rather forget. Panic flared in my stomach and brain. Every instinct told me to run. But I couldn't. I had to look after my charges. Besides, I was spellbound, drawn against my will, to the well around which they danced, putting one bare foot in front of the other, slender arms lifting and dropping in joyous dance.

Darkness darker than darkness is yours, O Mother,
It is graven within the hills, upon the dust, within the rock…

Water bubbled from the well and ran down the sides. "But that can't be," I told myself. It was dry a few hours ago. I had thrown a rock into it and heard it clatter in the depths.

The song reached a triumphant, jubilant tonality and stopped. Smell dissipated.

I was three or four paces from the boys when a scream erupted from the pit. It was horrendous, of such tremendous, terrifying proportions that it hurt every cell of the body. My heart missed a beat. Blood froze. The hair on my arms and on the back of my neck stood up. I clamped my hands over my ears and closed my eyes.

"Go away. Go away."

It did, ringing like a bell and climbing higher, until it disappeared.

Immediately, the dancers snapped out of the trance. Broke the circle and walked to their respective tents as if nothing had happened. All except Harun.

He cupped his hands and scooped water from the well. "Drink," he said, coming to me; and I did, unreservedly slurping, as if I had been dying of thirst and had not known it. When I finished, Harun kissed me on the lips. "Welcome back," he said, and returned to our tent, dropping to his knees as he crawled inside.

Dom hadn't moved. I made sure the other boys were safe in their tents and went back to the grove. Even though I was terrified, I had to find out who or what had produced the blood-curdling screams.

The crumbling stone wall around the well came up to my waist. It was held together by tangled roots and native grasses sprouting from cracks, drooping and colourless.

As though responding to my nearness, the strain started again. Ineffably soft, intimate, communing with me alone. I peered over the edge.

A face looked up at me, broken and distorted, dancing to the subtle movement of liquid.

Startled, I pulled back. The face performed the same action.

I laughed nervously. *It's your own reflection, idiot,* I thought.

I was about to look again when my attention was drawn to a curious sound coming from above. I looked up and saw that the previously dead trees had come to life, every branch covered with green leaf and butter-yellow flowers. Sage pods sprouted at high speed and burst, spraying the quivering air with coffee-coloured seeds. They were absorbed on the instant by the soil and germinated, pushing dozens of tender, fresh shoots around my feet.

New growth writhed and twisted, like eager worms, turning in moments to saplings, fed by trickling rivulets on dry soil. Life unfurled until I was surrounded by verdant greenery, where there had been, a short time ago, dust. Roots cracked open, shedding old skin and turning from black and brittle to mahogany. A milky substance oozed and mixed with water around my toes.

"Magnolia."

A voice, wavering and glassy.

"Who is it?"

"Magnolia," the cruelly caressing voice repeated. "Get me out of here."

More screams. This time my own.

Time kicked in…

CHAPTER 2

THIRTEEN HOURS EARLIER

My name is Magnolia Din-Olden. I'm Afghan-Aboriginal, twenty-eight years old, and I live in Alice Springs. The town was named after a white settler's wife and I can only hope she was prettier than the outpost that bears her name. All the same, I love the place and I wouldn't dream of living anywhere else.

On the day the story begins, you might have seen me crossing the hospital carpark, clutching a paper bag filled with pears and thinking of nothing more than seeing my grandmother, when a man blocked my way between two cars.

Morning, late March. The weather warm and the air rippling across the tops of cars, as if reality was disintegrating.

"Magnolia?"

His voice was a snake sliding through kangaroo grass, putting me on high alert.

I came to a halt between a red hatchback and a dusty white trailer with a workman's ladder secured to the top. Surprised that anyone had spoken to me (the residents of our fair hamlet usually step around me), I felt caught out, trapped. My insides quivered.

"What?"

I pulled the pears closer to my chest with the left arm and wrapped my right hand around the keys in my track-suit pants pocket, ready to strike if he tried anything.

He was tall and good looking. Black as coal, thin and gleaming. But the yellow eyes sent a shiver down my spine. I wasn't sure if it was fear or eroticism.

"I am Malachi."

He enunciated each letter of the name carefully, as if I ought to be familiar with it.

Looking at him through a tangle of hair, I became aware of a foul smell. It emanated from his mouth as he spoke, as if there was an open sewer inside him. I screwed up my face and scanned the surrounds for other people. There was no one. If he tried anything, I would have to back out between the cars and run for it.

"Someone wants to meet you," he continued.

"Oh, yeah, who?"

"George Green."

Again, he said the name as if I ought to know who he was talking about.

"Don't know anyone by that name. Excuse me, I've got to go."

"He knows you."

I looked up at him. He glared down at me. And for a moment, I was so afraid I almost pissed myself. I bit down on my fear, stepped back, and looked him determinedly in the eye.

Now that I really looked at him, Malachi was oddly familiar. His face was imprinted on a subterranean part my mind, as if the blueprint was part of my DNA.

"Have we met before?" I asked.

"In your dreams."

He grinned and I had the distinct impression this guy enjoyed hurting women.

"Yeah, well," I said, my insides quivering, "I'll be your worst nightmare if you don't get out of my way."

I was grateful for the fact that he didn't rise to the challenge. I don't know where I would have found the strength and the courage to do anything about it.

"Spoken like a true daughter of your mother."

"You know her?"

"The beginning, the end, all the way to the dawn."

"You're full of shit," I said. "Get out of my way."

He showed big, sharp teeth, like a cartoon shark grinning at a human dinner. And again, I had the feeling I was being toyed with.

"What does this George want?" I said, back-tracking as I talked.

He stepped closer and I noticed the strange way his limbs moved inside the oversized grey polyester pants. As if the legs were broken or there was something wrong with the knee joints.

"A job," he said.

"I have a job."

I stepped around the hatchback to my right and headed for the hospital's automatic doors. Malachi's next words stopped me in my tracks.

"Do you recognise this?"

I turned. A pendant hung from a silver chain at the end of one finger. Hypnotised, I walked back. It was my pendant. The one I lost many years ago. No doubt about it. I would know it anywhere. A silver ring encircled a black-and-white magpie with outstretched wings. I reached out to take it and he snatched it back.

"It's mine," I said.

"George Green will give it to you when you come to see him."

He withdrew a cream-coloured card from a pocket and, holding it between two fingers, passed it over with a flourish. I examined the address written in dark blue ink on elegant matt board.

"He lives around the corner from Nan's," I observed.

"How convenient."

"When does he want to see me?"

"Midday."

I looked at my wristwatch. Over an hour away. It was on the other side of town, but I could make it, if I cut short my visit with Nan.

"Tell him I'll be there."

I wasn't interested in a new job. I wanted the pendant, and I was willing to go against my better judgement, risk anything, to retrieve it. I turned to leave. Malachi's next words stopped me a second time.

"Give my regards to Cherry."

He smiled, the white teeth sparkling.

"You know my grandmother?"

"We go back."

"Funny, she's never mentioned you."

"Very remiss of her."

I didn't like the way he said that. There was a hint of mockery behind the words. In fact, I didn't like him at all. He was downright oily and repulsive.

Malachi's withdrawal, executed with stealth and agility, took place between rows of parked vehicles. It was only when he vanished behind a green four-wheel drive that I realised what had bothered me about him. His feet. They appeared to be on backwards. But surely that couldn't be. I was imagining things. How could a man have his feet twisted backwards and still walk? And there was something about the way the knees bent beneath the ill-fitting pants. Yet I was sure that he had walked away from me with the front of his body facing me and the feet turned right around in the direction he was going. Of course, that couldn't be right.

I told myself I was having 'a mental aberration'—an expression

I'd read in a novel and liked. It was the heat, getting up early for the morning school bus shift, and yesterday's migraine. Life was getting to me, making me see things. Still, the way Malachi's lower half moved was unsettling. It put me in mind of something I had read in a book or seen in a film perhaps. Try as I might, I couldn't think what it was.

It was a pleasure to step into the hospital's cool, clean foyer. And as I headed for the bank of elevators that would take me to the wards on the first floor, I was thinking I must not mention Malachi to Nan. She had enough on her plate as it was. Besides, I didn't believe for a minute someone like Malachi would know my grandmother.

CHAPTER 3

Despite my resolution to say nothing about Malachi to Nan, the first words out of my mouth when I reached Ward 7 were: "You won't believe what just happened." I bit my tongue, but it was too late.

She smiled and said, "What?"

I couldn't keep anything from Nan. It had been our daily ritual ever since I could remember, to sit down and have a good natter over a cup of hot, milky tea, while she smoked a cigarette or five in the backyard. I'd missed that ritual while she was in hospital.

Kissing her on the cheek, I dumped the fruit on the bedside table and plonked myself down in a chair.

Nan was short, round, and in her late sixties. Greying hair pulled back from chubby cheeks, she sat up in a narrow bed in a plain room with three other berths. Light blue curtains were neatly pulled back from windows to allow the sky to enter. Only one other cot was occupied and its occupant, an elderly Aboriginal man, appeared to be asleep. Nan's left leg was raised in a stiff horizontal formation under the white sheet. Though somewhat ashen in a teal hospital gown, she continued to look at me with bright, expectant eyes.

"Well, what happened?" she repeated.

"Met an old friend of yours in the carpark," I said, trying to make light of the unnerving encounter.

I took her soft, warm hand and gave it a squeeze. Air-conditioning hummed and chemical smells permeated the air.

"Who?"

"Malachi."

The smile vanished. Her eyes drifted from the ward to another time and place. Perhaps she might not have taken another breath if the man in the next berth had not chosen that moment to release a phlegmy cough that startled her back to the present.

"Are you alright?" I said to her.

"Don't know anyone by that name."

She was lying.

"An old flame, maybe?" I teased. "He was attractive, if you like 'em oleaginous."

"What's that mean?"

"Oily."

"You and your big words."

I dropped it. I could tell the conversation would go no further. I'd lived with Nan long enough to recognise her no-go areas. There weren't many, but they were significant. One was the absence of a husband. The other was my mother—actually, that was my forbidden zone, but we both adhered to it for different reasons.

"Anyway," I added, changing the subject, "he offered me a job."

The frown returned to her face. "Doing what?"

"Don't know. I'm going to find out later."

"Why?"

"Why what?"

"A stranger offers you a job in a carpark and you're thinking of accepting it," she said, raising her voice.

Embarrassed, I looked behind me to make sure the old guy wasn't listening.

"I didn't say I was accepting it," I whispered. "I'm just going to the interview."

"Why?"

I didn't want to tell her about the magpie pendant; that too came with a complicated history.

"You're always saying I should aim higher."

Nan shifted to a more comfortable position in the bed, the loose skin under her chin wobbling as she moved.

"That's true. Whatever this job is, it can't be worse than driving a school bus."

"Don't start that again."

The topic of my career, or lack thereof, had been thrashed many times over the years. Nan couldn't understand why, given my apparently splendid qualifications, I didn't have a job worthy of my talents, as she perceived them. As for me, I couldn't imagine working in an office, taking orders from someone I would doubtless come to despise. Driving kids to school, being outside, pretty much my own boss, was as close as I could come to holding down a job.

"I didn't pay for your education so you can drive a bus," she said, not for the first time. "You could do something with that nursing whatchamacallit."

"Nursing degree," I said, sorry I'd mentioned the encounter in the carpark. "And I didn't come here to talk about that. How are you?"

"Don't change the subject. I don't want you going to this interview."

"Please don't shout."

"I'm not shouting," Nan shouted; the guy behind me shifted in his bed, the stiff bedclothes rustling. "I don't want you going anywhere near this man."

"Thought you didn't know him."

"I don't want you taking risks."

"Yeah, yeah," I said, thinking that uncertainty, precariousness, was exactly what had entered our lives since last Friday.

We dwelled in silence for a while, each one lost in her own thoughts. I had known my grandmother all my life; we got on like a house on fire. Raised voices and arguments were not part of our relationship. But so much weirdness had happened the last couple of days that it was bound to come out one way or another.

"Did the cops interview you?" I asked.

"They were here earlier."

"What did they say?"

"Wanted to know what I saw last Friday."

"What did you see, Nan?"

I pushed the tangles of hair behind my ears and turned a steady gaze on my grandmother. Too afraid of upsetting her, I hadn't raised the subject with her earlier.

She shrugged, pulled a face.

"Nothing."

"You must have seen something."

"I learned long ago to close my eyes and let life roll on, as it should."

"Right," I said, thinking that didn't sound like her at all. She was usually forthright. We looked at each other for a moment, intimations of unspoken dread weighing down our lips. Me trying not to think about how life would change if my grandmother had died and she…well, all I could see was fear—dread and hurt she could not admit because she was such a tough customer.

"Well," I said, "you copped a bullet in the shoulder and another in the leg. That's more than enough for anybody."

"Should have been discharged today, if it wasn't for the pain in my leg," she said.

"You've only been here three days, Nan."

"How long do I have to stay?"

"Don't complain. You know what they're like in hospitals. Get you out quick as possible, even if you're bleeding."

She laughed. "Hurts like a bastard."

Nan was a straight-talker. It came from years as a barmaid and holding down a part-time job in a petrol station. She was not one to watch her language or to complain. Rolling up her sleeves and getting on with the job was more her style. You knew something was wrong if she grizzled.

"Get them to increase your pain killers."

"Honey, if they give me more of that stuff, I'm going to start floating around the room."

"Hey, Cherry, tell her what happened last night," said the man in the next bed.

I turned and looked at him, a black man with straight white hair combed back from a creased forehead.

"No one's talking to you, Jack," Nan said.

"Go on," the man persisted. "Tell her."

"What's he talking about?"

"Hallucinations," she said, glaring at him over my shoulder.

"What do you mean?"

Nan busied herself with the covers and pillows, straightening this, fluffing that.

"Nan."

"It was nothing, okay? Just a dream."

"She saw a man at the end of the bed," the man said behind me.

"You talk too much, Jack."

"Maybe it was a doctor or a nurse," I put in, leaning closer to my grandmother.

"Never seen a doctor who looks like that before," she said.

"What did he look like?"

"Tall and thin with eyes like a wild animal." Nan shuddered.

I pointed at Jack. "Maybe it was him going to the toilet."

"Hey," he said. "I'm better looking than that. Aren't I, Cherry?" He grinned and rolled over on his back to stare at the silent television suspended from the ceiling.

"You are, Jack," Nan reassured. "Anyway, he was gone when I turned on the light."

"Did anyone else see him?"

She shook her head. "It was late."

I gave her hand a reassuring squeeze, not knowing what to say. Nan had described, with uncanny accuracy, the man in the carpark.

"It was a dream," Nan said.

"I'm sure."

"But it reminded me of something."

"What did it remind you of, Nan?"

"It happened long ago, when I was fifteen," she said, looking across the room as if she could see through the wall. "In Ti Tree, where I grew up. One evening, I was walking past an abandoned house at the end of our street. Mum warned me not to go near the place because, according to Muslims, ifrits live in ruins."

"Oh," I said, thinking about Malachi.

"Anyway, I'm scooting past when I see a face in the window," Nan went on.

"Who was it?"

"It was almost dark," she said, ignoring the question. "There was a candle in front of him, throwing weird shadows over his face. He just stared, like the man last night, and then he licked his lips, as if he'd seen a nice juicy roast chicken straight out the oven." She shuddered. "It was revolting."

"You think it was an ifrit?"

Nan nodded, shrugged, shook her head. Yes, don't know, no, all in one eloquent gesture.

I didn't know what to say. Stories like this were common when you grow up with an Afghan grandmother and an Aboriginal father. Ancestral spirits, talking animals, djinns, sentient trees and rocks… It was part and parcel of who you are and the legacy you carry. You don't even think about it; it just is.

"Ifrit," I whispered.

"You know what that is?" Nan said.

I nodded. I had encountered the word in my favourite book, *The Arabian Nights*, and in the hadith she used to read to me when I was little.

"It's a kind of djinn," I said, "wicked and malevolent."

"Their feet are on backwards," Nan put in for good measure.

"Ifrit," I repeated.

Is that what I had seen, an ifrit, in the carpark? It was unnerving to hear the word spoken in a hospital. It sucked the light from the ward and muffled the sounds. Even the clock above the door seemed to be affected, the seconds hand jerking back and forth on the spot, stuck between ten and eleven.

"Cut it out, you two," Jack said. "You're giving me the creeps."

Nan laughed. The room brightened.

"Sorry, Jack," she said. "Got carried away."

The clock started to work again. It was almost eleven forty. I ought to leave if I was going to meet the man who had my pendant. It was a ten-or-so minute drive across town to Larapinta, the suburb where, according to his card, George Green lived a mere block away from the house I shared with Nan.

"Anangu got 'em too," the man said.

"What was that, Jack?" Nan looked at him over my head.

"We got 'em too. What you call ifrits. We call 'em 'feather feet'."

"Feather feet," I said, turning to look at him.

Jack nodded. "Yeah, from the Tjukurpa, creeping around at night, watching people sleep, leave no footprints."

"Shut up, you old fool. What are you trying to do, give me a heart attack?" Nan cried.

I gave an uneasy laugh and stood up.

"I should go. Let you rest," I said.

Nan nodded absently. I was about to plant a kiss on her forehead when she gripped my right wrist.

"Today is twenty-two years since your mum died," she said.

It was as if I heard her from a great distance. Her bed retreated from me as if down a long corridor. A loud thudding filled my ears, like the rush of blood. I was aware that one half of me was standing beside her, looking at her loving face, while the other half of me ran wildly for the exit. Anything to not hear her talk about her dead daughter.

"It'd be nice if you went to the mosque and said a prayer for her," Nan said.

"No."

"It's time you two buried the hatchet, that's all…"

I was already in the corridor with doctors and nurses coming and going, patients lying in dejected beds, bleeps and beeps coming from machines working to keep them alive. Yet I could still feel Nan's grip on my wrist, warm and moist where the skin had touched, and as I drifted out the entrance into the carpark, I imagined her talking to Jack about me.

"I hope she doesn't take unnecessary risks," she was saying.

"She looks like a sensible girl," Jack replied.

It was true. I was the embodiment of prudence, circumspection and caution. Never stepping out of my prescribed circle, and never seeking risk or instability. But I had every intention of going against my nature that day. All for the sake of a pendant that meant the world to me. And although my heart thudded with fear and my legs quaked as I walked to my car, I reassured myself that everything would be alright.

What was the word Jack used to describe an ifrit in the local Aboriginal language?

Feather Feet.

"Yes," I thought, "I prefer Feather Feet. It sounds less scary than ifrit."

Feather Feet leaves no trace. You don't even know it had been. Whereas an ifrit can cause great harm.

CHAPTER 4

George Green's house was located in the scrub, several hundred metres beyond the end of Rubina Street. I had lived in the neighbourhood most of my life and had never seen this place before. Given how all the residents knew each other more or less by name and lived in cookie-cutter brick suburban homes, I could not think how I could have missed the unusual mud-brick house with a turf roof. It was so different from the other residences. "Must be new," I told myself, shrugging it off. There had, after all, been much development around here the last few years. I followed a dirt path to the front door, knocked and waited in the dappled light filtering through spindly ghost gums.

A young man opened the door. He had a mane of thick, dark-brown hair and an incongruously white beard, closely clipped to a handsome face. The loose-fitting, bottle-green linen suit matched the colour of his eyes and his smile immediately dispelled any misgiving I might have had about visiting a stranger.

"Welcome," he said. "I'm George."

He presented a smart picture, making me aware I had not gone to any trouble with my own attire. Not that I ever did. Formless grey tracksuit pants and long-sleeve sports shirts that hid—among other offences—the lacerations on my wrists and forearms made up my wardrobe.

I stepped into a dim interior. George pointed to my left.

"We can talk here."

The study was a book-lined nook with a timber desk and computer in front of an open window. Cream-coloured lace curtains drifted in the breeze. George waved me to an armchair covered in faded blue velvet and took a seat opposite in a fancy wood chair with lions' heads carved into the armrests. He offered water. I accepted, and noted with pleasure the mint and lemon afloat in the tall glass.

"What's this about?" I said, coming straight to the point.

George crossed his legs and smiled.

"I have a job you can't refuse."

"You don't say."

Despite my timid appearance, I could be stubborn, especially when someone presumed to tell me what I could and could not do.

"I need you to drive seven boys home."

Not what I was expecting.

"And where is home?"

"Marree."

"That's a long way from Alice Springs," I stammered.

There was absolutely no way I was driving all that way. Anything could happen between here and there.

"You will be amply rewarded." George leaned forward. "How does two hundred and fifty thousand dollars sound? It will be transferred to your bank account before you leave."

"It's not that," I said, despite the fact I had never seen that much money in my life. "I need to be in town at the moment."

"For your grandmother."

I nodded. "Besides, I don't want the responsibility. Driving kids all that way is a big ask."

"You do it every day."

"Around town. Not across the desert. And that's another thing," I added, grasping at straws. "I have a responsibility to the kids I drive to school every day. I can't just dump them."

"I'm sure you will find a way."

I leaned back in the seat, sighed, and stared out the window. Life in Alice Springs was safe, comfortable, predictable. I knew how it would play out from one day to the next. I had gone to a lot of trouble to make sure it stayed that way. I had organised things so that nothing new or unexpected could shatter the placid routine I had constructed. Until Nan was shot in the leg, that is, proving the lie to the illusion that we control our lives.

"Meet the boys," George said, rising from the chair. "Everything will change when you see them."

"Why me?" I said, rising too.

George made a sweeping gesture with his right arm. "What have you got to lose?"

The presumption that I had nothing else going for me made me angry. Nevertheless, it was true. "My enviable position as a single twenty-eight-year-old woman who lives with her grandmother," I said.

"I fought long and hard for that reputation, you know."

George chuckled.

I might have added that I loved to drive. Despite being scared of my own shadow, there was no greater thrill than to put my rickety old motor through its paces on the way to work. And I adored sitting behind the bus's big wheel, trundling through town, taking kids to school in the morning and ferrying them home in the afternoon, through familiar streets. It was a form of freedom and power I could control. Sometimes, though, when restlessness bubbled inside and I didn't know what I was doing with my life, I wondered what it might be like to floor the accelerator and keep going. Pure fantasy, of course. I would never do it. Too scared of things going wrong. Too afraid of the unpredictability and randomness of life. It was easier to stay put than to go. But it was okay to dream, wasn't it?

"Come," George said.

I followed him down a corridor to a light-filled sitting room and kitchen at the back. It overlooked a backyard thickly planted with Witchetty bushes and desert oak. Seven boys sat at a table in the shade of a corkwood tree. The murmur of voices and subdued laughter came through the closed French doors.

"You see," George said with another sweep of the hand.

"Yes…"

I believe in all sorts of things. Magic, the sentience of the earth, and in the wondrous potential of the cosmos. I had read books on cosmology, astronomy, philosophy and esoterica, and I knew I was an insignificant dust mote in the vastness of the universe. I believed, or wanted to believe, which is perhaps the same thing, that there was no such thing as a random act. Everything happened for a reason and every act, no matter how minute, was interconnected. Humanity walked every moment through causal links, unknown and unseen, that waited to interlace and bring about a secret, sacred possibility. Despite wanting to believe I was a free agent, for me there was only an immutable plan, waiting to fall into place. That is why I was not surprised by what happened next.

I was entranced by the scene before me. A spell was cast by the bright, smiling, youthful faces. A feeling of lightness, like a fresh wind, swept through me, setting off mysterious chimes I hadn't known existed. They stirred currents deep inside, making me feel as if I was lifted, carried, and connected to each boy. They represented an answer to a question I had yet to ask.

What's more, they seemed familiar, as if I had seen them before. I knew them. And yet I did not.

The French doors opened and a girlishly pretty boy in a blue uniform and white skullcap stepped through. He was carrying a glass carafe that was too big for his tiny hands.

"Can I have more juice, please?" he said to George.

"Harun, meet Magnolia," George said.

The boy turned to me. "Hello."

"Nice to meet you, Harun."

I took his extended little wing in mine and knew what it must be like to hold a hatchling. I could crush it if I wanted to or, alternatively, give it love and affection.

The trusting, innocent face, the warmth of his skin, cut deep. For reasons I did not understand, I was profoundly affected. Tears brimmed and I had to turn away to regain composure.

"Introduce Magnolia to the others," George said. "I'll bring drinks."

Harun led me outside. Nightmare of nightmares, six pairs of eyes turned on me, making me feel scrutinised, assessed, judged. I shrank, horrified. What's worse, they were all boys. Like never before, I was aware of the picture I must present to these dazzling beings: a fright with unkempt hair and clothes dug haphazardly from a charity bin late at night. I had always wanted to make myself invisible and had thus far succeed. Now a spotlight was turned on, making me the centre of attention.

All rose courteously from the table, an orchestra of noise as chairs scraped on the paving and fingers touched the red checked cloth on which food and drink rested. All were attired in the same blue tunic, blue pants and white skullcap.

Harun introduced me to the gathering, adding that I was taking them home.

"That's up for discussion," I mumbled, pushing hair from my face and lacing it behind an ear.

Harun pulled me forward. I was surprised by the intimacy of his hand in my mine, the strength of it.

The others stood in line. Watching them, I thought of a documentary where the narrator noted how a school of fish was made of thousands of individuals but they moved as one. They turned and flashed in the water in perfect harmony, never bumping into one another or losing the fluid movement that was directed like a ballet. The boys reminded me of that school of fish.

Harun pointed to a boy with a five o'clock shadow.

"That's Adam."

"Pleased to meet you," the older boy said, bowing his head.

Harun pulled me along and pointed to the next boy in line.

"This is Rashid."

The others guffawed.

"That's not Rashid," Adam said. "That's Salih."

Harun was momentarily confused. "I thought it was Rashid."

"He can't recognise us yet," said a bulky boy with red hair. The others smiled and nodded in an indulgent fashion.

"Let me do this." Adam put a hand on Harun's shoulder. "Finish your lunch. Looks like you need more fuel."

Harun returned to the table and fell to eating in an oddly mechanical manner, shovelling food in his mouth as though refuelling.

Normally, when I meet new people, I don't remember their names seconds after they are introduced. There was no need. I was hardly going to become good friends with them and go out for coffee. Yet the names of these boys stayed with me as Adam took over the introductions.

"You already know Harun," he said, pointing to the seated boy. "He's the youngest." He turned to two boys who looked alike. "This is Salih and Zaman."

"They're twins, in case you're wondering," said the solid boy with freckles and red hair.

"Thanks, Rashid," Adam said. "I think the facts speak for themselves. Magnolia, this is Rashid. He's fourteen and he craves attention."

Rashid gave me a firm handshake, almost wrenching my shoulder from the socket.

"Next is Musa. He's eleven."

The others laughed good-naturedly as a broomstick of a boy with buck teeth stepped forward, floating inside the uniform.

"They are radiant," I thought. It was like looking into the heart of an exploding star.

Following Rashid's example, Musa shook my hand and stepped back.

"Last but not least," Adam continued, "is Kagan. Say hello to the lady, Kagan."

A small boy with beautiful lips stepped forward. "Hello." His voice was high, making me think of church bells in mountain air. Not that I had ever heard church bells ring in mountain air.

"It's nice to meet you," I said, feeling like the Queen of England. I pulled up the sleeve on my left arm and scratched vigorously, more out of nerves than anything else, and then I quickly yanked it down when I realised I had exposed the discoloured scars on my wrist.

No one appeared to notice.

"Have you been to Marree?" Kagan asked.

"No."

"You will now," Harun said, looking up from his demolished meal.

"I will?"

He nodded. "George said."

Disappointment flitted across his face when I said, "That's on the negotiating table. Finish your lunch, boys. Don't let me interrupt."

They returned to their seats and began wolfing down bowls of fragrant lentils that made my mouth water.

George appeared with a lacquered tray containing a jug of apple juice.

"Adam, pour a glass for Harun." He placed the tray on the table and looked at me. "Let's continue the discussion inside."

"Good idea," I said, glad to step into the dark interior, where I belonged.

CHAPTER 5

I took the same chair in the study. Feeling weirdly discombobulated after the encounter in the courtyard, I'd misjudged how low the chair was placed, sat too soon, and fell further than expected before my backside made jolting contact with the seat. It added to the discomfort I felt. To regain composure, I stared at the computer screensaver image—a flooded forest, tree trunks rising from the deluge to cast wavering reflections on the surface of the water. It was simultaneously restful and disturbing.

George's next words took me by surprise.

"You don't remember me, Magnolia."

He sat opposite and crossed one long leg over the other, a self-contained figure that seemed to have little to do with the world around him.

I narrowed my eyes and looked at him with renewed interest. "No." I shook my head, even though the question had been niggling me since I saw him. George Green was vaguely familiar, but I could not place him.

"Think," he said and when that yielded no results: "Thirteen years ago…when you woke up in your bed…" I held my breath and waited for him to utter the dreaded words. But he didn't. He was discreet and sensitive, and I was grateful for the small mercy that followed: "…to find a man sitting beside you."

I nodded, relieved. Of course. How could I forget? Much as I had tried.

The young man with dark hair and the white beard—so out of place on that unlined, young face, perched at the end of my bed.

"That's when you took my pendant."

He nodded, opened the desk drawer and handed over the item in question. I grabbed it, clipped it around my neck, and closed my right fist over the magpie. It felt cool and familiar, despite the fact I hadn't touched it in over a decade.

"Do you remember what we talked about?" George pursued.

I shook my head. It was a lifetime ago. Thirteen years and one month to be precise. I was fifteen years old.

"I thought it was a dream…"

"Do you remember the name I mentioned?"

I shook my head again. I didn't want to go there. Every cell in my body rebelled against it. Even so, I visualised the scene that played out on the day I had opened my eyes and sat up in bed to find a stranger in my room saying the most improbable things.

"Her name was Ali," I said.

George shook his head.

I tried two or three variations on a theme before hitting the mark. "Alila."

He nodded, satisfied. "What else do you remember?"

I stood before a black hole, afraid to look in and unable to look away.

George leaned forward. "This is important."

The room darkened. Walls closed in. A hush fell. I was underwater and could not hear a thing. After sitting in the chair, hunched up, feeling trapped and wanting to run away for several minutes, I looked at him and almost shouted, "I don't know."

"Take your time. It's important you get there by yourself."

Get there by myself? What was this, a counselling session? I'd had enough of them over the years. I closed my eyes again and walked around a blank spot in my memory, so dark nothing could be seen. "Concentrate on getting to the other side," I told myself, "like skirting a lake. See what's there, deal with the rest later."

"You said Alila wanted two things from me."

"What did she want?"

"That's when you took the pendant. Why?"

"Djinn are creatures of the air. If they take one of your possessions, you'll never get rid of them. They can find you anywhere."

He uttered the words as if it was perfectly normal to make such outlandish pronouncements in a room with a desk and a computer. I accepted it. Although my mind was already rebelling, rising in a foment against it.

"What was the second thing Alila wanted?"

It was hard to cast my mind back, especially as I had gone to so much trouble to forget.

"She wanted me to do something for her."

"Alila makes her claim now."

With these words, the study brightened. The air cleared. The walls withdrew. Birds sang. I saw and heard properly again. The shelves crammed with books. The computer screen with the image of a drowning world.

"Are you saying I have to accept this job? I have no choice?"

There was a look of pity in his gaze. "There's always a choice, Magnolia. You made yours years ago."

Only I didn't feel like I had; I was forced into it. The challenge I shot him with my eyes made him sit back in the chair. There was no point in arguing the absurdity of the situation. A djinni wanted me to chauffeur a bunch of schoolboys to Marree. Ridiculous. Yet this man believed it.

"What if I refuse?"

"Malachi will kill your grandmother."

He was matter-of-fact. Not a sign of malice or hostility.

"Are you threatening me?"

"It's a statement of fact. You owe Alila. She will not let you forget it."

"And you allow this?"

"I have no control over Malachi. He serves his mistress. There's nothing he won't do for her. I know that too well."

I wanted to call the police. But I remained seated, clutching the pendant, breathing slowly through the nose and out the mouth to control the mounting anger. I gritted my teeth and thought, "How dare this man make threats? How dare he tell me what to do? Who does he think he is? He can't control me." But I bit down on my rage. I also knew I needed to keep calm. I could not let my temper take over. No good would come of it. Besides, I had seen Malachi. I knew what he was capable of doing. The sly, crafty man who oozed sadism.

"Is he really an ifrit?"

George gestured with his hands as if to say it is what it is.

"And Alila is really a djinni."

This time he bowed his head in acknowledgement. "You know what a djinni is, don't you Magnolia?"

Of course I knew about the djinn. But they were myths, fables, cautionary tales. They did not exist. Even if they did, they were in the Middle East, not in Central Australia. They had no place here, where Aboriginal ancestral beings ruled.

My head swam thinking about it. The best thing to do was to stay grounded and talk about real things.

"It's a big responsibility," I stammered.

"You will not be alone. You will be accompanied by an adult."

"I need a reliable car."

"Taken care of."

"It's about twelve hours to Marree. Over a thousand kays."

George turned in his chair and drew a piece of paper towards him across the polished surface of the desk. "This is a carefully planned operation. Come here, I'll show you the course you *must* follow and the stops you *must* make."

I stood and leaned over him to study a crude, hand-drawn map of the Stuart Highway, where a thick red line snaked south from Alice Springs to Marree. It looked like a child had drawn it, adding to the absurdity of the situation.

George traced a finger along the paper as he spoke. "First day, you drive from Alice Springs to Kulgera." His finger tapped a spot south of the town. Comically, it was marked with an X, like a treasure map. "There's a campsite beside a cemetery. You stay there overnight. Tents and food are provided."

"Why don't we stay in a motel? The town's a bit dodgy, but it's better than sleeping in a tent."

"It's important you follow instructions to the letter."

I tapped the map. "Go on."

"The first day is the shortest part of the trip. Alice Springs to Kulgera. That's what—?"

"Three or four hours."

"The next day is a bit more arduous," George went on. "You drive from Kulgera to Coober Pedy. Then you make your way to William Creek"—his finger moved east from the Stuart Highway to the Oodnadatta Track—"You spend the second night in an abandoned train station south-east of William Creek. Here." Again, he tapped a spot marked with an X.

"Wow, first-class accommodation. Cemeteries, ruins. What's next, Dracula's castle?"

"Next day," he said, ignoring me, "you drive to the Marree mosque."

I shook my head. "Yeah, but I don't want to go to Marree."

"Why not?"

"My grandmother has a saying about Marree."

"Your grandmother isn't coming with you."

"She said if the shit's gonna hit the fan, it's going to happen in Marree."

George's smile was indulgent. "Altogether the trip will take three days. Monday Kulgera. Tuesday William Creek. Wednesday Marree. You will be back in Alice Springs on Thursday."

"If we leave today."

"Correct."

My voice rose to a pitch. "You want me to leave today? This is insane."

"There's a dark moon tonight. It will last three days. It's important you complete the trip when there is no moon. You return to Alice Springs on the night of the new moon, which is Thursday, in four days' time. Do you understand?"

It's true I did not have much of a social life. Like many solitary people, however, I had a rich inner world. It came from extensive reading across a broad range of topics and daydreaming. As I often said to my grandmother, I knew a little about everything and not a lot about anything. I knew enough about the phases of earth's natural satellite to know the significance of a dark moon.

"Is this some kind of witchcraft?"

"Call it a ritual."

Taking a deep breath, I turned around and faced two bookshelves crammed with paperbacks, leaflets and pamphlets, *The Arabian Nights* and Ovid's *Metamorphosis* among them.

"Who are these kids anyway?"

"They were at the mosque last Friday."

"No one said anything about survivors."

"You know what the media is like."

That did not sound right, but I was too tired, too bewildered, to argue. Suddenly, an immense lassitude took over and all I wanted was to go home and sleep.

"Can I tell you something?" I asked.

"Go ahead."

A peculiar calm descended when I stopped fighting and accepted the inevitable. It looked like I was going, whether I liked it or not. It did not matter what I revealed to this man because, for all intents and purposes, I had known him for a considerable time.

"It's strange," I said, unable to look at him. "My first impression of those boys out there was that they are in love with life. They're full to the brim with it. They are life. It's in the way they eat and drink and look at the world." I hesitated before going on. "They're so light, they made me feel heavy."

George was silent behind me.

I faced him. "I want what they have."

"What do they have?"

"Life." I turned my back on him again, embarrassed. "Freedom. Can I ask a question?"

"Go ahead."

"Why me?"

"You asked that before."

"You didn't answer."

"The winds blow where there is fear and anxiety. And with them come the djinn."

I faced him again and cracked a smile. "I've no idea what that means."

"It means you invited the djinn into your life and now you must deal with them."

More mumbo jumbo.

"When do we leave?"

"Immediately. You must be in Kulgera by nightfall."

"Who's the other person? He better know how to change a flat tyre or a blown gasket, whatever that is."

George rose to his feet. "Wait here," he said, leaving the room.

I sat and waited. George returned minutes later with a blonde woman in tight blue jeans and a tighter white, sleeveless shirt.

"You!" I cried, shooting to my feet.

CHAPTER 6

"Yep, me."

The woman grinned and the past rushed back.

Despite the astonishing thinness, Dominique Device was every bit as ravishing as I remembered. Except now she had short-cropped hair and a silver ring in the right nostril. Elaborate tattoo sleeves covered both arms.

When Dominique left Alice Springs thirteen years ago, I thought about her all the time. First thing in the morning, last thing at night. I missed her so much, I thought I would die. As weeks turned to months and then years, abandonment, loss, grief, loneliness turned to hate, anger and resentment towards my ex-girlfriend. These emotions, in turn, transformed to a dull ache that found home deep inside me. In time, the name Dominique Device became synonymous with abandonment, hurt and pain. With Dominique's departure, everything I secretly believed about myself was proven to be true. I was not loved and everyone walked out on me. Mum, Dad, Dominique… Even so, I could not have predicted how I would react if I met Dominique again. I had been fifteen years old at the time and Dominique sixteen. Now we were adults. Yet there she was, grinning at me, as if years had not passed. In that moment, love and hate collided and everything I'd held on to came pouring out.

"You must be kidding," I said to George. "You can't trust her with kids. She wouldn't know what to do with them, except maybe dump them by the roadside."

The grin faded from Dominique's face, her eyes hardened. "But you can definitely trust a suicidal neurotic to drive your precious cargo across the country. Is that it, Missy Din?"

My insides boiled. The old temper flared, and I almost lunged at her.

George stepped between us. "Dominique is coming with you," he told me.

"Why her?"

"You need a mechanic and a security guard."

"She couldn't secure her bra if she tried. If she wears one."

Dominique did not miss a beat. "When you've got 'em, flaunt 'em, baby. At least I don't slash and burn myself. What's with the sack cloth you're wearing, anyway? Are you ashamed of your body or does it pass for lesbo chic in this backwater?"

It was a low blow. Yet I was hooked. The remark about 'slash and burn' told me Dominique kept tabs. She knew about the years of self-harm I went through after she left—cutting myself with razors, deliberately burning my hands on stovetops, cigarette butts on thighs. Dominique knew, which meant she cared. The realisation surged through me, making me feel elated, hopeful and pathetic all at once.

"Enough." The steel in George's voice stopped further bickering. "You have issues. I'm going to let you figure it out for yourselves. Is that alright, Magnolia?" I nodded, without looking at him. "Dominique?" She nodded, too, glaring at me.

George left. We stared at the floor, like naughty schoolgirls caught pulling each other's hair. Neither of us spoke for what seemed an eternity.

Dominique was first to break the silence.

"Can we be adult about this?"

She moved to take hold of my arm.

"Don't touch me," I screamed, backing away.

She raised both hands in the air. "No touching."

Her fingers were adorned with chunky silver rings. Some skulls and snarling wolves' heads. Another looked like snakes' fangs curled back across the middle finger of the left hand. The fingernails were painted with chipped, dark-red nail polish. That, together with the pixie haircut and eyes outlined in black, made her look like a feral 1960s actress. If only she did not have those ugly tattoos on her arms, she would be perfect.

"Why did it have to be you?"

"I have no choice in the matter."

"What's he got on you?" I said, thinking of the pact I had unwittingly made with the djinn all those years ago—the year Dominique left.

She ignored the question. "For the record, I didn't know you were involved until I got here. George offered me a job. Flew me here business class, no less. Guess I'm good at what I do."

"What, ruin lives?"

"What are you talking about?"

"You ran out on me when I needed you."

"Move on, Missy Din." Dominique flopped into the armchair as if the air had gone out of her.

"Did it mean so little to you?"

"Alright, don't move on. See if I care."

My voice snagged when I said, "I can't move on. I'm stuck." I stared at the hallway, aware that George was probably out there, listening. I had never felt so low, humiliated and exposed. My eyes snagged on a small water colour hanging in the corridor. It depicted a windblown tree on a lonesome moor, and it expressed exactly how I felt at that moment.

Dominique stood up and came to me. "Sit down," she said indicating the chair previously occupied by George.

I sat. Dominique took the armchair, crossing her legs and folding her hands across her flat belly. We were close, knees almost touching. The nearness allowed me to examine her properly. Her skin was grey, pallid, stretched paper-thin over bone. She did not look well. She had gone to great lengths to camouflage dark circles under her eyes and spots on her face with thick applications of make-up and totally failed. I was embarrassed for her. I started off:

"You said 'See you on the other side.' But you weren't there when I woke up."

"I got scared."

"Scared?" Hot tears streaked my cheeks; the pain I had pushed down bubbled to the surface. I felt stupid, foolish, crying in front of a person I barely knew. Or knew only in the past and then only briefly.

"Scared," Dominique repeated. "I freaked out when I saw what you did."

"You instigated it."

"Doesn't mean I can't change my mind. It's not as if you get a second chance in life."

I sniffed. My fingers gripped the ends of my sleeves and pulled them down over my hands, terrified the evidence of my folly was visible.

"I saved your life," she went on.

"You condemned me to hell. I'm walking around, talking, but I'm dead inside. I died when you walked out on me."

I tried to stand, but she held me down with a firm grip.

"Forgive me," she said, sounding sincere.

I didn't know if I had it in me to forgive, let alone trust.

"Come on," Dominique said, leaning back in the chair and crossing her arms behind her head, exposing hairy armpits. "Doesn't your bible preach forgiveness?"

"It's called the Quran."

"Whatever. There must be something about forgiveness in the Koran. Or does it just teach people how to blow themselves up?"

Dominique's irreverence had always been her saving grace. At least that had not changed.

"I don't know," I said, melting a little. "It's not that easy."

"What have to you got to lose?"

I inclined my head at the door. "He asked me that too."

"What did you say?"

"I have nothing to lose," I said, feeling like a loser.

"And everything to gain."

Instead of making me feel better, the statement highlighted my supreme worthlessness. The failure of my life washed over me.

"It's only four days," Dominique said. "You'll never see or hear from me again after that. And we'll be rich. It's like taking candy from babies." She stood up, pushed my hair out of my face and saw the magpie pendant around my neck. "Still wearing that piece of junk."

"Dad gave me that piece of junk, thank you very much."

"Say no more," she said, casting a glance at the corridor.

"The magpie was Dad's totem. It's my good luck charm."

"How's your gran?"

"In hospital."

"I'm sorry."

"You weren't to blame."

I uttered the familiar refrain automatically, with a hint of a smile, so that Dominique was compelled to sing a couple of bars from our favourite movie song when we were teenagers and very much in love: "Put the blame on Mame, boys. Put the blame on Mame…" She pivoted on the spot, wiggled, smiled, clicked her fingers and swayed bony hips.

"Make no mistake," I said. "I'm not coming for you. I'm coming to keep the kids safe from you."

Another shrug. "Whatever rocks your boat."

"What do you know about this trip?" I said, dropping my voice. "It sounds dodgy. There's something…I don't know, that he's not telling me."

"I know all I need to know."

"What did he tell you?" I was wondering if Dominique had been clued in about the djinni and the ifrit. Now that I was speaking to a normal person, George's story sounded downright ridiculous. It was easy to believe he was a madman with more money than sense.

"Just that I'm your right-hand woman. Car repairs, support, that sort of thing."

"I think there's something fishy about driving seven Muslim boys across the country, after what happened at the mosque last Friday."

"I don't ask questions when someone hands me that much moolah."

I couldn't shake the feeling Dominique was also holding back on me.

"I'm the driver," I said, "and you're the bodyguard. Sounds like the start of a bad road movie."

"So long as we don't end up like Thelma and Louise."

George came into the room at that moment. "What's the verdict?"

"You win," I said to him.

"No, you win."

My eyes travelled from George to Dominique. Standing side by side, grinning at me, they looked like the proverbial cat with a canary in its mouth.

"I'll pack a bag and come back in an hour," I said, desperate to get away from their scrutiny.

"Make it fifteen minutes," George said.

I clicked my heels and skedaddled out of there.

CHAPTER 7

At home, I picked up the phone on the kitchen wall and dialled my boss at Charter Central.

"Ted, it's Magnolia. I hate to do this, but I need the rest of the week off."

"You better be sick as a dog."

Teddy Koopah did not approve of leave-taking.

I was planning on using my migraines as an excuse but, on a sudden inspiration, I told him I needed to take time off to care for my grandmother. Teddy had a soft spot for her.

"How is Cherry?"

"She's coming out of hospital. I need to pick her up and look after her for a couple of days."

"It's short notice, luv. Not sure I can replace you for this afternoon's rounds."

"Nobby Clarke's available. Give him a buzz."

"I expect you back Monday."

"No worries."

Then I dialled Nan's mobile. The first thing she said was: "Are you safe?"

"Of course."

"I was worried—"

"I have to tell you something and you're not going to like it."

"You're taking the job."

"How did you know?"

"You can't hide anything from me, lovely. What do they want you to do?"

"Drive some school kids down south."

"And?"

"That's it. You don't mind, do you? I know I should be here, but I can get Leah and her cronies to come in and see you every day—"

"Don't do it," Nan interrupted. "I've got a bad feeling about this."

"You won't believe how much they're paying."

"I don't care about the money. I lost your mother. I don't want to lose you as well."

"Two hundred and fifty thousand," I said, regardless.

She whistled, causing me to hold the phone away from my ear. "Sounds dodgy to me. You're not a drug mule, are you?"

"Nan, we'd be set up for life."

"Who's hiring you?"

"Remember the doctor who looked after me when…you know…when I wasn't well."

A pause. "There was no doctor, lovely."

"His name's George Green."

"I don't know anyone by that name."

I wanted to say, "That's what you said about Malachi as well." But I bit my tongue.

"He was there when I woke up."

"I was there when you woke up."

"He came whenever you left. I thought he was your friend."

"Why are you doing this?"

"I told you. The money."

"Why are you really doing it?"

It was a good question. I had been speeding along since going to George Green's house. Now I threw on the brakes. Nan and I were close. There were no secrets between us. Even so, I could hardly tell her that an ifrit was going to kill her if I did not do as I was told, let alone that I was doing a favour for a djinni.

"The truth?" I said.

"That'd help."

"Something came over me when I was in that house. It's as if I'm being offered a second chance."

"At what?"

All my defences came down.

"Life, Nan. Life. You have to admit, I've stuffed up bad. There's so much regret. So much I wish I could fix or undo. Get my life back on track…"

"We all have those moments, but we don't go shooting off across the country at the drop of a hat."

"Who wouldn't like to stand at the crossroads and be able to take a completely different direction to the one that has made them who they are?"

I was surprised by the sentiment. It sounded like a postcard cliche. Even so, I had not thought to sum up my life in quite those terms until that moment. And it seemed to be another kind of truth to the one I could not admit to Nan.

"I'll call every day. And I'll speak to Leah about visiting you."

"Are you going to be by yourself with those kids?"

"Here it comes," I thought. I counted four heartbeats before saying, "Someone is coming with me."

"Who?"

"Dom."

"I see."

My grandmother was well versed in the legend that was Dominique Device. She'd picked up the pieces after the relationship ended.

"It's not what you think."

"What do I think?"

I did not trust myself to speak. I had never been more ashamed of myself. Never had I felt that I risked so much for what was, in essence, so little. Yet I could not let the opportunity pass.

"I'm not doing it for her."

"Why are you doing it?"

"Maybe I am doing it a little bit for her. The door is still open on what happened between Dom and me. I want to close it."

"As long as you're sure that's all."

I thought for a moment. When the words came out, I talked as if I was discovering my thoughts as I spoke, which was ever thus with me. I did not really stop to think, question or probe into aspects of my life. Only went along, hoping for the best, and expecting the worst.

"I'm not in love with her, if that's what you mean. More intrigued. I want to know who she is. If that makes sense."

"You want closure."

I had no faith in the therapeutic cliches of 'closure' and 'moving on'. Far as I was concerned that was Anglo middle-class bullshit. You do not move on and you do not get over life's calamities. You learn to live with them. You made friends with them, sinking it all into yourself and making it part of who you are.

"Let's just say I want to close one chapter in my life and open another. All that aside," I went on, "I accepted the job because of the boys. You should see them. There's something really special about them and, I don't know, I feel like I have to look after them."

"You're always going on about wanting kids." I could hear the smile in her voice. "Here's your chance to find out what it's really like."

"Was it difficult for you?"

"I was a single mum. What do you expect?" She sighed and I could almost hear the cogs whir in her head, going back to the past. "But that's all done and dusted now, aye?"

A single mother. That was more than she had ever told me about raising my mum.

"What was Grandad like?"

"Ancient history," Nan said, her voice going cold. "Instead of asking questions about things best forgotten, why don't you go to the mosque and say a prayer for your mum? She passed away twenty-two years ago today."

"Can't."

Another silence.

"Nan, I just need you to say yes to this."

"I can't stop you. Your fate is written on your forehead. I only ask one thing."

"What?"

"Come back double the woman you were when you left."

I hung up and stood in the doorway between kitchen and living room, listening to my heartbeat. Then I went to my bedroom.

After throwing a few random things in a small overnight bag, I went to my dressing table and opened an Egyptian style jewellery box I'd bought from an op shop. I took out a small, embroidered pouch and peered inside. The clump of my mother's golden hair was oddly faded, gathering dust over the years. Together with my dad's magpie pendant, it constituted a link to a familial past I could not let go. Despite my feelings about Mum, her hair and Dad's pendant were, in a way, my good luck charms. I couldn't leave town without them.

I tucked the pouch with the hair in a side pocket in the bag and flung myself on the bed, knowing full well I did not have the time to indulge. Yet I was determined to be defiant, to assert myself. It was my rebellion. My way of giving George Green the finger, telling him he was forcing me to do this against my will. But I was going to do it in my own good time. And in my own way.

My mind wandered as my head sank into the soft pillow. The last time I saw Dominique we had been fifteen and sixteen years old, respectively. Both of us had sprawled on this bed, in this room. Back then, we planned to set off on an entirely different kind of journey. One from which you did not return. And here we were again, thirteen years later, setting off on yet another trip. I was even stretched out on the same mattress we sat on to perform that final act of love and devotion. Nan could not remove the bloodstains that seeped through the bedsheets, and since she could not afford to buy a new mattress for me, we turned it over and I slept on my own dried blood, night after night, on the altar of my folly and disgrace.

Was it punishment or twisted comfort?

Chapter 8

"Let's get this show on the road."

When I returned to George's place, Dom was in the passenger seat of a sleek, black van. Left arm hanging out the open window, she banged the panelling with the flat of her palm, cigarette between fingers, and looking very much the part of an anti-hero in a bad Hollywood film. The denim jacket and gold aviator sunglasses completed the picture.

"Hold your horses," I said, rushing over.

"Glad to see you went to some trouble with your travel outfit," Dom said, glancing at me over the top of the sunglasses.

She was being sarcastic. I had not changed out of the grey tracksuit pants and oversized black hoodie I had been wearing earlier.

Ignoring her, I threw my bag on the empty seat between us, slipped into the driver's seat, and turned to inspect my passengers.

"Roll call," I said, eyes registering which boy sat where and next to whom with the expertise of one who has worked with children for a significant time and knew the importance of remembering who, what and where in case of emergency. "Let's see if I can remember your names."

"You might want to pull all that hair out of your face first," Dom quipped.

"What are you, the fashion police?"

"You look like Cousin Itt," she mumbled.

Smiling to myself, I pulled the hair into a ponytail and tied it with an elastic band I found in my pocket. Then I turned my attention to my passengers in the first row of seats.

"Adam, Salih and Zaman."

"Well done you," Dom said around the cigarette in her mouth.

I surveyed the second row, securely clipped in with seat belts.

"From left to right we have Rashid, Musa and Hasan." I pointed to each boy as I pronounced his name, amazed I remembered.

"What's in a name?" Rashid said. "A boy by any other name would smell as foul."

"Speak for yourself, farty pants," Salih said. "Must be all the lentils you've been eating."

Laughter cascaded from seven mouths.

"That's all accounted for." I was sliding back in my seat when I remembered something. Or someone. "Where's Harun?"

A small voice piped up from the back.

"Here." Harun's head popped up from the last row, hands clutching the back of Rashid's seat.

"You're all by yourself back there," I observed.

Harun nodded, a tuft of blond hair poking fetchingly from under the skullcap.

"That's not right. You're too little. Rashid, swap with Harun."

"I like it here."

Harun's frame might be tiny, but his voice carried volume and authority. He peered at me in a way that put an end to further argument.

"If you're sure."

"I can stretch out to sleep," he said.

"Let me know if you need anything."

"Come on, Mother Hen," Dom prodded. "It's almost one thirty and we haven't moved yet."

I slid into my seat and spotted the bronze medallion hanging from the rear-view mirror. It depicted a scorpion with a raised tail.

"What's this?" I said.

"Good luck charm." Dom flicked the object with her forefinger and set it swinging. "For the long journey ahead."

"It's distracting," I said. "And kitsch."

Dom grabbed my wrist when I tried to take it down.

"No, Missy Din, it stays."

"You're kidding."

"Boss's orders."

"What is it?"

She shrugged. "Must be part of their weird-arsed death cult or something."

"Islam is not a cult. It's a religion, like any other."

"Could have fooled me."

"That's disrespectful and insulting. You should apologise."

Dom threw her hands up in the air and shouted, "Jesus fucking Christ.

Just drive, will you?"

Startled, I stared at her. I was, of course, familiar with her bad behaviour. Adulthood had done nothing to change it.

"It's alright, children," I said for their benefit. "Aunty Dom forgot to take her meds. And she's very sorry, isn't she?"

Dom did not reply. Just tapped an impatient finger on her knee.

I turned my attention to the car I would be driving for the next few days. It was impressive, and certainly better than anything I had commandeered before: a brand-new Fiat Ducato Luxury bus with tinted windows. Aside from three rows of seats, it apparently contained a covered section at the back with enough food and water to feed a small tourist resort for a week. The dashboard was loaded with mod-cons, including remote central door locking, MP3 player and Bluetooth, not that I knew how any of it worked.

"Let's hear you purr," I said, turning the key and pumping the gas. The 130 kW diesel engine leaped to life with a satisfying roar. My left hand fell on the automatic gear stick and stayed there as George Green emerged from the house, crossed the yard in a series of long strides, and came to a standstill outside my open window. He leaned in and whispered in my ear.

"If thou wouldst be with that which thou dost seek, follow where all is fled."

He stood back and waved me on. Puzzled, I steered the van out of the driveway. It was only when I stopped on the corner of Latz Court and Albrecht Drive to check for traffic that Dom spoke.

"What did he say?"

"Not sure." I turned right and navigated Albrecht Drive's gentle curves. "Something about going where no one else does…"

"He's got you pegged," Dom snipped. "Little Miss Intrepid."

"It's a familiar quote," I said, ignoring her quip, "but I can't think what it's from."

"Yeah, familiar as in driving around this dried up shithole all your life. Like a rat in a cage."

Nasty, but even I had to concede she had a point. Twenty-eight years old and I had not left Alice Springs' safe confines. Never been to another city in Australia, let alone another country. Did not even exhibit the slightest desire to travel. It did not make sense. George Green could not have picked a worse person for the job. But then, he hadn't. A djinni called Alila had chosen me for reasons I could not begin to conceive.

I looked at Dom from the corner my eye and the laughter that followed was magic. It was thrilling to sit beside the woman who had dominated my thoughts for years and to laugh again. I would have liked to say it was like old times. But it was nothing of the sort. Both of us had changed and gone on to have separate lives—lives that had nothing to do with each other, until a chance encounter brought us together again. Or was it chance? I could not help thinking that this was destiny, fate. That it was meant to be and that, somehow, I was being given a second chance.

Dom's phone pinged. She pulled it from the black bag at her feet and scrolled through the messages. At the end of the street, I turned left and headed towards the town centre to get on the Stuart Highway.

"Checked my bank account before leaving the house," I said, hoping to get her off the phone and talking to me instead. "The money's in there, like George said it would be…"

Dom nodded, fingers busily tapping the screen.

"More money than I've ever seen," I added, elated.

"You can splurge it all on sexy new lingerie from your favourite designers," she said, without looking up. "Big W, Savers, Kmart…"

"Very funny."

I was sorry I'd brought it up. All I cared about was having enough money in the bank for Nan and me to not worry about finances ever again, and to maybe buy a new car before my old bomb conked.

The Gap loomed ahead, a giant water breach that cleaved the MacDonnell Ranges in two and opened the way out of Alice Springs.

Hoping to engage the boys, I looked in the rear-view mirror and said, "See that?"

A couple of necks craned for a better view of the orange-brown escarpment. It looked like a dusty old chocolate honeycomb that had fallen from the sky and melted in the sun.

"The wonderful Australian desert's on the other side."

As the Gap came closer, I went into a kind of strange reverie, noting all the familiar things as they went past, stuff I had seen a million times, to the point where I had ceased to take notice, with fondness. New eyes even. It was as if I was seeing them for the first and final time. And as they went by, each one gained special, almost magical, significance.

There was the sign at the start of the bridge advising drivers to *Form One Lane*, channelling cars into a systemic, orderly line through the narrow opening. Next came the sign that announced Chinaman's Creek, even though everyone knew the Gap was called Ntaripe and was sacred to local Aborigine males before whites put a road and train tracks through it. Almost as an adjunct or a vignette, I spotted an Aboriginal guy and a white woman walking towards town, holding hands with a little black girl between them. All three stared ahead and walked with the unhurried, graceful stride of Aboriginal people undertaking a task in the broiling sun. Partly because of the speed with which I was travelling, and partly because of the fact we were going in opposite directions, they seemed to be frozen to the spot. Seconds before we shot through the Gap, I was gripped by fear. A voice in my head said, "There's nothing on the other side. You're going to fall off the face of the earth and never be seen again." I almost slammed on the brakes, but the van sailed through without incident. The highway open before me, soft and golden in the afternoon light, and I managed to rouse an approximation of hope about what lay ahead.

CHAPTER 9

Conceive a road that cuts through the centre of a vast country, top to bottom, north to south. Call it the Stuart Highway, after the first European to traverse these ancient regions. Two thousand, eight hundred and thirty-four kilometres in entirety, from Darwin in the Northern Territory to Port Augusta in South Australia. Next conceive of two women and seven boys in a van that smelled of new leather on that road, with nary a settlement along the way and only road-trains and the occasional tourist camper van to keep them company. That was us. We had to cover a mere 1,056 of the nearly 3000 kilometres to reach our destination in Marree—a drop in the sand, so to speak. But it was a long way for a woman who had not driven beyond the limits of the town in which she was born and raised. And although I was nervous, I was also mildly excited. I use the adverb because I had learned to keep my thrills in check; you never know when they could get out of hand and spoil a good time.

For the first hour or so, I focused on getting used to the Fiat. Compared to my bomb, this was luxury personified, elegant and powerful as it floated on the tarmac, the important looking dials and the extra height combining to make me feel significant and decisive as I guided the vehicle with growing ease. After passing a slow delivery truck on the town outskirts, I stepped on the accelerator and kept a steady pace at 130 kilometres per hour, the speed limit in the outback.

"Next stop, Kulgera," I said.

It was past two o'clock. At this speed, with only 317 kilometres to cover, we were certain to reach our first destination before nightfall.

"So cross your legs and hold on to your bladders," Dom muttered, "because Mad Maxine ain't stoppin' for no one."

The mocking tone made me smile. I had been dying to find out more about Dom's life and to reconnect, if that were possible or desirable after all the time that had passed. In an effort to be companionable, I said, "What have you been doing all these years?"

She kept staring at the phone. "This and that."

"Why are you qualified for this job?"

Obviously irritated, Dom looked up from the phone. "I guess because I worked as a bouncer at a shitload of nightclubs and I know how to take care of myself if and when some arsehole comes at me with a broken bottle or a knife. Any more questions, Missy Din?"

I was used to her flare-ups. "Yes, actually," I said, surprising myself with my own boldness around what was, in essence, a stranger. "Where do you live?"

"Here and there."

"How're your mum and dad?"

"Dad's six feet underground, where he deserves to be."

"I'm sorry."

"Why? Did you kill him?"

"No." I said, flustered by the thrusting and parrying. Why couldn't she talk like a normal human being?

"Then you've nothing to apologise for."

"How did he die?"

"A disease invented just for him."

"Oh, what was it?"

"Arseholeism."

"Good to see you getting on with your parents now that you're all grown up."

Dom snorted.

"I hope your mother is okay."

"She's perming her hair and trying to seduce every married man in her church, so she can't be too bad."

"What about you?"

"Am I seducing every married man in church?"

I laughed. "No, sorry, I meant, is there anyone special in your life?"

Immediately, I felt like an idiot for saying that. But it was too late to take it back.

Dom glanced at me. "Saw a good quote the other day," she said.

"What was it?"

"The road to hell is paved with banal questions."

The smile vanishing from my face. "I'm sorry. I was just…"

"I know, you're trying to be nice. Tell you what, let's pretend the last thirteen years didn't happen. We've been seeing each other all this time. So there's nothing to catch up on."

"Okay, sorry."

Dom turned her attention back to the device in her hand. "And another thing."

"What?"

"Stop apologising for everything."

Chastened, I kept my mouth shut and concentrated on driving. I hated the idea of being dull and conventional, and here I was doing just that with inane questions best suited to a gathering of middle-class matrons taking afternoon tea. Dom was obviously not interested in divulging her private life. Nor did she show the least interest in mine. The phone and whoever was at the other end occupied her attention. That was the reason I owned an old flip-top Nokia and had no plans to upgrade. Far as I was concerned, the mobile phone was there in case the school bus broke down or if Nan had an emergency. People with phones did not engage with those in front of them; they engaged with people miles away. Disconnected while being connected. And I…well, I was not particularly interested in connecting with anyone. I was happy living in my head.

Giving up on Dom for the time being, I turned my attention to my passengers. I did this by looking in the rear-view mirror which, over the next days, became a kind of roving eye in the back of my head. By tilting it up or down, left to right, I could see pretty much the entire cabin and its occupants—all except Harun, whose invisible presence continued to niggle. For some reason, I kept thinking he wasn't there.

Most of my passengers were staring out the windows, intent on the landscape. Tangerine earth below, bluest sky above, and against it all an extraordinary gradient of colour, some subtle as lichen and others lurid as honeysuckle grevillea. At one point, we sailed through a rocky pass dotted with ghost gums and spinifex—perfect after the monotonous flatness. Later, the twins, Salih and Zaman, exclaimed in unison when a ridge topped with desert oak appeared on the horizon.

"Looks like a fake movie set, doesn't it?" Zaman said.

The only one who was not impressed was the big redhead. Unlike the others, his mood had gone from jubilant to downcast the deeper we cut into the red centre. Searching for him in the mirror, I saw a boy with a long, despondent face.

"Rashid, everything okay?"

He nodded and went back to staring out the window.

Hoping to take his mind off whatever ailed him, I said, "Aboriginal people believe all this was created by giant spirits. The landscape contains hidden, secret meanings only they can see when they talk to their ancestors."

That roused Dom.

"Wow," she said. "Preaching nature worship to Muslims."

Surprised to hear her voice, I said, "No one appears to be offended."

Why would they be? If there's one thing I'd learned driving a school bus, it's that kids are flexible and resilient. They have a plasticity that allows them to adapt and absorb in ways an adult can't begin to understand. If these boys were anything like me when I was a kid, they would probably take my extemporary portrait of indigenous religions in their stride. I had floated between religions much of my life and it had not done me any harm. Islam on my grandmother's side and animism on my father's side. If I had to choose, I would go for nature worship any day.

Casting a sidewise glance at Dom, I saw that she had gone back to texting, fingers flying across the screen, fixated and caring for nothing else. The only break came when, twice in the last two hours, she shook out small, pink pills from the bag and threw them back with large draughts of water from a plastic bottle. I was full of questions, but I did not dare risk her acid tongue. I kept driving, the endless miles swallowed by the wheels as surely as the white line that disappeared under the chassis. After a while, it was pretty tiresome if you did not have someone to talk to. Going by the nodding heads in the back, most of the boys had also succumbed to the monotony.

"Life's full of surprises," I said to Dom. "When I woke up this morning, I couldn't have known I was going to meet you again and be driving across the country."

She emitted an unenthusiastic if somewhat sympathetic murmur in honour of the none-too-original observation. I would have liked to tell her that I was on this trip because supernatural forces had conspired to put me there. But she was having none of it. All manner of strange things had happened that day, turning my uneventful life into a kind of fairy story. And perhaps, given the fantastical things that had come to pass, I should not have been surprised by what came next.

A magpie started to fly alongside the van.

It hovered on the driver's side, effortlessly keeping pace with the speeding vehicle. Clasping the steering wheel with both hands, I peered at the corvid from the corner of my eye. It was big—large as a wedge-tailed eagle—and powerful, with a glossy head, whetted beak and a white-tipped tail. Puzzled, I turned my head to take a proper look. As if taking its cue from me, it stared directly at me with eyes that sparked with intent and comprehension.

Scared it might hit the van, I stepped on the accelerator. The Fiat leaped forward. Yet the bird remained firmly framed in the window, as if glued there.

"Can you see that?"

Dom looked at me. "See what?"

"That." I cocked my head at our strange visitor.

"I don't follow," she said, obviously seeing nothing.

"You don't see the bird?"

"A bird with tits or a bird with feathers?"

"Very funny. There's a big magpie out there. Tell me you see it."

"Seeing things after only two hours on the road," she said, shaking her head. "Christ knows what you're going to be like by the end."

Frowning, I turned my head to the right. The magpie was definitely there. I glanced at the speedometer: 120kmh. Can a bird fly that fast? I stepped on the accelerator. The van vaulted ahead. The bird fell behind. And, just as I thought I had left it behind, it slid into view. Beak. Head. Claws docked under the magnificent body. The thrust of the tail. The leaping forward on powerful wings. Unnerved, I tried to regain composure by telling myself it was nothing to worry about. The magpie was, after all, my dad's totem. That is why I was wearing his medallion. For all I knew, this was a good omen, his way of letting me know he was looking after me.

Moments before it vanished, the magpie cocked its head, the eyes lit up with a strange, gleaming light. An immense power leaped from it, zapping me between the eyes. It left me feeling weak and dizzy, as if it had sucked information out of my brain and put in a whole lot of stuff, too. Mission accomplished, it streaked ahead and disappeared.

"It's gone."

"What's gone?"

"The bird."

"Don't worry, we're almost in Kulgera."

Time flew by. Fifty minutes later, as the sun started to dip towards the horizon, streaking the land with shadows, she spoke again. "Dear passengers, we are about to pass the megalopolis that is Kulgera. Slow down or you'll kill someone on the grand boulevard."

More of the dry wit I'd once loved.

Far from being a heavily populated city, Kulgera was a hamlet, a series of wretched rooftops glinting to one side of the highway. A couple of motels, a police station, not a soul in sight. Gone before I had time to register its presence on the boundless plain. In this incredible remoteness, I was more likely to run over a camel than a pedestrian.

Dom reached into her bag and retrieved a shiny green pear. She cut it into small pieces with a small knife and offered one to me.

"Want some?"

I popped the fruit in my mouth and chewed, relishing the juicy sweetness. Pears were the only fruit I could tolerate. Pears and mangoes.

"Another one?" she said, extending another piece at the end of the knife.

Fearful of appearing greedy, I turned down the offer.

"You're allowed to have one more," she said, deadpan.

I took the fruit and chewed, feeling self-conscious and uncomfortable. There was something oddly erotic about the way Dom continued to feed me my favourite fruit, succulent and dripping at the end of a gleaming knife. It caused forgotten sensations to shift inside, reminding me that she used to feed me in exactly the same way when we were together. Only back then, she used to lie atop me and slide pieces of fruit directly into my mouth with her own wet, sticky fingers. Sometimes even mouth to mouth.

Salih brought me back to reality.

"My arse is numb," he complained.

They had all been asleep. Dom's voice must have awoken him.

"I'm dying for a piss," his brother Zaman said.

Adam, Musa and Hasan made similar remarks and squirmed in their seats. Rashid, on the other hand, maintained the silence that had become his trademark. From further back in the compartment, Harun kept up the state of non-existence that characterised his contribution to the caravan. I inspected Rashid in the mirror and made a mental note to have a private word at the first opportunity. He was obviously troubled.

Soon after Kulgera, I started to keep an eye out for the turn-off to the campsite where we were supposed to spend the night.

"It will be on the right." Dom pointed ahead as she checked maps on the phone. "Another three kays."

Much as I looked forward to getting out of the van and stretching my legs, I dreaded the idea of spending the night in a tent on the desert floor, crawling with spiders and snakes. Let alone axe-wielding maniacs, hunting vulnerable women. And I won't even mention what the notion of crouching over a makeshift toilet does to me. Yes, I definitely put the lie to the prevailing belief that lesbians love camping.

On top of everything else, I could not stop thinking about the magpie. It had not been an hallucination. The bird was real. Moreover, I knew enough about magpies in Aboriginal and Afghan lore to know that in both cultures they are omens or harbingers of things to come.

Only I did not know whether this was a portent of good tidings or bad. I gripped the magpie pendant with my left hand and hoped for the best.

"Please, Dad," I silently prayed, "watch over us."

Beside me, Dom said, "Slow down. Turn-off coming up. There it is."

Chapter 10

The dirt track led to a clearing in a sea of spinifex. Parking beside a scrappy stand of mulga trees, I sat behind the wheel and gazed at the forlorn sight ahead.

"There's something you don't see every day," I said in a dull voice.

"You can say that again," Dom mumbled.

A hundred or so wooden crucifixes painted white and garlanded with plastic flowers carpeted the western perspective, standing out vividly against the orange earth. Bleached by the elements, many of the blooms looked as if they had been carved from chalk and would disintegrate if touched. Some graves sported thoughtful borders of red brick. Most bled their precious contents into the surrounding landscape. About half a kilometre beyond the cemetery, the jagged silhouettes of four or five ruined buildings stood stark against the sky. The empty windows flared with the rays of the setting sun, seemingly staring like blazing eyes.

Strange and unsettling as it was, I had the distinct feeling I had seen this place before. It felt familiar, but I could not think why that would be the case. I had never travelled this far south.

"I can't believe we're sleeping next to a graveyard," I grumbled, shaking my head.

"I didn't book the accommodation."

Dom opened the door, put out her left leg, and immediately fell to the ground. I flung open the door and rushed around the car to her aid.

"Are you alright?" I said, helping her up.

She pushed me away.

"I'm fine. Just look after the kids."

She did not look fine. Leveraging the whippet-thin body onto her knees, she collapsed against the car with a grunt that belied her twenty-nine years.

"Are you sure?" I said.

"Back off."

The tone did not invite further argument. Fed up with the rudeness, I turned my attention to those who appreciated my concern. My passengers sat patient as dolls in the vehicle. I walked around to the other side of the van, yanked open the sliding door, and stood aside as they tumbled out, almost falling over each other, as they rushed for the trees, unzipping and pulling down their pants as they went.

"Don't step on spinifex," I called after them. "The spikes'll hurt."

Inside the mulga grove, they squatted in a line and proceeded to void their bowels. Taken aback, I did not know where to look, even though they did not appear to be in the least perturbed about performing such a private function in so public a forum. I shrugged, putting it down to the fact they were boys. I could not imagine making such a display of my own toilet habits.

"I hope you brought toilet paper," I said to Dom.

She seemed to have recovered from her earlier show of weakness. "Stacks," she said. Lifting the hatch, she tossed four rolls at me. "Take this to the little darlings."

I grabbed the paper and stayed put. "I can't do that."

"Why not?"

"They need privacy."

"Don't be stupid. Look at them, bums in the air, shitting for all they're worth. You think they care? Just go. Jesus fucken Christ!"

The vulgarity of the woman! Pushed to the limit of what I could endure in one day, I made my way as far as I dared into the trees and stood at a respectful distance. By the look of them, they could not care less, squatting and staring vacantly across the plain that, by degrees, turned from lavender to mauve in the evening light.

I was searching for a place to leave the toilet rolls when something grabbed my attention: a ring of stones, about waist height, amid a cluster of trees. The light in there was mellow and filled with shadows that scuttled with the dipping sun, bare branches hardly moving in the light breeze. Stepping closer, I saw that it was a well, wedged tight between two trees and encircled by a riot of roots, hideously twining, like living organisms, around the wall. It looked as if they were the only things that kept the entire edifice from toppling over.

I closed my eyes as another sense of déjà vu swept through me. This place was definitely known to me. I had been here before. But when? On top of that, the sight of the well, crouched amid the foliage, unnerved me at a primal level. For a moment, as I stared, there was nothing in the world but me and it, caught in a spotlight, an emblem of my worst fears. Terror welled in my chest. I stepped back, panic welling in my gut. Every instinct told me to run. But I could not move. I was rooted to the spot and, distantly, a voice called my name.

"Magnolia, Magnolia."

I turned my head, fearful of who or what I might see.

"Bring the dunny paper."

It was Adam. His voice broke the spell. Reality snapped into place.

"I'll leave it here," I stammered, placing a couple of rolls on the ground a polite distance from the intended users before scurrying away.

I had barely turned away when I was overcome by a sudden urge to void my own bowels. At first, I tried to ignore the call. But I couldn't; it must be obeyed. I moved a discreet distance away, on the other side of the well, behind some scrub, and dropped my tracky dacks, horrified and hoping no one saw. Everything I had eaten and drunk in the course of the day (which was not much) poured from me in a rush. I was almost done when Dom appeared and, without a word, did likewise. I did not know where to look. She and I had been intimate once. This pushed boundaries beyond all comfort levels. When it was over, I adjusted my clothing and scampered away. She followed soon after, fixing her jeans. With her t-shirt pulled up, I saw her hip bones jut out under the pale skin. There had been a time when, as girls, we lay naked next to each other, delighting in the comparative dark and light of each other's skins, and taking pleasure in the warmth and softness of each other's bodies. Now Dom looked sickly, unhealthy, unappetising.

"What just happened?" I said.

She shrugged. "Search me."

"Not until you wash your hands," I quipped, walking to the van to do exactly that.

Bewildered, I felt as if I had done more than just answer nature's call. I was certain, deep inside, it had something to do with the grove, or more accurately, the well. An uncompromising, magnetic force had pulled me there and compelled me to make an abhorrent offering. I'd felt it the minute I approached the mulga—a low vibrating hum that tugged at the innards, making me feel as if I had taken a powerful laxative. The combined force made me, and everyone else it seemed, offer a libation to the earth.

I know it sounds bonkers, but there it is.

Hoping to restore normality, I turned to tell the boys to wash their hands and saw Hasan lean over the well.

"Is there water in here?" he said.

Harun joined him. "Anyone who drinks this water now will be thirsty again," he said. "If we drink when the offering's consumed, we will never thirst again."

Salih and Zaman joined them.

"The offering will bring new life," Salih said. "When we drink, the waters will become in us—"

"Hey," I called. "Come away from there."

They looked at me as if they had never seen me before. Or as if they could tear me limb from limb for disturbing whatever it was they were doing.

"Come on, get away from there," I repeated.

Faces softening, they returned to the clearing as light dimmed around them, bringing out umber tones in the earth and the pink and cobalt in the sky. Birds sang. Insects buzzed. And I could not help noticing that only Rashid skedaddled out of there as soon as he finished.

"What were they talking about?" I whispered to Dom as we washed our hands.

"Sounds like weird-arsed Muslim bullshit to me."

"That had nothing to do with Islam."

Dom had other things on her mind. "It's going to be dark soon," she said. "We need to set up camp and feed this lot before turning in." She began to toss tent bags from the van. "Come on, you lot," she called. "Set up the tents like we showed you." The objects of her clarion call came forward in groups of two and one from each pair picked up a bag as Dom continued to call instructions. "Set 'em up around here." She indicated a space in the middle of the clearing, between the cemetery and the van. "In a horse-shoe shape, the open end facing this way"— she pointed at the trees—"Rashid, you share with Musa. Adam, you're in with Hasan. Salih and Zaman, we wouldn't dare separate you. Move it."

Because of the uneven numbers, Harun was the only one without a partner. Dominique did not appear to notice how crestfallen he was when she lobbed a sleeping bag at him and told him he was sharing with her. She handed me a small shovel and said, "Bury the shit, will ya? Then dig a hole for the proper dunny over there." She pointed to a spot at the far end of the camp.

I took the shovel and walked away, feeling like I was her helper, instead of the other way around. *How different we are*, I thought. *Was I aware of it when I was young? Or are the polarities obvious now because I am no longer in love?* There was no answer. All I knew was that Nan was always big on two things: education and God. Thanks to her, I was the beneficiary of a pretty sound education, first at the Lutheran school and then at the Charles Darwin University. Despite her parents' best efforts, Dom barely scraped through primary school and did not finish high school. Far as I knew, she did not have a tertiary education. When we were teenagers, she joked that I talked with the plummy voice of characters I watched on British TV shows, while she sounded like a character from *Planet of the Apes*. It was funny then. It did not seem funny now.

In those days, my grandmother and I watched endless English television shows in which elegant ladies disported themselves with aplomb and spoke in crisp, rounded vowels. I had fun imitating them, walking around the living room like a grand lady, much to Nan's amusement, and talking in a BBC accent. Inevitably, I ended up sounding, in my everyday life, like a distant echo of those characters. A caricature. In the schoolyard, my clear intonation and odd phrasing sounded peculiar coming from a brown-skinned, mixed-race girl. My classmates thought I was 'bunging it on'—an affectation. Truth was I could not help it. It was what it was and although I had done my best to erase any trace of the fake English accent, it occasionally surfaced. When kids made fun back then, I was grateful to Dom for coming to the rescue. She was, to all intents and purposes, my knight in denim and soiled runners. Now she was a foul-mouthed, inked and pierced feral who was vaguely distasteful. Yet I still craved her approval.

These thoughts and more flitted through my mind as I dug a trench for the latrine. When I finished, I turned my attention to the unenviable task of burying the waste we had contributed to the land earlier. Swinging the shovel by my side, I walked over, careful to not step in anything. Finding nothing where Dom and I had been, I went to the spot where our charges had squatted. Again nothing. Not a sign of waste or dampness on the ground. It was as if the soil had absorbed everything. At first I thought I was looking in the wrong place, but after going around a bit, checking for tell-tale signs, I had to admit the evidence had mysteriously vanished.

CHAPTER 11

Twilight. Best time of the day. Optimum time in the desert, too: the air is lovely and still, the light mellow and crystalline. I was in the cemetery, standing amid the crucifixes, holding my phone to my ear and waiting for Nan to answer. I turned on the spot as it rang, taking in the surrounds and loving the rosy pink that brushed the horizon as the sun went down behind the ruins. I was surprised there was reception out there, but I guess we were close enough to Kulgera to pick up the fading remnants. From this vantage point, I could see we were in a valley between a series of gently rounded hills, all of which kept announcing their familiarity to my bewildered mind. The mounds flowing one after the other, and the rich, earthy aromas rising from the soil brought to mind other things I felt I ought to recall but did not. Had I been here before? The question niggled, making me feel baffled and confused.

Taking in the view, I searched for some detail, a vital clue, that might trigger an onrush of memory. Something was missing from the landscape and I found the absence, unnamed though it remained, disconcerting. I shook my head and tried to get rid of the disquiet I felt, as the phone continued to buzz in my ear.

"Come on, pick up."

Never particularly patient, I focussed on the five tents in the clearing as I waited for Nan to answer. Salih was feeding the fire with dry branches, Dom stirred a pot over a propane gas heater, and Hasan and Musa placed enamel crockery and cutlery on a rug. It was a very domestic scene, as if Dom and I were mothers to a motley crew of lost boys.

The phone stopped ringing. I thought it was going to message bank when a woman's voice said, "Hello?"

Leah Unger, Nan's best friend.

"Where's Nan?" I said.

"The loo. I'm visiting her."

"How is she?"

"Fine. I'm glad you called."

"Something happen?"

"We're a little concerned."

"About?"

"Where did you say this George bloke lives?"

"At the end of Rubina Street, in the scrub a little ways."

"I went there today, hon. There's no house."

"You probably didn't look in the right place."

"Mags, there is no house. I searched. I even spoke to neighbours. No one knows anything about a house out there."

I had no words. And even though I was irritated by the fact Leah was being a busybody, I had to concede I had known her since I was a child; she meant well and she could be trusted.

"Are you there?"

"Yes." I turned my back on the campsite. "Listen, Leah, I don't want you or Nan going near George Green. Stay away."

"Why?"

"Because I said so."

I heard muffled hospital noises behind Leah's sharp intake of breath. I knew her patience was being tested. Other sounds intervened, bringing Alice Springs comfortingly close. An announcement on an intercom, snatches of television news, people talking, a toilet flushing. Life ongoing, and here I was so far away.

"Mags, between you and me," Leah said, dropping her voice, "I think you should be here. Cherry's not good."

"Did something happen?"

"She's having a bit of a turn."

"What do you mean?"

"She reckons she saw some weird guy standing next to her bed last night—"

"I know about that."

"There's more. This afternoon she woke up from a nap and the same man was sitting beside the bed."

I was silent.

"Get this: his hands were under the covers. Cherry said he was pressing down on her wound, causing her pain."

"You're joking."

"I wish I was."

"Did anyone see him? Did she report him to security?"

"No one saw him. Not even the guy in the next bed." Leah took another breath; I heard movement, sounds fading, coming to the fore. "Sorry," Leah said when she spoke again. "Just stepped into the corridor. Don't want Cherry to hear me from the toosh."

I kicked impatiently at a stone, waiting for her to finish. I wanted to get back to camp, to sit with my new family, to eat and to gaze at the stars, not be dragged back to a life I'd left behind.

"It's probably the anaesthetic," I said. "And the pain killers—"

"I don't think you understand, Mags. Cherry knew this guy."

"What?"

"Up in Ti Tree," Leah went on, "where Cherry grew up. There's absolutely no way he could turn up now. No way."

"Why not? Ti Tree isn't far from Alice."

"Hold on a sec," Leah said.

I heard muffled voices at the other end. Leah came back.

"Cherry wants a word," she said in an urgent whisper. There was the noise of a handset being passed over and my grandmother's voice came on.

"Hello, lovely. You having a nice time?"

She was obviously putting on an act. I reassured her the trip was going as well as could be expected.

"Just called to say goodnight," I finished.

"Goodnight to you too," Nan said. "Don't listen to Leah. All social workers think the world has 'deep-seated issues'."

I smiled, almost seeing the contemptuous inverted commas Nan would place over the last three words. We parted soon after, promising to speak the next evening. I pocketed the phone, turned to go back to my little band and bumped straight into Rashid. I let out a yelp.

"You startled me," I said. When he did not say anything, I backed away from his imposing bulk and looked up at him. "What's up, Rashid? You haven't been yourself all afternoon."

"I don't want go home," he said in a small voice that belied his size.

"Why not?"

"I want to stay here."

Alarm bells rang in my mind. Over the years, I had encountered kids on the bus who did not want to go home and I knew what it meant. Child abuse.

"Is there a problem at home, Rashid?"

"No," he replied, staring over the crucifixes.

"Okay," I said, at a loss. "Is there anything you want to tell me?"

"I'm not allowed."

"By whom?"

I might as well have addressed a block of granite. A wave of hopelessness passed over his face, like a blackbird's wing. He turned to leave. I grabbed his arm and stopped him.

"Everything will be alright," I said, aware how glib I sounded. "Trust me."

He tilted his head and gave me a curious look. I had seen a similar quizzical gaze pass over me twice that day. The first came from Adam. The second from Harun. Both had turned on me the same keenly observant scrutiny, casual yet shrewd, as if they could not get a handle on me. As if I was a mystery to them, making me feel as if I had done something wrong or as if I had disappointed. Afterwards I felt deflated, as if I had indeed let them down, and not knowing why or how. Wanting to avoid that eventuality with Rashid, I looked for a distraction. Anything to take his mind off whatever ailed him.

"Look," I said, pointing at a cylindrical stone marker not far from where we stood. "A Muslim grave in the middle of all these Aboriginal graves."

Rashid peered at me as if I had lost my mind.

Desperate, I raised my voice and called to the others.

"Hey, guys, come over here. Have a look at this."

Rashid frowned and walked away as his friends streamed towards me. I hated myself for driving him away, but I could not help it. There was something off-putting about him and the way he looked at me.

When the others congregated around me, I pointed at the marker.

"Here it is."

The inscription carved into the worn grey stone was barely legible in the fading light.

> *Ghul Mohammad Died 1903*
> *Said Omar Died 1905*
> *Here Lie 2 Brave Afghan Cameleers.*

A series of illegible lines and scrolls followed.

"How come Muslims are buried here?" Hasan queried.

"Muslims have a strong presence in Central Australia," I told him.

"They do?"

"Ever heard of the Ghan?"

Hasan nodded. "That's the train that goes from Adelaide to Darwin."

"We were supposed to go to the Ghan museum last Friday," put in Salih, in a slightly querulous tone.

"Well," I said, "'The Ghan' is short for 'The Afghan Express'. Who knows why?"

All-round silence.

"The train honours the Afghan cameleers who came to Australia in the late nineteenth century to help British explorers find a way to the country's interior. They opened up the roads that brought the white men that chucked blackfellas off their land." I took in the gathering, aware I was treating them like students. "Any of you from Afghanistan?"

"My great-great-great-great grandfather came from Afghanistan," Salih said.

"Actually," said his brother Zaman, "he was our great-great-great-great-great grandfather."

"Whatever," said Salih. "He married an Aboriginal woman."

I smiled. When I met them that morning, at George's house, I had noted how strange it was to see the twins look distinctly Middle Eastern and yet speak with a strong Australian accent. In my naïveté, I had presumed they were new arrivals and had expected to hear a foreign accent when they spoke. Nothing doing. Salih sounded as Australian as I did. All of them were Australian. Born and bred on this soil, far from wherever their ancestors originated. I smiled at my own presumption, silently acknowledging one of the things I liked about this country. There was no such thing as a 'real Australian'. Since British arrival, the nation had been a mishmash of peoples and cultures from around the world. It did not matter where your forebears came from, you could still be Australian. Except for Aborigines, I believed. For some reason, they had fallen between the cracks in their own land.

"In that case," I said to the twins, "you can probably trace your lineage to one of those cameleers."

Adam pushed to the fore. "Are you Aboriginal, Miss?"

No one had ever asked. Given the colour of my skin, people presumed I was indigenous or a mixture thereof. Taken aback, not knowing how to answer, I hesitated before saying, with a slight shrug, "I used to think I was Aboriginal when I was younger, but only because my mother and father lived with Dad's people in an Aboriginal community. When I moved in with Nan, I stopped thinking of myself as Aboriginal."

"Why?"

I shrugged again. "I don't know. I felt like a phoney. I didn't feel connected to the culture or experiences to be able to share it with other people, where Aboriginal culture is more ingrained in their lives."

Adam nodded, waiting for me to continue.

"It's the same thing with my Afghan ancestry," I went on. "My grandmother thinks of herself as Afghan, even though she was born here. So were her parents. But I don't think of myself as Afghan. I was born here. I know little about the culture or the history of the country…" I drifted off, conscious I was talking too much and being the unwarranted centre of attention. "You guys probably feel the same way," I added, hoping to divert attention away from myself.

"I think I understand," Adam said.

Harun slipped his warm paw into my left hand and looked up at me, like a kitten calling for attention.

"Mostly," I said to Adam, "I remember what my father used to say."

"What did he say?"

"When people die, their bodies become part of the story of the land. Every place they visited when they were alive, every object they touched, carries the essence of who they were. In that way the landscape became the story of their lives. And they became the story of the land."

"The land is alive," Adam said, dreamy. "The earth is living…"

"I guess that's what it comes down to," I replied, staring into his violet eyes. "The earth is sentient and we're part of it. Not separate or outside of it. Part of it."

Harun tugged at my hand. "Where's your mum and dad?"

Another question people never asked. But I had a ready-made answer for that one, just in case.

"Mum went away and never came back," I said. "Dad died of a broken heart."

That was the fairy tale version I told myself and I intended to stick to it, without deviation. I was surprised by the ease with which it came out, never having said as much to anyone, let alone a bunch of strangers. Not even Dom knew the full story. Only Nan had been entrusted with the keys to the kingdom and she knew better than to divulge the truth.

"Do you have brothers?" Harun said.

I shook my head. "Just me."

"I'm your little brother."

The smile made me feel like bending down to drink him up, like a fresh draught of water.

"I'd like that very much," I said, giving his fingers a gentle squeeze.

"Come and get it."

Dom's voice shattered the mood. She banged a tin plate with a spoon, making a hell of a racket in the silence that had fallen with the parting of the light. Birds rose from perches, wheeled in the sky, and sought shelter in the toothy ruins on the far side of the cemetery.

Chapter 12

"Rashid," I said, "you barely touched your food."

"Not hungry."

"Would you like something else?"

"There's nothing else." Dom spoke out of the side of her mouth. "Just lentils and more fucking lentils."

Rashid shook his head, refusing to make eye contact. He had been avoiding me since our earlier encounter in the graveyard, preferring to stare at the gathering gloom as he sat between Adam and Musa. Adam whispered to him and Musa rubbed his back, offering what comfort he could. I sensed that if the two boys did not sit either side of him, Rashid would bolt for the desert and never be seen again. What could be bothering him? Why was he behaving like that? I wished I could talk to Dom about it, but I did not want to do that in front of Rashid.

"Don't want it?" Musa said to Rashid. Rashid shook his head again. "More for me." Musa grabbed his mate's bowl and shovelled food into his mouth with a blue enamel spoon that clacked pleasingly against his teeth.

"If you're not careful," Adam said to him, "you'll get too big for the bus."

The ensuing laughter spurred the skinny boy to a renewed feeding frenzy, buck teeth moving up and down like a rabbit. He obviously enjoyed provoking laughter in his friends.

Despite my concern for Rashid, it was a pleasant first dinner under the stars. I had always feared being in the open at night, feeling vulnerable, exposed. But as I sat cross-legged with my new family, dipping warm flatbreads into spiced lentils that perfumed the cooling air, I felt that I might be content. Happy, even. I belonged. I was accepted, part of a group that had invited me in. That had never happened before. Not even with the mainly white lesbians I'd met in town over the years.

The temperature dropped with the onset of night, making it necessary for Dom to distribute black, hooded fleece anoraks to everyone. Quickly donned, they made us resemble Bedouins in the Arabian desert or druids at a sacred grove.

Dom folded a spoonful of lentils in a piece of flatbread and shoved it into her mouth.

"What a dump," she said, eyes roving the darkness. The wind had picked up and the crucifixes emitted an unnerving glow, flickering in response to the guttering flames. "Imagine living out here."

"I wouldn't live anywhere else," I said, meaning every word.

"I'd rather be in the city, watching TV, knowing there's heaps to do if I felt like going out and having fun."

I pointed at the fire with my spoon. "This is all the TV I need. It's nature's television. It contains all the entertainment you could ask for."

Dom looked at me as if I was barmy. "Right," she said, dragging out the vowel as long as she could. "No wonder you never left Alice Springs."

"I belong here. Nothing wrong with that."

"I don't want to belong anywhere."

"What are you afraid of?"

"Not being able to leave when I feel like it."

I gave a rueful smile. This was probably not the right moment to tell her there was a time I would have followed her to the ends of the earth.

"Listen," I said, instead. "How well do you know George?" I chewed my food and waited for her to answer.

"Like I said, met him last Thursday. Never seen him before." Dom shrugged inside the anorak. "Why?"

"We don't know him from a bar of soap and yet we're following his orders without knowing why—"

Dom puckered her lips. "You don't know a bar of soap when you buy it in the supermarket either, but you still strip naked and rub it against your skin."

I rolled my eyes. "You know what I mean."

"I know exactly what I'm doing and why, Missy Din. Not my problem if you don't."

"Why are you here? Aside from the money, I mean."

Dom hesitated before saying, "Money's all the reason I need."

Her willingness to be bought was distasteful. But could I really blame her? I was as guilty as she was. When I thought about the crazy things George talked about that morning, I could not believe I had not gone straight to the police. He made threats and the most outrageous claims, and then he hooked his minnow with the promise of money. Greed. That is what it came down to. That is exactly why I did not tell him to get lost. Money-grubbing avarice.

"What's on your mind?" Dom said, folding another piece of bread in half and tucking into it.

"A friend of Nan's said George's house isn't there."

Dom snorted. "Houses don't just disappear." She filled a tin mug with tea from a kettle hanging over the fire and rose to her feet. "Going for a smoko," she said, heading towards the cemetery. She was a few paces away, on the other side of the tents, when I heard her say, "Hello, sweetheart. How are you?" My heart missed a beat. For a second I thought she was talking to me. Then I realised she was speaking to someone on the phone, using the same words, the same tones, she'd used when she addressed me in another life. Feeling like a fool, I fell on my back with a grunt and covered my eyes with a forearm, mixed feelings wheeling inside me, like stars above.

"Girl," I said to myself, "you're a mess."

Harun's voice broke my reverie.

"Magnolia, can I ask you something?"

I opened my eyes and looked at his face afloat against a background of heavenly bodies. I sat up, happy to be drawn away from my blighted thoughts.

"Sure."

"Can I share a tent with you?"

"You're sharing with Dom."

"She shouldn't sleep in the same tent as me."

I thought he was talking about Islam's injunction against women commingling with men outside the immediate family.

"If you look at it that way," I said, "I'm a stranger to you too."

Harun shook his head. "You're one of us. She's not."

Gazing at him, I was hit by another jolt of love—a bizarre reaction, given I had met him that morning. Yet I felt overwhelmingly that I knew him and that we were tied together with unbreakable garlands of devotion.

"Wait here," I said, rising to my feet and walking away.

Dom loitered behind the van, speaking on the phone and smoking cigarettes that befouled the pure air. As I approached, I heard her say, "Won't be long, baby. We'll be together soon. Sweet dreams." She made kissing noises and slipped the phone into her back pocket. Then she yanked a cardboard box from the van, plonked it in my arms as if she had been waiting for me and yelled, "Time for bed, gentlemen."

The group rose to its collective feet without argument.

"I have a proposition," I said.

"No, you can't sleep with me."

I ignored the remark. "Harun's sleeping in my tent while you keep the first watch. If he wants, he can move to your tent when I take over."

We had agreed earlier to take turns keeping watch while the other slept. Neither one of us believed we were in danger, but both of us thought it wise to err on the side of caution, given we were two women camping with children.

"Suit yourself," Dom said. "I thought you might like a good night's sleep. Tomorrow's a long haul."

Smiling, I turned to inform Harun that his wish had been granted… and froze. There was no one there. The boys were gone.

"Where did they go?" I said in a tiny voice.

Looking around, I felt a stab of panic. In the dark, recharged by the fire flaring upwards in fine lances of red and orange, I could not see a single boy. Only Dom, the tents, the van, and the eerily flickering crucifixes. My charges had vanished as though they had never existed. I looked wildly around, and felt myself to be alone. A swift and awful feeling of loneliness passed over me. I wanted desperately to run, and then I saw Dom point at the trees. I peered in that direction; the boys were peeing against the well. Harun squatted and went one better.

"I dug a latrine for that," I yelled at them, but they ignored me. "I wish they wouldn't do that," I said to Dom. "The well is probably used by local people."

Dom could not care less. "Okay," she said, "we need to put two bottles of water in each tent, in case the little darlings get thirsty during the night. You carry the box. Come on. Should be fun. You, me, doing things together…" She gave a pretend shiver of delight and rolled her eyes with fake pleasure. "So romantic."

Frowning, I followed. "Why don't you like them?" I said, pausing in front of Adam and Hasan's tent.

Dominique put the bottles inside, zipped up the flap, and moved to the next one. She did not say anything until after she'd placed two bottles inside Rashid and Musa's tent.

"I heard what that little shit Harun said before."

"About you not being one of us?"

Dom nodded, taking two more bottles from the box and placing them in Salih and Zaman's tent.

"He's just a kid."

"Please. He'd sell his Muslim grandmother to the Israelis."

I suppressed a smile. Much as I liked Dom's unfettered speech, it could go too far sometimes.

"Now that you mention it," I said, "they're not very Muslim."

"No kidding."

After we finished dispensing water we stood beside the fire, warming our respective rumps. It was surprisingly chilly, the warmth sucked from the air as soon as the sun disappeared. Dom threw a mulga branch on the fire.

"I've been with them for several hours and they haven't prayed once," I observed.

"How often should they pray?"

"Five times, if they're devout."

"Maybe they haven't been brainwashed yet."

"Show some respect."

Dom laughed and gestured at the copse. "Maybe taking a dump is their idea of praying."

Disgusted, I peered over her shoulder and saw the boys gathered around the well, heads bowed and holding hands.

"See?" Dom said. "Prayer."

"That doesn't look like a Muslim prayer to me."

Dom released one of her curt laughs.

"Alright, you lot," I said, charging across the clearing. "To bed."

Seven mask-like expressions stopped me in my tracks. Chilled to the bone, I stared in horror. The boys I thought I knew were stripped of their disguises, presenting a visage that was as remote as the hills, eyes ablaze with frenzied fervour. I was reminded of zealots, burning bright and blinded to all but a mission only they perceived. I was rooted to the spot for a heart-stopping moment, caught between the rational light of the camp and the irrational pull of the well, convinced I had stumbled onto something I ought not to have seen.

They are more than schoolboys.

The thought flashed through my mind and was gone, leaving me in a state of confusion. Certain I was witness to a lie, an illusion, I was about to turn away when Rashid approached.

"I tried to tell you," he said and walked away.

Harun flashed a smile. With that small gesture the warmth, life and vibrancy returned to their faces. Seconds later, I was surrounded by jubilant celebrants who escorted me to camp on feet that kicked up dust as they danced lightly on the ground.

"To bed," I said in a weak voice. "All of you."

Harun was asleep when I joined him in the tent. Making as little noise as possible, I slipped into my sleeping bag, dreading yet another sleepless night and not wanting to resort to the sleeping tablets I had brought for that purpose.

When I next opened my eyes, I knew I was inside a dream. Because the scene in front of me was impossible. George Green sat cross-legged beside me, dressed in an elaborate turquoise robe, hands lost inside voluminous sleeves. The ascetic face, as he leaned over me, was bathed in green light that emanated, seemingly, from inside the man. He pulled a scroll from his sleeve, unrolled it, and began to read…

CHAPTER 13

The Tale of Alila, the Accursed Djinni

It is said, O Mistress of the Age, that in days of yore, when djinn did wander upon the earth, before man was a glimmer in the Aeon's eye, there was a great and powerful djinni. Greater was she even than Asmodeus, cunning and fearsome.

Alila was her name, wondrous and fair. By the fire of scorching desert winds was she created thus, and the ifrit Malachi was her minion true. All who gazed upon Alila, seraphim, ghouls, marids and angels alike, did bow before her and bend to her will.

Thousands of years old was she when mankind appeared upon the earth. Second was she to none, for she saw clear as mountain air the dim past and unknown future, trailing before and after, from beginning till the end of time. All was known to Alila. Fierce was her vanity, and pride was her second name.

She did challenge the will of the Aeon, false god that he was, when he created man out of mud.

"Is not the race of the djinn greater than the race of man?" quoth the djinni great. "Oh Blind One, can you not see that man is pestilence, a canker foul upon the earth? He is not deserving of love. Ruin he will bring to creation fair and you will rue the day you made him thus."

Displeased, the Aeon chastened Alila with these words: "All creation is born equal to damnation and salvation alike, including the djinn. None shall rise above and all shall follow Law for I am Truth. My heart is wide and I am capable of loving the djinn and human kind in equal measure."

Knowing better than he and seeing to greater heights beyond all seeing and all knowing, Alila refused to bow to the greatness of mankind.

Angered, the Aeon quoth: "How you are fallen from our pleasure. How you are cut down to the ground, you who weakened nations and gathered unto herself appellations great. For you have said in your heart I will ascend above the will of God, above even His creation, man. Yet shall you be brought down to the pit and slumber in the bowels of the earth, to be forgotten, though you can live to greatest age beyond reckoning."

Hearing this, Alila bewailed her sorry state.

"Oh, mercy," cried the fallen djinni. "How will I be saved?"

The Aeon turned from her. "You will sleep," pronounced he, "in the earth until such a time as one who is half fire and half clay gives you entry to the world. Then and only then can you wed your smokeless fire with the mud of those who are neither living nor dead. For it is through that which you despise most that you can nourish your uprising."

Alila cried, "When will that be?"

"When the dark moon aligns with the truth that cannot be denied."

So saith the Aeon and cast Alila as a profane thing from the mount into a fathomless chasm, to await until such a time as prophesied.

CHAPTER 14

I sat bolt upright and stared into the semi-dark. Was it a dream? Of course it was. What else could it be? But what did it mean? George Green had told a story about Alila, the djinni to whom, according to him, I was bound. If he was to be believed, Alila was trapped, bottled up, and her salvation depended on someone made of smokeless fire and mud. In other words, half djinn, half human. Is that why I was driving seven boys across the desert during a dark moon? To bring Alila back to life? I could not imagine why anyone would want to do that. She sounded awful, a bitch who had contempt for humanity. Let her rot.

And who was half djinn and half human?

The more I thought about it, the more the dream faded, details becoming indistinct and hazy. My head whirled as dream collided with reality to form a vague image in my dazed brain.

But I could not dwell on it. Harun was not in the tent and my attention was drawn incrementally elsewhere. Beyond the confines of the stuffy tent. A steady chant, rising and falling, now a wailing and now a drone, drew me out into the world.

I stepped into blinding incandescence. Putting up a hand to protect my eyes from the light, I saw that the world was frozen. Every gesture, sigh and breath. Dom by the fire. The flames. The air itself as I paced through a timeless realm. All were bound by an unmoving spell.

Everything motionless. Everything, that is, except the seven boys, holding an ecstatic chorus around the well as starlight bathed their naked forms in silver.

> *To raise greenwoods are yours, Alila.*
> *To be black, to be white are yours, Alila.*

Convinced I was still dreaming, I made my way to the trees. The well was full to the brim with water, overflowing in crystalline rivulets that sparked and shimmered. Bare feet splashed in muddy puddles as the boys bowed their heads to drink and to take the life-giving purity into bodies that were transparent so that I saw, as I approached on stealthy legs, the internal workings, blood and water running inside them. Did I really see the form of a young woman coiled inside the chest of each child or was it a mental aberration?

> *To turn a man into woman and a woman into man are*
>   *yours, Alila.*
> *Fecundity, replenishment, to grow, to spread, are yours, Alila…*

The stench of attar of roses was strong, choking me, making me nauseous.

As I stood, bewildered, frightened, not knowing what to do, Harun approached with water cupped in his hands, running between fingers.

"Drink," he said, ecstatic. "Drink."

I did, wholeheartedly, take a draught and then a second, and swallowed it down until it felt that barren gardens came to splendid life in me. Even as I noted, as in a dream, Harun's genitals. They were female, like the others. When they had most certainly been male earlier, when I saw them defecate.

There was no time to think about that, because one by one they walked past me and went to the tents.

I turned to the well—the source, I was convinced, of the wonderment of this peculiar night. I was two or three steps away from it when terrible shrieks erupted from the depths, harrowed, distressed, strong enough to shatter illusions. When the cries stopped, the hitherto dormant mulga grove burst into vivid, exuberant life, needle-like leaves unfurling from dark branches and yellow flowers bursting with promiscuous abandon.

After all that, the last thing I expected to hear was a woman's voice call my name.

"Who are you?"

"Magnolia," the voice repeated. "Get me out of here."

The scene wavered. The trees were overlaid with a fine film that contained fainter still imprints of a dozen waterboard houses arrayed against brittle hills. A young girl with a dog in her arms slept in a chair. The uncanny screams that followed shattered the scene like glass. The hallucination fell apart and, just as it looked like the weirdness was over, light burst from the well, shooting up into the sky, like a spotlight.

I reeled, fell flat on my back.

Time kicked in.

CHAPTER 15

"Did it rain?"

Dom yawned, scratched her scalp, and stared at the rejuvenated mulga. She still wore the jeans and anorak from the previous night. The hood was thrown back to display hair that stuck up like filaments on her head. The first remark was followed by, "What the hell is that?"

The latter remark was aimed at the light emanating from the well.

It was early morning. A pearly grey blue with the occasional cheep and twitter from hidden birds. I had not slept. The road-trains stationed in Kulgera for the night had taken to the highway half an hour earlier. The boys were still asleep. I led Dom to the edge of the grove and told her everything that happened the previous night. The chanting, the eerie song, the screams and the regeneration of trees that followed. Everything except the dream about George Green in my tent. And boys with female genitalia. They seemed part of an unfathomable mystery.

"Then this happened," I said, indicating the light coming out of the ground as if it was a big deal Hollywood premier at Grauman's Chinese Theatre.

"I slept through all that?"

"Kind of…"

I told her that she had been in a trance for most of the night, disappearing into her tent soon after the incident with the well.

"Still pretty groggy, actually." She passed a hand over her brow and stepped closer to the well, craning her neck upwards to take in the full length of the shimmering lustre emanating from the ground. At the apex it spread like a mushroom head against a cloudless sky. Dom whistled between her teeth and beckoned for me to come closer.

I approached reluctantly.

"It's not smoke," she said, awed. "More like vapour or gas."

She was right. Despite a light breeze, it remained unmoving and intact.

Nor did birds and insects fly through it; they flew around it. Inside, I saw a gently subsiding mist, made up of millions of tiny droplets of water that twinkled and sparkled, as if they were precious gems, so solid I could not see through to the other side.

"Did George know this was going to happen?" I asked.

Dom put up her right hand to stop me talking.

"Can you hear that?" she said, bringing an ear closer to the light.

I nodded. The barely discernible sound of chimes, mixed with the trickle of water, sighs and whispers, was simultaneously unnerving and calming. There was a torpid heaviness to the air under the trees. It was difficult to breathe. The whole set-up felt wrong.

"Feels like we're standing under a nuclear bomb," Dom whispered.

"We need to get away from here," I murmured.

"Agreed, o captain, my captain."

"Wow, you've read Walt Whitman?"

Still focussed on the light, Dom said, "No, but I've seen *Dead Poet's Society*. I'm not as stupid as you think."

"I don't think you're stupid."

"Sure you don't." Her face was a scornful mask. "You always were a snob, Missy Din. No one was good enough."

"That's not true," I said, knowing full well it was. Coming from nothing, belonging to no one, I had to raise myself up somehow. Looking down on others was the easiest way to do that.

Dom gave a derisive sniff and poked a finger into the light.

"Don't," I cried.

Too late. The crackling discharge was followed by an eruption, like the cries of outraged seraphim; Dom was lifted bodily from the ground and flung several metres away. She slammed against the van with a thud and slid to the ground.

"Dom."

I ran to her, gathered her in my arms, and rested her head on my knees, vaguely aware that the pendant around my neck was warm against my skin.

"Are you alright?" And when she did not reply: "Dom, answer me."

Eyes closed, Dom turned her head and groaned. "What happened?"

"Are you hurt?"

"Don't think so…" She moved arms, legs, head.

"Good, because I really think we should get—"

The words froze on my tongue.

A man was watching me from among the trees. Bright amber eyes in a black face, almost indistinguishable from the shadows. Grinning,

Malachi stepped naked from between tree trunks, knees bending the wrong way at the joints. He raised one arm and pointed at the light.

"She is risen," he hissed, the flame-like irises dancing in his head. The pointy sex organ was a pendulous growth that emitted a steady golden stream at his feet. I knew it was time to pack up and get out of there when he turned into my grandmother, right down to the hospital gown and frowsy hair. "He found me," Nan said in a broken voice, hands reaching out.

She vanished; Malachi flickered back. He smiled thinly and dived head-first into the well, the aqueous voice trailing behind him as he descended. "Coming, O mistress mine."

Chapter 16

"Hitchhiker," Adam said.

"What? Where?"

I had been driving for approximately two hours, my mind in turmoil as we headed to Coober Pedy, when Adam's voice broke into my thoughts.

"Up ahead. Hitchhiker."

I barely registered the woman zip past on the right side of the road. All I noted was a feminine figure in fluttering white robes twisted around her body, head turning as the van barrelled past. She receded in the side mirror, leaving behind an impression of dust flying around a head wrapped in linen, like an Egyptian mummy.

"Hope she finds a ride," I said to Adam.

Dom opened one eye. "What's going on?"

"A hitchhiker."

"Out here? He must be desperate."

"I think it was a she," I said.

"Dead by dawn." She nuzzled into her corner. "Mind if I sleep? I'm seriously zonked."

"Getting thrown against a car will do that for you."

"Wake me up if the world needs saving." She closed her eyes and drifted off.

My thoughts went back to earlier preoccupations. I had been thinking about what Nan, or rather Malachi, said back in Kulgera. "He found me." A loaded statement. It implied they knew each other, as Malachi had stated in the carpark, and that he had been looking for her. Nan was hiding from him. Why? I had wanted to call her immediately, but my desire to get away from that horrible place was stronger. Opting for a speedy getaway, I helped Dom pack and hit the road as quickly as possible. I could call Nan from the car, I had reasoned. But reception had been choppy after Kulgera. Then it dropped out altogether. Dom had plugged her phone in the charger, but there was a lot of static and reception kept fizzing into a kind of cosmic output. My Nokia was useless. In the end, I decided to try again later.

Far as I was concerned, Coober Pedy could not come soon enough; I wanted people around me. Houses. A semblance of civilisation. Surely they were just beyond the horizon, where the tapering end of the highway jabbed at the soft underbelly of sky. Beside me Dom slept fitfully. My other passengers were similarly engaged. I had found it hard to look at them after last night, having difficulty with the idea of boys with female genitalia. Had that been an hallucination, too? Surely everything that had happened at that eerie place was a figment of my overwrought imagination, I told myself. Either that or I was losing my mind.

I was nervous, as if something or someone was catching up with me. Fingers fidgeted on the dashboard. I contemplated putting on music, decided against it, preferring my own thoughts to noise. Music while driving always brought unwanted memories, reminding me of the times my mother and I piled into Dad's purple Holden and drove to see his mob, radio playing crackly country and western on low volume as the miles unfurled. They were among the few joyful times I recalled from childhood, and I often wished I was still in the back of that smelly car, family intact.

Shaking my head to clear it, I looked up at the rear-view mirror and saw that only Adam was awake, a thoughtful expression on his handsome face.

"Penny for your thoughts," I said.

"I was thinking about the light coming from the well."

When the boys emerged from their tents earlier that morning they appeared to have no memory of the previous night's revelry. They had been immediately drawn to the light. After what happened to Dom, I had told them to stay away. Even so, all except Rashid managed to get close enough to slip their hands into it, without being jettisoned, as Dom had been.

"What about it?" I said.

"I wasn't expecting it to be so…beautiful."

"You knew it was going to happen?"

"Yes."

"Do you know what it is?"

"Of course."

"Want to share?"

"She's awake."

"Who?"

"Meter Neros."

"I don't know what that means," I admitted.

"Water Mother." Harun's voice carried up and over the seat that blocked him from view. It was like receiving words from a Sibylline oracle.

"I didn't know you spoke Latin," I said.

"It's not Latin," Dom muttered.

"Oh, what is it then?"

"Greek." With her eyes closed, it looked like Dom was talking in her sleep.

"Ancient Greek," Adam corrected.

"You speak Ancient Greek?" I cried, head whipping around to Dom.

She opened one eye and peered at me. "Told you I'm not as stupid as I look." She closed her eye and went on. "But no, I don't speak Greek. Ancient or new. My last hook-up was Greek, and I recognise the words. Besides, everybody knows only actors use Latin to cast spells and summon demons. People who really know what they're doing use Ancient Greek." She opened the eye again and gave me a mocking jab.

"Is that what's happening here," I said, "evoking demons?"

The outrageous remark was unremarkable in the middle of the otherworldly landscape. No one thought to answer my question.

"Alila is not a demon," said Harun. "She is a goddess."

"I had a dream last night," I said at length.

"What about?" Adam said.

"George Green was in my tent."

"Was he just?" Dom's voice was loaded. "Don't tell me you're changing teams."

Ignoring her, I went on. "He told me about a djinni called Alila. Apparently, she was cursed." I shook my head, unsure of the details. "And she was imprisoned by God and had to wait to be freed."

"Go on," Dom said, when I stopped.

"George used strange words when he talked about God."

"Strange how?"

"He used words like 'Aeon' and 'false god'. And he suggested God was not aware of a greater truth." I shook my head again. "It didn't make sense."

"It does if you are familiar with Gnosticism."

"You know about Gnosticism?" This time I could not rid my voice of incredulity.

Dom sat up properly. "Like I said—again—I'm not some dumb bitch."

"Dom, I don't think—"

"Save it. Gnosticism is a mystic wing of Christianity, like Sufism in Islam."

I was dumbstruck. Could not believe that sentence came from Dom's mouth; I had really underestimated her.

"Go on," I said, interested to see where this was leading.

"Long story short," she continued, "in Gnosticism there's a true God, who didn't create anything. He or It simply exists. This true God brought forth the substance of all there is in the world. At the same time, portions of the original essence have been projected so far from the source that they changed."

I nodded and Dom continued.

"These discharges are false gods. They're called Aeons. According to Gnostics, the god who created this world is an Aeon."

"A false god?" I said.

Dom nodded. "But he doesn't know it. He thinks he's the real deal."

"In other words, the Christian god, the Muslim god, the Jewish god, and so on, they're fake."

"According to Gnostics."

"That means Alila is a false god too."

"Except, according to your dream, Alila is older than the god who created this world. By the sounds of it, she tried to stop him from creating us. He got pissed off and tossed her in the clink. Typical male! Some things never change."

"How do you know this?" I asked, looking at her.

Obviously satisfied with herself, Dom put her feet on the dashboard and said, "Mum and Dad were hardline Methodists. You remember. That house was like a mausoleum. Suffocating. Do this, don't do that. Say this, don't say that. Ugh, it was fucken awful. Couldn't wait to get away.

"But I still wanted to believe in God. I wanted to believe in something more than my shitty self. Just not their idea of a higher power that wagged a finger whenever I did something wrong. Stumbling onto Gnosticism in the encyclopaedia was my escape."

I was about to say I found it difficult to believe Dom had ever opened an encyclopaedia, let alone read it, but I bit my tongue. I remembered the *World Encyclopaedia* with the gold and brown spines carefully arranged on a dust-free bookshelf in the Device living room— the only books I recalled seeing in that beige house. I liked her neat and presentable parents. I just did not approve of the way they did not listen to their daughter and felt it was their duty to tell her what to do.

"So you're a Gnostic."

Dom shrugged. "It's a belief system, not a religion. One that treats me like an equal, not like shit because I'm a woman."

"You're full of surprises." I smiled, the cogs in my brain shifting in her favour.

"Yeah, I'm a regular jack-in-the-box. Now if you don't mind, I want to get some shut-eye." She dipped in her bag, retrieved another pill, threw it down the hatch and closed her eyes.

"What does all of this have to do with us?" I said to no one in particular.

The question fell into a well of silence. No one replied. After a while I dropped the subject, discomfited by the idea of gods and demons roaming the desert, even though back home it comprised the bread and butter of my daydreams.

A good half hour or so later, Adam spoke again.

"There's the hitchhiker again."

The woman went past on the right side of the road, an exact replica of her earlier appearance. The identical billowing white sails. The covered face. The head turning to follow the passing vehicle.

"Can't be the same woman," I said. "She'd be way back by now."

When the impossible began to happen, and continued to happen, over and over again for several alarming minutes, I tapped Dom on the shoulder.

"Time to save the world," I said.

Dom cracked open an eye. "What now?"

"Tell me you see that."

"Not another bird," Dom said, sitting up.

"Not a bird."

Frowning, she looked at the scene unfolding outside my window.

"Fuck me dead." And after further consideration: "My advice, don't stop. Keep going."

My heart thundered, my arms trembled at the wheel, because the world on my side of the van had turned white. Or rather it had turned into what appeared be a mass of trembling, gently subsiding linen stretched across the land. It reminded me of a bizarre version of wash day, with hundreds of bedsheets strung out to dry on the world's longest Hills Hoist. Only this went on for kilometres. There was no end to it.

It started with the hitchhiker flitting by every couple of seconds. Soon as the car passed her, then she reappeared. Appeared. Disappeared. Appeared. Disappeared. Faster and faster. Until she flashed by on dizzying high-rotation; until it looked as if the woman was unspooling like a massive bolt of white fabric against red soil.

No matter how fast I went—and I really did plant down my foot—she managed to keep up. The speed building to a frenzy as the van shot down the highway at astonishing speeds, the hitcher resembling an old-fashioned film reel on fast forward, repeating the same action over and over again with accelerating, maddening, tempo. Until even daylight flickered. Until I thought I was going to scream and never stop.

The steering wheel juddered in my sweating hands. My right leg jiggled. The van's frame vibrated, threatening to tear apart. I glanced at Dom, panic-stricken, beseeching her to do something. To stop this.

"Don't worry," she said, surprisingly calm. "I don't think she'll try anything. And if she does, this'll take care of her."

The last thing I expected to see was a stainless steel revolver with a black handgrip drawn from Dom's bag.

"Put that away and be serious," I said. "I really need your help."

"Done." Weapon dropped into bag and bag pushed under dashboard with foot. "The best thing you can do is slow down. You'll have an accident. Like I said, I don't think we're in danger."

I lightened the burden on the accelerator. Speed bled off. Dom was right. The last thing I wanted was an accident or to get booked for speeding.

By this time, the landscape on my side was a white movie screen, the other side totally normal.

"What's going on?" I managed, throat dry.

"I think this is your djinni."

"How can you be certain she won't hurt us?"

Dom took her time answering.

"Well?"

"First, I think the scorpion medallion is keeping her out. Second, I saw things when I stuck my finger in the light."

"What did you see?"

"Some fucked up shit."

"Specifics, please."

"Weird stuff. A jumble. Like quick impressions. Hard to distinguish. It felt like I stuck my head in someone else's head and copped a download of their life." Dom paused, reached for the water bottle in the holder between the seats and drank. "Before she zapped me out of there I saw…lots of stuff."

"Like?"

"Alila is weak and she needs to build up her strength." She chewed her lower lip, thinking it over.

"That confirms what George told me in the dream. Anything else?"

Dom shook her head, lost in thought. There was something else but she was not going to divulge.

"Did you know this was going to happen?" I said.

Dom nodded. "Sort of. Nothing specific. To be honest, I didn't think it was true. I mean it's so far-fetched when someone tells you about it in their sitting room."

"That's what I thought, too. You believe it now?"

She nodded again, her face reflecting conflicting emotions.

"You're not telling me something," I said, glancing at her.

"Yeah, nah, everything's fine…"

"Dom, you're lying."

"Question is what do you know about all this, Missy Din?" she said, after a brief silence. "What do you know about this djinni?"

It was an effective way to deflect attention away from herself. Not knowing where to begin about Alila, I focused on driving for the time being and searched my brain for all the stuff I had read over the years about Alila. I wanted to open the window, let in fresh air, but I was scared that thing might come in. I had eaten little at breakfast and my empty stomach was filled with so much cortisone and adrenaline from the stress and anxiety, I felt sick. More than anything I was scared for the kids. They had gone into some kind of a weird trance when the djinni appeared, staring ahead, like zombies.

"Well," I said, finally, "Alila was a fertility goddess worshipped in pre-Islamic Arabia."

"No shit." Dom yelled, switching on a big smile. "You mean the misogynists were ruled by a woman?"

"Muslims are not misogynists," I said over delighted hoots and claps.

"Sure they are. Look how they treat women."

I breathed through the nose to compose myself. "It's complicated."

"Yeah, well, they'd stone a dyke like you to death. So tell me how Islam is the most feminist religion in the world." Dominique made quote marks with her fingers.

I did my best to not be drawn in. "I'm more interested in Alila, actually."

"Was she a dyke, too?"

"Be serious."

"I am serious."

"Why do you always talk like that?"

"Like what?"

"I don't know. Rude. No respect or consideration for anything."

"Respect is earned, not given."

"Where did you read that? *The Book of Wise Sayings*?"

"TikTok."

Even though I was exasperated, I loved it when Dom talked like that. She was free. Did not care what anyone thought. Whereas I took everything and everyone into consideration before opening my mouth or making the slightest move. It was crippling. I was a prisoner in my own body. How I wished I could be like her.

"Anyway, according to myth," I went on, "Alila was a complicated figure. Some Semitic traditions say Alila is the female form of Allah. She ruled what is now the Middle East before Islam. Some believe that the Black Stone in the Qaaba represented her."

"The what inside the what?"

"The Black Stone is a holy relic inside the Qaaba, an ancient building located at the centre of the Grand Mosque in Mecca. It's the most holy site in the Islamic world."

"That'd be right," Dom quipped. "Patriarchy unseats matriarchy and steals holy objects. Nothing new there."

"The point is Alila was a pagan deity no different to Isis or Aphrodite in ancient mythology. She wasn't real."

"Tell her that." Dom pointed at the drama unfolding outside.

"Depending on which region you come from," I continued, "Alila was either Allah's wife, his older sister, or his daughter."

"Probably all of them. The old gods fucked anything that moved." Warming to her subject, Dom reached into her bag, drew a cigarette, tapped it on her knee, caught my disapproving glance and slipped it back in the pack. "God, you're boring."

"Here's the crunch," I said. "Yesterday George said something really interesting."

"What?"

"He said I had to do take this job. I couldn't turn it down."

"Why?"

"Because I owe Alila."

"What can a sweet, innocent girl like you possibly owe a non-existent deity?"

I hesitated. "George said Alila saved my life, thirteen years ago."

Dom whistled, long and low.

At that moment, two things happened simultaneously. The whiteness outside the window disappeared and, just as the road sign for

Coober Pedy appeared, Rashid started to scream.

"I see you," the boy yelled, thrashing in the back of the van. "I see you."

"Calm down, Rashid."

I leaned over him, my body shivering as the adrenaline drained from my muscles, leaving me weak and faint. Dom and I had run to his aid after I pulled over on the highway.

Bringing Rashid under control was not easy. He was big, with powerful arms and legs that thrashed and kicked in the van's narrow confines. He was obviously in the grips of a terrible nightmare.

"Rashid, it's alright," I said, looking at the other kids. They had emerged from their daze and watched with stony expressions. "You're safe."

Dom crawled into the van behind Rashid. With some effort, she managed to wrap her arms around his massive frame, holding him down while I leaned over his prone figure, rubbing his forehead, calling his name, patting his hands. To no avail.

"Is he having a seizure?" I said, panicked.

"Don't ask me," Dom said. "You're the nurse."

That snapped me out of the panic. The nursing certificate. I had not practiced, of course, but the dregs of training remained. Taking a deep breath, I forced myself to calm down and inspected Rashid. Although there was rapid, random muscle movement, he had not lost consciousness. When I checked under the eyelids, his eyes had not rolled back in his head or dilated. He had not lost control of his bladder and his face had not turned blue, which meant he was breathing.

Unbuttoning the top three buttons of his tunic and pulling open the collar to give him air, I told Dom to turn him on his left side to aid breathing. Dom followed orders, handling Rashid with surprising gentleness.

"I'll call triple zero," I said, reaching for my phone.

"No ambulance."

"His life could be in danger."

Dom shook her head. "He can't go to hospital."

"Why not?"

Dom did not reply. So many no-go areas, I thought. So much rudeness. I backed away from the vehicle and stood on the roadside. Hands on hips, I looked around and tried to think of what to do next to help the boy. I had parked at a crossroads, where a dirt road intersected with the highway. This close to town, there ought to be someone who could help. All I saw was a blasted landscape of gleaming mullock heaps, spoils from the opal mines that dotted the desert. The bleak terrain looked positively apocalyptic.

When I looked back the way we had come, I was startled to see a massive wall of roiling dust advancing on us from the north: a dust storm. Thankfully, it was still several kilometres away.

"I'll call George," I said, leaning inside the van. "He should—"

A kick to the stomach catapulted me from the van. I flew backwards through the air and landed with a jolt on my back. Winded, I lay in the dust, gasping with shock, clutching my gut and trying to catch my breath. The pain brought tears to my eyes. My head whirled. Over and above that was the sudden rage. It flowered in my gut as I lay in the dirt, curled up and fighting the urge to smash Rashid in the face. Hit him, make him feel what I felt. How dare he kick me after everything I had done for him.

Slowly, breath by painstaking breath, I forced the black snake back in the bottle and put the cork in it. The impulse to hit and pummel subsided.

Rashid had regained consciousness. He leaned against Dom, right leg raised and aimed at me. His eyes whirled in his head, like a frightened horse.

"Don't come near me," he cried.

I had not moved; I was lying on the ground, leaning up on my elbows to see inside the car.

"I see you," Rashid repeated.

My voice was weak. "See what?"

"I trusted you, and you lied."

"Lied about what?" Dom said, gently pulling him towards her and stroking his brow.

Rashid said, "She knows."

Puzzled, hurt, I turned over and vomited. When I finished, I wiped my mouth with the back of my hand and sat up. That's when I saw the woman.

She stood where the two roads intersected. Her rippling robes lashing the air, snapping in the oncoming wind and flying around her, like tattered wings, the face a black maw inside a deep hood. There one minute, gone the next.

Dom came up to me.

"He's okay," she said. "Had a bit of a scare, that's all. I'll sit with him while you drive. We need to go."

No asking after my wellbeing. No nothing. Just pulled me to my feet and pushed me into the car.

Seated, I sipped tepid water from a bottle and looked at them in the rear-view mirror. Water helped ease the fire in my gut. But I did not know what hurt most, my abdomen or my feelings. I thought Rashid was my friend. Now he hated me and I did not know what had changed. Truth is, I could not bear the fact that he hated me. I wanted—needed—to be liked. Not just by him, but by everyone. To be accepted and drawn in. Not driven out.

"Drive," Dom said, squeezing in beside Rashid.

Feeling dejected, I started the engine and headed for town. Acutely aware of the empty seat beside me, I sat alone, while they clustered together, pushing me away. They did not care. They did not see me. I thought they were friends. They were not.

No matter what I do, I thought, I am always outside. But I will show them what I'm capable of doing. Then they will see. The past follows me wherever I go, threatening to undo my efforts. If I could only start over. I don't need Dominique. I don't need a bunch of weird kids. I have myself. But how painfully alone it can be sometimes.

CHAPTER 17

"Turn left and go straight," Dom directed from the back of the van.

I followed instructions, turning into a gently bending road that went past a police station and headed for the town centre. The backs of houses and industrial complexes came into view as the begrimed vehicle slowed from eighty to fifty kilometres an hour to accommodate changing speed limits.

I took in the legendary outback town as I navigated the rundown outskirts.

The gibber plains and distant mountain ranges made Coober Pedy appear small and insignificant, nothing more than a series of tumble-down fences, clusters of tin roofs, lacklustre vegetation and black tarmac in between. It was hard to believe most residents lived under-ground to escape the tremendous heat. The notion of building a town in such remote, inhospitable regions seemed foolhardy and heroic in equal measure, an attempt to stamp civilisation on a landscape that was as desolate as Mars. It would not take much to wipe out the place, I thought. Yet it had existed since the early days of the twentieth century, an anomaly that defied expectation.

"Turn left," Dom said as the van approached a T-junction, "and go through the next roundabout."

My stomach growled with hunger, reminding me it was almost half past twelve. I was contemplating lunch when Salih spoke.

"Here comes the dust storm," he said. There was a note of triumph in his voice as he pressed his nose to the window and looked back the way we had come.

The sky to the north was the colour of rotten oranges. Grey-green, high as a mountain, a colossal dust cloud hurtled towards town, blotting the sky and reducing light to a bare minimum. Lightning flashes inside the accretion resembled jagged legs of behemoths stalking the land.

"Looks like a bad one," I said.

It started as a low-range howl, the strong wind buffeting the vehicle and setting shop signs into agitated motion. Trees and bushes bent almost to the ground. People ran for cover in the shopping strip, squinting and keeping down heads. Plastic bags took to the air and skated on pavements. Newspapers danced. The roar of a jumbo jet fell from the sky and when the storm hit, the van was instantly enveloped in a rain of fine dirt particles that pelted the panelling and pinged off windows.

I found myself driving in a world of seething reddish-yellow. Visibility dropped to a few metres. Normal sounds ceased. There was only a booming from the edges of the known universe. Beyond was a haze in which shadowy figures darted, phantom-like, in and out, only to vanish. I was not sure if some of them were human or not. Cars switched on lights and slowed, so that headlights pierced the miasma like gleaming eyes in a dark room. I did the same and, somehow, that made everything worse. Shafts of crimson sent searching fingers through the obscuration, reaching for me as I struggled to stay on the road. Buildings became indistinct, the street vaporous, on the verge of disintegrating.

"Here," Dominique said, pointing ahead. "On the right."

A petrol station came swimmingly into view on the next corner. I indicated a turn and inadvertently mounted the pavement with a jolt as I steered into the driveway. My passengers were flung about in their seats. Thankfully, the air bags did not go off. I apologised, pulled in next to a bowser and turned off the engine, relieved.

"Here?"

"Yes."

"What now?"

Dominique settled in between Musa and Rashid. "Why don't you look under the bonnet or something?" she said.

"In this storm?" I said, outraged.

I was really starting to resent the way she was bossing me around. After all, I was supposed to be running the show and she was meant to be the aid.

"You're the one who's always going on about how you much you love the sand and the desert," she said. "Here's your big chance to get acquainted with both."

"You can be a real bitch sometimes."

"I'm sorry you think that."

"Well, I do."

"I thought I was a bitch all the time."

I thought it best to get out of there before I slugged her. Clenching my jaw, I edged out and stood beside the car. Despite the wind that pulled at my hair and clothing, it was eerily quiet. Sand stung my face and the backs of my hands, like a million tiny pinpricks, making me feel as if tiny insects were assaulting me.

A beanpole of a man in a backwards baseball cap and dirty navy overalls darted from the service station and uttered words filled with sand.

"You right, luv?" he shouted a second time.

"Yep, good," I yelled in his face. "I'll take care of everything." I pointed at the bonnet, nodded, a silent mime.

He gave a thumbs-up and scuttled indoors, no doubt glad to be out of harm's way.

There were things to do before hitting the Oodnadatta Track. I pulled a red bandana from my back pocket, tied it across the lower half of my face and set to making sure we'd be right for the rest of the journey. Working methodically, I checked the tyre pressure, water, oil, and topped up on petrol. Far as I knew, William Creek Road was sealed most of the way to its namesake hamlet. From there, I had to take the Oodnadatta Track to Marree. That was almost two hundred and four kilometres of unsealed road—easy in a decent four-wheel drive like this. It had not rained, which meant the roads would be in good condition, if maintained. Even so I must make sure everything was in order with the vehicle before leaving Coober Pedy. One stuff-up and I was lost, especially as there was no phone reception.

I finished playing mechanic, paid, and threw myself into the car, relieved to be out of the elements. There was a terrible hush inside the cabin. My passengers huddled together and stared at the scorpion medallion hanging from the rear-view mirror.

Was it my imagination or was it pulsating? As I looked in growing wonder, a faint orange light throbbed, pulsed, like a beating heart. I turned to Dom.

"Is that thing glowing?" I said.

No response. Several minutes passed. I was fidgety, nervous, could not keep still. Odd sensations passed through me, leaving me feeling light-headed, weak, confused.

"Should we leave now?" I asked. "Or wait till the storm's over?"

The church-like hush, the sense of anticipation, building to a pitch.

The medallion continued to pulse, the light in the cabin intensifying, dulling, intensifying and dulling.

Finally, unable to bear it another moment, I turned to Dom, but she got in before me.

"It's lunch time," she said. "Get something to eat." She pointed across the road where a souvlaki joint was barely visible on the opposite corner.

"Why don't we all go?"

"We'll wait here," Dom said, barely moving her lips. "Here's some money." She reached into her pocket.

"I've got money," I snapped, keenly aware she wanted me gone.

Before leaving, I asked the boys if they wanted anything. No one replied. Smarting from the rejection, I left the van, slamming the door behind me. After checking for traffic, I ran across the street, keeping my head down and my mouth closed. The wind slammed into me in the middle of the street, almost knocking me down. I struggled to keep my footing.

A bell rang over the door as I stepped into the shop. I closed the door, killing the wind as surely as turning off a giant fan.

"What'll it be, luv?"

A middle-aged man with a round, unshaven face stood behind a counter with a glass front, surveying me with a wide grin. Greek pop music played from hidden speakers on a wall.

I scanned the menu neatly written on a blackboard above the man's head.

"A souvlaki, please. No onions," I said, leaning on the polished silver top.

"Good choice. We make the best souvlaki in South Australia. Want a drink with that?"

"A bottle of water."

"Still or sparkling?"

"Still."

"Bubbly gives me gas too," he said. "Fart like a truck."

I smiled, handed over fifteen dollars and took a stool at a bench facing the street. Pulling over a stack of newspapers and magazines, I settled down to catch up on celebrity gossip while I was there. The van was barely visible through the haze. Only an amorphous black blob in a seething sea. The medallion must be lit up like a Christmas tree because, quite suddenly, a blaze came forth from the car, lighting up the surrounds.

I saw, or thought I saw, a tall man with the long, fluid motions of spindly limbs approach the van.

The sliding door opened. Rashid emerged and stood beside the man. In the next instant, the thin man lifted the boy bodily in the air. Dust thickened above them and, from where I sat, it seemed all of nature's fury drew back, like a panther or a wolf, and then leaped hungrily on Rashid, engulfing him. When the dust cleared, man and boy were gone. There was only a circle of fading light inside the van's cabin.

"Here's your souvlaki, luv," the man said, bringing over my order. "Didja cop the storm on the highway?"

I shook my head and told him we'd missed it.

"On ya, luv," he replied. "You wouldn't wanna get caught up in that soup." He gestured outside the shop. "Where are you from, anyways?"

"Alice Springs."

He nodded, waiting for more information, and when I wasn't forthcoming: "Where you off to, then?"

"Marree."

"Tourist?"

"Nope."

He nodded again, eyes locked on me.

I took a bite of the souvlaki. It was excellent, warm and fresh with plenty of juicy tomato and lamb. Made a change from lentils. My eyes fell on the newspaper in front of me. I stared, blinked. Had trouble swallowing. Coughed. Thought I was choking. A roar built inside my head as I absorbed the shocking headline and took in the black-and-white composite photo accompanying the story.

"Terrible business," the man said, also looking at the paper. "Poor kids. Didja hear the latest?"

"What?" I said.

"Their bodies disappeared from the morgue coupla days ago."

The roar in my head changed to an irritating buzz. My vision faltered. I coughed, spluttered, thumped my chest…

The man's "You okay, luv?" sounded distant and faint.

Headshots of seven boys. Familiar faces, smiling, staring, drowned the music from the speakers. Another kind of cry built up inside my skull, animal, bellowing, furious. Grabbing the newspaper in a fist, I leaped to my feet and, without warning, my legs gave out from under me. I toppled to the floor, pulling everything on the counter down with me. The back of my head struck the ground and I knew no more.

CHAPTER 18

"Wakey-wakey."

Gently, the voice pulled me back. Reeled me in. Eyes fluttered. Opened. Deep intake of breath. From my position on the floor, I stared up at the grey dropped ceiling with banks of light fixtures, smoke detector and air grille. Into that pushed Dom's face. Oval shape, golden hair, flushed cheeks, the bluest eyes in the world gazing into mine, like a dream, afloat above me. Like old times. The lips parted and I thought she was going to kiss me. Wake me up from a bad dream, like a fairy princess. Instead:

"Welcome back."

"You'll be fine in a sec, luv." The Greek's head appeared beside Dom's.

Aided by Dom, I sat up, feeling confused, embarrassed.

"What happened?"

"You fainted."

"I hope it wasn't the souvlaki," the man put in.

"Get some water," Dom told him.

He left.

She helped me to a chair at a nearby table. "You right?"

I nodded, stared into space, unable to get my bearings. I was confused. Could not remember what happened. Why did I faint? Then I saw it. The newspaper at my feet, pushed under the bench along the shop window. And everything came back in a rush. The photograph. The dreadful, bewildering headline. The man's words: "Terrible business. Poor kids."

Poor kids, indeed.

What about me? They made a fool out of me. Did not tell me the truth. But what was the truth? Surely the newspaper's claims could not be true.

The shop owner returned with a white plastic cup. "Here you go, luv. Feeling better?" The anxious face was eager to please. "Nothing like this has happened before. You must be allergic to tomatoes or something. Some people are, you know."

"I'm fine," I said, staring at the street. The storm was breaking, leaving skeins of red to float in front of a powder-blue sky. The shop's windows were streaked with dirt. Already people were outside, cleaning up after the storm. A woman wiped a table with a wet rag and set chairs aright on the pavement. Cars reappeared as if nothing had happened. Business as usual. "Where are the kids?"

"Right there." Dom nodded at the street.

The van was parked outside the shop. The sliding door was open and Adam was leaning against the vehicle, staring at me through the window with one leg up against the panelling, arms folded across his chest. No sign of the others and for some reason that bothered me. It brought to mind Rashid's weird departure. The man lifting him up. Surely I had imagined that, what with dust flying around and poor visibility. The boy was probably safe with his family by this time.

"Rashid's dad picked him up?"

"One down, six to go," Dom answered.

I nodded and put the boy from my mind. There were other, more troubling things to think about.

It was a good fifteen minutes before I was able to get back behind the wheel. The nausea and the awful lurching in my stomach retreated. The knowledge of what I had seen in the newspaper remained. I could not shake it off. All the things I ought to have known. The things Dom and George kept from me. A secret from which I was barred. Now that I knew, I could not believe it was possible. How could it be? If I could accept an ancient djinni prowling the outback, I ought to have no trouble coming to terms with the newspaper's horrendous revelations. I was desperate to ask Dom, to fling the knowledge in her face, but not in front of the shop owner.

She asked if I was ready to leave. I nodded again and asked the man if I could keep the newspaper.

"All yours, luv." He gestured with a big, hairy hand. "It's old news anyway, God help 'em." He crossed himself three times in the Greek Orthodox manner.

I picked up the paper, rolled it up and stuffed it in the back pocket of my tracksuit pants. *Ammunition for later,* I thought as we left the premises.

"Have a safe one," the man called, waving from the door.

Now that the storm had moved on, the sun was bright, the air gritty with sand. There was a lovely clean smell, fresh, as if it had rained. Mounds of dirt piled up against buildings and lay thick in gutters, a grim reminder. Like a right gentleman, Adam stepped forward to help me into the car.

I shooed him away. "I'm fine. Don't fuss." I was angry with all of them.

"What's wrong with you?" he said.

"Probably all the bulldust I've been breathing for the last couple of days," I mumbled.

He exchanged glances with Dom. She shrugged.

I climbed into the car and slammed the door shut, putting all my strength into it and feeling a voltage of the earlier fury well up again. Dominique Device. George Green. Adam, Harun. They had played me for a fool when all I wanted was to help, to be part of the group, to protect. Then I hated myself for being angry. For falling for it. For feeling negative emotions. For being naive and foolish. I ought to have known this was going to happen. That I could never be accepted, never be part of a group.

Dom climbed in beside me and turned on the air conditioner. "Hot," she said, wiping beads of perspiration from the skin above her damp shirt.

Seating arrangements had changed now that Rashid was gone. Harun sat directly behind the driver's seat with Musa and Adam. The twins pressed close together in the row behind them, whispering.

Harun placed a consoling hand on my left shoulder. "Are you alright?" he whispered.

"Yes," I replied. I wasn't. Far from it.

Taking a deep breath, I reached up with both hands and pulled back my hair, tying it in a knot at the back of my neck. That felt better. I could see, feel the cool air pumping out of the air-con on my skin.

I patted Harun's hand. "Put on your seat belt."

I got back on the road. At the edge of town, I turned left on to the William Creek Road and headed east, aware that from there on I was well and truly in the wild. About as far from humanity as you can get. Yet I was not afraid. Despite everything, my heart soared to see the rocky outcrops give way to red gibber gravel. Tufts of pale green grass to the horizon. Emptiness as far as the eye could see. It was real. Not fake, like my passengers. Like the lies I had been fed the last couple of days.

For the next little while, William Creek Road was sealed. The van cruised at one hundred kilometres an hour, passing glistening mullock heaps, derelict outposts and dried riverbeds whose white stones glistened in the sunlight. Black birds rose like evil presentiments. Two camper vans headed in the opposite direction went past, trailing clouds of dust. It was an hour or so later, when we had passed the fourth abandoned car—a ute rusting by the roadside—that I said, "When were you going to tell me?"

"Tell you what?"

I flung the newspaper in Dom's lap.

The headline read: '7 SCHOOLBOYS GUNNED DOWN AT ALICE SPRINGS MOSQUE'.

CHAPTER 19

FIVE DAYS EARLIER

"Mags, turn the TV on the twenty-four hour news channel. Hurry." Groaning, I pressed the phone to my ear and leaned against the kitchen wall.

"What's wrong?"

I was wearing a white t-shirt that came to my knees and black, no-nonsense knickers. The house phone had woken me and now I stood, dazed, on the cool linoleum floor in bare feet, listening to Leah Unger. Her voice was too loud for that time of morning.

According to the clock on the wall it was 10.20.

Hanging up, I shuffled to the lounge, turned on the TV, and collapsed on the couch. Wincing at the loud noise that blasted from the flat-screen (Nan must be going deaf), I turned down the volume, pulled chilled feet under me, and listened.

A blonde female reporter's voice, high, excited, stumbled over words. Staccato sentences snagged my sleep-dazed brain.

> *The dead…*
> *Numbers unknown…*
> *Police cordoned off area…*
> *Horrific scenes…*
> *Carnage…*

The reporter's face filled the screen. Behind her, through the dust storm that had swept through Alice Springs that morning, was a familiar tree-lined street. Anxious faces peered over the woman's shoulder as she spoke.

> *Terrified residents fled when a gunman opened fire on this quiet, suburban street.*

I could not follow what she was saying. "What?" I leaned forward.

I had come home early the previous day with a migraine—worse than usual and probably brought on by another sleepless night. It lingered behind the left eye, causing it to throb. The Mersyndol tablets must have stopped working. Maybe I ought to switch medication again. For some reason the migraines always got worse this time of year, subsiding to a debilitating ache the rest of the time. News items like this did not help, especially as I hadn't had coffee yet. This is precisely why I did not watch TV news: it was full of horrors. Better not to know.

I walked to the phone, dialled Leah's number and walked back to the couch with the receiver, long cord trailing behind me.

"Leah, what is this?"

"What's what?"

"The stuff on television."

"Don't know what you're talking about."

"You just rang to tell me to turn on the TV."

"No, I didn't."

"You didn't call me a minute ago?"

"I'm at work. What's this about, Mags?"

"I think someone's shooting people on Scholten Drive. It's on the news."

Leah swore and hung up.

Puzzled, I turned my attention to the television. If Leah hadn't called, then who did? Scholten Drive was only a couple of blocks away.

On the TV, the female reporter pushed a microphone into an African woman's face. She was short, middle-aged, and wore a white, tasselled headscarf.

> *You're a witness? What did you see?*
> *Man, shooting people at mosque.*
> *What did he look like? Can you describe him?*
> *I only see them from behind.*
> *You said* them. *How many were there?*
> *Two. No, one.*
> *What did you actually see?*
> *No much. I scared and go inside. I only see one boy fall—*
> *A boy?*
> *I hear POP, POP, POP and run.*

"My god."

Someone was shooting kids? I stared at the screen aghast, unable to believe my ears. How could such a horrible thing happen in Alice

Springs? What was the world coming to?

On the screen, the reporter stood next to a young Aboriginal man. A bright yellow shirt set off a shiny face. Orange dust drifted around him and settled on his shoulders as if he stood in the heart of a great fire. The Scholten Drive mosque was partially visible behind him, somewhat blocked by a white mini bus and an ambulance, blue lights sweeping the haze. Officialdom moved through the open gates in the driveway. There were stretchers, medical kits, grim, determined, faces.

"I jumped him but he hit me in the face and drove off," said the Aboriginal guy. The camera zoomed in on his bruised face. "There's dead kids all over the place, man." He gestured behind him, distressed.

The reporter turned to a grey-haired police officer who confirmed that a search was underway for the alleged gunman who had driven away in a black vehicle. "He's armed and dangerous. Residents are advised to stay indoors and keep safe."

On hearing the warning, my mind went to the most obvious person. "Nan."

I headed to her room. The mosque on Scholten Drive was her place of worship. She ought to be in the lounge room, watching this. But she was not in her room. A quick search of the house revealed that my grandmother was not there. I returned to the kitchen and inspected the whiteboard beside the fridge. This was where Nan compiled her shopping list and left messages for me. The two sentences scribbled in blue Texta froze my blood.

GONE TO MOSQUE. BACK FOR LUNCH.

Praying to a god I did not believe in, I picked up the phone and pressed 1 for her number. It went straight to message.

"Come on, answer."

She didn't.

I called the mosque next. Engaged. A monotone beep sounded a bleak note against the horror of what was happening blocks away.

In the bedroom I quickly pulled on yesterday's tracksuit pants and a fleece hoodie. Although it was mid-morning, the light outside belonged more rightly to twilight, an orange shifting screen that made the world unreal. I jumped into my dark-blue Pulsar and drove, turning on the wipers to prevent sand building up on the windscreen.

I could barely see past the bonnet, the dust was so thick and light so poor. It was only when I came to the end of Latz Drive and turned right into Albrecht Drive that I switched on the headlights. Two beams cut through the haze as the car inched forward. Details of a porch or a gate hinted at the suburb hidden in the powdery consistency that layered everything. It would be easy for an assailant to vanish in this as quickly as he doubtless appeared.

In a weird kind of way, I like dust storms. They allow you to move invisibly without being noticed, like a ghost, a presence lacking substance. I was thinking this when, with a gasp, I hit the brakes and wrenched the steering wheel to the left, mounting the nature strip and almost colliding with a sapling that had seen better days. Ahead was a wall of people.

I sat in the car for a couple of seconds, trying to control my heartbeat. When I regained composure, I left the Pulsar and walked in the direction of the mosque. Existence on the street was reduced to an orange-red cloud from which the outlines of men and women appeared and disappeared like phantoms. Sand stung my face and got in my eyes and mouth. Squeezing between a tall man and a short woman, I rounded the corner into Scholten Drive. The mosque was half a block down on the left. The start of the normally quiet street was blocked. Gawkers pressed shoulder to shoulder, peering over heads and making it difficult for ambulances to manoeuvre. A few people held up phones to take pictures.

I shouldered through the throng, feeling the tension in the back of my neck, and the return of the migraine as it pulsed in my left temple. It was warm and muggy, perspiration running from my armpit down the side of my ribcage. Two police officers were stationed halfway down the street, keeping the way open for emergency vehicles. Everyone else was kept out. Reporters milled about, asking police officers if there was new information. It was only when I stood outside the cordon that I spotted the white minivan I had seen earlier on television. Parked in front of the mosque, the bullet-riddled vehicle was the centre of orderly police activity.

I approached a short police officer with a beer gut. "I have to go through," I said. "My grandmother's in there."

He put up a hand with a gold wedding band on a plump finger. "No can do. There'll be an official statement about the victims soon."

The word 'victims' made me queasy. I backed away and looked for another way to get to the mosque. That was when I spotted Leah Unger with a couple of women across the street.

"Come with me," Leah said when I told her Nan was probably in the mosque.

Leah was in her mid-fifties, curly chestnut hair framing a strong face and intelligent eyes. She led me down a lane behind the houses facing the mosque and we emerged further along the Drive, away from police activity. Only a handful of locals had congregated at this end. No one stopped us when we clambered down the dry creek bed, walked under the overpass and scaled the crumbling banks to climb over a wobbly tin fence to the rear of the mosque.

Leah tried the back door. "Locked," she whispered. "Try the front."

Pressed together, we made our way along the west side of the building, keeping close to the brick wall and trying to make as little noise as possible.

"What's Cherry doing here this time of the day?"

"Don't know." I shook my head. Nan and her cronies usually prayed later, before going for coffee and cake. Then I remembered the previous night's conversation. "Last night she said she was part of a welcoming committee for a school group."

Leah stopped in her tracks, causing me to bump into her. We were behind a squat brick tower crowned with the green Islamic crescent.

"Word is the gunman was targeting the schoolkids," Leah whispered. "Four or five are dead."

I did not trust myself to speak; I could not lose my grandmother as well. That would be too much after losing both parents. I pushed back against the pain in my temples and momentarily closed my eyes against the blinding light.

Leah took my hand. "You be strong now."

I nodded.

"Let's face the music," she said.

Together we stepped like frightened yet oddly determined adventure story heroines into the bustle of the forecourt.

Across the way, five bodies lay where they had fallen, covered with blood-soaked sheets abuzz with flies. An ambulance with open rear doors had backed into the drive and a female paramedic attended to an adult male on a gurney. His left arm and shoulder were wrapped in bandages. The ambulance doors closed, the vehicle pulled away with a soft whoop of sirens and was replaced by another. Two men emerged from the cabin and gently, as if handling fragile goods, proceeded to zip the first corpse in a grey body bag, leaving behind a chilling chalk outline on the concrete. A heftier body, red hair poking from under the white sheet, lay further along the driveway. A large hand was visible, fingers curled like a dead crab on its back. The sight of the lifeless body, knowing it would never move again or know the touch of mother or father, almost pushed me over the edge. But I held on. Had to for Nan's sake.

"Who would do such a thing?"

Leah shook her head, clearly distressed.

I was wondering if my grandmother was similarly prone under a sheet when a young constable with black, curly hair approached.

"What are you two doing here?"

"It's alright, officer," Leah said, pushing in front of me. "We're with the mosque."

"You haven't seen a short woman in her sixties, have you?" I asked.

The man shook his head. "Best get back inside, if I were you."

He pointed at the nondescript building behind us as a microphone came to crackling life on his right shoulder. The cop turned his back, speaking urgently into it, as Leah and I stepped inside. The interior was as unremarkable as I remembered from my one visit many years ago. A plain rectangular room with banks of fluorescent lights in the low ceiling. A green and red carpet before a mihrab contained a pulpit with a microphone. So charmless, I thought, it would scare God away. If He existed.

Leah made a beeline for a bulky African in a white jalabiya and skull-cap.

"Karim, is Cherry Din here?"

The man looked at me when he heard Nan's name.

"Daughter of Iblis," he whispered. "You dare enter Allah's house?"

Leah stepped between us, a short woman caught between two tall people.

"Now is not the time," she said. "Is Cherry here?"

Karim glared at me over Leah's head. "You sin against nature," he hissed, eyes boring into me. "It's all over town and you dare parade your sins inside this holy place? I see..." He nodded. "This terrible thing, it is happening because of you. You cause this."

I was so shocked, I could not speak. I closed my eyes and lowered my head, taking deep breaths to control myself. For a moment I could not move, let alone say anything in my defence. I had never felt the need to apologise for loving women. As far as I was concerned, it was not wrong. If someone took issue, it was their problem, not mine. But to be accused of causing the deaths of others—that was too much. Unacceptable. I could not, under any circumstance, allow this ignoramus to make such vile accusations.

"Karim, please," Leah said. "There's no need for this."

The migraine throbbed behind my eyeballs. My hands felt like they belonged to someone else as they tightened into fists by my sides. I forced myself to open my eyes and saw, first a blinding light, and then an all-encompassing blackness.

"With all due respect, Karim," Leah was saying, "you're way out of line."

In the next instant, I pushed her aside and lunged at Karim.

He was bigger, stronger, but I had years of built-up rage and the element of surprise on my side. Besides, Karim did not expect a mere woman to attack him inside a house of worship. Attack I did, grabbing him by the throat and head-butting him on the nose. There was a crack. The man howled with shock and pain. He fell back, cursing, a hand clamped over his face as blood pulsed between fingers.

His voice was muffled when he yelled, "Leave, witch," pointing with a bloodstained hand.

Swearing under her breath, Leah guided me away. Behind us, like a malediction, Karim continued to shout.

"Your grandmother is dead. You killed her. Whore."

Nan was not dead. She was badly wounded. Even so, the incident, and the imam's imprecations, planted a seed in my mind. One day, one way or another, I would be responsible for Nan's death. That was how it went with me. Mother, father, and eventually grandmother. It seemed I was cursed, and my curse was to kill anyone I loved. It was probably just as well Dom left when she did. Otherwise, I would have caused her death as well.

Chapter 20

And here I was, reaping the rewards.

Did all that happen five days ago? It seemed a lot longer. An eternity of hell, fear and anxiety. Sitting inside the van, looking at the unforgiving landscape around me, I could not believe it. Yet, somehow, it was true. I had been wrangled into a plot—a conspiracy that was connected to events that had happened to me thirteen years ago, and now to these kids.

"Why pretend they're dead when they're not?" I yelled.

I glanced at Dom and turned my attention back to the road. I felt like I did that day in the mosque, with Karim, when he told me Nan was dead because of me being a lesbian. It had felt good to hit him. To see him in pain and bleeding. Afterwards, as Leah told me off, I did not feel in the least guilty about it. Had not seen fit to apologise. He had it coming. Scary thing was, that is how I felt at that moment. All I wanted was to explode inside the car, cause harm and injury. I quivered with rage.

"Say something."

Dom remained obstinately silent. What could she say? According to the *Central Advocate* in her lap, the boys I had been ferrying across the desert for two days were dead. They were killed by a terrorist who was still at large. Yet the six kids who shared the vehicle with me—the headshots and the names under them testified to the fact they were the same—were clearly not dead. They were alive. They did not have a scratch on them.

Dom clenched her jaw and hid behind her sunglasses. *Obstinate bitch*, I thought, fighting another urge to thump her.

"Answer me."

"After the boys were killed, the bodies were taken to the morgue—"

At last!

"I know. I was at the mosque."

Dom lifted her glasses and peered at me. "You were there that day?"

I nodded.

"How come?"

"My grandmother was there. Bastard shot her. She's lucky to be alive."

"I'm sorry," Dom said in a tight voice.

"They should bring back the death penalty for him. What happened after they were taken to the morgue?"

I didn't like to talk about the boys as if they were not there, but it could not be helped. I was past niceties. I had to know what was going on if I was going to continue with this charade. Even then, I might still walk away.

"How many kids were at the mosque last Friday?" I asked.

"Seven," Adam, one of the supposedly dead boys, replied.

"Right, seven boys were killed. Seven boys were taken to the morgue. What happened next?"

"Early Saturday morning," Dom said, "I helped George remove the bodies from the morgue and take them to his house."

"Why?"

Dom replied in mini sentences, as though she resented every utterance.

"His house is built on a cave system. The soil has…I don't know, special properties. If you bury a corpse there, it comes back to life. I helped George bury the boys Saturday and they came back to life Monday."

"More lies!" I cried, smacking the steering wheel with the palm of my hand. It hurt. Almost as much as the presentiment of low-grade pain in my temples, and I had forgotten to bring migraine pills.

"Why would I make it up?" Dom said.

"You tell me."

"I wouldn't have believed it if I hadn't seen it with my own eyes."

"You expect me to believe this nonsense, after what you did to me?"

"What are you talking about?"

"You abandoned me. You skipped town and left me alone. Or did you forget that? Did it mean so little to you?"

"That was a lifetime ago."

"For you."

Both of us absorbed that sad declaration, like dust settling on furniture in an abandoned house. I continued to drive, the landscape growing more arid and starker with each passing kilometre. The bitumen was a corridor on the wide expanse, covered by a network of dried creeks and riverbeds that crisscrossed each other. I saw it from high above; it looked, for all the world, like the cuttings I had made on my inner thighs, scars and welts intersecting, some fresh, others faded, and some strong and new. One for Mum. Another for Dad. Yet another for being bad and hard to like. Another for releasing all the mental torment and agony I felt on a daily basis. Why was I so unlovable? Why did people walk out on me? Why did they treat me so badly? On it went until my skin was a roadmap of pain, until I felt like I floated above rooftops, temporarily free of guilt and suffering.

"I helped George bury the bodies," Dom repeated. "Three days later, I saw them sit up, alive. I don't care whether you believe me or not. It happened."

"Harun," I said.

His eyes met mine in the mirror.

"Is this true?"

He gave a decisive nod, eyes steady as lamps on a windless night.

"Don't be afraid," he said. "Everything's going to be alright. Trust me."

Hearing the same words I'd used on Rashid in Kulgera made my skin crawl. The vertigo that had gripped me in Coober Pedy returned. My head swam. The landscape wavered. I took two deep breaths to clear my head and concentrated on driving. *The grey bitumen*, I thought, *the white line down the middle. They are real, dependable. They can be relied upon.*

Abruptly, the tarmac ended. The tyres shot off on the unmade road, making a harsh grinding sound on hard-packed soil. "Follow where all is fled," I thought as the unsealed road proceeded, unbending to the horizon.

"If what you say is true," I said, "why bring them back to life?"

Dom did not reply.

"Answer me." My head whipped around so fast that my neck snapped, intensifying the pain in my temples.

Dom flinched. The car swerved, almost mounting the verge.

"Keep your eyes on the road," she said, reaching for the steering wheel.

I swatted away her hand, brought the car under control. "I'm waiting."

"Alila wants the boys."

"Why?"

"She feeds on resurrected children."

I slammed on the brakes so fast it brought the van to a skidding halt in the middle of the road, throwing about everyone inside.

"For heaven's sake!" I shouted, reaching for the door handle. "You're mad. I'm getting out of here." I knew I was acting badly, endangering the kids, but I could not help it. The old temper had taken over. I had been restraining myself for the last hour, gritting my teeth so hard my jaw ached. I could not hold back any longer.

Dom stayed my progress with a hand on the upper arm. "Mags," she said, voice steady. "I want you to calm down and drive. Will you do that? This is important."

We stared at each other, breath accelerated, heart racing. Me half out of the car and Dom holding me back. Finally, I calmed down, shook her off, put the car in gear and drove.

"What Dominique means," Adam said in due course, "is that Alila feeds on children who have the seed of life and death in them."

"Why?"

"To regain her strength," Adam replied.

"In other words," I said, "this is meals on wheels for a monster, and I'm the driver."

"Alila is not a monster," Harun said.

"Okay," I said with renewed determination. "How do we stop her?"

"We don't stop her," Dom said, alarmed.

"Of course we do. She's coming after the kids. We've sworn to protect them."

"You swore to protect them. I swore to make sure everything goes according to plan."

"It's fine, Magnolia," Salih said. "We are willing."

The calm acceptance coming from that trusting boy was infuriating. It made me want to shake him. To put up a damned good fight.

"Then why did you propose shooting Alila back there?" I said to Dom. "Why stop her if she's supposed to get them?"

Dom was surprisingly matter-of-fact. "George explained it to me," she said. "It's like the fairy stories where the prince goes through all these tests before he wins the princess's hand. It has to be a trial. It has to be hard. It can't be easy. And it has to happen in incremental stages. It must be an ordeal for Alila because nothing worth having is easily got. It has to be a challenge. She has to earn it. But she only has a small window of opportunity."

"The duration of a dark moon," I said.

Dom nodded.

"What happens if Alila doesn't get the boys during the dark moon?"

Dom shrugged. "She's only half revived, I guess."

In esoteric terms, the dark moon was a powerful liminal phase, transient and evanescent. A time when Earth's satellite was between waxing and waning. Magical traditions used that as a time for summoning deities and for honouring underground forces. The work must begin on the first day of a dark moon and end on the third and final day, as the sliver of a new moon appeared. Anything after that was null and void.

The trick, I thought, was to throw a spanner in the works. If I could do that, I may be able to save the boys.

"There's nothing you can do about it, Mags," Harun said as if he had read my mind. "We offer ourselves willingly. Except for Rashid."

"And look what happened to him," Zaman said.

I did not trust myself to drive after that pronouncement. I indicated and pulled over, even though there were no cars in sight.

I turned to Zaman. "Alila took Rashid?"

Shocked by the fierce expression on my face, Zaman pressed to his brother and looked away.

I turned to Dom. "Well?"

"Rashid was the first," Dom confirmed.

Her words barely penetrated my skull. In my mind's eye I saw the van at the petrol station. I saw again the sinister dust thicken over Rashid as he stood beside what appeared to be a man. The elongated figure lifting the heavy boy in the air and the cloud pouncing, like a cobra. When it cleared, no Rashid, no man. Despite the evidence of my eyes, I had told myself it had been Rashid's father, come to claim his son. I saw what I wanted to see. I believed what I wanted to believe. I watched it happen and did nothing. I clamped a hand over my mouth and almost vomited, sick with the awful realisation.

"That wasn't his father," I said.

Dom shook her head.

"Who was it?"

"Malachi. He collects them and gives them to Alila."

"And I told Rashid everything was going to be alright. No wonder he hated me."

The atmosphere in the vehicle thickened.

"Why didn't George tell me any of this at the start?"

"You wouldn't have believed him."

"No…"

"You wouldn't have taken part."

"Of course not."

"Mags, you have to understand," Musa said, "Alila is our mother. She's your mother, too."

"No real mother would treat her children like that," I said, facing him.

"We want to go back to her," Zaman said. "We were taken from her and we want to return."

I did not dignify the ludicrous pronouncements with a response. I put the car in gear and drove on, aware that I was no longer in control of my faculties. The migraine had intensified, electric currents shooting through my head, bad as it had ever been. My sight grew fuzzy as I commandeered the vehicle, head filled with the buzz of a million bees. I blinked to clear my vision. It did not help. I stopped at an intersection to check for non-existent traffic—had to check twice because I did not trust my senses—turned right onto a stretch of road with mounds of hard-baked earth banked on the edges and made a beeline for William Creek, hoping it was not too far away. Because I really could not take any more of this unreality. That is what it was like. Unreal, as if there was no ground under my feet. And I needed desperately to land on something solid. The stones pinging beneath the vehicle were the only things that grounded me to an unstable reality, but they were fleeting, hard to grasp.

"You're killing children," I said after a while.

"You can't kill what's dead."

"Call George. I need to speak to him."

Dom checked her phone. "No reception."

"Show me."

The signal bar was grey. Dom tossed the phone on the dashboard, and I drove on, mind in turmoil, turning over things I knew about djinns.

According to tradition, King Solomon controlled the djinn with a signet ring inscribed with a hexagram. The way a vampire is wary of garlic, djinn are said to be heedful of iron, citrus and salt—the latter of which was in plentiful supply in our provisions.

"I'm going to protect you from her whether you like it or not."

I did not realise I had spoken aloud until I heard Dom's rejoinder.

"You're making this harder than it needs to be."

And before I knew it, we were yelling at each other as I continued to drive an erratic course.

"We can't just hand them over to a demon."

"Why do you care?"

"Children are precious. They ought to be protected. Not treated like garbage. Not that you'd understand. Your womb is probably dry as the desert."

That hit the mark. I could tell from the expression on her face, and I almost regretted saying it. I opened my mouth to apologise and closed it again. Let her suffer. When Dom spoke, her voice was a tight constriction in the throat.

"Talking about yourself again, Missy Din. Mummy and Daddy left you with Grandma and you never got over it. Boo-hoo, bring out the fucking violins. The world did you wrong and we all have to pay for it. So fucking what? It's not the worst thing that can happen. Others have it worse than you, believe me. Cherry's a good woman. She brought you up good. I'd be proud to have her as a mother. What more do you want?"

"I'm going to save these kids and you can't stop me."

"You don't have to save us, Mags," Harun's voice floated from the back. "Just make sure the journey is beautiful."

"Shut up," I yelled. "You don't know what you're talking about. I'm going to look after you, whether you like it or not. As for you," I added, turning to Dom, "George put me in charge of this operation and you're going to do as I tell you. Do you understand?"

She stared at me. Then she drew the handgun from her bag and aimed it at my abdomen.

"I've got too much riding on this," she said, her voice flat with menace. "I'll be damned if I'm going to let you ruin it."

CHAPTER 21

There aren't too many choices after a person points a gun at you. Either you do as you are told or you spring a leak. I knew better than to argue. My priority, as I saw it, was to save the kids, not to score points with a gun-toting woman with her own agenda.

"Put that away," I said, keeping my voice steady. "You made your point."

Despite the assured tone, my heart raced and my right knee jiggled as I pressed the accelerator; I was that scared. Of the gun's lethal potential. Of the likely prospect of losing my temper and lashing out. But how could I warn Dom? How could I tell her about what I was capable of doing: the attack on the imam, and a nursing student who called me 'an Abo dyke'. I had reduced her to a screaming mess with half her hair torn from her head. Charges were dropped because of the racial slur. But I knew, from that moment, I was a walking time bomb. If I went off, there was no telling what damage I could cause.

"I'm glad you see it my way," Dom said.

Instead of putting the gun in her bag, she tucked it into the waistband of her jeans and continued her admonitory glare.

"I can't let you ruin this for me," she repeated.

"So you said."

I drove on, thinking, *I will get you back sooner or later.*

Within the hour the sun's indistinct orb was behind low striations of cloud that covered the sky. A misty, somewhat reluctant drizzle began to fall, peppering the denuded plain. Turning on the wipers, I endured several seconds of sludge before the glass cleared.

"I can't believe it," I said, speaking more to myself. "Rain, after all this time."

"Won't last," was Dom's terse response.

We spoke in low tones, like two friends who had had a bitter argument and regret the entire, sorry business. We could not, after all, continue to work together with rancour between us.

"I hope we get to William Creek soon," I babbled. "I don't want to drive in rain. Floods can be dangerous out here."

"It's a cloudburst, that's all."

I was not so sure and said as much.

"Pull over if you're tired," Dom said.

"I'm fine."

Despite the long drive and having eaten little that day, I was holding up pretty well. If it hadn't been for the infernal migraine skulking in my skull, moving from left to right temple like a ball in an unwinnable tennis match, I would have said I'd never felt better in my life. More alive, attuned, open to the world and zinging with energy. Nevertheless, I was mentally exhausted, my brain whirling and unable to take more craziness.

The sun broke through a dense cloud bank and the dehydrated land changed yet again. Orange become crimson, palest greens shot through with intense emerald. Browns to shimmering bronze. The pleasure of seeing rain, even though it was nothing more than a fine, soaking film; the fresh smells coming off the earth… And that was how it began. A type of hypnosis took over, my brain slowed, the eyes became heavy and fixed, thoughts drifted, and I realised I had not paid attention to the road for several minutes.

Amid a chorus of shrill voices, the van veered to the left, mounted a grassy verge and, poised at a precarious angle, tilting to the right, nose pointing to the sky, almost tipped over, engine whining as the front left wheel spun on emptiness. Remote voices called my name, hands gripped my shoulder; I snapped out of it, took control and reversed the vehicle onto the road. No problems. Except everybody was shaken and talking all at once.

Apologising, I pulled over.

I was about to turn off the engine and have a little break when the sliding door was flung open. My passengers tumbled out and ran behind a stony outcrop, presumably to relieve themselves. Only Harun remained in the car.

"Don't you want to pee?" I said, in a thin voice.

He shook his head. Looking at him in the mirror, it seemed to me that he had forgotten to breathe. As the atmosphere thickened inside the cabin, I found that I was also holding my breath, telling myself something was about to happen and I should get the other boys in the van. There was a subtle pressure of expectation, and although I did not look at it directly, I knew the medallion hanging from the mirror had begun its phosphorescence, emitting the soft orange light I had seen in Coober Pedy—moments before Rashid was taken.

"You right?" Dominique said, staring at me.

I nodded, shook my head. "Don't know. Sorry, this is a bit too much for me," I said in a distracted manner. I felt like an idiot, like crying and resigning from the human race. But I managed to hold it together and present a picture of a mature woman doing her job under extraordinary circumstances.

The heavens opened at that moment. The shower turned to a downpour. The parched earth opened its mouth to drink it in. Seconds later, the tick of the cooling engine was replaced by the hiss of water sweeping across the bonnet. Thunder growled and lightning flashed, illuminating the cabin with thick, radiant strobes, and bringing a glint of menace to the medallion, which continued to emit a golden gleam.

Unnerved, feeling that I ought to rally the troops against imminent danger, I stuck my head out the open window and yelled: "Hurry up. You'll get soaked."

Nothing happened for a second or two. The engine tick, tick, ticked. Rain hissed. Harun stared at the pendant, hanging like a presentiment between me and Dom.

And just as a shard of light from the medallion struck my eye, blinding me temporarily, causing the pain in my head to flare like a needle jab, two things happened at once.

Harun collapsed in his seat with an audible sigh and seemed to pass out.

Almost immediately, the view through the windscreen turned to chaos.

At first, I was not sure what was happening. Movement, noise, running. A welter of disparate images, broken, fragmented, jangled across my confused brain. The most unlikely impressions flashed before my eyes. Then bizarre, jarring sounds coalesced to form a coherent vision, or as reasonable as it was likely to get, given what was happening.

A large circular object wreathed in flames burst from behind the rocks where the boys had gone to pee and shot across the road. Astonished, I gasped and watched open-mouthed as all of them ran after it. At first I thought they were chasing it away, shouting. Then I realised they were waving and cheering. Some even sported jubilant smiles. Sheets of rain swept across the scene and bounced off the bonnet as I emerged from the car and stood in dumbfounded amazement, unable to comprehend what I had seen as the thing shot past.

Dom remained in the car. I looked across at her. Judging from the expression on her face, she too was gobsmacked.

The wheel of fire—for that was the only way I could describe it—stopped and pivoted to face me. In that moment, everything snapped into place. I realised I was looking at Malachi, the ifrit, tall as a house and surrounded by a ring of fire. The malicious face, the backward feet were unmistakable.

But it was what he held in a flaming talon, high above his head, that shocked me.

Musa, the skinny boy from Port Augusta.

Malachi stood by the roadside, grinning and shooting a challenge with yellow, reptilian eyes, seconds before letting off a triumphant screech and vaulting north.

Gun in hand, Dom emerged from the van and fired an ineffectual couple of shots behind the creature. Job done, she tucked the weapon into her back pocket.

"Righto, you lot," she yelled to the remaining boys. "Show's over." She sounded almost bored.

"Go after it," I yelled, outraged. "He's got Musa."

She could barely look at me. "No point. It's too fast. Besides—"

"I know, it's supposed to get him."

"Now you're learning."

"Not on my watch, he's not."

Malachi was mounting a pitted hill to the north, flames roiling behind him.

"I'm not giving up on Musa," I said, hair plastered to my skull.

I was about to run after Malachi when Dom called my name. I turned and, for the second time that day, stared down the barrel of a gun.

"Get in the car," she said, waving the weapon. "Now."

"No."

"Don't make me use it."

"I dare you to shoot me."

Despite my trembling legs, I took off after Malachi, certain a bullet was going to lodge in my spine. Instead, Dom's voice lanced the air behind me.

"Come back, you stupid bitch."

Chapter 22

I could not recall the last time I ran, let alone this fast, arms and legs pumping as I put my entire being into the act. Despite my fears, Dom's bullets did not rain on me. Warm, heavenly water did, soaking me to the skin and reducing the ground to slush. Mud stuck to my sneakers and turned them to cumbersome boots that threatened to hold me back. My ill-fitting clothing hung off me, uncomfortably bunched in all the wrong places. Furthermore, I could barely see through the strands of soaked hair that had fallen, yet again, in my face. I stopped to get my breath and stared ahead.

Malachi crested another hill and disappeared on the other side, flames dancing around his head like piqued orange feathers.

I started to run, stumbling and falling several times, until I was caked with mud, red and brown as a figure from prehistory. Pausing at the top of the rise, I saw Malachi cross a plain the colour of burnt citrus. The ifrit was almost the same shade as the soil, except for the fiery mane that trailed behind, lending the air a dancing, livid, quality. I slipped and fell on the way down, completing the task on my backside and bruising an elbow in the scree. The seat of my pants torn, I picked myself up and dashed after the creature, determined to save Musa.

I was so hot and flustered, so focussed on the task, I did not notice the magpie pendant hanging from my neck had heated up. It was only when I went to tuck it under my t-shirt to stop it bouncing against my chest and rebounding under the chin that I realised how hot it was in my hand. More so when it came in contact with the sensitive skin between my breasts.

Puzzled, I looked down, tripped on a rock and fell face first in the sludge.

When I looked up again, coughing and spluttering, Malachi was gone.

I stood up and stared through the teeming rain, unable to understand what had happened. Heart racing, I glanced the way I came and saw a forlorn moonscape ringed by purple mounds and jagged ridges. The van, Dom, the boys, were nowhere in sight. The only thing left for me to do was to go forward and hope I came across Malachi. Sloshing across fast-running rivulets of orange water, I walked to the spot where I last saw the ifrit. It was only when my toes balanced on the edge of a precipice that I realised how close I had come to falling.

Gasping with shock, I stepped back and studied the incredible sight before me. I was at the top of a tremendous drop. Metres down was a rocky gorge, winding for many kilometres, like a snake, from west to east. From where I stood, it looked like a monstrous crack in the earth, festooned with palm trees and eucalypts and watered by a swollen creek that rattled noisily over shattered boulders. It resembled a lush fantasy land lost in time.

Malachi had to be down there. I had to follow. First: find a way down. Several minutes later, after walking almost the entire length of the gorge, staring down at the cliff face, I found what I was looking for: a flight of crude steps cut into the sheer wall. They were rough and slippery. I would have to be very careful. One false step and I would plunge to my death. I took a deep breath and began the perilous descent, grabbing hold of rocks and vegetation along the way to stop from losing my footing on slick surfaces. A fine, soaking mist permeated the surrounds, dampening the earth. Fissures softened, giving plant life in the lower reaches a chance to regenerate.

Being fearful of heights, I had avoided looking down. When I was halfway, I did.

Friendly treetops came up to greet me. I was clinging to a wall a few metres above a gently subsiding canopy of eucalyptus leaves and murmuring palm fronds weighed down with moisture. Birdsong rose above the rush of water.

Relieved, I continued the descent. It was as I broke through the leafy canopy to penetrate the torpid realm beneath, that I looked down again and saw a remarkable sight.

Not the forest floor, but a room dominated by a double bed whose sole occupant was a girl covered with a red blanket.

I closed my eyes, shook my head, and opened my eyes. The mirage remained.

"Get a grip," I said aloud and slapped my face.

Problem was I recognised the room. It was mine, as it had been in my teens. The girl on the bed was my younger self. The red blanket was not a blanket, as I thought, but blood. As I stared, the dazed girl sat up and looked at me with the kind of startled fascination I knew was reflected on my own face. When she extended her arms, I saw that the wrists were slashed to ribbons and bleeding.

A door appeared behind the bed.

But there has never been a door in that wall, I thought. *The bedroom door is at the foot of the bed.*

In spite of that indisputable fact, the door that ought not be there opened to reveal a human figure.

Unaware of what was going on behind her, the girl fell back on the mattress and closed her eyes.

The room faded and I found myself looking at a normal forest floor.

Puzzled, unable to understand what had happened, I finished the descent and stood amid the trunks of close-growing trees. The only certainty was that I had seen the horrible moment when I had tried to kill myself. But what did it mean? And who was the figure in the door?

"There is no time to dwell on that now," I told myself. "Find Musa and get back to the car."

I took in my surrounds. I was in a narrow gully with a creek beyond a stand of trees, pale roots exposed along the water's edge. The escarpment heaved up on all sides, closing me in and reducing the sky to a narrow grey slit above. The craggy bluff was layered like a multicoloured cake: pale green, orange and chocolate. At intervals, it was festooned with hanging fronds that resembled jewels around a grand dame's weathered neck. It really was a lost world, peaceful and still, and yet suffused with pensive melancholy.

"Where are you, Musa?" I whispered.

I could not call his name. It seemed sacrilege to raise one's voice in this sacred place. Instead, I grabbed the magpie pendant in my right hand—it had cooled by this stage—and said: "Ancestral spirits, I'm sorry to bother you. My name is Magnolia Din-Olden. Daughter of Jimmy Olden and Laila Din. I'm not here to hurt you or to steal. I'm looking for a boy. Please help me find him. I will take him away and leave you in peace."

I had heard my father utter similar words to ancestral spirits once and I thought they might help.

After a moment, the pendant warmed slightly in my hand. I pivoted on the spot. Faced south. Nothing. Faced west. Nothing. East. An increase in heat.

A thought occurred to me as the magpie continued to warm in my palm: *My father is using his totem bird to communicate with me.*

It was comforting. The chill departed from my bones. Quite suddenly,

I did not feel alone in this lonesome place. I was held, consoled, ready to go forward.

Before setting off, I had to leave a marker to find the stairs. Not caring any more who saw the scars on my wrists, I tore off the hoodie's left sleeve and tied it around a sapling to mark the spot. Then I began the hunt for Musa, pushing through foliage and soaking myself anew as water cascaded from branches and leaves.

I could not get over this place. It was paradise. The press of the walls, the hush that came with the sultry atmosphere, the sound of the creek sloshing over rocks, and birds that sent sharp, clear, notes across the confined space were exhilarating. This was nature's cathedral. A female underworld, the sense of being inside a woman. No hard edges. Only smooth, flowing curves of golden rock, chamber opening inside chamber, the deep waters and the expectant moments before creation began. The word 'holy' hovered on my lips several times as I looked around, awed.

After a while, I came to a bend in the cliff face. A massive crag pushed into the water in front of me and curved away on the other side. At the same time, the bluff on the opposite bank came in, pushing in and twisting away as it formed a new rift. I waded through the shallows, washing away the mud on my sneakers and pants, and found myself in a smaller fissure on the other side.

It was a bubble in the rock, with a small pool in the middle that reflected the trunks of ghost gums along the edges. The reflection took my breath away, forcing me to look up. Ochre walls soared overhead, closing in to form a domed roof with a large hole in the middle—a monstrous eye or a teardrop configuration. At that moment, the sun broke through the clouds, sending a shaft of light to illuminate the pool, like a stage set.

Stunned, yet feeling oppressed by the closed-in space, I set forth on a barely visible path through thick undergrowth, pushing bending boughs and large fronds that yielded before my progress and flipped back with a rustle when I passed. I could barely see ahead, so dense was the vegetation. There was no room for man or beast to pass if I met one coming the other way.

That was how the certainty came upon me that another living being stood somewhere in the jungle, metres ahead or behind or to one side, watching, waiting. Ready to pounce. The sensation came upon me so suddenly, with such conviction, that I wished, for a moment, I had taken Dom's gun for protection. Though what good it would do against Malachi I could not think. If that was who waited for me.

This presence felt entirely different. The ifrit gave off a jagged energy of accumulated, frenzied malevolence and tumult. This was of an altogether different nature. It had the texture and weight of an all-encompassing stillness, the motionlessness of primordial jungles; the insinuating hush that breathed in underground caverns. If I walked past it in this leafy corridor, I would not see it, but I would feel it.

The migraine had disintegrated without me noticing. But the muscles in my neck ached with tension. I continued to push forward, despite the desire to turn tail and run. The sensation did not lift; it intensified. I was surrounded, observed, by a swarming presence.

Beyond a flat, dark-green leaf beaded with water, I saw the trail broaden and open to a clearing. I need only put up with this dread for a moment longer. Then I would be safe.

Pushing aside a leaf, I stepped forward. As I was about to let go, a hand touched me. It ran over the back of my fingers all the way to the wrist, light as a feather, gentle as a lover's caress, and was gone.

I yelped, let go of the leaf. There was no one there. Not even a spider. Nevertheless, I felt a prodigious presence surge over me, even as I squealed and rushed headlong through the undergrowth, panicked, almost screaming, desperate to get away.

Terrified, I collapsed on a rock beside the pool and, hunching over, closed my eyes. *Silly girl, silly girl,* I thought. *What were you thinking, coming all this way? So much for 'follow where all is fled.' You have definitely strayed, and you are about to pay a high price. You idiot! You should have listened to your grandmother and stayed home.*

The sensation came on stealthy wings, present in the initial stages as an opening up or a greater vibrancy in the air, a shimmer behind my eyelids, and became a reality from which there was no escape. It was only by freezing to the spot and making myself very small, so that I may be overlooked, that I gained a greater awareness of the presence. Vast and wondrous it was, swooping from the sky and settling on great haunches at the opening in the roof. As though a pagan deity had come home to roost. I became aware of eyes, distant, arrogant, disdainful; the gorge was filled with the creature's essence. I was frozen in a moment of greater insignificance against a colossal fixity of purpose, beyond comprehension.

It was not malevolent. It was not benevolent. It simply was. In its overwhelming might it was beyond reckoning. Before it I counted for nothing. It could absorb me and not know it. Yet, at the same time, I felt as though I was held, supported, could easily lose myself and be content.

I opened my eyes, expecting to see it. But there was nothing. I was certain of one thing: it was definitely not Malachi. This was altogether different. Could it be Alila, the Water Mother, in this torpid realm?

Hoping to alleviate the pressure in my chest, I took two deep breaths. Vision wavered. I closed my eyes and saw behind my eyelids a woman suspended in amber, hair afloat, like seaweed.

"Mum?"

There was an audible intake of breath around me. An "Ahhh" of deepest satisfaction, followed by a contended sigh; the presence lifted, leaving behind a token of its occupancy in the topmost branches. After a while it dissipated altogether and was gone.

When I opened my eyes, Musa was standing on the opposite bank, perfectly reflected in the water so that it looked like two boys stood one above the other, connected at the feet.

I called his name and ran to the edge of the water.

The boy did not show any sign of recognition. A beatific smile suffused his thin face. The eyes were distant, seeing beyond me. It was at this point that I noted the wreath of vine leaves crowning his head. My eyes looked down the length of his body and saw that he was covered with a wondrous cloak of purple grapes, a beautiful, bewildering entanglement of leaf and fruit.

"I'm coming," I called, and flung myself into the pool.

As I vaulted across, Musa opened the cloak to reveal himself. Only there was no boyish body of flesh and blood beneath. The legs were a twist of wizened, woody stalks that supported slender tendrils and glossy green leaves with clusters of ripened grapes growing beneath, so purple they were almost black.

I screamed, tripped, and fell at his feet. Only they were not feet at all. They were the gnarled roots of ancient grapevines buried in the soil. My horrified cry echoed in the enclosed space, sounding like mocking laugher.

Musa cradled me in his woody lap. Looking into my face, he opened his mouth and, in a voice that combined resigned compassion with feminine-masculine tones, said, "It is as it should be, Magnolia. I play my part as you will play yours in due course."

As his face melted, turned to a viscid condensation of red fluid, the woman I had seen at the crossroads appeared behind him. She was still enshrouded in white, like a mummy, the face hidden inside the hood's gaping maw. More alarming, she appeared to be surrounded by a wavering, vegetable-green darkness that expanded to create the illusion of a submerged world.

As I watched with growing horror, Malachi appeared beside her. Gently guiding her head, he said, "Drink until you have had your fill."

The blackness inside the fabric turned to a ravenous, vortex-like mouth that, by degrees, sucked in Musa's liquified form until there was nothing left. At the last moment, before the boy vanished, Malachi leaned forward and, with a long arm, dealt me a great blow to the chest.

I flew across the water, went chokingly under, and when I emerged, spluttering, coughing, I…

CHAPTER 23

…lay on my back, staring at the sky.

Groaning, I turned over and saw the van not too far away.

No idea how I got there. All I knew was that the rain had stopped, and I had failed to save Musa. Just like I failed Rashid. I was covered, head to toe, in mud, the lumpen clothing forming a bulky weight around my thighs. The left sleeve of my shirt was missing, revealing scars that besmirched my arms, from elbow to wrist—those shameful emblems that pulled me back to a past from which I could not escape. Looking around, overwhelmed, confused, I was not sure if I had moved beyond this spot when I fell earlier, while chasing Malachi. Maybe I had hit my head, passed out and imagined everything that happened? Was the ravine real? Over and above all of that, I did not know if I cried for Musa or because Dom's appearance in my life had brought to the surface everything I'd fought to suppress. *Why is this happening?* I thought. *Why am I going through this pain, when all I want is a life of numbness?*

I lifted my head and looked at the van, parked down by the roadside, looking small and insignificant in the tangerine expanse. Figures came to life in front of it. I heard raised voices, saw arms pointing in my direction. If I could, I thought, I would make Dom suffer as I'd suffered, make her twist at the end of a knife, as I had. I would visit punishments on her she would never forget. Yet the stringy little woman seemed impervious as stone.

The same woman found me minutes later. Kneeling in the mud, Dom lifted me to my feet and guided me with professional alacrity—cigarette dangling from mouth—to the vehicle, saying things like, "Don't cry. It's okay. You couldn't save him. It's not your fault. You tried." But my tears continued to flow. The Fiat's door slid open, I was lowered to the floor. "Stay here."

"I don't understand. Why is this happening?" I said, looking at my open hands, empty and useless.

Dominique returned with a hand towel and a bottle of water. She used them to clean my face, arms, neck. As much of me as was exposed. Surprisingly calm, gentle, given what had transpired between us earlier. She paused briefly when she came to my arms and saw the grotesque, frenzied, crisscrossing scars. To her credit, she said nothing about them.

Instead: "Hope you brought a change of clothes. You look like you've been mudwrestling."

I did not see fit to tell her the overnight bag contained only a change of underwear, toiletries, and a box of sleeping pills. It hadn't crossed my mind to bring a change of clothes.

I grabbed the water bottle from her hand and guzzled the contents, hoping to wash away the bitter taste of self-loathing. Nothing doing. Through the wash of tears I saw the kids arrayed behind Dom, staring at me as if they were looking at a madwoman.

"I'm sorry," I said to no one in particular. "I couldn't save Musa. I tried but…" Fresh tears rolled down my cheeks, probably leaving ugly streaks on my face.

"It was useless to try," Dom said.

"It's not your fault, Magnolia," Adam said, crouching in front of me. "It was meant to be."

I was not listening, or I could not accept what I heard. Musa's face—his transformation from boy to grapevine—haunted me. So bizarre I could not possibly tell them what had happened; they would never believe me. Nevertheless, the eerie metamorphosis swept through me a gust of horror, anger, repulsion. I was overcome by a stupefying sense of fury and despair. I felt that I had let down not just a boy, but innumerable children of all classes, races and tongues across the world, born to be sacrificed to expediency. Rashid among them, lost in Coober Pedy because I was too blind to see. The dissolution of this rage into my sorrow drove me to a sudden frenzy of activity. I began to tremble with the shock.

I rose to my feet and looked at Adam. "That's nonsense," I said. "Nothing is preordained. You have a choice. If we banded together we could have saved that little kid's life."

"You think so, do you?" Dom said, coming up to me. She spread her legs and put her hands on her hips, the front of her shirt carrying an imprint of my muddy hands. "And I suppose you thought it was a good idea to run off by yourself. Anything could've happened to you out there and we'd waste time looking for you. We're supposed to be in Marree tomorrow, don't forget."

"I couldn't stand by and let Malachi take Musa."

"For the thousandth time, you have no choice. Let that sink into your thick skull."

"It's happening as it's supposed to happen," Harun beat home the point.

He was completely unaffected by his friend's abduction. Rashid before that. Two boys gone and no one cared.

"Nothing is preordained," I said for Harun's benefit. "You don't have to sacrifice yourselves to Alila just because someone said you have to."

"For the final time," Dom said, "they're cattle."

"Don't call them that." I turned on her. The rage came back and I really believed I could hit her. Knock her down and cause real harm. Dom must have seen it, but she was not one to back down.

"Why not? That's what they are. Alila eats them the way you eat lamb chops. That's why they were killed and brought back."

She stopped, perhaps realising she had spoken carelessly.

"Hold on. Are you saying they were deliberately killed?"

Dom turned her back, swore, kicked at dirt.

"Answer me," I shouted.

She flinched. Then she gave a barely perceptible nod.

It took a moment for the gesture to sink in. "This is sick. Does George know?"

"He organised it."

"You're monsters. Both of you. And for what?" Tears filled my eyes again. I wiped them angrily away with the back of my hand, leaving great smudges under my eyes. "If George organised the killings, you must know who did it."

Dom was silent.

"Who killed them?"

She shrugged; shook her head; would not look at me.

"Have it your way." I turned to the five boys standing in a haphazard fashion in the middle of the road, puddles gleaming at their feet. "What about you? Don't you have a say in this?"

They stared at me as if I was some kind of new incomprehensible creature.

"There is no point in having an opinion," Harun said. "It will happen as it's meant to happen."

"So you're happy to be a puppet on a string," I said, rounding on him.

He shrank from me, pressing against Adam and staring at me with those big eyes of his. Oh, how I hated the person I saw reflected in them!

"We're not puppets," Salih said. "We know what we're doing."

"It's you who doesn't know what she's doing," Zaman finished for his brother.

"You who is off track," Harun said, picking up his friend's train of thought.

My resolve began to weaken in the face of such certainty. What if they were right and I was wrong? It would not be the first time. After all, I hated being told what to do. Being forced to yield to someone else's will, and here I was doing precisely that to these kids who all too willingly sacrificed themselves for a cause, no matter how sick. And then Dom spoke and brought the house of cards tumbling down.

"They have no say in the matter," she said in a tired voice. "Why can't you understand that?"

"I understand," I said, turning on her. "I'm just not playing along. I will never play along so long as children are hurt."

"We are acolytes," Salih said, desperately. "You too."

As usual, Zaman finished the sentence for his brother. "We offer ourselves for a greater good."

"Don't you have any fight in you?" I came up to Zaman. "You're young. Don't you want to live?"

"We live in the Mother," he said.

"And she in us," Salih put in.

I knew that belief in an afterlife was central to the meaning and purpose of Muslims. But I also understood that was not what Salih meant. How could it be when he all too willingly sacrificed himself to a djinni, the very thing Muslims fear? Furthermore, I saw with my own eyes what happened to Musa. I could not imagine what horrible fate befell Rashid. Did similar fates await these kids, too?

"Sounds to me like you're all in an abusive relationship with your mother," I said. "Comes a time when you have to stand up against her."

Dom pushed through the gathering. "I hate to interrupt this little chinwag, but we can't stand here all day. We have to get to our next stop before nightfall."

At that moment my attention was drawn to the sound of an approaching vehicle. It came from the direction in which we were headed. Moments later a dirty jeep with a surfboard on the roof pulled up in front of us, forcing Dom and me to hustle the kids off the road. A sunburned young man with a scraggy beard and a mass of bleached dreadlocks poked his head through the open window. He was good looking in a skanky sort of way.

"G'day, Swampy," he said, giving me the once-over. "You look like you could use a bath." Squalls of laughter followed.

I turned my back on him and ushered my charges to the van.

"Youse need help or sometin'?" he said.

Dom walked over to him.

"We're fine," she said. "How far's William Creek?"

Another quick up-and-down. "Half an hour, I reckon."

Dom nodded, stuck her head in the car and sniffed. "Got more of that good stuff you've been smoking?"

The man released another hyena laugh. "Sure have, sweetheart." He reached into the glove compartment, produced a fat, badly rolled joint, and handed it to her.

"Nice." She ran it under her nose and gave it an appraising squeeze. "Wanna share?"

"Nah. You keep it. Already had two. Gotta keep me wits about me while drivin'. Gotta get to Coober Pedy to make up with me girlfriend." He looked over Dom's shoulder at me. "Pretty little thing like you shouldn't look like the Swamp Thing but…"

He laughed when I glowered at him.

"And smile, why don'tcha."

The man let off another animal cry and drove off, leaving us in the dust.

I gave him the finger, hating to be told to smile like a dingbat by an idiot.

Dom tucked the joint behind her ear and said, "Can we please go?"

William Creek was a pub and a camping ground smack-bang in the middle of a vast and untenable emptiness. A dusty charter plane with 'Joy Rides' written on the sides crouched disconsolately beside skeletal trees, a runway visible in the distance. While Dom and the boys grabbed a drink at the pub, I paid for a room, had a shower and changed into a pair of Dom's blue jeans and an emerald short-sleeved t-shirt with 'Supreme' written on the front. Not at all the kind of clothes I would normally wear. Far too revealing. Refreshed, springy dark hair spilling down my back, I walked into the pub—a long room, plastered floor to ceiling with travellers' memorabilia—and found Dom perched on a stool at the counter, staring at her phone. Two empty beer glasses were arrayed in front of her. A third was half full. Across the room, Adam did his best with an old-fashioned pinball machine that pinged and clanged, filling the constricted space with oddly merry noises. The remaining boys cheered him on.

The publican turned an appreciative eye on me when I entered. He was a portly gent with a red face, short dark-brown hair and an ineffectual moustache.

"Hey, love," he said. "Were your parents thieves?"

I frowned. "No. Why?"

"Because I think they stole the sun and the moon and put them in your eyes."

Dom echoed his good-natured laughter, which only served to make me more self-conscious. I hated being appraised like a horse and commented upon.

"Give me some mineral water," I snapped.

Dom tossed the mobile phone in her bag and gave me a quick up-and-down.

"My clothes become you."

"Took the words right out of my mouth," the publican chimed, handing over a chilled plastic bottle.

I took it from him and turned to Dom.

"They're a bit tight," I said, squirming inside the unfamiliar clothes and pressing the flats of my wrists to my thighs.

"When you've got it, flaunt it," she said in a dead voice. "No point hiding your assets under all that baggy crap you wear."

"Maybe I just want to be comfortable," I mumbled.

"Spoken like a true dyke," Dom snorted.

This time there was no doubting the quality of the publican's laughter.

"Have you got reception?" I said to Dom.

"Yep."

"I'm going to call my grandmother."

"Want my phone?" she said, reaching for her bag.

"No, thanks. Recharged mine."

Taking the water and my phone outside, I sat on a wooden bench against the pub wall and dialled Nan's number.

"Hello?"

"Nan, it's me."

"Lovely, how are you?"

I could tell from the strained voice that something was up; I said so.

"I've had a bit of a setback," Nan said after a couple of prods. "Nothing to worry about."

"Out with it," I said, staring at a row of dusty camper vans parked beneath desiccated eucalypts. "What's going on?"

"Everything's just getting on top of me, that's all." She started to softly cry.

"What does the doctor say?"

"I don't want to bother him," she said after a couple of sniffles.

"For heaven's sake, Nan, that's what the doctors and nurses are there for."

Brief hesitation before she said, "I don't know how to tell him. I mean, who'd believe me? I'm not sure I believe it myself…"

"What are you talking about?"

I held the phone to my ear with my left shoulder, unscrewed the bottle top with both hands, and swallowed some water to clear my throat.

"I think I'm losing my mind," Nan said in a barely audible voice. "Strange things are happening."

"Like what?"

"The man with the yellow eyes came back last night."

"What?"

"The pain in my leg…he's causing it."

"How?"

"He sticks his fingers in my wounds. Through the bandages. Through the skin. It hurts so much. I wake up screaming."

"Nan, you must be having a nightmare. Who wouldn't, after what you went through?"

"It's real."

"You just said you wake up screaming."

"Yes, but he's real. And he said he's going to make me pay for what I did to him."

"Do you know him?"

Another small hesitation.

"Well, do you?"

"Yes."

Dom emerged from inside the pub and tapped her wrist.

"Time to go," she mouthed.

I nodded, gestured one minute, and hunkered over the phone.

"Who is he, Nan?"

"You can't name an ifrit. It's bad luck."

"Malachi," I said. "There, I said it and nothing happened, has it?"

"No, but…"

Dom stared at me when she heard Malachi's name. Then she lowered herself on the bench. "I'll be damned," she mouthed, still staring at me. "Speaker phone," she said, aloud; and when I indicated that the Nokia did not have such luxuries, she pressed her left ear to the phone. The heat of her body against mine was intoxicating.

"Don't worry," Nan was saying, "the imam's coming. He'll recite a prayer to protect me."

The dwindling band of boys stepped through the pub door and milled around under a big, wide sky heavy with cloud. The wind picked up and made their uniforms flutter around their thin ankles. They seemed incongruous on the red Australian soil in their askew skullcaps and creased blue tunics; and then it struck me that it was not so unusual after all. Islam came to Australia pretty much as soon as white conquerors, if not earlier from Indonesia. If anything, it was Dom, the only Anglo in our little party, who was out of place as she used those emaciated arms of hers to light another cigarette and blow smoke in my face.

"Nan, how do you know Malachi?" I said.

As though a great weight was lifted from her shoulders, Nan said, "I thought it was all behind me. But it's not easy to walk away from the past."

"No," I said. "You can't walk away from the past, but you can set it right."

"That's why," Nan said, "I want to tell you about…"

CHAPTER 24

The Tale of the Ifrit and the Black-Haired Girl

Know, O beloved granddaughter, light of my eyes, that an ifrit did come to me when I was young, and the blood ran fervid in my veins. Fiendish and slippery was he, doing Allah's bidding and leading women astray.

Know also, O child of my child, that an ifrit, once it comes into being, exists across time and place, no matter when or where it springs into existence. Nor are they bound by the normal strictures that encircle mortal lives, short as they are. So that an ifrit or djinn, although he is created today, may live and exert influence on times long gone before, in the here and now, and in years to come.

Acquaint yourself then, daughter of my daughter, with these facts.

When I was fifteen years old and growing up in Ti Tree, north of Alice Springs, I walked home one summer's eve, after visiting a friend on the other side of town. It was dusk. Peace had settled on the land and stars pierced the sky, cold and distant though they be. It was thus ordained that I had to pass a ruin that put the wind up me even in the bright light of day, let alone at night when marids and ghouls are out and about. I could have taken the long way around, but I was lazy and could not be bothered, which is probably why Allah saw fit to punish me.

See if you will the abandoned warehouse. It stood on the edge of town, covered in graffiti, and slowly sinking into the earth, black doorways yawning and shattered windows staring, so that birds flew in one wind-filled hole and out the other.

Now see me, the skinny dark-haired Muslim girl, pretty as a rose, it was said, walk by, pretending I was not in the least scared and trying not to look at the hovel, though of course I did. From the corner of my eye, I espied a light in one window.

How can there be a light, thought I, when no one lives there? And when a face appeared above the candle stub, my initial gasp of horror turned to a sigh of relief. It was someone I knew well enough.

Malachi, a homeless Aboriginal guy who drifted around town, living here and there, tolerated by all and aided by some.

It so happened, by the will of Allah, I pitied Malachi. He must be wretched indeed, I told myself, to shelter amid the cobwebs, owls, and fallen timbers, when he could as easily sleep under the stars or 'neath a tree on the other side of the highway.

Malachi called out. "Hey, girlie. Yeah, you, the pretty one. Come over here, will ya."

Drunk as usual. But he meant no harm. Everyone knew that. I went over to see what he wanted. I was a big girl, wasn't I? Can't be scared of every little thing. Malachi probably just wanted a bob or two, or to ask me to buy him grog at the store over by the highway. It would not harm me to do him a good turn, would it?

But no, the man dragged me inside by the hair and forced himself on me; rolled with me in the dust and rubbed it in my mouth and in my hair, while I fought and screamed beneath him. No one heard, of course, and no one came to my aid, so far was I from ears that might hear and eyes that might see. When he finished, he pushed me aside and fell asleep, leaving me to stitch my clothing like so many shattered fragments of my life together again.

I turned up on my parents' doorstep, bleeding where it mattered most, clothes torn, a mess.

And that was why, as my mother tended to my every need, bathed, cleaned, scrubbed and prayed, my father went to teach the drunk a lesson. Only it did not stop at that. It never does. My father killed Malachi, albeit unintended. After he robbed Malachi of life, he dumped the body down a dried-up well inside the warehouse and left him to marinate in his own blood.

Perhaps it is easy to say this after the fact, but had my father been in full possession of his faculties, had he thought on the custom and tradition his ancestors had been brought up on in Afghanistan, he would have done well to drive an unused nail into the blood of the dead man. That would have stopped Malachi from turning into an ifrit, as all murdered men must, left to wander the earth as unsettled spirits intent on doing harm.

But my father was in agony. He was not thinking straight and he most certainly did not think to observe custom. Why would he? He was in Australia, far from the lands of his forebears, where such superstitions held sway.

Even so, Malachi was reborn that night, a fearsome ifrit sworn to blood vengeance on those who robbed him of precious life.

This, then, is all I have to relate of 'The Tale of the Ifrit and the Black-haired Girl'.

But by no means is it the end, for Allah is All-Knowing and only He can tell when a story reaches the zenith point.

An older, greyer Cherry Din stopped talking on the phone and released a heavy sigh. In it I heard all the pain, fear and agony of her life.

"That's the first time I told anyone that story," she said. "Though I've played it often enough in my head."

I didn't know what to say. And so, like all wise people, I kept quiet.

"What happened afterwards, Cherry?" Dom said after a while.

"If I went past the ruin, I saw him in the window," Nan said in a hushed voice, "watching, waiting, for the right time."

"And…" I said.

"I got pregnant. My father called me a prostitute, a slut. Said I deserved it for disobeying orders. So I came to Alice Springs to have the baby. Brought her up by myself and tried to turn a bad deed into a good one. What else could I do?"

I had trouble uttering the next four words. Yet, somehow, I managed to cough them up. Because to utter them was to make them real, and to make them real was to bring lunatic sense to Nan's story.

"Nan, are you saying Malachi is my mother's father?"

"Yes," she said.

"That means he's your grandfather," Dom whispered, her breath tickling my ear.

She pulled away from me as if I was tainted. Shaking her head with disbelief, she stood, lit another cigarette, and paced in front of me.

"Explains a lot," she said.

"What's going on?" Adam said to her.

I could have hit her when she told him Malachi sired my mother. But her words had the complete opposite effect on the boys; they gathered round and stared at me with renewed interest. With a sense of wonder and revelation.

"Nan," I said. "I will sort this out. Don't worry." My mind whirled. I had no idea what I could do to protect her. All I knew was I must offer the woman I loved above all others some comfort.

"You believe me," Nan said.

"Of course."

"Thank you."

"Malachi will not hurt you again. I promise."

I hung up. We piled into the van, and I drove away. The mood, as we left William Creek, was dark and foreboding as the clouds hanging over us.

CHAPTER 25

"We have to turn back."

The rain was heavy. The wipers could not keep up, sloshing back and forth like demented arms trying to keep back the tide.

"Keep going," Dom muttered, staring at the car's GPS. "We're not far from where we're supposed to stay the night."

"We're going to get washed away, or stuck in mud."

I looked at her, anxious and afraid. Her profile wavered in the light from the dashboard, making her look as if she was floating underwater.

It had started to drizzle soon after we left William Creek. In minutes the skies had opened to release a deluge of biblical proportions. Rain powered from the sky, making a racket on the roof and reducing visibility to a few uncertain metres in front of the vehicle. The earth opened up, drank it down and spewed the excess, forming frothing puddles around a van that inched forward carefully, as earth slipped away under the tyres. Rivulets streamed across the road in a boiling mass of brown water. To make matters worse, light was failing fast. I turned on the headlights, giving life to a liquid world.

The hush inside the cabin gave weight to my anxiety. This is why, I reminded myself, you do not crave adventure. Too unpredictable, too dangerous, is the world. And here you are, stuck in the middle of this madness. Still, I was a responsible human being; I had to think of the children, and so I guided the van over unstable ground, gripping the steering wheel as I peered past wipers turned on high, headlights lurching in wild arcs as the van dipped and lurched out of potholes.

The Fiat emerged from a puddle that came up to the doors just as the left side of the road collapsed, blocking the way back. *There goes any chance of returning to William Creek,* I thought. For several minutes after that I did less than thirty kilometres an hour, sweating as I tried to keep the car on the road.

"This is not good."

"You're doing fine," Dom said, her voice almost drowned by the noise on the roof.

"The desert's going to turn into a lake if this keeps up."

"It'll stop."

"We must get to high ground. Where's this homestead supposed to be?"

"It's an abandoned train station. Shouldn't be far. George said to look for a dirt track on the right side of the road, ten kays from William Creek."

"Good luck with that."

My passengers were handling the situation better than I was. Chatting, faces pressed against glass covered with condensation, this was a big adventure for them, a voyage towards the one true aim for which they had been created. I remembered that they were not boys in the normal sense of the word and the disquiet I felt increased, adding to the suffocating closeness in the claustrophobic cabin. As someone who had always drifted through life, never committing to anything, it was hard for me to understand their absolute dedication to a principle. Yet a small part of me was envious, too. They had something I did not. A reason to live. Or to die for, for that matter.

What did I have?

Nothing.

I just went along, like a dumb animal, from one day to the next.

A murky sun was setting behind a mountain range to the south-west when a violent lightning bolt revealed our salvation. A structure on a hill leaped momentarily to the fore, then vanished. As the electric discharge danced on the heights, I saw the outline of a building that resembled a horror movie house, details etched against an indigo sky: two chimney stacks and a series of jagged roofs. The tremendous rumbling and crashing that followed silenced even the boys.

"Did you see that?"

"That's got to be it," Dom said.

"Hope so."

A track of white quartz appeared soon after, glistening in the semi-dark. I turned onto it and it delivered our troupe, via a winding route, to a hilltop in fifteen spine-jolting minutes, rain turning the road to polished silver.

Headlights swept the scene as I swung into a wide-open clearing. Two sandstone buildings, one smaller than the other, stood next to each other at the apex of the hill. Only the hiss of rain could be heard and, every once in a while, the wind moaning in a chimney. Rusted train tracks disappeared into the dark on both sides, as if falling off the edge of the world. I peered at the crumbling buildings, a sense of foreboding in my stomach.

"Ifrits like ruins," I said, remembering Nan's story. "But it beats getting washed away in a flood."

The building to the right was no more than a facade with a doorway, a chimney and no roof. The cottage next to it had a roof and looked like it would be suitable accommodations for the night. I pulled up in front of it, headlights illuminating a frontage with two windows either side of a door.

"I'm going to make sure it's safe," I said.

In truth I wanted time alone. My feelings about Dom were so mixed up I did not know if I was coming or going. The more time I spent with her, the more uncertain I became. I was not in love with her; of that I was certain. Or so I told myself. But something else had kicked in—the need for someone to look after me. Someone who would make everything alright with a magic pass of the hand, while holding up the promise of maltreatment down the track. Mix that in with the resentment I felt towards her and there was a volatile mix.

"Take the torch." Dom tossed a yellow battery box with a large reflector onto the driver's seat.

I grabbed it and ran to the cottage. Standing in the doorway, I turned on the torch and flashed the beam on my surrounds. The roof had collapsed over the front two rooms and part of the hallway, littering the floor with debris. Floorboards had disintegrated long ago, leaving spongy-looking joists on which to stand. The place stank of rot, earth and animal droppings. Miraculously, the ceiling had held over the back section—a kitchen, with a fireplace, walk-in pantry, and a window with a view over the back of the property.

It seemed a safe, relatively dry place to spend the night. Or as safe as it could be, given djinns and ifrits were said to be drawn to dilapidated buildings.

Thinking about ifrits brought back Nan's story.

Malachi, that hideous misshapen creature, was my grandfather— or rather his human counterpart was. My grandmother was raped, and my mother was the product of assault, setting off a chain reaction that brought me to this point. I shook my head in wonder as I guided the torch around the kitchen. No wonder there had never been talk of a grandfather, let alone photos of family members. Nan would have been sixteen when my mother was born. A single mother bringing up a child in Alice Springs. Must have been tough. Yet Nan never complained. It was not in her nature. She forged on and looked on the bright side of life. While I wallowed in misery, feeling sorry for myself; I had practically built a personality on suffering. Take that away and what did I have?

"I'm not ready to go there," I said aloud, my voice sounding ghost-like.

I went to get the others, the failure of my life trailing behind me like a train wreck.

Half an hour later, we were set up for the night. While Dom lit a fire in the grate and heated the evening's meal on a butane stove, I found a piece of sharp quartz and set to work. Standing on a portable cooler in the hallway, I scratched a symbol above the kitchen doorway.

Harun came up and asked what I was doing.

I put the finishing touches to the design and leaped off the cooler. "Keeping you safe," I told him.

Dom looked up from stirring a pot. "By drawing graffiti on a wall."

"It's not graffiti. It's—"

"A hexagram."

It was Adam. He was looking at the design I had drawn above the doorway.

"That's right," I said. "A hexagram. It keeps djinn and ifrits away."

"You know this how?" Dom pulled over a stack of bowls and began to serve the ubiquitous lentils.

"The hexagram is on the Seal of Solomon," Adam said.

"Correct." I said. "It's engraved on the ring given to the wise king by Allah."

"Fairy tales to the rescue," Dom sang.

"They're age-old stories of wisdom. In one *Arabian Nights* story a man wards off a djinni with salt. Citrus is used in another story. We've plenty of both in our food stores."

"Are you going to pickle Alila or kill her?" Dom said. "She's a djinni, not mutton. She's supposed to eat them. You don't eat her." She passed a bowl to Salih and ladled more food into another bowl.

Frowning at her, I climbed onto the window ledge and scratched another hexagram on the outside wall, rain pelting my face. I joined the group in front of the fireplace after running a line of salt across the kitchen doorway and windowsill.

"That should keep them out," I said, settling down.

The boys attacked their meals with characteristic gusto. Dom picked in a disconsolate fashion at her own food. After all the stress, I was content to take my time over the meal, lean against the wall and enjoy the almost cheerily crackling fire. Twice, in quick succession, Dom went to urinate in one of the other rooms. I noticed her stomach was swollen. In between, there was only the sound of rain dripping in another part of the house. All else was calm.

Buried in my own thoughts, I thought that maybe the horror was over. Perhaps by resisting Alila I had averted disaster and saved her remaining victims?

"Want more tucker?" Dom said, returning to the room. She nodded at the pot of lentils.

I shook my head. "I've grown to hate the sight of lentils."

"Lentils are the food of the gods," Salih said with his mouth full. "They purify the body."

I shook my head. "You can have mine," I said to Dom. "You look like you need it."

"What's that supposed to mean?"

"Too skinny," I said from the side of my mouth. "Need more meat on your bones."

"You a chubby chaser?"

I contented myself with a satisfied grin. I was itching for a fight, but this was not the time.

Dom was not letting it go. "My weight is none of your business. Got it?"

She stood next to the window and lit a cigarette. I was going to tell her smoking was bad for her, thought better of it, and bit my tongue.

Harun drank water from a bottle and looked at me.

"You shouldn't have done that," he said.

"Done what?"

"The hexagram. The salt. Alila won't like it."

"I don't care what she thinks. I call the shots here."

I did not know where the determination to fight the djinni came from. This defiance, this indignation, was not me. I usually let things slide and take their own course, content to sit back and watch. Where was this fixity of purpose coming from?

"Time for bed," Dom said, flicking the cigarette out the window.

After the others turned in, I placed my own sleeping bag under the window and slid into it, relishing the cocooning warmth. The position gave me a clear view of the hallway, all the way to the front door. No intruder was going to get past me.

Dom draped a few blankets over the boys, turned down the LED lamp, and sat on her sleeping bag at a respectable distance from me.

"I don't get you," I said at length, keeping my voice low.

"What don't you get, Missy Din?"

"How can you show such care and consideration for the boys by covering them up with a blanket and then feed them to a demon?"

"I'm good at compartmentalising."

"Whatever that means."

"It means when there's a job to do, I do it, without letting my personal feelings get in the way."

"You wouldn't say that if you had children."

"There speaks the voice of experience."

Weirdly, her tart response softened the hard mettle in me. "I wouldn't mind having kids," I said. "But I'm scared."

Dom pulled out the joint she had cadged from the surfy and lit it, releasing a sweet aroma into the room.

"Of what?" she said, taking a puff.

I fought the urge to tell her to put it out, shrugged, and smiled sadly to myself.

"My mother wasn't particularly good at being a mum," I said. "Guess I'm scared I'll become like her."

"You're not your mother," Dom said, passing the joint.

I had never smoked tobacco, let alone marijuana. Or even drank alcohol. Smiling, I shrugged again and took a toke. Might as well get adventurous. Smoke filled my lungs. I almost coughed, held it back and felt my lungs expand, head reel. I breathed out, liked what I felt and took another puff, before passing it to Dom.

"My mother died young, and I guess I always wanted to give her the gift of life."

"Meaning?" Dom said.

"I wanted to live the kind of life she might have led if she had lived."

"What, by staying in a dead-end town like Alice Springs?"

I shrugged, not knowing what to say.

"You're you," Dom said. "You have to break away from all that bullshit and follow your own path. Life is short and you don't get to do it twice. It's about survival. You should try it some time."

The words emerged from my mouth before I realised I had uttered them: "Explains your behaviour back then."

"I think we have very different memories of that day, Missy Din."

She passed the joint. I sucked on it, allowing the acrid smoke to fill my lungs. Holding it in. And then releasing it with a sigh. Oh, it was nice. My head opened up and floated away. My insides quivered and released.

"You led me on," I said, handing it back to Dom.

"I tried to save you. Hell, I did save you. You're alive, aren't you?"

"You made a fool out of me. You left me behind when all I wanted was to be with you."

"Abandon those who abandon themselves," Dom said, putting the joint between her lips.

Oddly, there was no anger or acrimony in the words; perhaps they were being softened by the dope. Just statements of fact, emerging because they had to.

"Is that what you think I did?" I asked.

"I know it."

The joint was back in my hand. We sat metres apart, leaning against the wall, unable to look at each other. Instead, I stared at the fire, my mind a playhouse directed by the licking flames. My earlier feelings towards Dom had subsided, leaving behind a dull ache, a sense of profound loss. Followed by a dizzying sense of buoyancy and elevation. I felt as if I was suspended above my problems. As if I was awaking from a dream, knowing it was not real and that I could not reclaim it.

"Besides," Dom said, "this isn't about me. It's about you and your mother."

"You're a psychologist now, are you?"

Another puff and back to Dom. The joint was almost a wet stub between my fingers. And boy, did it feel good. I felt fluid, not fixed, free.

"Being abandoned by your mother and father," Dom went on regardless. "That's all you talked about when we were kids."

I was surprised to hear that.

"Really?"

She nodded, passed back the joint. "Mum and Dad didn't love you. That's why they left you with your grandmother. You know what I reckon?"

I shook my head, dreading what she was going to say.

"I reckon you turn people into your mum and dad and play games with them. Well, I'm not your mother."

"You know nothing about me," I said, the words sounding hollow. I took another toke, wanting to hold on to the lovely drifting buoyancy.

"You tried to take me down with you," Dom whispered. "But I refused to be taken down. I saved your life. That has to mean something."

"I lost face," I said, knowing full well that was the crux of the problem.

"No, you didn't. No one knew. Even if they did, so what?"

"I knew. That's all that matters. I trusted you. And you threw it in my face."

Thunder filled the silence between us—a deep rumble that shook the foundations. Fire popped, crackled, hissed in the grate. Rain whispered in the bushes, and water dripped in a recess.

"I missed you so much," I whispered. "I missed you every day. Why did you go away?"

"I was scared."

"Of dying?"

"Of you."

Dom could not have uttered more damning words.

"Of me?"

"You were so desperate, so determined to do yourself in, it scared me."

"They wanted to separate us."

"You can't blame me for choosing life. You can't."

In the next bout of silence, I finished the joint and ground the remains under my heel. As I did so, I had time to contemplate events so far. It had been a bizarre couple of days. So much had happened, so much of it strange and inexplicable. It was hard to believe it had been crammed into two days. The horror of losing Rashid and Musa. Hearing Dom's confession. Seeing my younger self in that impossible room in the gorge. Even wearing Dom's clothes seemed offbeat and outlandish; they made me feel like a different person. Like the real me. And yet, out of everything that had happened, the most prominent thing was the conversations, the small exchanges, with the kids. The way they treated me, the way they turned to me, even if in the end they were disappointed. They behaved as if I ought to know. As if I ought to understand… And yet I did not; I had no idea what was happening, how such things could occur, with me seemingly in the centre.

I was scared—scared because of the hunger in their faces and terrified because they thought—I could admit it—that I was one of them. Harun said as much. Of course, I was not one of them. I was not a zombie, prepackaged food for a monster. All the same, things were beginning to penetrate my thick skull. Something was going on and I was mixed up in it. The connection with Nan, Malachi and my mother indicated as much.

I spoke barely above a whisper, like a scared girl. "Can I ask a question?"

"Go ahead."

My thoughts were muddled. I wanted to lie down and sleep. But I managed to say what needed to be uttered.

"What does this have to do with me? Why am I here?"

"That's two questions."

"Tell me."

"You really don't know?"

I shook my head and regretted it. The room swayed and I almost vomited.

"George said this'd make you remember."

To my surprise, Dom scooted across on all fours and pressed against me. Tentatively at first and then more insistently. She was warm and tantalising. After the initial shock of her body, I relaxed and felt the contours of her—thin and emaciated and filled with sharp angles that had not been there before. Oh, the nearness of a human being. This human being. It was nice. More than nice. It was old times, when nothing stood between us, and the world was ours for the taking. Just Dom and me. Tears welled.

"Close your eyes and think back to when you were fifteen and I was sixteen," Dom said, voice a soft caress.

Feeling silly and unable to explain why I was crying, I closed my eyes. Again, the room swayed, lurched to one side, tilted sideways. Tears really did flow. Possibly, I told myself, it was because Dom sat me down like this in the long-ago fairyland of our teenage years. The sitting down was always followed by a talking-to on a topic I failed to grasp, whether it was how the world worked on a minor point, or a boy problem, though admittedly the latter had not been a reality once I met Dom. From early on, I knew Dominique Device, the Anglo girl with the blonde hair and buttery skin would chime across all the years of my life.

"Now think about your fifteenth birthday," Dom said.

I stiffened, my mind fought, clawed. I struggled to open my eyes. Too late. I plummeted. It was like an elevator going down too fast. My stomach lurched. When I opened my eyes minutes later, Dom said, "What happened?"

I could not answer. My mouth was sealed. So long as I held it inside, it would be fine and good. It would not be real. It would be make-believe.

"Look at me." Dom's voice was more gentle than it had been the entire time. It confused me; I did not know what to make of it. I faced her. She tipped my chin up with one finger. Her breath touched my skin, and even though it was rank with cigarettes it was still Dom. "Look at me," she repeated. And it was only when our eyes met and she kissed me full on the lips, like she used to, that past and present merged. I remembered everything. Or almost.

CHAPTER 26

THIRTEEN YEARS EARLIER

I first saw Dom when her family moved next door, going back and forth from the massive removalist's truck and their newly acquired double-fronted brick house. The truck contained a seemingly endless array of boxes and furniture. And although the girl in the butt-hugging denim shorts and sweat-stained Judas Priest t-shirt was slightly built, she shone bright as the noonday sun, lugging boxes with a surly face. Her skin was the colour of summer peaches, her hair as gold as high-flown corn. She was, in a word, perfect. A princess in a fairy story. I was hypnotised. From the first, my mind teemed with romantic fantasies.

Even so, it was almost two months before we talked. In the initial stages, we had everything going against us. For one thing, Dom was a year older than me; and, therefore, a higher grade in high school. For another, I could not imagine a girl like her, who was picked up by boys in cars that vibrated with loud music of a Friday and Saturday evening, showing the least interest in me. Nevertheless, I was content to spy on my object of desire from a distance, and to dream. The former happened surreptitiously across the schoolyard, through the curtains of my bedroom window, or, when my grandmother was out, through a crack in the fence.

The inaugural meeting was memorable if mortifying. It happened at the tail end of a stinking-hot February afternoon, one of those stultifying Alice Springs days when sullen cloud pressed on the town, sealing in heat and threatening rain that rarely came. Thunder rumbled across the MacDonnell Ranges as I lay on my bed, alternately dozing or reading, in front of a fan that blew hot air over my melting form. From my prone position, I could hear the hiss of waterspray and Dom squealing with delight as she hosed herself down in the backyard, flaunting strict water restrictions.

A part of me was outraged. Another part was thrilled, wishing I had the guts to do the same. I lay for a time, alternately angered and admiring, imagining all manner of gratifying sights taking place on the other side of the fence. A wet girl frolicking under a spray of water. If only I could watch!

It was a matter of waiting for my grandmother to leave before I crept to my spot.

I approached the crack in the fence, put my eye to the hole, and reeled back in horror, falling on my butt. A blue eye stared back at me. "Boo!" it said. Humiliated, blushing furiously, my first thought was to rush inside, shut the door and never leave the house again. Before I could move, Dom's head popped up over the fence.

She wore a tiny two-piece bikini, the apple-green halter top showing over the wood palings. With pale skin, gold hair plastered to her scalp and bare shoulders dusted with sparkling water droplets she was a nymph from the pages of myth. A slender arm extended towards me, and words meant only for me issued from the perfect mouth.

"Why doncha come over? Water's nice 'n cold. And my fucking olds are out."

I did not think twice. Clambering over the boundary, I spent the afternoon running around the yard with fake grass, as Dom squirted me until I was soaked through. When her parents came home they found two saturated girls cavorting and squealing. Mr Device's hoarse cries put an end to the fun and games.

"What's going on here? Don't you know there's bloody water restrictions?"

From that day on, Dom and I were always in each other's company. We walked to school together and marched home to spend evenings in each other's company, doing homework or lying on Dom's bed to listen to raucous new music I had not listened to before.

One evening, towards the end of the second week, we lay on Dom's rumpled bed, listening to Shakira's "Knock on My Door" — an admittedly odd choice of music for Dom. Our hands crept closer on the sheets. Fingers clasped, first tentatively and then more firmly. Then we faced each other across the white expanse of pillows, lips met, and with a swift movement, Dom threw her right leg over me. Crying out delightedly, she clambered on top, allowing me to push hot, fervid hands under her t-shirt to caress breasts that were more fulsome than they had a right to be on such a petite figure. It was a dream from which I did not want to awaken.

Awaken I did.

As brazen Shakira enticed her lover to knock on the door, telling him she will most assuredly be in town and he ought to ask for more, Dom's mother walked in the room, holding a tray of cool drinks. The prim woman with the perfectly set dye-job screamed, dropped the tray, the door slammed shut behind her. From the hall could be heard a muffled, "Oh, my dear Lord. You disgusting girls. Get out of my house."

"You better go." Dom grinned, sat up and adjusted her clothes.

Horrified, I headed for the door.

"Not that way." Dom pulled me back. "The window."

I fled into the night like a thief, but not before Dom bestowed a kiss on my lips.

"One for the road." She smiled, caressing my cheek. "See you tomorrow."

"Are you going to get in trouble?"

She nodded and shoved me out the window. She did not appear to be bothered about what might happen. I was mortified. Shame and embarrassment swept through me like a gale-force wind, knowing my grandmother was bound to find out. I could not be in the same room as Nan when the news broke, as it must. Judging from the shouting coming from the Device household, the storm had already broken and would soon spill over to our side of the fence. I could not face my grandmother. So I went to the sports oval behind the house and stayed there till late, lying on my back, staring at the stars and building up the courage to go home. When I did, I got the surprise of my life.

Nan sat in her favourite armchair in front of the TV, a grin plastered to her face.

"I guess, my girl," she said, cocking an eyebrow, "you've been getting cross under a rainbow."

At first I thought she was referring to the rainbow flag. But, always an original, she was most definitely not.

"It's an Afghan proverb," she stated. "It says if you get angry under a rainbow, your sex will change."

I was incredulous. "Like boy becomes girl and girl becomes boy?"

Nan nodded. "That's right. And if our dearly beloved neighbour, Tony Device, is to be believed, you've been getting mighty pissed off under a lot of rainbows."

"But I'm not a…"

"I know, honey. You're not a boy. You're a very pretty girl. But you're a girl who maybe likes other girls. And who's to say you bloody well can't?"

It was the last thing I expected to hear from a devout Muslim. And I knew everything was going to be fine when Nan opened her arms and pulled me in a tight embrace that smelled of cardigan, cigarettes and bathing soap.

I sobbed with relief. Not that I was ashamed of my attraction to girls. Not at all; I saw nothing wrong with that. I just did not want my grandmother to reject me. I clung to her and whispered, "Thank you," over and over.

Dom's parents were not as understanding, and although Nan tried to calm them, the Devices' staunch religious convictions could not be overturned. What was more, they declared me a baleful influence on their daughter and forbade us from seeing each other. By the end of a fortnight, plans were made for Dom to attend a girls' school in Perth, as far away from me as possible without shipping her to another country.

That was why in little under a month after the first dizzy kiss, we sat on the edge of my bed one Friday afternoon, contemplating razor blades. Nan was at the mosque and she was not expected for several hours.

"Are you sure about this?" Dom said.

The suicide pact had been her idea, flung before me like a magic carpet the previous evening when we met in secret at the sports oval behind our houses. "We should just kill ourselves," Dom had said, highhanded as she lay beside me on the grass. "Then they'll be sorry." She had probably not meant it. It was merely something to say, a gesture spoken with teenage fervour. Even so, I latched on to it like a piranha with fresh meat.

"Absolutely," I said, staring at the dazzling array of razor blades on the bedside table; there were six in two neat rows of three. "It's the only way we can be together for ever." I spoke with the ardour of a teenager who believed in the eternity of the moment and the impossibility of alternatives. It was my fifteenth birthday and I was convinced that killing myself and taking the love of my life with me was the most romantic gift a girl could possibly receive.

"I'm a bit freaked out," Dom admitted.

"Just think about what's on the other side."

"Why, what's on the other side?" Dom cried. She had been raised a Methodist; and although she was hardly practicing, suicide remained a mortal sin.

"Me, of course." I took her hand and kissed the knuckles. "We will be together. Forever. Will you wait for me if you get there first?"

She gave a reluctant nod, unable to look me in the eye.

"Say it."

"I will wait for you."

"Promise."

"I promise."

"Say my name."

"I promise, Mags."

I kissed her on the lips and let go her hand. Then I reached across to the dressing table and picked up the small whiskey bottle I'd placed there earlier. It was beside my diary with the baby blue cover. I had opened it on impulse that morning and noted that the day I entered the world and the day I was destined to leave it fell on a new moon.

"There's a dark moon today," I said.

Dom looked as if she could see through me.

"It's a good time for new beginnings," I continued.

"Or endings."

"Have a swig of this." I passed the whiskey to her.

Dom grabbed the bottle as if to a lifeline. "You've been at it," she said, noting the half-empty bottle.

"Dutch courage," I replied, shrugging.

We'd decided earlier to let Dom run the show; she was the strong one. The one to take the lead, but I saw then that it was up to me. Dom was not capable. She faltered precisely when needed. According to the clock by the bedside it was 1.15 p.m. My grandmother would be gone for at least another two hours. By then, Dom and I would be beyond saving.

"Is there something you want to say before we do this?"

Dom lay on the pale blue pillows and shook her head, looking at me like a trapped doe. It occurred to me that the alcohol coursing through my veins was probably making things easier than they might otherwise have been.

"Move up," I said.

She shuffled across, I lay down beside her and tucked Dad's magpie pendant under my t-shirt. Picking up two razor blades, I handed one to Dom and held the other in front of my face, studying the grooves in the polished metal that allowed the blade to fit snugly in the old-fashioned razor.

"On the count of three."

I took the pendant between thumb and forefinger, kissed it, and tucked it back again.

"Love you," I said to Dom. "See you on the other side."

She did not utter a word.

I said, "One, two, three."

I was amazed by the ferocity with which I took to the task. Closing my eyes, I gritted my teeth, preparing for horrendous pain, and slit quickly three times vertically through the skin of my left wrist. I felt as if I could cut through the arm down to the mattress, before switching hands and attacking the right arm with equal relish, knowing to aim for the radial artery so that even if I were found before I died there would be little chance of survival.

What surprised me most, as I sliced at my flesh, and the wound gaped open, was the release, the liberation of the pain I'd held on to for years. The relief was backed up by an opening up, a lightness of being. The agony flew away, leaving me free as a cloud.

After the initial shock, there was no pain. Only an ebbing and flowing, a rising and falling, a sliding on broad, flat waters, before a series of frantic movements beside me supplanted the inevitable. Whatever was going on in the room was removed from me, happening at the edges of consciousness. It did not require attention. I need only allow myself to be carried away.

Besides, someone had switched off the lights. It was pitch black. I could not see anything.

The sound of a door opening and closing brought me back. Feeling drowsy, numb, I opened my eyes, sat up, and leaned back on my elbows. My heart lurched to know Dom was gone. I was alone, again. Frightened, I raised my head and saw her on the other side of the room, descending a flight of stairs beside the closed bedroom door.

I said, "Dom, what are you doing?" before realising it was not her. It was a woman, covered head to toe in mud or red earth. Our eyes met. Then the woman's gazed shifted to something behind me, to the right of the bed. She stared for a moment or two, puzzled, and then vanished.

Curious, I turned my head. The effort proved to be too much. I swooned, fell back, and knew no more.

The next series of events came to me as disconnected images and longer scenes that advanced and withdrew, sometimes slowed down and other times speeded up. A camera flash went off in my head, illuminating the stage one minute and plunging it into darkness the next. Each time the lights came on, a different scene presented itself, to be replaced by another after an interval. There were times when I was not visited by a mirage, as I supposed them, and I drifted, thinking the performance had ended, when it started again. In this manner, I was flung about, not knowing if what I saw and heard was real or imagined. I could not even be certain as to the order in which events occurred. After a while I lost my way inside a labyrinth.

I was pressed against the ceiling when a man in loose green garb walked into the room. He picked up the body from the blood-soaked mattress and carried it out. Not down the corridor and out the front door, to a waiting ambulance, with curious onlookers, but sideways, through a gap in reality, so that he bypassed streets and houses to bring the body to a dimly lit room I had not seen before.

The body. It was no longer mine. I had nothing to do with it.

Even before the man reached the bedside, I had passed through the ceiling and shot through the roof. I discovered the brain was wider than the sky. Worlds fell away. I was everywhere and nowhere. I saw everything and nothing all at once. Infinitesimal vision. A deluge of imagery, sounds, sensations. In the moment before I dwelt in possibility, a door opened in the wall behind my bed and I saw a woman stand back, well away from the light, waiting to come in.

The door closed.

The universe did fade.

Sound stopped.

Magnolia ceased.

Sublime, it was. I was zilch and the whole shebang. I dispersed, was carried, a spore, across the cosmos and beyond, to realms white, deeper than oceans.

In due course, I became aware that a Horrendous Enormity was with me. Far back. Invisible. Perhaps only eyes that turned and locked on me. I was seen. Oddly, I was not afraid. Only aware of being watched, progress followed.

Consciousness for a mind without body was expansive, all-encompassing. There were no limits. Consciousness for a mind inside a body was a different matter. It was enclosed, limited, narrow. The body defined the limits of awareness, of experience. From boundless to singular; from breathing solar winds, to breathing common air.

And soil. Lungs inflated, deflated. Heartbeat. Limbs thrashed. Total paralysis, terror, panic, alarm. Pain. Oh, so much pain. Yet oddly distant and detached. As if it was happening to someone else.

With consciousness came the awareness that I was buried alive.

I could not breathe. I could not open my eyes. Soil pressed against my face and filled my mouth. Panicked and clawing; and when I sat up, gasping inside a shallow grave, I saw that I was in a cave of living rock. Other graves lined the wall. Empty of the seven sleepers, they contained or would one day contain—I was not sure. Light flickered on walls adorned with handprints, outlines of human figures, some with large, round heads radiating light and big watchful eyes, bounding animals in red ochre.

I was naked, except for the magpie pendant.

A man came down the stairs and kneeled beside the grave, thick hair obscuring his features. He took me in his arms and ascended seven steps to emerge through a door in the floor. Seven. I counted each footfall as though it was time moving forward, taking me away from that awful place. The clock on the wall announced the time: 1.15 p.m.

Still holding me in his arms, the man stepped sideways through trimmings of air, molecules, atoms. Space crimped as it combined with rapid movement along dark halls, to deliver my body to my bedroom. The journey was akin to stepping sideways from a grand hallway into the servants' corridor that runs parallel behind walls in a great mansion. Servants move about all over the house and no one knows. Except, in this instance, the man ferried me from one house to another, without stepping into the street.

Moments before we stepped into my bedroom, I saw a woman suspended in inky blackness. I closed my eyes and turned away.

The man put me in a clean bed and went away.

Singing brought me back. A dirge filled with sorrow and hope as ancient and indomitable as the mountains. Gasping, I opened my eyes and saw that I was in my own bed, covered with a quilt adorned with tiny red and blue flowers. A prized possession my grandmother's forebear brought from Afghanistan when he came to Australia in the late 1800s.

Nan, pale and overweight beneath a cotton dress with thin straps on meaty shoulders, sat in a chair beside the bed, singing a tuneless melody. Light fell on her through the window.

I looked at my arms. Outside the quilt, palms up. Ugly purple and pink scars. No bandages. After what I did to myself, I expected stitches, a period of rest, recuperation. Yet the wounds were closed, to all intents and purposes healed. How long had I been unconscious?

"Nan?"

She started in the chair. With a joyful cry she caught me in a tight embrace.

"Baby girl. You're awake. I was so worried."

Tears streamed down her face and wet my cheeks.

Confused, I took in the room over her shoulder. I was in my own bedroom. No doubt about that. In my own bed. Not a spot of blood any-where. And even though that did not make sense, given what had taken place, my first thought was for Dom.

"Where is she?"

"I'm here now," Nan said, cradling my head against her shoulder.

I pulled away. "Where's Dom?"

"Gone."

Thrashing and kicking in the bed, I tried to throw off the quilt.

"Why am I alive if she's dead?"

Nan sat back in her chair. "Dom isn't dead. She left town."

"No."

It was too much. I was alive and Dom, my own Dom, had left. The person I trusted most had walked away.

"Yes."

"Where did she go?"

Nan shrugged. "Don't know."

A scream built up inside me. It rose from the abdomen to the chest and exploded from the throat. I buried my face in the pillow and wailed, a dingo in the most forgotten part of the continent. The cry cut through my grandmother and echoed across the width and breadth of the desert.

A force was disturbed. It turned and listened, registering that it had been called. But it was not time to fully awaken. The wailing was the first call, an indication that time was near. The door was ajar, but not fully open. The force had to wait for another dark moon in thirteen years' time. And although it had been buried for aeons, it possessed infinite patience. A decade or so more was nothing. Black waters held it. It could wait. Before it gave itself to dreamless sleep, it relayed a message to its minion. Unlike itself, the henchman was not spellbound. He was free to wander, to keep an eye on things and to do its bidding. The vassal, in turn, alerted the Green Man. So that when I came to my senses a second time…

…he sat at the end of my bed, dressed in a bottle-green linen suit. He was young and disarmingly handsome; and although the luxuriant hair piled atop his head and falling across his brow was dark brown, the clipped beard was as white as the hair on an old man's pate.

"Who are you?"

My throat was sore. I could barely speak. The room swirled. The man wavered, broke apart and came together again. He was not real. But he was present. He had weight, because the mattress sank where he sat.

He said, "Magnolia, you must stay awake. You are not yet fully returned. If you sleep, you may not awaken again. Sit up and talk. Do you understand?"

Alarm swept through me. Who was this man? How did he know my name? What was he doing in my room? Not fully returned from where? I ought to scream, call for help, but I found that I was not afraid. There was no threat in him. I got nothing from him. No vibration, no energy, no human warmth. He revealed nothing other than the mere fact of his existence.

"Are you real?"

"As real as anything can be on earth."

"Are you a doctor? Did you patch me up?"

I displayed my bare arms. Then, realising what I had done, I quickly pressed my forearms against the bed covers. A wash of emotion followed: shame, embarrassment, humiliation. I was one of those cowards people talk about, a weakling who tried to kill herself, without a thought for her loved ones. And failed. The fresh disfigurements I had inflicted on myself made me think of other such cuttings I intended to make in future. These blemishes, becoming part of the 'cuttings' I already planned to make on my arms and legs now that I knew how good it felt to cut my skin. The relief it brought. The new injuries would be canyons against a welter of faded yet intersecting riverbeds and creeks, a scarlet landscape of torment, that would elevate me. Take me away.

"I restored life to you," the man said.

Suddenly, I was angry. "You had no right."

"Alila is grateful to you."

"I wanted to die."

"Your life—that's your reward."

"Life is not a reward. It's a curse."

My words gave the man pause. To this point his face bore no expression. He was unreadable. When he heard my words, his face darkened.

After a while, I said, "Why is she grateful? What have I done for her?"

Might as well play along; it was only a dream.

"It's not what you've done. It's what you will do. And for this Alila is grateful. She is thanking you in advance."

"Who's Alila?"

"You will find out in due course."

"How does she know about me?"

"The spirits see the living when they enter the world of the dead."

"So she's a spirit."

"She is a djinni."

"What does she want?"

"Two things. First, a personal item from you."

I was casting my eyes around the room, looking for something to give him, when his hand closed on an object on the bedside table.

"How about this?"

It was the magpie pendant.

"You can't have that," I said, lunging for it. "It's a special gift."

"All the better."

The man slipped the pendant into a pocket and grinned. I could not be bothered arguing. For me this was a game, a delusion. Everything would go back to normal when I woke up properly.

"What else does this Alila want?"

"All you need to know for the time being is you can't sleep. You must stay awake and talk until you fully return to yourself."

Return to yourself. An odd way to put it. But I didn't have the energy to question him. Perhaps he was a foreigner and used English in a peculiar way.

"I'm not saying another word," I said, "until you tell me what she wants."

The man considered, turning to look away from me. It was as fine a profile as I had seen. The clean lines of his face belonged in a Persian miniature touched with gold leaf.

"You are the door through which Alila will re-enter the world."

"What does that mean?"

He placed a finger on my lips; the finger slipped inside my mouth, past the teeth, and touched my tongue, the invasion horrifying and electrifying.

"This is the door," he said.

He removed the invasive digit, and it felt as if he had taken my insides with it.

I knew then that this could not be real. I was still dreaming or hallucinating or whatever was going on in my mind in the wake of the suicide attempt. Exhausted, I slipped under the covers, lay my head on the pillow, and looked at the electric clock on the beside. 1.15 p.m. Had the clock stopped?

"I want my grandmother."

"Tell me a story," he said.

"Don't know any."

"Everyone has a story they carry inside themselves about their lives."

"Not me."

"People live inside the stories they tell about themselves. And they use those stories to interpret everything around them."

I looked at his unmoving, unsmiling form and for a moment, he disappeared. In his place I saw a girl, dark hair pulled back in a ponytail, a frown sullying a pretty face. She turned to me and said, "Get me out of here."

She faded; the Green Man reappeared and with a slight tilt of the head, cocked a very fine eyebrow as if to say, "Well…?"

"Once upon a time," I began, "a young girl did something terrible. So horrible and shameful was this act that no matter what she did thereafter, she couldn't break free from its baleful influence. She was trapped inside herself, inside an impossible room that existed perhaps only in her own mind, waiting for someone to free her…"

I paused.

"Go on."

I shook my head. "Too scared."

"Of what?"

"Of what will happen if I tell."

"Stories have the power to free as well as to trap," he said.

Even as he spoke, he and the room melted. I saw two women sheltering from a storm in a hilltop house.

"I died," I said…

CHAPTER 27

…to Dom. "And George brought me back. The way he brought them back. That's what he meant when he said Alila got him to save my life. I thought he was a doctor who patched me up. But he literally brought me back from the dead, like Lazarus in the Bible."

Careful not to disturb the salt I had placed along the ledge, I stood at the window, looking at a night that was not night at all. In the wet blue, I saw clearly enough down to the plain and across to a distant mountain range, lit up with the raggedy play of lightning. The spectacle made me feel lonely and insignificant.

Dom said, "Yes."

"You knew."

"George told me."

In the distance, three jagged legs of lightning danced nimbly over the earth, illuminating a mountain and the undersides of clouds with licks of purple, pink, red. Rain on the roof was the sound of the sea. With it came the frothing wash of unwanted thoughts. *I am like the boys,* I thought, *a puppet brought back to life to satisfy the needs of a demon. But if they can accept their destiny, why can't I?* What was I fighting against? It wasn't as if I had much to live for. Why not give in and accept the fact that I too was food for the gods? At least then my life would have meaning, purpose, aim. But no, I could not lie down and take it. I would fight tooth and nail to save my charges and stop that bitch Alila.

A tremendous crashing and rumbling of thunder brought me back.

"What did George tell you exactly?" I said.

"Long story short, you bled to death. In the time it took your grandmother to come home, George buried you in a cave under his house and you came back to life three days later."

"That doesn't make sense. Nan got home minutes after she got the call—"

"From me."

"She came home," I continued, "and found me in bed, asleep… Or something like that. It's confused."

"George works outside of time. Half an hour for Cherry was three days for you."

"That's handy."

"Like I told you," Dom said, coming to stand beside me, "I wouldn't have believed it if I hadn't seen that creepy guy with the weird legs…"

"Malachi?"

Dom nodded. "He met me at Alice Springs airport."

"He's definitely a sight for sore eyes."

"That's no way to talk about your grand-pappy."

We smiled shyly at one another.

"That's what convinced me all this was real," Dom went on. "Him and…seeing a bunch of dead kids sit up in their graves. Good as new, like you."

The last statement was not an entirely accurate summation of the situation. Dom must be aware that I was not 'good as new'. Far from it. I changed after the resurrection. It had been a terrible awakening, a terrifying ordeal. Traumatic. Distressing enough for me to close down, bury the facts and not think about them again. Until this minute. Dom's departure had been the final blow.

Had the boys experienced the same anguish and suffering when they awoke Monday morning? Is that the reason they turned to me for reassurance the way a flower turns to the sun for sustenance? Only to be rebuffed, disappointed, of course, because I had no idea what they wanted from me. Well, I knew now, and I would make it up to them.

"If I get my hands on the maniac who shot them," I said, "I'll kill him."

On the other side of the room, Adam, Harun, Salih, Zaman and Hasan sat up in their sleeping bags and listened to us talk. Their faces beamed with silent rapture, probably glad I had finally found my way to the truth. Only Harun's face was sunk in shadow, firelight flickering behind him and creating a nimbus around his head. All the same, I was sure he watched as intently as the others.

"What are you staring at?" Dom growled at them. "Haven't you seen a lesbian come out dead before?"

They tittered and lay down. Even so, I was sure they remained awake and listening.

"I thought you didn't believe in killing," Dom said, referring to my earlier remark about the terrorist.

"I don't. But I'd happily kill him."

"Anyway, time you got some shut eye."

That was when I leaned across and whispered what I had been holding onto for ages. "I thought I was nothing without you," I said. "There was a time when I would have done anything to make you love me."

"I'm not worth it," she whispered back.

"Don't say that about yourself."

Dom pulled away. "I'm a bad girl. Real bad. I left you for dead and I've done worse. Far worse. I just hope I get the chance to do one good thing before I cark it. Otherwise I'm a goner."

She left the room, stood at the front door and lit a cigarette, match flaring in the dark. Taking advantage of her absence, Adam came to me.

"Did you know about this?" I asked him, keeping my voice low.

"Part of it," he whispered.

"Why didn't you tell me? I feel like an idiot."

"You're supposed to discover these things for yourself. It's more meaningful that way."

"George brought us back to life to feed a monster. There's no meaning in that."

"That's our destiny," Adam said, the sweep of his hand taking in the others. "Not yours."

"What's my destiny?"

He shrugged. "Only you know that."

"What about Dom? What's her part in this? She better have one because she's a dead loss as a body guard."

Adam smiled. "A shepherd needs a cudgel."

He smiled again and I thought: *He really is beautiful. He will grow up to break many hearts.* But he was not going to grow up, was he? He was supposed to die. Never see manhood.

"I don't get you," I said.

"What don't you get?"

"All this stuff about sacrificing yourself so that Alila can live. You're better than that. You have a will of your own."

"Do you always go against your mother's wishes?"

"I don't know. I didn't have a mother for long."

"If things were different, if your mother came back into your life, what would you do?"

"I'd be a good little girl," I said, without thinking about it, "and do everything she told me. I'd never disobey her."

"Are you sure about that?" Adam said.

Dom returned at that point and told him to get back to sleep. When he rejoined the others, she looked at me. "You too."

I did not need to be told twice. I slipped into the sleeping bag and pulled the hood over my head, glad to close my eyes and descend into nothingness. The last thing I heard was Dom shaking another couple of pills from the bottle. This, in turn, reminded me that I had forgotten to put my plan to stop Alila into action. It was too late to do anything about it tonight. Maybe tomorrow? Sleep gripped me and I gave in to its seductive pull.

CHAPTER 28

I stepped out of the sleeping bag as though sloughing an old skin. It fell at my feet and I wandered, barefoot, rejoicing in nakedness, from the kitchen, into a corridor devoid of rubble and perfectly lined with gleaming floorboards. Doors on either side opened on to perfect rooms. Light played on newly plastered walls as though the house was underwater, the sky ablaze with stars even though there was a ceiling over my head.

A large magpie waited on the doorstep, the beak turned in sharp profile, glistening eye on me. I followed its ponderous gait into open desert. It was like stepping into a new world. My senses sharpened to the point of being overwhelmed. The aroma of wet soil was enough to make me reel, each grain of sand visible, every blade of grass. Every plant that grew and creature that crawled was audible. The air vibrated with mournful chants and clap sticks. A haunting melody filled me with a yearning for something that had no name.

The magpie walked to the back of the cottage. In the starlight I saw a pond ringed with bullrushes. The bird plunged its head into the water. The head that emerged after a quick dip belonged to my father, Jimmy Olden. A man's head on a magpie's body. The curls of black hair soaked through and plastered to a gleaming forehead. Almost black lips smiled as he extends his right wing and I smiled with him. So glad to see his face again. The feathers were warm and smooth in my hand, comforting. With the other wing, he pointed at the water.

I dropped to my knees and gazed on my own reflection.

"Truth is inescapable, daughter," he said.

A pretty woman gazed at me from the water. The hair was pulled away from the face and knotted at the crown of the head to reveal a high brow and skin polished to a lustrous sheen. The eyes sparked with intelligence, casting light on cheekbones and an upturned nose. Gorgeous.

As I thought this, the girl in the water smiled, revealing white teeth whose lustre rivalled the moon. Behind her, constellations revolved. My own falling star, a tear, fell from my eyes and rippled the surface.

In the depths I saw myself in my sleeping bag inside the cottage. Five naked boys with female genitalia pressed against my own nakedness. I held Adam to one breast and Harun to the other. Salih, Zaman and Hasan had pushed so far into my torso they had merged with my flesh, arms, legs, heads poking out in a monstrous, grotesque, body-melt merger.

Horrified, on the verge of screaming, I pulled away. In that moment, before I turned away, I saw a woman with long hair swim swiftly up to me, a thin smile on her lips.

CHAPTER 29

"Mags, wake up."

I opened my eyes and sat up, images from the dream flooding my brain. Jimmy Olden's words echoed: "Truth is inescapable, daughter."

What truth was he talking about? My life had been one big denial, sidestepping one issue after another just to keep up the semblance of sanity and a normal life. There was no end to the tricks and deceptions I had played on myself, and on others, to keep going. How was I to know where one truth or lie ended and the other began?

But I had no time to think about any of that. Salih kneeled beside me, shaking me by the shoulder.

"What is it?"

"Something's going on outside."

I was instantly on my feet. A scan of the room told me Dom was absent. Adam and Zaman stood at the window. Harun and Hasan crouched beside the fireplace. I squeezed in between Adam and Zaman, and noticed the salt I placed along the ledge had been broken. The boys must have done it when they leaned on it.

I told Salih to bring the salt from the food storage. The fire had almost burned down, too, and I was grateful the LED lamp continued to push back darkness.

Salih gave me a plastic container full of salt. I used it to replenish the line on the window ledge. Then I poured a good handful of salt into my pocket, for good measure.

"Put it back," I said, handing the container to Salih. "And throw some wood on the fire."

He was obedience personified.

"Okay," I said, gazing out the window, "let's see what's going on."

Rain had stopped. The pond at the back was a gleaming reminder of the dream. The valley below was almost purple. A mountain range glowed palely on the horizon. Keeping down my voice, I told Adam and Zaman to get away from the window, waving them away with my hand. If someone or some thing was out there, I wanted them well away from danger. Dom must be on reconnaissance. As the thought passed through my mind, the light in the room intensified, growing stronger by degrees.

It was not coming from Salih's feeble stoking at the fire. Nor was it coming from the LED lamp.

It was coming from outside, a staccato, pulsating rhythm growing in intensity.

Zaman said, "Wow," and pointed.

A giant wheel of white light rolled past the window. It disappeared down the side of the building and came around, almost instantly, before I could draw breath, completing the revolution in no time as it encircled the buildings. It did this over and over again. After half a dozen revolutions, the light turned to a flaring phosphorescence cut through with pale blue and scarlet flashes. It was hypnotic. An elongated form with a large head could be discerned inside the light.

"Malachi," I said.

"He's come for one of us." Adam pressed against me.

I pushed him away from the window. "Stay here. Look after the others and don't go out, no matter what happens. I'll see what Dom is doing."

The fact that Malachi did not attempt to enter the room was a good sign. The old charms worked.

I was in the process of stepping out of the room when Malachi stopped revolving around the house. Light died. Night closed in. Silence. Water drip, drip, dripped somewhere inside. Air tightened with tension as I waited in the doorway to see what the ifrit was going to do next.

Nothing happened.

"I'll go now," I said, afraid my voice betrayed the fear I felt.

Can the boys hear the thunder in my chest? I thought as I walked away. *Can they see my legs quake?* I was more terrified than I had ever been, my stomach flooded with adrenalin as I walked the length of the corridor with the torch, looking behind me to make sure they stayed safely in the kitchen.

"I am going to confront the creature who is my grandfather," I told myself. "I exist because of his actions. Yes," I went on, "your fear is justified. So go a little easy on yourself." Then I thought, *Stuff it, I've been going easy on myself all my life and look where it got me.*

I was standing at the entrance to the cottage, wavering, when Harun came after me, stepping lightly over the struts in the floor, arms spread to give him balance. He grabbed my free hand and said, "Stay."

Touched, I kneeled and said, "It's going to be fine, sweetheart. I need to see where Dom is."

"She will die."

"No one's going to die," I said. "Go back to the kitchen."

"It's her destiny."

"You mustn't say things like that."

"She killed us. Now it's her turn."

The allegation was presented as cold fact. No blame, no anger, or resentment, in his voice. Nevertheless, the two sentences shattered my world. The words passed through the bone of my skull, into the brain, and bounced like ball bearings down an endless corridor.

"What did you say?"

"She was the gunman at the mosque," Harun said.

The pounding in my head was accompanied by a sudden loss of vision. I almost toppled over backwards. When sight returned, I was rigid with a killing rage I could all too willingly unleash on anyone that came close. Only I did not know if I was angry with Dom, Harun, or myself.

"She betrayed you," the boy went on. "Let Malachi take her."

I rose to my feet. Distantly, I knew I wanted to knock down the boy. Make him stop talking. The lips moved. The eyes held mine. I heard him through a brain-shattering pounding, an entanglement of anger, rage and confusion that connected with a string of insults, slights and hurts I had suffered at the hands of that vile woman. In that moment I knew I could kill. If I had a gun, I would use it on Dominique Device. Empty it into her chest, into her face. Make sure the pretty young thing from next door resembled a side of beef.

Harun was right. Let Malachi finish the job.

Through a mighty fog, I became aware that Adam had joined us.

"Is it true?" I said to him.

His silence told me everything.

"Let Malachi kill her for you." Harun again. "You know you want to."

I did not like the way he smiled at me. I looked at Adam, pleading with my eyes to make the younger boy stop talking.

"You've said enough," Adam said to Harun. "Come."

Harun faced Adam, face ablaze. "You can't let her go. It's not how things are supposed to be. You know that."

His voice shattered the night. I was certain he could be heard kilometres away. I wanted to stop him from saying things I did not want to hear. And then I wanted to go outside and work with Malachi, blood of my blood, and finish Dominique.

"Harun," Adam said, "you don't know what you're talking about."

He led the protesting boy away. For a while I stood there, unable to move or think. My feet decided for me. They moved of their own accord. To what purpose, I could not tell. All I knew was I had been duped again. I had put my trust in Dominique and she killed the boys. I had loved Harun and he obviously despised me. They had taken me for a fool. If I continued to move, directing the broad sweep of the torch beam and stepping through the door, it was not to save Dominique from Malachi. My grandfather, I could admit it now, could have her. I moved because, like a shark, I had to keep moving to stop from dying. I had to get away from the people in whom I had put trust, and who had betrayed me.

I was rounding the corner along the side of the cottage when the torch failed. I flicked the switch on and off, hoping it would come on. Nothing happened. Then I realised I didn't need it. I could see without it. Ahead, light streamed from the kitchen window, flooding a pond ringed with reeds, like a stage set.

"O granddaughter, come and take thy final choice..."

The voice was sibilant, a hiss that elongated vowels and emphasised consonants. It was how a snake might speak. The lean figure stood on two absurdly attenuated legs whose knees bent backwards and whose feet were twisted right round. It emitted light, like a glow-worm, through translucent skin—a poisonous, glowing green. Some of the internal organs were visible, blue veins coursing through the body, as well as the landscape behind it. Arms with taloned fingers reached to the ground. The oval head was raw meat, the lidless eyes bulbous. Two fangs, protruding from the lower jaw and bracketing the mouth, finished off a not-too-pretty picture.

I froze, shaking my head as I pressed against the wall.

"You're not my grandfather."

Now that I looked at Malachi I saw the impossibility of my earlier thoughts. I could not align with something as utterly inhuman as that creature. It was absurd to think otherwise.

"Cherry would disagree."

"You raped her."

"What stupendous issuance we made."

"You're insane," I said, taking a step back.

"Your mother, your good self," Malachi continued, moving forward slightly. "Where is she, by the way?"

"Who?"

"Your adoring mama."

I could not find the words to tell him.

"Oh, that's right," he teased. "She doth suffer a sea-change, into something rich and strange."

"No." I did not like where this was going.

"But she left behind a precious pearl. A granddaughter fair for the grandparents to dote upon." Another stealthy step forward. "Oh, Magnolia," he said, voice dropping, clawed hands reaching out, "you are the perfect vessel. Well met." He bowed as the lips roiled across the face like molluscs.

"Well met yourself, fucker."

Dominique emerged from a cluster of bullrushes, aimed, and fired a bullet into Malachi's back and another to the head. The noise was explosive. I screamed and threw my hands up. The ifrit screeched, reeled, and toppled over. Blue ichor spurted from the wounds, starting spot fires where it made contact with vegetation.

I shouted, "No, no, no," until I was hoarse.

Dominique rushed the slumped figure, held it down with a foot to the chest and put another bullet to its forehead.

"That's for putting your hands on me without permission," she said.

Malachi let off a piercing scream. Thrashing and flailing on the ground, waving arms and legs, and in the process, knocking Dominique off her feet. The gun flew from her hand and landed out of reach. Dominique fell. As she struggled to get up, slender fingers locked around her ankle and drew her nearer. Another arm emerged from the right side of Malachi's torso, gripped Dominique's throat and began to squeeze. She turned the same shade of red as Malachi's face. Her tongue poked from her mouth, eyes popped, as her own hands closed around Malachi's forearms, desperate to stop him.

Not sure what I should do, I picked up the gun and ran to where Malachi and Dominique enacted their struggle. I had never fired a gun in my life. But I had to do it now. I aimed, gripping the pistol in both hands, the way I had seen actors do on television, and indecision set in.

The gun pointed first at Malachi.

And then, barrel trembling, at Dominique.

I hesitated. Time stopped.

Malachi took advantage of the moment. He tossed Dominique on her back. Then he flipped over, straddled her chest, and squeezed the slender neck. Ichor continued to pour from the wounds, setting alight the hair on the left side of Dominique's head. She shouted and thrashed in the dirt, trying to extinguish the flames.

Frozen with indecision, I saw Dominique's bloodshot eyes through Malachi's transparent head. Looking at me through the creature's cranium, Dominique's eyes travelled between my grimly determined features and the gun barrel.

"Kill her," Malachi said. "No one will blame you. You missed me and hit the woman by mistake. Who's to know?"

The ifrit was right. Dominique deserved to die. She had betrayed me, killed the boys and shot Nan. A bitch like her should die. My finger tightened on the trigger. The weapon wavered. Yet I could not do it.

"Who is to care?" Malachi went on. "She's trash. No one will miss her."

He slammed Dominique's head on the ground with such ferocious strength that I heard her teeth rattle. There was a sickening crunch as the back of her skull made contact with the ground. On the second attempt, the back of Dominique's head broke through a tangle of grass and reeds and floated inches above the scummy pond surface. Seeing an opportunity, she plunged her head backwards in the water and doused the fires in her hair.

"Kill her. There are no witnesses."

My eyes meet Dominique's for the second time. As the grey tongue protruded from her mouth and her eyes bulged, I realised she was on to me. She knew I meant to kill her.

I looked away and saw Adam watching me from the kitchen window.

That broke the spell. Fear and guilt swept through me. Or maybe I knew I would not get away with it this time. Time leaped into motion. The gun moved from Dominique's face to the back of Malachi's head.

In that instant, Dominique vanished. She was replaced beneath Malachi by Cherry Din—a young girl lying under a monster as he assaulted her. The slender legs flailed, the skirt fell back to reveal sleek thighs, the hands thrashed. "Stop," Cherry screamed. "No."

Cherry disappeared. Dominique was back under Malachi.

"Do it," Dominique hissed. "Just fucking do it."

It was as if she had spoken to Malachi. His skin changed. The transformation started on the head, neck, shoulders, and spread through the rest of the pallid body. He was reverting to his original form, fire.

Dominique let out a piercing scream.

If I didn't act straight away it would be too late for her. I stuck the gun in my back pocket, grabbed Malachi by one scaly ankle and dragged him with all my might toward the water. He delivered a vicious blow to my face with the other foot. My head flew back, neck snapped, teeth clashed, but I managed to hold on and drag the creature closer to the water. For some reason my hand was not burning.

Dominique let go another agonised scream as Malachi wrapped his arms and legs around her and glared at me with an eye that left me in no doubt he was truly acquainted with hell.

Dominique screamed again. Her t-shirt was on fire.

The pool was a couple of steps behind me, yet it felt like an eternity before I reached it. By that time, Dominique's t-shirt was alight, as was the hair on one side of her head, the skin on her left cheek blistering and turning black. The cries for help were terrible.

I gritted my teeth and continued the grim task of pulling Malachi inch by agonised inch to the water's edge. In the final stages of the transformation, the ifrit's body took on the consistency of burning coal; and it was at this point that my runners touched water.

With a desperate cry, I hauled the grotesque lovers across the squelching mud into the pond.

It was a baptism of fire. I fell back in the water, pulling Dominique and Malachi with me. Malachi shrieked in the wake of furious hissing. The pool bubbled like a witch's cauldron. Steam rose in the chill air. Yet the water remained cold around me.

Malachi released Dominique. I retrieved a handful of wet salt from my pocket. Knee deep in water, I waded across to him and plastered the creature's face with the salt and rubbed it in. Malachi let go another roar and, before falling back, eyes blazing, limbs thrashing, our eyes met.

I saw a bright red light sink into a well of loneliness, going back through the ages, until it blinked out. Seconds later, the blackened skin turned to ash. After a while, that also dispersed and floated away. By the time the water stopped bubbling and the smell of sulphur faded, Dominique and I were the only living creatures in the pool. My grandfather was vapour.

<h1 style="text-align:center">CHAPTER 30</h1>

After putting an unconscious Dominique to bed and playing nurse with the first-aid kit, I decided it was time to put my plan to action.

Alila must be stopped. The insanity had gone far enough. I could not allow it to continue another moment.

Reaching into my overnight bag, I retrieved a box of sleeping pills and popped three tablets out of the blister pack. A slug of water from a bottle encouraged their descent into Dominique's lying, treacherous throat, where I hoped the soporific effect would spread through the body and keep her out of action for a while.

The plan, such as it was, went something like this: keep Dominique knocked out for a couple of days, secure the remaining boys in the cottage until the new moon on Thursday, and shatter the narrow window of opportunity Alila had to prey on them. When the ritual period was over, the djinni's plans would be thwarted and the kids would be safe. Or so I hoped.

Granted, it was not much of a plan. And I was not certain it would work. But it was the best I could come up with at the time.

Exhausted, I tossed the sleeping pills in my bag and turned my attention to other matters. That is when I noticed two of my charges were missing.

"Where's Harun and Hasan?"

Adam sat with Salih and Zaman in front of the fireplace. He pointed at the alcove beside the kitchen door.

Bewildered, I walked over and looked inside. It was empty, but dust had been disturbed on the floor. Stepping in, I tapped with the tip of my right foot. Hollow.

An entry to a basement, I thought, bending to probe layers of accumulated dirt. My fingers snagged a metal ring. When I pulled on it, a trapdoor creaked open to reveal a square hole, stone steps descending into the dark.

"Are they down there?" I said to Adam.

He nodded.

Glaring at him, I found myself descending another flight of stairs for the second time in a matter of days. It was the last thing I wanted to do. I was mentally and physically exhausted after the ordeal with Malachi and Dominique in the pond. Yet I had sworn to protect, and protect I would, whether they liked it or not.

As I placed one foot in front of the other, I was obscurely reminded of yet another flight of steps, many years earlier, when I was younger. Only in that distant time I was in the arms of a man with pale green eyes and a white beard. The two images came together in my mind; for a moment, as I gazed into the black void beneath me, I was not sure if I was ascending or descending the present staircase that, for me, was the same as the one in George Green's house in Alice Springs. Even the texture of the walls was the same—red, orange, black and brown striations, scored and pitted with age. Ochre handprints pressed to stone, a stylised kangaroo, humanoid figures, cavorting animals. I had seen the same images in George's basement.

Was it the same cave? How could it be? An image from that time flooded my mind. George holding my naked form as he made his way up the stairs to emerge inside a walk-in pantry in his own home. And when he stepped into the kitchen the clock on the wall said it was 1.15 p.m. All the timepieces were stuck at that precise moment in time.

Stuck. That is how I felt. Fixed in place and unable to move. Yet, conversely, I had not stopped moving. I had lived my life in almost constant motion, as if I was afraid to stop and consider my situation.

Standing in the basement, I directed the light onto my surrounds. A low, narrow chamber with a dirt floor followed the course of the house above. Two sets of small footprints disappeared into the gloom on the other side of eight open graves, dirt piled beside each one.

Shuddering, I turned away and shone the torch into a narrow tunnel. The height of the ceiling dropped considerably as I followed the direction Harun and Hasan had apparently taken. Ahead was a tapering passage leading to a larger cave system. Cold air blowing in my face was proof of that. After several minutes, a faint light caught my attention, a flickering orb in the immense darkness.

Moments later, I stepped into a shimmering jewel box. The roof soared as limestone stalagmites shot from the floor to greet stalactites that reached gleamingly down to earthbound sisters. Water dripped and trickled, creating musical reverberations.

Spellbound, I admired the sights. It was another world, going off into infinite space and keeping its secrets to itself. A body of water caught the amber light and cast dancing, silvery configurations on walls and ceiling. The still surface, broken by drops of water from above, reflected the otherworldly confections attached to the ceiling, creating a mirage at the end of the chamber that resembled the mouth of an ancient beast with smashed teeth.

At first, I thought the light came from the fantastic mineral formations. Then I realised, as I stepped forward, wonderstruck and admiring, that it emanated from a small terracotta oil lamp. It was atop a twist of multicoloured limestone, the flat surface acting as a plinth. When I stood breathing over it in my excitement, the flame danced in the nozzle, setting wild shadows in motion.

For the next little while, as I made my way further into the caverns that opened one after the other, I encountered six more lamps, burnished terracotta sending forth a lick of flame atop a flat surface that appeared to have been formed for the occasion. Cavities opened like puzzle boxes, one inside the other, and the further I penetrated into them, the more splendid they became.

I passed a room in which blue light shimmered beneath a lofty ceiling. The walls of another chamber resembled billowing pink and turquoise clouds, rocks polished to such a sheen that I could see my reflection. Yet another chamber was composed of basalt columns that resembled organ pipes, rising and falling in scale and creating broad steps that took me high above the floor to an opening that passed through to the cave system's crowning achievement: hundreds of colossal crystals thrust from the ground, forming a forest of pillars that supported the roof. I clambered through with difficulty, slipping and falling once or twice. The way ahead was barred by a screen frozen in wave-like motions, a semi-transparent curtain drawn between rooms. On the other side I spotted the familiar glow of yet another lamp.

By squeezing through a fold in the partition I entered a large cavern dominated by a single remarkable occupant. A palm tree, the towering trunk twisting and coiling like melted toffee into a fantastical spiral shape, with an eruption of lustrous green fronds at the top. It was the sole occupant of an otherwise empty chamber. Yet it claimed the might and majesty of the realm, especially when moonlight came through a hole in the roof. Rain fell with a patter on leaves. An embrasure in the tree trunk held a final terracotta lamp, with the familiar lick of orange flame.

Despite the size of the chamber and the freshness allotted by air and rain coming in through the hole in the roof, the room was humid, oppressive. I was reminded of the grotto in the canyon, with the eye in the sky. This place felt the same—a home for prehistoric beasts and beings from another world. Yet there was the stirring, lofty profundity of a sacred temple about it, too, light and beautiful, round and smooth as a womb. A wholly feminine space. I held my breath, suspended between sublimity and dread.

The palm tree knew I was there. It watched and waited.

With considerable effort, I turned away and looked for Harun and Hasan. I had lost track of their footprints long ago, presuming they too had followed the enticement of lights. I called their names and, as if summoned by my words, they stepped out from behind the tree, holding hands and smiling.

"Look, Hasan," Harun said. "Mags's come to the rescue." His voice was mocking, addressing Hasan even as he kept his eyes on me. A serene smile played on his lips as if his body was flooded with endorphins and dopamine, triggering a tranquillity hardly warranted by the bizarre situation. Hasan was the same. "Are you good at maths, Mags?" Harun pursued.

I nodded, dumbfounded.

"Seven times seven."

"Forty-nine."

"Seven lamps for seven boys ferried across the country in four days," the boy continued.

"I don't follow."

"The mother wants you to think about numbers, Mags. Seven steps. Seven boys. Four days. What's that?"

"Fifty-three."

"Think about the symbolic meaning of numbers and what they represent. Then you might understand what is going on and why you can't stop it from happening."

"I don't know anything about numerology."

"You're not as smart as you think."

"I'm your friend."

A cruel laugh. "This isn't about friends and enemies. It's not a game. It's a matter of life and death. You play your part, I play mine, and everything will work out just fine. Everyone is playing their part, except you."

"I don't care about Alila," I said, voice quivering.

"She cares about you."

"I care about you. I'm taking you back. Come here, Hasan."

I extended my right hand and waited. Neither moved. They merely gazed at me. Slowly the smiles broadened on their faces, hinting at hidden knowledge beneath the calm. In an act of pure frustration and exasperation, I grabbed Hasan's hand. The response was immediate.

The boy had been standing on four large palm fronds that radiated from beneath his feet. The moment I seized Hasan's hand, the leaves leaped up and enfolded him inside an envelope that sealed him off from my efforts to affect a rescue. Startled, I yelped, leaped back, withdrawing my hand with some difficulty through the tightly bound leaves. Hasan did not resist. He did not even make a sound as the leafy bundle was lifted from the ground by a cord that yanked him to the top of the tree. He dangled there, like pupae in a cocoon.

I called out his name and rushed to the base of the tree. But I could not reach him. He was too high up for me, and it was impossible to scale the smooth trunk. Desperate, I turned to Harun.

"Help me get him down."

Harun did not move. I tried to scrambled up the tree on my own; although I found purchase for my hands and feet in the twists and coils in the trunk, I was ultimately defeated. The toffee-like surface was too even and polished. A few feet off the ground, my strength gave out and I slid down, until I stood doubled over and lay panting on the ground.

After my third or fourth attempt, Harun gave a gelid smile and moved his eyes the length of the tree trunk to where Hasan hung, turning inside the casing. I followed his gaze. As I watched, the leaves around Hasan underwent rapid change, crinkling and shrinking to compact the body inside. The foliage changed from viridian to tawny brown. The satchel quivered. The outline of a human form wasted away inside was replaced by what appeared to be a pulpy mass of rounded nodules pressed against the shell.

Head thrown back, I waited to see what happened next.

The cocoon split opened with a light explosive sound and thousands of crimson berries rained down on me.

Surprised, I bent over and covered my head with my hands.

"Alila blesses whoever does not spill blood in this sanctuary," Harun said. "We are food for the djinni."

And, indeed, the berries were instantly absorbed by the loamy soil as if they had been slurped greedily into the earth.

My horror was added to when I turned to face Harun. He opened his mouth and mushrooms began to stream from his throat, choking his voice. Bright red caps with white spots that quivered with the sudden onrush of freedom, followed by a profusion of different shaped fungi.

They emerged from between his lips, twisting and gyrating, before thrusting out from the side of his face, streaming down the cheeks, up the nostrils, in and out of the eye sockets, ear holes, emerging from the mouth and diving back again through every orifice in his face.

In seconds, Harun's head was covered in a hood of multicoloured living matter. He lifted his hands and displayed hideous horseshoe-shaped hoofs in all the colours of the rainbow.

Finally, when I thought it could not get worse, a pinkish, thread-like appendage emerged from one of his nostrils and twisted around the throat, tightening until the boy's eyes popped from the sockets. What little skin was left on his neck folded over and in between the tendril's loops.

Realising he was about to choke, I fell on him and began to claw at the organic matter. I worked silently, determinedly, occasionally releasing a fearful cry as I tore chunks of the boy's face. It was useless. The fungi continued to proliferate until Harun was botanic, head to toe.

"Leave off, woman, and let it be."

A female voice.

I spun around. I saw no one. Only the tree.

"You look but you truly do not see."

That was when I did see. Feminine features pressed into the tree trunk. Grotesque as it was, I could not look away. I saw a crude, heavy brow, eyelids closed over large eyes, a nose, strong chin.

Appalled, I stepped back and almost tripped on the uneven floor.

"Do not deny the acolyte his pleasure. Your turn will come soon enough."

The words emerged from a horizontal slit in the wood. Each word was accompanied by a flow of viscous crimson liquid that poured from mouth, nose and eyes, dyeing the jaw in a veil of glistening red.

"This can't be real. I must be dreaming," I said.

Low rumbling laughter from the tree.

"Who is dreaming whom?" the woman teased. "Is it me or is it you?"

Appalled, unable to absorb what I was seeing, I backed away. "Who are you?" I said.

The eyes opened, green as gemstones. "Mother of all Mothers, Beginning of all Beginnings."

"What do you want?"

"I want what you want."

I was irritated by her composure. Besides, she made no sense. We could not possibly want the same thing. I wanted to kill her. Surely she did not seek her own demise. But I knew that if I continued to listen I would fall under her spell. The best thing to do was to get away from this awful place. I continued to back off, keen to put distance between me and her.

That is when I bumped into something behind me. Startled, I turned and started to scream.

Harun was an upstanding mass of fungi, revolting to behold. Even as I stared, the yellow florets on his face folded, the outer shells withered to reveal soft, feathery cores. Yellow spores burst over his face, breaking apart and sailing away until there was nothing left of the head. Only an upright torso with a neck stump and two legs, wreathed by hundreds of gyrating mushrooms, like well-dressed ladies at a ball.

The transformation reached an apotheosis when Harun began to secrete a white fluid that made him look as if he had been dunked in milk.

The face in the tree opened wide its greedy mouth and sucked in every drop.

I wailed and fled.

"You shall seek me in the darkest pit, and I shall be there," the woman gurgled behind me.

I ran along ever darkening corridors, desperate to return to the real world, yet knowing whatever constitutes reality was forever beyond reach.

CHAPTER 31

I angled towards a band of light that fell warm across my face. My eyes opened and perceived an indistinct form bending over me, pressing something to my lips. Remembering the face in the tree, I yelled and flailed my arms. I was rewarded with the sound of breaking glass. I sat upright, head spinning, and saw Adam kneeling beside me.

"I was trying to give you water," he said.

"Sorry, I thought you were someone else."

For some reason, I was simultaneously angry and sad.

"Only me," he said.

"What's the time?"

"Almost eight thirty."

"Morning?"

He nodded.

"What happened?" I propped myself against the wall and rubbed my head. Dominique was still asleep beside me, head to one side, mouth open beneath bandages that had slipped to reveal layers of livid skin.

Adam shrugged. "You came back last night and went straight to sleep."

Memories rushed back. The underground journey. Hasan and Harun. The face in the tree.

"Sorry," I said, rising to my feet. "I couldn't find Hasan and Harun."

Better to lie than admit the truth.

Adam showed no interest whatsoever in their fate. He behaved as if they had never existed. It was inhuman, and it made me shrink from him. What did it take to acknowledge his friends were dying and that their lives mattered?

"You don't care, do you?" I said.

"I accept."

"You accept that your friends are dead."

"They're not dead. You know that."

I looked into the grave young face. Aloof and largely silent, Adam had been a quiet kid, caring for the others and supporting Dominique and myself all along. I had been so smitten with Harun, thinking I had found a little brother who understood and accepted, that I hardly noticed that Adam had been a kind of lieutenant at my side. I felt ashamed to have ignored him. But that was the story of my life, wasn't it? I invested in the wrong people and ignored those that mattered. Dominique, that snake in the grass, was the first in a long line.

"I feel like I failed all of you," I said to Adam, knowing full well I was doing it because it was easier to fall back on self-pity and blame rather than front up squarely to the present.

"That isn't true."

"This whole thing has been an exercise in neglect and futility," I replied, hedging closer to the truth.

"That's one way of looking at it."

I gestured helplessly. "Don't you see? My parents didn't look after me properly and, despite outward appearances, I'm doing the same to you. It's a pattern."

"Magnolia, you're part djinn." Adam sounded as if he was sick of trying to explain things to me. "What does that mean?"

"Explains my hairy legs."

"Sorry?"

"Djinn offspring have hairy legs, like Queen Sheba."

"That's a myth—"

"I thought it was because I was a lesbian," I interrupted, "with too much testosterone. But it's because Malachi sired my mother, and my mother made me when she got with Dad."

"Magnolia, what does the word 'djinn' mean in Arabic?"

"Don't know."

"Hidden. It means hidden."

"So…?"

"What is concealed in your life?"

"Hello! Where do I start?"

He breathed in through the nose and released it through the mouth, exasperated. "Do what you always do. Begin in the middle, work your way to the beginning and then go to the end. There's a reason for everything that's going on. Salih, Zaman…"

The names of the twins brought me back to the moment—any excuse to get away from the incessant, unbearable interrogation. They were not in the room.

I pushed away from Adam. "Where are they?"

"Outside, saying farewell to Malachi. You killed a powerful ifrit last night. He deserves a proper send-off."

I rushed to the window. It was a hazy day, still and peaceful. Bulky, flat-bottomed clouds drifted across the sky. On the plain, the desert showed marked signs of rejuvenation as varied shades of green shot through with blotches of saffron and caramel spread across the land.

Salih and Zaman stood beside the pond, last night's battleground, their backs turned to me. I was about to tell them to get back inside when my eye was drawn to an indistinct figure on the opposite bank, wavering among the reeds and bullrushes. The boys were not looking at the water, as I had thought. They were staring at the man. But who was he? It could not be Malachi. He was dead. I had seen to that.

The wind picked up, causing the reeds to bend with a rustle that turned to a menacing hiss, obscuring the view. Sunlight danced on the water, momentarily blinded me.

I turned away to protect my eyes. When I looked again moments later, the man was gone.

Had it been a man, or was it my imagination? Could it be the killer from the mosque come for the remaining boys? Then I remembered. There had never been an assassin. There had never been a right-wing terrorist who hated Muslims, like the newspapers claimed. It had been a ruse. A ploy to fool me and the authorities. Dominique killed the children. A nasty, cold-blooded prelude for something more sadistic. The blind animal rage I felt towards Dominique mounted. Looking down on the supine figure, still asleep thanks to the sleeping pills I had administered, I felt like giving her a kick to the ribs.

Biting down on the urge, I poked my head out the window and told the brothers to come in. "Now," I added when they hesitated.

It was only after I made breakfast for all of us that I inspected Dominique's injuries. Caring for her the previous evening had been the hardest thing I had ever done. Every fibre in my body rebelled against ministering a monstrous individual. With every bandage I tied around the wounds, with every ointment I applied to the burns, I felt that I betrayed all that I stood for. Not to mention betraying those she had killed or injured. Yet I could not allow another human being to suffer and not offer assistance. That was why I had become a nurse: I cared about people.

Now Dominique lay on her back, head turned to the side on a white pillow, breathing noisily through the nose and looking like a crazed hillbilly. The full damage to her face was made clear in the light of day. The left side was a mass of charred, peeling skin. The upper arm, shoulder and neck were livid, the hair burned to the blotchy scalp. Yet the face and the eyebrows were miraculously untouched.

Why are my own hands unharmed after touching Malachi's scorching skin? I wondered. But I did not have the time or the energy to dwell on that question now.

"There's no burns cream left in the first-aid kit," I said to Adam.

More was needed if I was going to look after Dominique and keep us at the railway station another day. A substitute. An idea suddenly popped into my head. I could make a cream. I knew how. But first I must take care of a few important things. Making sure to obscure my actions from Adam, Salih and Zaman, I slipped Dominique another two sleeping pills. Then I made sure the Solomon's seal was clearly inscribed above the kitchen door and outside the window; I replenished the salt on the window ledge and the kitchen door. Given the remaining disciples accepted their fate, I could not expect them to remain in the house, but I could absolve myself of further responsibility by making sure the djinni did not come in and take them.

I needed to make more burns cream for Dominique. But, in truth, I had to get away, clear my head and retain a semblance of sanity in the midst of madness. Aware I was pulling a fast one on the boys, I tossed a large bottle of water and a sealed plastic container in a black cloth carry bag and made sure the van's keys were in my—or rather Dominique's—jeans' pocket; I didn't want her to take the boys and leave without me, should she by some miracle awaken.

When all was done, I turned to Adam. And, as I did so, I caught sight of my own shadow moving on the far wall. Where previously I would have seen a woman's bulky frame in formless tracksuit pants and hoodie, I saw a tall, slender creature in tight-fitting clothing. I looked down at myself and took in the sheath-like blue jeans and the equally figure-hugging emerald blouse and I could barely believe I was seeing my own body, let alone my own self. Dominique's clothes felt right and natural on me. I did not feel the need to hide. I didn't even care that the short sleeves revealed, to anyone who cared to look, the scars that scored both arms, like tribal talismans. I wore them with a certain kind of embarrassed pride.

"I have to go," I said to Adam. "You're in charge."

"Where are you going?"

"I need some stuff to make a lotion for Dominique's injuries."

Feeling like a part of me had given up on him, I left the abandoned train station and headed out across the hilltop.

Long ago, in a happier life, I had watched my father make a witchetty grub and snake vine poultice to relieve a friend's burns. Though I had followed him and watched with a keen eye, he had been largely oblivious to my presence, talking to himself as he worked. In the scrub north-east of Alice Springs, he walked from one witchetty grub bush to the next and dug the ground with a long stick to expose larvae feeding on the roots. After gathering a large number of the critters in a jar, he scrounged a bunch of snake vine from someone's yard and pounded the leaves with the grubs to produce a nasty looking brown paste that he rubbed on the injured man's arm.

At one point, I remembered Dad holding a writhing grub at the end of his weathered fingers. "You can eat this," he said, popping it in his mouth. "It's yum."

"Yum," said my five-year-old self.

"But don't eat this." He displayed a wreath of snake vine. "It stinks and it burns your mouth. It's yuck."

"Yuck," I repeated.

It was my earliest memory.

From the hilltop, I descended to the plain below and stood on the Oodnadatta Track. It was a still, muggy day, the cloud cover so thick and low that it lent the air a peculiar blue-grey sheen, unmoving and pensive in the immense silence. In this profound and total absence of sound I found myself slipping between levels of quietude, like stronger or weaker sea currents that go by unnoticed, like a slight tickle felt against the ear, small murmurs, whispers, that led me on, deep into the desert's virgin peace. Much of the road had been washed away by the rains and needed urgent care. Not a car or human being in sight. Only the vicious, eternal beauty, lonesome and elevating, and the soaring sky above. I breathed in deep, feeling my lungs expand. Already I felt better for having left the claustrophobic house on the hill and the passive, herd-like occupants. A noisy gang of budgerigars flitted above bright puddles, bringing a smile to my face. Uncertain which direction to take, I aimed for a long, dark spur to the north-east.

"If thou wouldst be with that which thou dost seek, follow where all is fled," I thought as I walked. Where was that quote from? And why did George Green whisper it in my ear last Monday afternoon, seemingly an eternity ago?

I had almost lost a sense of my own physicality, legs weightless beneath me, mind dissolving, when I reached the base of the spur some twenty minutes later.

A jagged ridge of black stone stretched for a couple of hundred metres across the hilltop. A stegosaurus could have died up there long ago and left its cantilevered spine to dry on the chocolaty landscape. Wondering what astounding geological cataclysm could have formed such spectacular formations, I made my way to the top, passed through a natural archway in the rock and found myself looking down on a narrow valley hemmed in by another, smaller ridge half a kilometre away.

"My name is Magnolia Din-Olden," I said, speaking aloud to any ancestors that lived there. "I'm looking for bush medicine. I promise I will only take what I need and then leave."

On the descent I continued my dialogue with the spirits of the place, telling them what I was doing there, hoping they did not mind my intrusion because I was in need and I would appreciate their help and protection. The chatter made me feel better, less alone, more secure and connected. It almost got rid of the feeling that I was being watched by teeming eyes.

Stopping in front of a witchetty shrub, I picked up a flat stick and set to work, digging at the sandy soil to expose the larvae that clustered around the roots. It was tiring work yet calming too. The labour released me from the relentless churn of my thoughts, away from the fear and uncertainty of the previous night, the loss of the boys, the knowledge of Dominique's appalling actions, Adam's persistent words. It was amazing how quickly the mind gets used to a new reality. If someone had told me a few days ago I would be battling an ancient djinni, or I would be digging for witchetty grubs, I would have laughed. Now I accepted without question. It felt so natural I could imagine myself doing it for ever.

When I found the grubs, I picked them up gently so that they did not secrete the defensive liquid that rendered them useless for eating, and put them in the sealed plastic container I had brought. Working in this manner, wandering across the valley, I filled the container with grubs in little under an hour. At no time did I see a snake vine, though I did encounter iridescent lizards sunning on lichen-covered rocks.

Soon after mid-afternoon, tired and sweating, I returned to the spur and settled on a flat rock to rest, the indistinct sun casting long shadows at my feet. I felt light and open, as though I could fly all the way back to the train station. I was thinking how this itinerant life might suit me after all when I became aware of an irregularity in the shadows at my feet.

The outline of a man, standing behind me.

Alarmed, I leaped up and scuttled away, almost tripping and falling. When I was a safe distance, I looked back.

Except for wind ruffling the pistachio-coloured linen suit, the man was still as granite, the sun creating a nimbus around his head.

"You," I said, heart pounding. "What are you doing here?"

George Green did not utter a word.

I approached him, warily, as though he might be a mirage, so unnerving was the stillness and the steady gaze. The first thing I did, when I was close enough, was to slap him hard across the face, putting all my strength into it. The blow was audible. George did not flinch. The contact did, however, prove his materiality.

"We need to talk," he said, as if I hadn't hit him.

"You put her up to it."

George gazed at me, weary beyond his years. He sank on the rock I had vacated and stared across the valley.

"You hired Dom to kill the kids," I repeated.

"Harun is mistaken."

"He ought to know, he was there…"

"He is, nevertheless, wrong."

I forced myself to calm down. "Okay. What happened?"

"Dominique was meant to kill the children. She agreed to it. But she couldn't go through with it at the last minute. Malachi finished the job for her."

It was the last thing I expected to hear. It gave me pause. Made me realise there was a part of me that had wanted to believe the worst about Dominique. It would justify my anger and resentment.

"Go on."

"When Malachi realised Dominique couldn't go through with it, he took possession of her body and made her pull the trigger. Djinnis and ifrits can do that, you know. Dominique thinks she acted of her own volition. She didn't. Malachi was inside her. That's why she feels violated."

In a way, I was relieved to hear this unexpected news. It meant Dominique was not a cold-blooded killer, even if in principle she agreed to do it. Her conscience kicked in at a crucial point and stopped her from committing an atrocity. Knowing this made things easier for me. I could not have gone through with the rest of the trip, believing Dominique had killed, and continue to be civil.

"This changes everything," I said.

George sat as if he was truly made of stone.

"Why did Harun say she did it if she didn't?"

"To spur you to action and perhaps to hurt you a little bit. Who knows?"

"I trusted him."

"Perhaps he meant to shake you out of your complacency and indolence."

I shook my head, unable to believe I was having this discussion.

"You revived the boys," I said, hoping to bring the conversation back to where I could exercise some control over it.

Another nod.

"And you brought me back from death's door years ago."

"True."

"Then you can bring back the boys Alila has taken."

"That's not how it works," George said, smoothing his pants leg across the knee.

I pushed my face up against his. Anger bloomed like a flower, until I was barely able to contain it, like the time I beat a schoolboy senseless with a Coke bottle when he called me a 'boong'.

"Then tell me how it works, George," I shouted, spittle flying, "because I'm very confused right now and I feel like I could pick up a rock and bash your head in. You have no idea what I've gone through the last couple of days. What you put me through…" My voice broke. "Most of them are gone. I can't protect them. I failed… I failed."

I wept. Great heaving sobs with no embarrassment or restraint that persisted for several minutes, until I was empty and had nothing more to give. Then I faced George. For his part, he remained seated throughout, unperturbed, one leg drawn up under him, large hands clasped on his knee, regarding me with glacial reserve.

I did not know what to do next. This was not normal. There was no possibility of comfort or reassurance in this unyielding man, and I was suddenly afraid. More afraid than I had been during this whole time. I did not know George. I faced not a human being, I told myself, but an unmoving boulder, as old and uncaring as the hills. It made me feel small and terribly alone.

A falcon adrift high above let off a cry, and it seemed the sound came from my own guts.

"Sit," George said. "Let's talk. There's not much time."

I obeyed. So caught up had I been in my own drama that I had not given a thought to how he arrived at this remote location.

"Where's your car?" I said, looking around. "How did you get here?"

"I'm not here. I'm in Alice Springs, visiting your grandmother in hospital."

"I should say 'Don't be absurd', but after everything that's happened the last couple of days, I don't know what to think any more."

George produced a sleek mobile phone from his pocket and passed it to me. "Call her," he instructed. The expression on his face was that of a man about to open a box filled with juicy secrets.

I palmed the phone. "There's no reception out here."

"Dial your grandmother's number, Magnolia."

I pressed the numbers on the pad and put the phone to my ear. Nan came on after a couple of rings.

"It's me," I said, voice flat.

"Hello, lovely," Nan said. "What a mad coincidence. Your ears must be burning."

"Why?"

"Because I'm sitting here with your boss, George Green."

My eyes moved across to George, still most assuredly perched opposite me.

"Ask to speak to me," he mouthed.

"Nan, can I speak to him?"

"He said the trip's going according to plan," Nan persisted.

"I need to speak to George, Nan. Sorry."

"Everything alright?"

"Yes. I really need—"

"I know. You need to speak to George. Here he is."

I looked at George seconds before his voice said, "Hello, Magnolia," from the other end of the phone.

"Who are you?" I whispered, without taking my eyes off the man sitting across from me.

Both men spoke at the same time.

"I've asked myself that question many times."

There was no doubt the voice on the phone belonged to George. A measured, reassuring rumble at the base of the throat, distant, almost mocking, as if it were emerging from a vessel, with its own pent-up sadness waiting to be released.

"How did you do that?"

"Some questions don't have answers," said the voice on the phone.

"What do you want with me?"

"The question is, what do you want with me?"

"You came into my life, buster. I didn't come into yours."

"I come as someone you invited."

"I would never invite someone like you into my life."

The George sitting in front of me roused himself, blinking as if he had emerged from sleep. "We don't go where we are not invited," he said.

"I want to speak to Nan," I said to the phone.

"That won't be necessary," replied the man at the other end of the line.

"You harm her and so help me…"

"She's safe," said George on the phone. "You saw to that, didn't you?"

The man sitting opposite me chuckled.

"How can you be in two places at the same time?"

The phone pinged in my hand: a text message. I looked at the screen as a picture came through. It showed Nan sitting up in bed, smiling as she pushed her head up against George Green. I stared at the image, dumbfounded.

It was the man at the other end of the line who answered my prior question. "Give me back the phone and listen to what I have to say."

"I'm listening," I said, passing the phone to George.

"I'm not sure you're ready for this," he said, shaking his head. "Despite what he said."

"I'm ready as I'll ever be."

George shook his head again, adjusting his seat on the hard surface. "You don't have a skerrick of patience or understanding, Magnolia. You're brutal, base, self-deceiving."

"Nice to meet you, too."

"You don't know yourself. How can you have perseverance with me when I explain things your brain can't comprehend?"

He was right on that score. I was often dishonest with myself, preferring to live in illusions that sheltered me from reality, and I was given to stupid, impulsive acts I regretted as soon as they happened.

"I give you my word I will try to understand."

George made a dismissive gesture. "Pfft, I've heard that before."

"How do you do that, anyway?"

"Do what?"

"How can you be in two places at the same time?"

"That's what I hope to explain."

"I'm listening."

George looked at me sceptically. "Listen then," he said, "to the tale of…"

CHAPTER 32

The Tale of Khasis, the Green Man

There was, in times of yore and in ages long gone before, a spirit called Khasis. Guardian of arcane knowledge and fertility, he presided in The Land of Zalaam, a place of darkness on the border between man's haunts and Mount Qaf, home of the djinn. Such was his agility that, when summoned, Khasis moved easy as breath from humblest hut to brightest palace, communing with man and djinn as though they were equal and alike. It was said that the spirit was not enchained and could be in two places at the same time. And though he was revered by all, he remained humble and modest, putting trust in kindness and generosity above all else.

For all that he was sad and lonely, a disembodied shade, witnessing from afar the daily courtships and couplings of mortal and immortal, knowing he was barred from their august company. For only flesh can know the pleasures of the senses and lose itself to touch.

This preyed upon his mind and disquieted him, so that Khasis often yearned to know what it means to have a body, to truly love and to be bound to another. But he had no one to talk to and no one thought to ask what he thought or wanted when they genuflected before him, with only a question or request for themselves on their lips.

One day there came to Khasis an ifrit named Malachi.

"O Khasis," said Malachi, "of a truth I desire to know thee and rejoice in thy company during my lifetime."

When Khasis heard these words, dark became light. He turned on Malachi the full force and joy of his existence. At first they spent time together in their natural state—that is to say, Khasis as pure consciousness and Malachi as smokeless fire. Great was their bond. Not a day passed when they did not talk and exult in the nearness of one being to another. Even so, neither possessed a body and, much as they wanted to, they did not know earthly pleasures, beyond talk and agreeable companionship.

A time came when Malachi appeared before Khasis as a youth in the first bloom of beauty. He was like the full moon on a still lake, naked and splendid in head and limb. Stars not yet born gleamed in his eyes and Khasis understood why Malachi claimed he was created in times yet to come and had gone back to primordial past to be with him.

Khasis could not turn away. He was bewitched.

"Wherefore art thou clothed in this beauteous body?" Khasis asked, and Malachi explained that, being a shape shifter, he could take any form he wished.

"I am no orator," Malachi went on, "but my feelings towards you manifest themselves upon this canvas, making themselves plain to see. You have made me thus, dear friend, and now it is your turn to feast your eyes on your creation."

Khasis was overwhelmed. Words deserted him; his mind was in turmoil. Malachi only felt his presence and knew him to be near. If he knew of the tumult in his friend's mind, he gave no indication. With all his might Khasis wanted to touch Malachi's surpassing beauty and seemliness and perfect symmetry, but it was impossible. He did not have hands and there was no possibility of him growing any. Nor lips to kiss. Nor indeed eyes to see. He was pure enveloping presence, incorporeal and insubstantial. He swarmed around Malachi and knew only deep elation and devastating frustration.

"What will put out the fire that you have lit in me?" Khasis said.

"My lips," Malachi answered.

Khasis fled, despairing, for he knew not how he might achieve such a miracle.

Next day, Malachi returned. He had with him a fine-featured young man with long, dark hair and a dazzling white beard. At first Khasis thought the man was real. Then he realised he looked upon a life-size statue fashioned from finest porcelain.

"What is this?" Khasis asked.

"It is for you," Malachi replied, eyes brimming with love for his friend. "You can enter it and know what it is like to have a body."

Khasis did not have to be told twice. He entered the figure and in seconds his life force turned porcelain to flesh so that he walked and talked and looked at the world as if for the first time.

That night Khasis lay beside Malachi and knew the intoxicating pleasures of the flesh, lips on lips, belly on belly. The next night and the next. Until there came a time when Khasis almost forgot what it was like to not have a body, to be pure spirit, unencumbered consciousness.

One day Khasis was called upon by a great king in the land of Hatusas and, much to his alarm, he realised he could not exit the body fashioned for him by Malachi. He was entrapped by love. And when he begged to be released, Malachi laughed and said, "O my friend, know that only one can break the seal and release thee from thy fleshly tomb."

"Who might that be?"

"Alila is her name, my mistress height, to whom I am beholden and to no one else."

Khasis had heard of Alila. Her legend preceded her, asleep though she was in the earth these many thousands of years. Thus it was that the perfidy of Malachi's mind was revealed to Khasis, and the craft by which he had been seduced. It broke his heart and he was not able to look on Malachi as he once had, with love and adoration.

"Then take me to your mistress," Khasis cried, "so that she may free me."

Malachi shook his lovely head and told Khasis it was not possible. Alila was imprisoned and he, Malachi, was her right-hand man for so long as she remained within the earth. He laughed again and revealed the full betrayal that had been worked upon the ensorcelled spirit.

Khasis was to remain corporeal, Malachi declaimed, until such a time as Alila had no further use of him.

"When will that be?"

"Millennia from the point on which you stand."

"How might this happen?"

"By resuscitating eight of Alila's acolytes during the time of the great transfiguration."

Eight, Khasis knew, because the capability and strength of the number is said to hold feminine energy, which gives the power and determination to achieve one's aims. The shape of the number eight (8) ignites the soul as the cyclic path of breath moving through the body in a symbol of infinity.

From there on Khasis could not remain in The Land of Zalaam; he was too heavy for the spirit world. He fell to earth and roamed the land, an eternal wanderer living here and there, performing good deeds and always keeping in the back of his mind that he was slave to Alila's pleasure and that he was her instrument, for she was the only one who could break the spell which held him in thrall.

Centuries passed. Khasis witnessed the rise and fall of empires. In time also, he was revered by peoples across the width and breadth of the world, and he gathered unto himself many names. He was Utnapishtim in Mesopotamia; Vishnu in India; al-Kidhr, the Green One, for Muslims in Arabia; and Saint George for the Christians of Asia Minor. Eventually Khasis settled in Constantinople during the time of the Eastern Romans and adopted a Greek name, Yorgos Prasinos, George Green in its anglophone variant.

For a time, he plied his trade in the great city as healer and mage for Jewish, Armenian, Greek and Turkish ladies, and as mystic guide for Sufis and Whirling Dervishes. He lived in a great house near the docks where ships from the four corners of the world berthed, and at night he visited the taverns and coffee houses frequented by the sailors and seamen who brought with them hours of respite in momentary love and wondrous tales of discovery from beyond Anatolia's borders.

That is how, in 1606, Khasis learned of the founding by European explorers of a Great Southern Land and knew this to be his ultimate destination.

In 1881 Khasis uprooted once more and made his way along the remnants of the ancient Silk Road to Hindustan, there to join cameleers who were shipped by their British lords across the ocean to Australia.

<h1 style="text-align:center">CHAPTER 33</h1>

It was a sobering narrative, one that made me see the enormity of what I was up against. Listening to George was like hearing a tale from of the *Arabian Nights*. Outlandish as it was, I could relate to one point: the betrayal George suffered in Malachi's hands. The two-faced lover, seducing, enticing, saying one thing and doing another. I knew all too well how it felt to be on the receiving end of such invidious perfidy. How crushing it was and how one never really recovers. How the fire burns, even when you think it is quenched. Knowing George suffered in a similar fashion made him relatable. I thought I could understand what drove this inscrutable man. Yet how was it possible to comprehend a creature who claimed to be many thousands of years old and not human at all? There were so many questions. The first thing I said was:

"He's dead."

George gazed at me.

"Malachi," I clarified. "I killed him."

"I am the poorer for it."

"He betrayed you."

"He is betrayed who seeks to be betrayed. Besides, Malachi was my first friend and lover. He knew everything there is to know about me: the beginning, the end and everything in between. I forgave long ago."

"How can you forgive someone who betrayed you?"

"I could not ask for Malachi's demise," George replied. "Killing is not an answer. It's the beginning of a more complex question."

I turned away, ashamed and knowing full well that the flint-like rage I often felt found expression in violent fantasies that appalled even me. Was I really capable of such horror? Yes, I was. I had killed Malachi, and I had come close to killing Dominique. Who knows what else I was capable of doing? Even so, I was not willing to let George off the hook that easily.

"You don't approve of killing, and yet you ordered the cold-blooded assassination of innocent children."

"Many acts which seem to be evil or malicious are merciful and have greater significance than first appears," he stated.

"In other words, the ends justify the means."

"Do you know about the Harrowing of Hell?"

"Enlighten me."

"It is in the Bible. Peter 3:19-20. In a nutshell, it describes Christ's descent into hell in the time between the crucifixion and the resurrection." He paused, obviously finding it difficult to talk about the subject.

"Go on," I encouraged.

"In point of fact," George stated, "Jesus didn't go to hell. He went to what you might call limbo. Though the experience of going there was a thousand times worse than any hell you can imagine."

He paused again and this time I let him be. When he composed himself, George spoke in haste, as if he wanted to get it over with.

"There came a time, when Alila sent Khasis on his first mission, so to speak. At that point, Khasis lived in Palestine and his name was Yeshua, the name that underwent later alteration from Iesous in Greek to Jesus in English and to Isa in Islam."

"Jesus Christ, you're Jesus?" I cried, shooting to my feet.

George smiled for the first time. "No. At the time, I was an itinerant preacher known as Yeshua. He was killed for his political and philosophic beliefs and buried in a cave such as the one you were buried in after the suicide."

"There are other such caves?"

"Seven, to be precise."

"So you're not the son of God."

"Hardly. The myth of the son of God developed decades after I left Palestine. It has nothing to do with me. It's a fabrication, a moral and ethical confabulation based on older stories."

"That's a relief," I said, grinning. "Otherwise I'd go straight to hell for slapping Jesus."

The smile we shared cleared the air, bringing us closer, on the same level. I sat near him.

"Go on," I said again.

"To cut a long story short," George continued, "when Yeshua was in the cave awaiting resurrection after the Romans crucified him, Malachi came and told him he had to travel to Zalaam to rescue eight souls. They had been trapped centuries earlier by a Babylonian patriarch called Nuktu. The eight spirits, Malachi revealed, had been in another life Alila's most fervent female worshippers. In the days prior to the Great Inundation, they refused to bow to Nuktu's patriarchal god. In retaliation, Nuktu cursed them so that when they died in the fullness of time their souls were stuck in limbo. It was up to Yeshua, Malachi said, to navigate the tightly wound maze that is Zalaam, find the spirits, and free them."

"Why?"

"Because a greater purpose awaited them."

I asked what purpose. I was also aware of time passing. It was late afternoon by that stage. I wanted to go back to the railway station, but I also knew that the fantastical stories were key to understanding what had happened in the last few days. They may even weigh heavily on the future.

"And so," George continued, "while Yeshua remained inert in the cave for three days, Khasis, the spirit trapped in his body, travelled to Zalaam. You can imagine how it was for him to be home again after all this time. Centuries had passed on earth, you see. Many, many centuries. Aeons. In that time man had emerged from his cave, spread across the face of the world, and built great cities and monuments. Empires rose and fell. Yet there was Khasis again, breathing freedom's air in his own realm, knowing this was where he belonged. This was home. For all that, he could not stay. He was bound to the body in the cave by invisible cords and he had to return soon enough. In point of fact, he could feel the physical weigh him down in the astral plane. He was truly in hell, he told himself. The agony of being there and not being able to stay was unbearable.

"It wasn't hard to find the eight spirits. They gave off a rarified energy that did not belong to that mysterious in-between place. Khasis found them and, using his arcane knowledge of such things, broke Nuktu's enchantment. Off the eight went, knowing that one day they would be called upon to make the ultimate sacrifice in the name of Alila."

"I repeat," I said. "What did the eight spirits have to do?" I looked across the valley, atwitter with unseen birds as shadows deepened around the rock face. "What was their purpose?"

"When time was ripe, they had to step into the bodies of eight children raised in the Islamic faith."

"Eight spirits, seven boys," I said. "It doesn't add up."

George's eyes flared. "Don't be obtuse," he said. "You are the eighth. You are as much a part of this as they are. That is why you are on this journey. I implanted the spirit of Alila's head priestess, Ninsar, into your body when you were resuscitated after the suicide."

"I'm possessed?" I said, jumping to my feet again.

"Demonic possession and transmigration of souls are two different things."

"Then why can't I remember this Ninsar?"

"That's not how it works," George said, sounding rational even as he outlined the most irrational propositions. "You don't recall a past life for the simple reason that the brain would be overwhelmed by the sheer volume of information. You'd never be able to function."

"But am I me or am I her?"

"You are you. Or, rather, you combine elements of Magnolia and Ninsar."

"If I don't remember what she knows, what's the point?"

"Ninsar will know what to do when the time comes, and you will enact her will as if it is your own."

I did not like the sound of that. Something else occurred to me. "I'm not Muslim."

"You were raised in the faith by your grandmother."

"I'm an apostate."

"That's one way to look at it. Another way to look at it is this: one part of you represents the three religions of the book, Judaism, Christianity and Islam, and the other part of you represents an ancient culture that maintains deep spiritual connections to the earth. Both elements are essential in facilitating Alila's return."

"Why is Islam important to this?" I said, pacing the hilltop, feeling trapped by his words.

"The race of the djinn is rooted in Islamic faith. They are elemental fire spirits that play much the same part angels and demons play in Christianity. More important, the Judaeo-Christian faith and its offshoot Islam are patriarchal myths. They worship a sky god, far removed from the female-centred earth cults of earlier practices. All three creeds of the book separate followers from nature and teach them to look upon the earth with disdain, as something to control and subdue. Earlier cults, on the other hand, were agrarian. They worshipped the female principle and revered nature."

"So all of this is about stopping global warming," I said.

He looked at me with a mixture of pity and resignation.

"The external is internal." He touched his chest. "And the internal is external." With a grand gesture he took in the entire width and breadth of the land.

"Glib is as glib gets."

I stopped pacing, my mind refusing to go where he was pushing me. It was easier to hold on to self-perpetuating anger and injustice. "For all that," I said, "you were willing to shoot children so that their corpses could be reanimated or possessed by the spirits of dead people. It's sick. You're as much a monster as Alila and Malachi. I'm glad I killed him. And I promise you I will destroy Alila as well."

George looked past me, as if I was a gnat circling his nose.

"As I said before, acts which seem evil have greater significance than first appears."

I turned my back on him, disgusted. When I spoke again, my focus was locked on the distant hillock with the train station and its precious occupants.

"You keep telling yourself that, buster, and you'll always be a puppet dangling at the end of Alila's fingers. Me, I don't want any part of this. I think for myself. And I'm telling you, mistreating children is wrong."

"The boys were killed for two reasons."

"And I can't wait to hear what those wonderful reasons were."

"To provide vehicles for the spirits of Alila's acolytes," he continued. "And to provide sustenance for the djinni."

I whirled on him. "Yes, but will Alila stop at seven boy nuggets to recharge her batteries?"

"Seven is a significant number."

"Why?"

"Seven is the number of the completed cycle and of its renewal. That's why we have seven days of the week, seven rungs of perfection, seven petals of a rose. Seven also symbolises the fullness of time and space. And, as you know, the circumambulation of Mecca is completed in seven circuits, and so on…"

"It's still wrong to harm children. No matter what the cause," I said, beginning to sound defeated even to my own ears.

George folded his arms across his chest. "Why do you care so much, Magnolia? Why not let them go?"

That was all I needed to hear. It brought back the full force of anger and determination, the urge to kick and fight.

"I care," I yelled, pushing my face up against his, "because children are special. They ought to be looked after, protected, loved, nurtured. Not dumped by shitty, no-hoper parents who don't care what happens to them. Not sacrificed by a bunch of loons to some bloodthirsty cult. That's why I care, and I give you my word"—I pointed a trembling finger at him—"I will stop this."

My voice echoed, sounding oddly hollow in the immense landscape. My throat was sore from yelling. Hands clenched by my sides, I allowed the tears to flow again, knowing full well I was only trying to save myself. This was a selfish act. What annoyed me was that George appeared to be doing his best not to smile.

After a while, he said, "I told you you don't have the patience to understand." He walked across to me. "You were brought back to life because you are the doorway through which the Mother will return."

"Tell her this door is firmly closed," I said, swiping at my eyes with the back of a hand.

"Don't be afraid to be strange, true, impure and dissonant. Cherish your flame."

"Cheap philosophy 101."

George looked at me with what I could only interpret as displeasure. Or so it seemed.

"If I were you," he said, "I'd go back to the house, put the boys and Dominique in the van and drive to Marree. You can make it before nightfall."

That was how he revealed he was on to me. A simple sentence that put on full display my utter transparency. Everything seemed so final, so pointless. It meant I was caught in a nightmare, with no way out. And I wanted very much for that to not be the case. I wanted freedom, autonomy. Not preordained fate. One way of holding on to the former was to keep the outrage and the injustice burning. I walked in circles, feeling trapped and powerless, clutching my sides and breathing heavily, almost doubled over with the weight of what lay ahead.

"I will leave now," I said, straightening. "They will be wondering where I am."

George was at my side on the instant. I felt his breath on the back of my neck, an awful presentiment. The large hands fell on my shoulders even before the words came out of my mouth.

"You never left," he whispered.

The weight of his flesh lifted from my skin and in the time it took for me to turn around, he was gone. I was alone inside the train station's main building, the facade with the door to the right, open country to the left.

"You will find snake vine beside the north wall."

For a moment, I was not sure if it was George's voice or the wind moaning in one of the chimneys.

I found the vine and then I went indoors, totally confused about what to do next.

CHAPTER 34

If it's true the human eye perceives a small portion, a tiny wedge, of the sheer scale and vastness of what is in the world for the ocular senses to perceive, then what am I not seeing? I wondered.

I was bothered by the question of how much the human eye can see, or not see. It ate at me after the meeting with George Green. If people can see a minuscule slice of what is in the world, then the rest—the sheer immensity—is invisible to humans. If a cat sees far more than people do, I reasoned, then there was something false in our understanding of what constitutes reality. According to science, when we look, we do not objectively see what is in the world. The eye picks up bits and pieces, like confetti thrown in the air and raining down, a fragment here, a fragment there, and transmits them to the visual cortex, where they are put together as inferences based on past experience of seeing. We complete the picture with all the other things we have seen and then transmit that to the world. The amount of information flowing out of the visual cortex is ten times the amount that goes in. We are not filling in the gaps. We are filling in most of the picture. People are projectors, not just absorbers. If seeing is subjective, what does completely objective *looking* look like? What is hiding in nooks and crannies, or in plain view, knowing it cannot be seen? And what was I projecting on to the world from my own inner workings?

Holding this knowledge in mind, I turned from the kitchen window and studied the room. I saw Dominique in her sleeping bag, turning every now and then and making small whimpering noises, Adam dejectedly staring at the fire with Salih and Zaman beside him as water heated for hot drinks.

But is that all there was to see? What if there was something else in the room that I did not perceive? What if this small room contained multitudes, worlds within worlds, like a Matryoshka doll? If I could see it, what might I see? Ever since I saw my teenage bedroom in the gorge, I'd had the sense that none of this was real. That I was circling around a major event in my life, trying to make sense of it. Or that it was a reality superimposed over another perhaps greater reality—a dream or an alternate plane, playing in the margins of consciousness and laying before me the different paths I could have taken had I played my cards different at a vital juncture.

Surely if George could be in two places at the same time, anything was possible.

Even so, I saw nothing more than what was in the room—four walls, a rotting ceiling and three boys in front of the fire.

"How are you?" Adam said, coming up to me.

I nodded, then shook my head. "Not so good," I admitted. It was a relief to be able to say it aloud.

"What's bothering you?"

"Everything."

"If I ask you something, do you promise not to get angry?"

I gave him every assurance I would not.

"Why do you insist on saving our lives?"

I was going to repeat what I'd said earlier. That children are sacred. Their lives matter. They ought to be looked after, not sacrificed to expediency when adults tired of them. But every one of these injunctions stuck in my throat like fishbones. They still held true, but for some reason they also sounded false, even to myself. Something else was going on and I was failing to see it.

"We accept what's going to happen to us," Adam continued. "Why can't you?"

"It's my responsibility to look after you."

"How did you feel when Dom's parents stopped you from seeing their daughter?" he asked.

I did not have to think twice; the feelings were still raw and on the surface. "Awful. Terrible," I said. "I was so angry and resentful of these stupid adults telling us what to do."

"Yet they were certain they knew what was best for you and their daughter."

I nodded, the sadness and frustration of that long-ago time resurfacing in great heaving waves that broke on stony shores. Losing Dom just when I had found her, just because her idiot parents thought it was wrong for a girl to love another girl.

"How did you feel when your grandmother accepted you?"

Again, the response was instantaneous. "Liberated."

"Humph," he said, looking at me sideways.

Not liking where this was going, I looked around for something to change the topic.

"Guess I better make that poultice for Dom," I said.

Adam sighed as I stepped away from him.

Real or not, I had found the snake vine where George's voice said it would be—in the lee of the fireplace. I had plucked it in greedy handfuls from the hardy ground, stuffed it in the container with the witchetty grubs and brought it to the kitchen a short time ago.

Now, I scrounged a glass jar from the supplies and, using the back of a wooden spoon, I mashed the vine and the grubs to make a thick, grey paste. The smell was vile.

"Ugh," cried Salih, screwing up his face. "It stinks."

Using two fingers, I gently rubbed the paste on Dom's burns. Looking after her was a lot easier now that I knew she had not killed anyone. Malachi had, and he could rot for all I cared.

Adam looked down on me as I worked on my patient.

"Dom isn't going to thank you for rubbing that stuff on her," he said.

He spoke in a guarded voice, as if he was timidly hedging towards another, perhaps more serious topic.

"She'll have to put up with it if she wants to get better," I replied, seeing the humour in rubbing the two-faced bitch with gunk that smelled as if it had originated in a latrine. More than that, I was feeling proud of myself for having subverted Alila's grand scheme by keeping the troupe at this location an extra day.

As if he had read my mind, Adam said: "We're meant to be in Marree."

"A change is as good as a holiday."

"Why are we still here?"

"Because Dom's not well and we have to make sure she's fit to travel. We'll go tomorrow."

"It will be too late. There will be a new moon."

I sealed the jar, wiped my fingers on a rag and tossed it aside. "Save your breath. I'm not changing my mind."

Adam crossed his legs at the ankles while continuing to lean against the wall. "It's a strange life," he observed, voice softening.

I finished wrapping Dom's head and shoulders with clean bandages, closed the first-aid kit and stood. The sun was almost below the horizon. Already the air was chill, sucking the heat from the day as clouds moved east, leaving a clear sky. On the plain, thick fog pressed around the base of the hill, stretching away to an endless ocean.

"Tomorrow is today and yesterday is today," Adam said. "The day you were born is now and the day you will die is now as well. As is everything you have done and will do in between those two points."

"Time is an illusion," I stated, looking at him. "There is no past, present or future because all time exists simultaneously."

Adam nodded, his eyes shining as though a great truth had been revealed. "Everything is happening right now. Past, present, future."

"If that's true, then why can't we access all those other realities"—I looked searchingly around the room—"why couldn't I remember dying and coming back to life in George's cave?"

"You were traumatised," Salih said from the other side of the room. He sat cross-legged next to his brother, who was drinking chrysanthemum tea from a white enamel cup. "You woke up alone and frightened, not knowing what was going on. It was easier for us. We knew what to expect."

"We knew about the transmigration of souls," Zaman finished.

"You didn't," Salih continued. "George was there when we woke up. So was Dominique. They prepared the way. For some reason, you woke up earlier than expected. That's why there was no one there for you."

"That's why you went into shock and shut down," Adam said.

I looked from one boy to the other. "How do you know this?"

"You are us and we are you," Adam stated.

I pointed at Dom. "Does she know any of this?"

"Some," Adam said.

He walked to the fireplace and helped himself to tea.

"If all time exists now," I said, "why can't we access it?"

"You have to open the door," Adam said.

"Last time I did that, I let in a monster."

"Alila is your salvation."

"Are you familiar with Stockholm Syndrome?" I said, tiring of the back and forth.

I was halfway across the room, intending to put the lentil stew on the fire, when Zaman said, "Look, tears for Malachi."

His words stopped me in my tracks.

"What did you say?"

"The fog," Zaman replied, pointing out of the window.

"Fog is fog."

"No." Adam joined me by the boy's side. "Alila is grieving for Malachi."

Fog surrounded the house, long, wispy tendrils lapping at the edges of the pond. The valley was totally obscured, making it look as if the hilltop was an island afloat in clouds.

Finding it hard to believe a monster mourned another monster, I was turning away, intending to prepare dinner, when Dom's phone pinged with an incoming message.

"I thought there was no reception," I said.

"She's been getting texts all day," Zaman said. "I heard them come through."

Perplexed, I kneeled beside Dom's supine figure and retrieved the phone from her bag. The screen lit up when I pressed the *on* button. There were several messages from someone called Athena.

My jaw dropped when I saw the image behind the incoming messages.

The face of a very young blonde girl shot to the surface against a dark background. The large blue eyes were filled with fear, the pale lips formed soundless words, and tiny fists beat at the glass.

I screamed and dropped the phone when an iron grip closed on my wrist.

"What are you doing?"

Dom was awake, sounding groggy, slurring words.

Flustered, I said the first thing that popped into my head. "Athena's been texting."

"That doesn't mean you can go through my stuff." She snatched the phone from the ground, wriggled up to a seat and inspected the screen. After a while, she put away the phone and turned to me. "I hurt like hell," she said, "and I'm dying for a drink."

I brought water and she gulped down two glasses, one after the other.

"My head hurts," she said, setting aside the glass. "How long have I been out?"

"All night and all day."

I watched her as the facts sank in.

"That means it's Wednesday night."

I nodded.

"Why are we still here?"

"You were unconscious," I said, getting flustered. I had expected her to be unconscious until Thursday morning.

"We're supposed to be in Marree," Dom yelled, struggling to her feet. She wobbled, almost fell, grabbed the wall behind her.

"I didn't want to move you. I couldn't risk it. Besides," I added, grabbing at straws, "you should see what's going on outside."

She hobbled to the window and was presented with an undulating whiteness. It looked as if the sky had sunk to earth and planned to stay there for the foreseeable future.

"We're not going anywhere," I said. "Not till this clears up."

"No, no, no," she said, hobbling around the room and shaking her head. "You have stuffed up big time."

Music to my ears. The dark moon was almost over and three boys still lived—after a fashion. That meant Alila was not strong enough to make a full resurgence. I turned my back and smiled, aware Salih, Zaman and Adam were watching.

"It's nice and cosy in here," I said, putting on a cheery voice. "Eat something. It'll build up your strength."

"No," Dom shouted. "We have to leave now. Right away. Start packing." Though groggy, she began a halting progress to the far end of the room, picking up stuff as she went. "Don't just stand there, help me."

"It's alright, we can leave in the morning."

Dom turned on me the full force of her fury. "It's not alright, you idiot. You have no fucking idea what you've done. Get out of my way. You're not going to fuck up my life again."

Her frantic advance around the room stopped when she collapsed against the wall and sank to the floor, obviously in pain and weak. She burst into tears when her backside touched the ground. I had never seen her so dejected.

Her misery was my triumph. If her fury was any indication, I had thwarted Alila's resurrection. Even so, a part of my mind was on the picture of the girl in the phone. Who was she and why did she look as if she was trapped in the device?

<h1 style="text-align:center">CHAPTER 35</h1>

Fog outside the window. It was unnerving to see it come up to the rotting wood frame and not venture in, despite there being no glass to stop its advance into the room. It merely flattened and remained there, like an animal's furry paw come up against the Solomon's seal I had drawn above the window. Nothing existed, except the miasma. The world, everything in it, disappeared. If this was Alila's show of grief for Malachi's demise, it was indeed extravagant. The servant must have meant a great deal to the mistress.

I sat by the fire, watching Adam, Salih and Zaman prepare for bed. One by one, they slipped into sleeping bags, zipped up to the chin, and passed out. Dom had retreated to the far corner to sulk. The atmosphere in the room was brooding, melancholy, as if Alila's bereavement had infected us as well.

"You can't blame me for the fog," I said to Dom in a low voice.

"No, Missy Din." She flared up again. "You are responsible for all this."

What would she say if she discovered I had been giving her sleeping pills as well?

"What happens now that the ritual isn't complete?"

The question had been worrying me since sundown. If this was the final night of the dark moon, and three boys were still extant, what would happen if Alila was not fully resurrected? Would she go back to her eternal slumber? Or…?

"What does a dangerous animal do when it's cornered?" Dom responded.

I did not like the sound of that. Would it make Alila an incomplete creature, a tiger without teeth? The questions did not even address the fact that there were still three boys who were, to all intents and purposes, dead and wandering the outback. In trying to save them,

I had condemned them to a half-life. I had not thought to ask what would I do with them if and when things went back to normal. They could not go back to parents who would, no doubt, be horrified to discover their dead offspring ringing the doorbell.

Tired, uncertain and apprehensive, I prayed to whatever forces might be listening, asking for the fog to disperse, so that I may leave this oppressive, lonely place. It had served its purpose. Now I wanted to get away.

Out of habit, I fiddled with the pendant, knowing I had been favoured with a symbol of my father's blessing. Other than warning of danger, I did not know what else it was capable of doing. Despite that, I held on to it and prayed.

"If you can hear me," I pleaded, picturing Dad's handsome face, "please help."

I snuggled down in my sleeping bag, pulled the hood over my head and closed my eyes.

"Don't mind me," Dom muttered from her corner. "I've only got third degree burns to half my body."

I told her to toughen up and drifted off.

Caught in that half-world between wakefulness and sleep, I remembered another time when I was in a peasouper like this.

I was four or five years old and I had gone with Mum and Dad to a remote Aboriginal community to visit relations on Dad's side of the family. One morning, Mum woke me up and said we were going for a walk. It was dark out but, being used to her peculiarities and her vacillating moods, I did not think anything of it. Nor was I surprised that my father and aunts and uncles were not there; they often went off, leaving Mum and me behind.

Mum and I wandered hand in hand out of the house, me almost running to keep up with her. Together, we stepped into a dense fog. It was like the end of the world or a time before the earth existed, so heavy and solid I could not see in front me. Nevertheless, I held my mother's hand and followed where she led, the cold prickling my bare arms and running chilly fingers down my neck. I knew that at sunup it would disperse and bring on a bright new day.

After a while, my mother's hand slipped from mine and I watched as she drifted away, leaving me alone. Thinking it was a game, I called after her. At first, she teasingly answered. Once, twice, the disembodied voice came from out of nowhere. Eventually she stopped answering so that, frightened and alone, I stood in a world without beginning or end, up or down.

For the longest time, or so it seemed, I walked aimlessly, placing one foot in front of the other, calling for my mother. No one came. No one spoke. Not a whisper. Eventually, I bumped into a stone wall and realised I had walked all the way to the well that was a fair way from the cluster of houses. I crouched at the base of the wall and wailed.

After what seemed an eternity, the fog billowed, like a monster leaping from behind a velvet curtain, and my father popped out. He carried me back to the house, whispering, "Shhh, baby girl, don't you cry. You're safe. Dad's here."

There was an almighty row afterwards, Dad accusing Mum of abandoning me and she accusing him of not loving her. I did not trust her again, and the thought of that incident caused anxiety to flare in every part of my body.

With these thoughts in mind, I fell into a peculiar lucid dream.

I was in the ruin next door, mist creeping over gleaming paving stones and drifting in and out of windows. In a detached sort of way, I was vaguely aware that I was holding onto two small hands whose owners were invisible or sunk beneath to earth and therefore invisible to me; when I looked down at them, they were alternately obscure blurs, like smudges in a photograph, or somehow under tons of soil.

Distantly, I became aware of a figure up against the walls, flitting, circling and causing the fog to swirl in a dance.

"Who's there?"

It approached, drifting as if its feet did not touch the ground. When it was close, I saw that it was a blonde woman in a pale green dress.

"Mum?"

I stepped closer, surprised to see her.

It was definitely my mother. But there was something wrong with her. She moved in a stiff, one-dimensional sort of way, as if she was a cardboard cut-out or a stylised drawing.

"Mum," I repeated, voice softening.

She stared at me, expressionless, head tilted to one side, like a dumb animal that did not know where it was. She extended long, pale arms and I saw that the stub of a candle burned in the palm of each hand. Her demeanour changed when I stepped closer. The face moved in an odd mechanical way, as if invisible fingers had drawn a different expression on it—soft, kind, loving. The top half of the body leaned forward, the dead eyes brightened. She smiled, like a jaguar in a tree.

The transaction, when it happened, was so slight as to be unnoticed. The invisible hands I had been holding slipped from my grasp and there was the sensation of blurry forms scurrying from me and going to my mother. At the same time, she placed the candles in my hands, only now they were two dead baby magpies.

Distressed, I made a sound in my throat—"Oh"—just as a man's voice rang out of the miasma.

"Laila, where are you? Come back."

My mother's head snapped to the left as if a spell was broken and she drifted away, floating backwards like a paper cut-out. The two dead magpies in my hands turned into heads with wings and flew after her. It was only after they had disappeared that I realised the heads had Salih and Zaman's faces on them.

I sat up in my sleeping bag, covered in sweat. If I trembled, it was because of the memories that pulsed through me, like scorching underground springs. The damage I had suffered in that woman's hands. The dreadful late-night conversations I heard.

"Jimmy, let's have some fun."

"We can't do that anymore, love. We got a kid now."

"I hate her."

"That ain't true."

"You said you'd love me forever."

"I do."

"She's coming between us."

"Don't be silly."

"I should have had an abortion."

I had lost count of the times I heard these words when I lived with my parents. Fighting back tears, angry with myself for allowing the ancient detritus to affect me, I lay down and tried to get back to sleep.

Not long after, a pale light shone on my face. Thinking it was Dom, I raised my hand up against it, ready with a gruff word.

A man's voice said: "Come on, sleepyhead. Wakey-wakey."

By the time I stood up, the light was at the kitchen door. And by the time I made my way to the corridor, it had gone to the cottage entrance, shedding soft phosphorescence on walls mottled with age and dereliction.

I followed. Why not? It was bound to be yet another dream. There could be no other explanation for the drifting luminosity and the sense of wellbeing permeating my body. Yet there was no mistaking the very real chill on my skin and the sound my bare feet made on the ground. It was real, vivid. A dream, yet not a dream. A moment caught between reality and dreaming.

The light stopped at the door and flickered. Moments before it vanished, I was presented with the outline of a man's profile. Curly hair, small beard. My father, Jimmy Olden. There was no mistaking the lanky form, the inwardly drawn shoulders, and the manner in which shirt and jeans hung from the bony frame.

Gone in an instant, he left behind a residue of his being. In his place was a large bird. I recognised the magpie instantly. It was the one that that had flown alongside the van on the Stuart Highway—was it three days ago? It filled the doorway with its impressive bulk, the size of a small dog. The head terminated in a sharp beak and the tail trailed off to a narrow black band. As I stared, the bird turned its head and looked at me with the same red eyes I had looked into when I was driving. Then it lifted its head, exposing an elegant throat, and began to sing.

First a warbling for a full minute. Then it threw back its head, expanded its chest, pushed back its wings, the beak opened and released several high-pitched rallying calls that continued for several minutes; a series of aggressive beak clappings ended the display. After a moment's respite, it started again.

It repeated the same pattern three times. The sound was deafening, a trumpet blast that roused the heavens and carried across the width and breadth of the country. The reverberation pierced my body as would a spear, echoing inside the milky haze, until it finally rose to the air and traversed time and space.

It was so loud I had to clap my hands over my ears, gritting my teeth and shutting my eyes against the noise. At one point I was afraid my ear drums might burst, or that I would be pulverised. I knew it was no dream when I opened my eyes and saw Dom and Adam at the kitchen entrance, staring at me with stunned expressions.

When Dom quizzed me with her eyes, I indicated with a slight movement of the right hand that they ought to remain where they were.

I could not have guessed what any of this meant or what might happen next.

Which was why I was not prepared for what followed.

The fog started to break up. Or at least that is what I thought was happening at first. Then I realised that rather than disperse, like mist touched by morning sun, the fog was being torn apart, like white wallpaper stripped off a wall to reveal black beneath.

And then I realised what was really happening.

Slivers of black fell to earth, raining down around the cottage, leaving the mist intact and unaffected in every single detail. One or two black patches turned to a few dozen, to hundreds and then thousands, until a seemingly black rain washed the earth with feathery tar. The relentless downpour went on for quite some time. When it stopped, the ground was covered with thousands upon thousands of magpies, standing cheek by jowl next to each other, staring into a distance that was filled with more of their fellow creatures. It was impossible to count them. Their number was equal to the stars in heaven.

The van, parked in front of the building, was invisible under their weight. In a mad moment, I hoped they did not poop on it.

The magpie opened his bill and released a complex series of melodious warbles pitched at a conversational level. His carolling was picked up first by one and then a second bird. Before long, the song travelled through the entire company and was swallowed up inside the turmoil, through which it echoed and re-echoed to infinity. Then, on cue, every bird unfolded glossy wings and lifted into the air. They moved as one, a living carpet, a solid mass, that lifted higher and higher. With them went the fog, on collective backs.

"It's working," Adam said, coming up to me.

"They're using their wings to push the sky up," I said, astounded. "Like the Dreamtime story about the separation of earth and sky."

Though I did not know which tribal group the story belonged to, I knew this was an almost identical re-enactment of the tale about the first sunrise. Long ago, the story went, the earth was dark. There was no light, and a huge cloud covered the earth. It was cold and damp. Creatures crawled along because there was no room to stand. One day the magpies decided to pick up sticks and push up the sky, until the clouds were high up in the air and all the birds and animals had plenty of room to move. As soon as this happen, the earth was flooded with light, warmth and colour. It was the first time the animals had seen Sun-Woman. The magpies were so happy they burst into song and continue to sing at dawn to this day.

That was exactly what happened on this particular morning. With a final heave of their muscular bodies, the magpies pushed the clouds up into the sky, allowing the sun to flood the desert, bringing light and colour to the land. Spirits soaring, I stepped outside. Adam joined me on red soil that sparked with renewed life. And I was rewarded with an equally bright smile from Dom.

The sun was molten sliver on the horizon, the sky a symphony of orange, pale green and lavender. The outlines of trees stood stark and unmoving in the distance and the few remaining clouds were streaked with veins of molten red, purple and blue, the dawn of a new day.

I turned to see where my magpie was and found him on the Fiat's roof. Our eyes met as he began a new song. This time his warbling was directed at me, and I knew from the high, ringing tone that it was a song of reassurance.

When the solo performance ended, the bird drifted away on invisible currents.

"Time to leave," I said, turning with no small amount of relief in my voice.

In the kitchen, my heart sank all over again.

Chapter 36

"Where are they? What have you done with them?"

The front of Dom's shirt was balled up in my fist. The tip of my nose touched the tip of hers. I was so angry spittle flew from my mouth as I shouted. In my fury, I lifted her almost off her feet, forcing her to stand on tip-toes.

"I don't know," she said, quiet as a mouse.

Salih and Zaman were missing, their sleeping bags empty and cold to the touch, as if they had been long gone.

"Don't lie."

"It's the truth."

"As if I'd believe you."

"Ask him."

She tilted her head at Adam, standing by the door.

He nodded a tight-lipped assent.

I released Dom's shirt-front and pushed her violently away. She hit the wall behind her and yelped with sudden pain.

"If you handed them over to that bitch, I swear I will kill you," I said, pointing a finger at her.

Dom stared at Adam. The tension in their faces told me I was scaring them, but I did not care. All I wanted was for the twins to be safe.

"You're both in on this together," I said, through gritted teeth.

Adam stepped forward. "Magnolia," he whispered, "Dom's telling the truth. Zaman and Salih weren't here when we woke up."

"Then where are they?" I screamed.

He shrugged those thin shoulders of his and for a moment I really did believe I could hurt him, too. After all, he had allowed Harun and Hasan to go into the basement. And now this. Just when I thought we had made a breakthrough of some kind.

Furious, I strode to the window, desperate for fresh air. It felt as if the room had grown too small, too hot and stuffy; it could not contain me and the rage I felt. I would burst through its walls. My face was on fire. I gasped for air, legs quaking. They were all complicit; I was the only one standing up to Alila. I stared at the landscape, serene and distant, hands on the window ledge, willing myself to calm down. That is when I noticed the line of salt had been broken.

"Who did this?"

"Who did what?" Dom said, wary.

"The salt is gone."

Both scurried over and had a look for themselves.

"I didn't do it, if that's what you're implying," Dom mumbled.

I leaped out the window and stood on the other side.

"The hexagon's been rubbed out as well," I said, looking above the lintel. A sense of betrayal and futility swept through me. It was infinite. They had done this. They had done this together and they thought they could get away with it. That I would be fool enough to believe them.

"What's that?" Dom said, pointing to the right of where I stood.

Two sets of small footprints following a bigger set of prints, towards the main railway siding.

"What have you done?" I said to Dom.

She frowned. "Look again, Missy Din. I'm wearing leather boots. Those are sneaker prints. Far as I know you're the only one wearing sneakers around here."

My head felt suddenly very light, thoughts fizzing inside the bone casing like champagne bubbles in a crystal flute. Feeling like I was going to tip over and vomit, I stood beside the large set of footprints, pressed both feet firmly into the soil, and then stood aside to study the results. Identical.

I looked at Dom. "It doesn't make sense."

"Maybe next time you'll think twice before you start flinging around accusations."

"But it couldn't have been me. I would never harm Salih and Zaman. You know that."

She sat on the window ledge, swung her legs around, and lowered herself on the ground beside me.

"Well," she said with a satisfied smirk, "unless there's someone else wearing the same runners as you, it looks like you handed those kids over to their doom."

Briefly, last night's dream flashed through my mind. I saw myself holding two small, invisible hands. Then came the image of my mother, followed by winged heads that sported Salih and Zaman's faces.

When I told Dom about it, she said: "Looks like we're finally playing on the same team."

"Get bent."

"Get bent yourself, Little Miss Smug."

"You know nothing about me," I yelled.

"You don't know your own mind, let alone the mind of others," she said and walked away.

Desperate and ashamed, I looked up and saw Adam framed by the window. He looked back at me, serene and utterly unaffected by what was going on.

"I thought it was a dream," I pleaded. "But it couldn't have been. It was Alila, using whatever strength she had to trick me into giving her the boys."

He gave a puzzling little smile and turned away.

"We leaving or what?" Dom called from inside.

Sure, I thought, we can get away from here. But I will never get away from me. I follow wherever I go. And where I go, disaster follows.

CHAPTER 37

"I suppose you think you won."

An hour or so after we hit the road, Dom spoke up from the back of the van; she had refused to sit beside me when we left the train station. I was fine with that. It was starting to look like my efforts at reconciliation were doomed to failure anyway.

I glanced in the rear-view mirror and saw her sitting beside Adam. Burned, slathered in dried, flaking witchetty grub lotion and covered with bandages that had slipped off, she was a sorry sight—a far cry from the vital young woman of a few days ago.

"I hadn't thought of it that way," I said, still smarting after the loss of Salih and Zaman. "But I suppose I did win. Today is a new moon. Adam is alive and it's too late for Alila to make a full recovery. That's all I care about."

"Do you ever stop to think how your actions impact others?" Dom said.

I fought back the impulse to tell her that the correct word was 'affect', not 'impact'. Instead, I mumbled: "That's good, coming from you."

Adam sat poker-faced beside her, staring at the changeless landscape.

"You're no different to my mother and father," Dom said.

"How so?"

"Remember how they reacted when they found out about us?"

"They went ballistic and tried to stop us from seeing each other."

"Precisely. And here you are doing the same thing to these kids now. You are so determined to stop Alila, you never once stopped to think about what they want. Or what I want, for that matter."

"She has a point," Adam ventured.

"Don't you start," I said, raising my voice.

I would be lying if I said Dom's final thrust did not break skin. By this stage, it had dawned on me that I was fighting a losing battle. No matter what I did, the outcome was still the same: one more lost boy. Moreover, no matter how often I told myself that I acted out of love, kindness and consideration, doubts lingered. Was I doing it for them? Or was I doing it for me? What if Dom was right? What if I was just another adult imposing her own thoughts and beliefs on children? Telling them what is good for them. What they can and cannot do. All the things I hated about adults when I was their age.

Confused, my convictions on very shaky ground, I stopped at a T-junction to check for oncoming traffic. Nothing, of course. Straight ahead, birds swarmed blackly over a turquoise ripple in the air, a shimmering haze really. Kati Thanda, Lake Eyre, precious because it is so transient and ephemeral. Here today, gone tomorrow. Real one moment, unreal the next. The perfect symbol of the ruthless, ever-changing desert.

I would have liked to go there. It would be full of water after the rains. But it was a lengthy diversion and I was desperate to get to Marree, to be among people, houses, civilisation, after everything that had happened.

"Alila will have to find another way to rise up in the world," I said, turning right and heading in a south-easterly direction.

Despite the rain, the road was in relatively good condition. Rutted but drivable. I was able to keep a steady speed of eighty or so kilometres an hour.

Marree popped up an hour and a half later, like a boil on a kangaroo's arse. It hardly qualified as a town. More a huddle of houses, with a thin layer of bitumen haphazardly thrown over crusty earth to create the illusion of human permanence. Even then the veneer wore off fast, allowing sand and soil to peek through potholes filled with muddy water. Across the abandoned railway yards to the right, sway-backed buildings of timber and tin cast long shadows along the empty station platform. It looked like the end of the world. Even so, I could have leaped out of the car and kissed the ground, so pleased was I to be among the last vestiges of human occupation again.

"Where to now?" I said, slowing down to fifty kilometres to observe the speed limit.

"The mosque," Dom grumbled.

"Where is it?"

"Corner of Birdsville Track and the Outback Highway," she said, pointing ahead.

I drove along until I came to an intersection a little ways out of town.

"That must be it," Dom said, pointing to the left.

A clump of dusty green bushes stood back from the Birdsville Track. I turned left onto the famed road, parked under a gum tree, turned off the engine and got out, desperate to stretch my legs and rub some life into my numb backside.

A rather wobbly, primitive-looking structure stood close to a brackish waterhole.

"Don't tell me that's the mosque," I said.

"Alright, I won't," Dom mumbled.

Adam stepped out of the van just as an old woman emerged from the bullrushes around the waterhole She was holding a rusty bucket and wore a black patch over the right eye.

"Oh," she said, putting her left hand to her breast. "You gave me a fright."

She looked like an old witch who might be seventy or a hundred. Bone-white hair down to the shoulders, one startlingly blue eye showing in a heavily lined face.

"Who might you be?" she said, putting down the pail.

"We're passing through," I said.

She nodded. "Muslims?"

"I am," I said. "Well, I was raised as one."

She nodded again. "I'm Shahrazad."

"From *The Arabian Nights*," I said, smiling.

"Beg yours?"

"Shahrazad is the heroine of *The Arabian Nights*. She tells stories for 1001 nights to a homicidal king to save her life."

She gave me a curious look. "I don't know any homicidal maniacs, but I wish I knew a genie or two."

"Why?" I asked.

"A genie would give me three wishes, wouldn't she?"

"Suppose so," I said, thinking that was not always the case. Some djinn are so incensed about being trapped in a bottle or a jar or a ring for thousands of years they vow to kill the person who frees them.

"My first wish would be to fix up this place," the woman said.

"It's definitely seen better days," I said, casting an eye over the structure.

It was nothing more than four large tree stumps holding up a grass roof, with a low parapet of mud-bricks running around it. It looked like it might blow away in the first stiff breeze.

"Do you own this place?" Adam said, joining us.

"No." The woman turned that keen blue eye on him. "I just look after it. Getting a bit much for me now, though."

"I see," I said, feeling the need to step between them.

"It's the oldest mosque in the country," she said, still eyeing off Adam.

"When was it built?" he asked, and I felt the need to reach out and hold him back as he stepped closer to the woman.

"1861. It was for the Pashto cameleers who lived north side of town, with the local black fellas; the whiteys kept to the other side of the tracks, you know. Then someone had the smart idea of building the new mosque on the main street—you would've passed it on the way in—and this one was forgotten."

"Djinn don't like mosques," I said.

"Only the ones who belong to Iblis," she responded, her eye moving from Adam to me.

Dom joined the party at that point.

"Listen, I'm knackered," she said to me. "If we don't set up camp soon and get some tucker, I swear I'm gonna fucken pass out."

The woman gave her the once-over. "Are you camping here overnight?" she said.

A sharp "yep" was the extent of Dom's engagement with her, before she hobbled off to the van.

"It's okay, isn't it?" I said to the woman. "I mean, it's not private property or anything."

"You're welcome," she said. "Just let me make the place presentable."

She picked up the pail of water, waddled into the structure and sloshed the contents on the ground. Then she set to meticulously sweeping the hard-packed floor with a straw broom, giving rise to pleasing damp aromas. "There, nice and clean," she said when she finished.

Her venturing freely into the mosque dispelled any fears I might have had about her being an ifrit or a djinni. Still, there was something not quite right about her and I could not wait until she left. It wasn't just that eager eye staring out of the inscrutable face, while the other remained terribly hidden. But Shahrazad was in no hurry to depart.

Settling on the parapet, she said, "You can stay here but there are conditions."

"Of course," I was quick to say.

"Because," she went on, "this isn't just a place of historical import-ance. It's the house of Allah. We must show respect. No graffiti. No alcohol and no foul language." The latter was obviously aimed at

Dom. "And try not to burn down the place, like a couple of hooligans tried to do last year."

"I bet you get all sorts around here," I said, trying to make light of the situation.

"We do," Shahrazad said. "Oh, my, do we ever. Have you heard of…

The Tale of the Impious White Girl and Her Black Lover

"The story goes," Shahrazad said, "and this happened almost thirty years ago, an impious Muslim girl, pretty as the morning star and just as cold, came to this mosque with her Aboriginal boyfriend. Spiteful and rebellious as she was, she had only one thing in mind: to go against her mother and the laws and edicts of the land.

And so she lay in the dirt, beneath the sheltering straw of this here holy building, and drew the young man to her, saying, "Take your Roving Mule and let him run wild in my Hotel of Happiness."

Though not of the faith, the young man had more sense than his girlfriend. He saw the situation for what it was, saying, "Light of my eyes, darkness of my soul, this is a house of worship. It's not right to pass the time in such a manner here. Let's do it outside."

"No," she cried, clinging to him tighter. "Do as I ask."

"Think of what your mother would say," he said. "Not to mention your vengeful god. Let's get out of here and consummate our love where the moon can see and be envious of our happiness."

But the spirit of madness had taken hold of the girl. She poo-pooed him, saying, "Take your stick and beat me with it." And she gouged deep furrows in his back until he bled. "Take me, you coward. Plow me and plant your seed."

And he said, "You know no shame," secretly delighting in the way the white girl with the blonde hair did not care about anything except her pleasure.

She persisted in pinching, punching, scratching and pulling his hair until, at last, he relented and gave her what she wanted, right there, where pious men had kneeled upon prayer mats and offered devotions to God.

After they had done what they had come to do, they went to the pool and washed away the sin, unaware that a djinni, one of the devout followers of King Solomon, witnessed the perfidious act and offered up this curse on girl and boy:

"May your offspring wander the earth in perpetual unhappiness and misery, seeking that which can never be found."

"And so it came to pass," wrapped up Shahrazad. "The Story of the Impious White Girl and her Black Boyfriend spread across the width and breadth of the land, and that is how it was remembered when it was time to record it."

"Well, I'm sure there's something in that for all of us," Dom quipped when the old woman finished.

"Oh, yes, and what's that?" I asked, having found the story disquieting.

"Don't shag in front of genies who like to watch," snapped Dom. "Now, if you don't mind, ma'am, I need my friends to help me set up camp for the night."

But I was not done with the old woman. The story of the heady Muslim girl and her sagacious boyfriend had stirred something in me. The lovers reminded me of my own parents. I meant to say as much, but what came out was this:

"Shahrazad, if you don't mind my asking, what happened to your eye?"

She did not bat an eyelid, so to speak. No doubt she had been asked before.

"That, too," she said, "is related to the impudent lovers and the evil that came from their sacrilegious act."

"How so?"

"As the wise say, it's always best to be eyes without tongues."

"Say what?" Dom crossed one leg over the other and leaned against a tree.

"See but don't talk," amended the old woman. "Wagging tongues bring even the best of us down to the level of the offender."

"What happened?" asked Adam.

"Back then," responded Shahrazad, "I was younger than I am today."

"Weren't we all," said Dom.

I told her to be quiet and Shahrazad resumed the tale.

"Back then, I was younger than I am today. Though old enough to know better. You see, I was present the night the lovers desecrated this holy place. In those days, it was my mother (Allah bless her soul) who cared for the mosque and I, concerned about her welfare, had walked here—an isolated spot, you must admit—with her to make sure she was safe.

"We had cleaned the place, my mother and I (Allah bless her soul) and came down to the water to rest before going back to town when the lovers arrived in a beat-up old bomb."

"Oh," I said, remembering my father's Holden.

"Yes," said Shahrazad, swivelling her weird eye at me. "And so we hid, my mother and I, in the reeds. We watched and waited. We knew from the way they talked and treated each other that they were trouble, and we didn't want them to burn down the place. In hindsight it might have been better if they had burned it down.

"At any rate, they did the deed and because it was dark by the time they went to wash themselves they didn't see the mother and daughter, hiding, holding their breath, among the reeds. They left soon after.

"'I smell sex,' said my mother the minute we stepped inside the mosque. 'Bring water to wash away the sin.'

"And so it was I who stood alone by the cooling water, among the whispering reeds and chirruping frogs, when King Solomon's djinni uttered the curse upon the young lovers. I've always had the ability to see and hear the invisible. That's how it came to be that I heard his every utterance, and I knew the lovers had committed a great wrong, punishable in severest terms. I can also attest that it was the evil djinni Jarjaris, a descendent of Iblis, who tempted me to gossip about the lovers and to spread their misdeeds far and wide, so that soon it was talked about from Marree to Alice Springs.

"To answer your question," she said, turning to me.

"Long story short," said Dom.

"I lost my eye," Shahrazad went on, "because the girl's mother drove from Alice Springs to Marree to pick a fight with me. She said I had sullied her daughter's name. Even though it was already mud. We exchanged words. Afghan Muslim against Turkish Muslim, which is never right. Tit for tat. One thing led to another. Words came to blows and before you know it, she bends down, picks up a rock and throws it at me.

"God willed it to go straight into my right eye, instantly blinding me." Pause for dramatic effect. "Such was my punishment for the sin of gossip, and I wear it to this day as a sign of repentance."

I sat there, feeling as if someone had hit me in the stomach with a sledgehammer.

"Well, well, well." Dom finally broke the silence. "Good old Cherry. Didn't know she had it in her."

She had put two and two together and come up with the worst possible scenario.

"Did you know," I said to the old woman, "that you were talking about my mother and father?"

"Like I said," Shahrazad replied, "I see things others can't. I knew you were your mother's daughter the minute I saw you."

"How is that possible?"

"I can enter the lowest levels of heaven and hear the angels talk."

"That's beautiful," I said. "What else can you see?"

"That you are doomed."

I rose to my feet very slowly. "I'm not doomed," I said through gritted teeth.

Shahrazad heaved herself up with an audible groan. "She has awakened from the dream of life," she said. "It's you who, lost in stormy visions, keep with phantoms an unprofitable strife."

"Did she just curse you?" Dom said, turning to me.

"No," I said, "she's paraphrasing a poem by Shelley."

The three of us watched as the old woman wandered off down the road. The light was so intense beyond the confines of the small oasis that the rest of the world looked like a black-and-white film negative. Every shrub and blade of grass was bleached of colour. By the time Shahrazad reached the turn-off, she resembled a black rag wavering in heat. Moments later, she was the merest flicker of an illusion, melting between earth and sky. I hoped I would never see her again.

"So," Dom said, grinning. "Now we know why we're here."

"Want to tell me?"

"It's the beginning place."

"I don't understand," I said, still dazed by Shahrazad's story.

"This is where you were conceived," Dom said. "Where Mummy and Daddy did the dirty deed. Where everything began for little Miss Magnolia."

She was right. If Shahrazad was to be believed, I came into being twenty-eight years ago on this very spot. This desolate place was ground zero for me. But I still did not know what any of it meant. Why was I there? What was I supposed to do?

Questions with no answers. Everything was closing in on me and I was beginning to feel like a mouse in a trap.

"Explains Nan's motto," I ventured.

"What's that?" Dom asked.

"If the shit's gonna hit the fan, it's gonna happen in Marree."

CHAPTER 38

"I need tell you something, Missy Din."

"A confession!"

"Be serious."

"Sorry. Go ahead."

"I don't know where to begin." Dom stared at the desert, flaring and sparking in the last light of day. "I was never good with words."

"Do what I do when I'm stuck."

"What's that, bullshit?"

"No, start in the middle and work your way to the beginning."

"What about the end?"

"That can wait till you finish."

I was rewarded with a rueful laugh.

It was twilight, peaceful and almost silent. Dom, Adam and I sat inside the mosque, nervously picking at an early dinner. Mellow light as different shades of yellow, purple and red flooded the land. Birds twanged and chirruped. A slight breeze agitated the leaves overhead, causing them to murmur in response to the flustered whispers emanating from the bullrushes by the waterhole. Adam was stretched out beside us, hands behind his head, staring at a mauve sky streaked with thin cloud.

"That's just it," Dom said, her features arranging themselves into a confused expression.

"What's just it?"

"I don't know how it ends, and I don't think I'm going to be around to find out."

"What are you talking about?"

"I was primed for this job," she went on. "As long as everything went according to plan, I knew more or less what to expect. I had a part to play and I played it—well, if I may say so. You threw a spanner in the works. Now I have no idea what's gonna happen. It's new territory and I don't feel right about it." She tossed back some water and stared at the empty glass as if it contained answers to the questions churning in her mind.

She was right. I felt it too. The rules of the game had changed, and I was responsible. Going on what that old goat Shahrazad said, my family history was even more deeply embroiled in current events than I previously thought. Perhaps that was why I was preoccupied, reassessing events, trying to figure a way out of the maze. At first I thought this crazy adventure had nothing to do with me. That I was simply swept up in events beyond my control. Now it seemed that something of a more personal nature was at play. Malachi sired my mother when he raped my teenage grandmother. Nan's father accidentally killed Malachi, paving the way for Malachi to become an ifrit. And I was conceived on this spot twenty-eight years ago. But what did any of that have to do with Alila and the seven boys? I had no idea. But even I could not deny the fact that I was elated, oddly buoyant, and for the first time in my life I felt like I had a purpose. I was enjoying all of this, even as it frightened the life out of me. Still, I could not walk away from the fact that the situation also felt askew — the whole setup in this quaint building felt odd, unreal, precarious. As if we were sitting ducks. Yet I clung to hope.

"Maybe we should call George and tell him what happened," I said.

"I did," Dominique replied.

"And?"

"He didn't respond."

"Oh… But honestly, I think everything is going to be fine now."

"Famous last words. Alila waited a long time for this. She's not going to give up that easy."

"You don't know that."

"Remember when I stuck my hand into the light in Kulgera?"

I nodded.

"I saw stuff."

Adam came up on an elbow and looked at her. "What did you see?" he asked.

Slumped on the floor, picking at the checkered tablecloth with fingers that were missing half the rings that had previously adorned them, Dom was a changed woman. Earlier, soon after Shahrazad left, I drove to the Marree chemist and purchased some first-aid material for her burns. Now, a skin coloured compression bandage covered the left side of her face and neck. The left shoulder was similarly enveloped in an elasticised sleeve and the other cheek gleamed with ointment the chemist told me to apply to her face.

"What did you see?" I repeated.

"I'm going to die."

"You saw your death?" I whispered.

"No. Doctor told me in Melbourne."

I shook my head. "I don't understand."

"I've got cervical cancer. I was diagnosed four months ago."

I was not as shocked as I might have been. Startled for the second time in as many minutes, perhaps, but not blown away. "I've got cervical cancer." With these words everything fell into place. The pill popping, the extreme weight loss, the almost constant need to urinate, fatigue, back pain, bloated tummy. I had put Dom's behaviour down to the travails of a long road trip. But it was cancer.

"Are you having treatment?"

Dom shook her head. "Nah, don't want any of that shit in my life, thank you very much."

"Why didn't you tell me?"

"I'm telling you now."

"Why now?"

"Because the situation calls for it."

"How?"

"You have to do something for me."

"What?"

"I thought I had a couple more months—you know, to take care of things. Settle my vast estate, multimillion dollar investments, secret bank accounts in the Cayman Islands, and all that. But I don't. I'm going to cark it today."

"What are you talking about?"

"I saw my death when I put my hand in the light." Dom shook her head again. "Can you believe it? I'm going to die in a shithole in the middle of fucking nowhere." She let go a banshee yowl, which caused birds to flutter out of the reeds. Even Adam was startled.

She picked up her spoon and violently shoved lentil stew in her mouth, smearing her face and the bandages with sauce. She went from looking like the phantom of the opera to a ghoul.

"Wipe your mouth," I said. "You've got sauce on your face."

It was a stupid thing to say, given the circumstances. But it was all I could come up with. I needed time to process the news that my first and possibly only love was going to die, get taken out, not by cancer, but by some quirk of fate. I would not see her again.

"My mum used to do that," Dom said. "'Wipe your mouth', 'Elbows off the table', 'Watch your language', 'Where are you going?', 'What are you doing?'." She tossed back her head and let off another howl. "God, I fucking hated all that controlling bullshit."

"Anyway," I observed when she settled down. "I liked your mum and dad. They meant well."

"You know what they say about good intentions."

There was no need to reply. Poor Dom, I thought. She was barely recognisable. If I were honest with myself, I would admit I found her grotesque and slightly repellent. Pathetic, even, now that she had lost her mojo. The girl I loved resided in the past. Probably she'd never existed outside my own fevered imagination. The woman opposite me was reality. And although we shared a past, we had little in common. Both of us coasted on memories. Or, more accurately, I coasted on memories. Dom cruised on mutiny—a mutiny that was about to end, if she was to be believed, leaving no discernible mark behind.

"Hello, are you with me?" Dom clicked her fingers in my face and I snapped out of my reverie.

"Sorry, what did you say?"

"I want to ask a favour."

"Of course."

"You can't say no."

I nodded, thinking I never thought I would see the day when this aggressive, unyielding woman would ask me for a favour. How far I had come from the person I was at the start of the week. It was almost as if I had shed my old self when I put on Dom's clothing in William Creek.

"Actually, you can't say no," she said, "because you're the one who stuffed everything up for me. So you're gonna have to fix it as well."

A fly targeted a smear of sauce on her plate. She swiped it away and fixed her eyes on me.

"Well?" I said.

"I have a daughter."

I blinked. "You're full of surprises."

"Well, you know me…"

"Of course, the picture on your phone," I said, recalling the unsettling image on Dom's phone.

"Athena," Dom said, nodding.

"Goddess of wisdom and warfare."

"Best thing that ever happened to me."

"Why are you telling me this?"

She took a deep breath and tapped her knee with her chipped nails. "I want you to take care of her. I mean, you're the last person I'd ask to look after my kid, but given the circumstances I don't have an option, do I?"

"Gee, thanks…"

"You have to admit you can't exactly be trusted with children."

"That's not fair."

"Lost six kids in two days. Hardly a good track record."

"Then why ask me? Why not the father?"

"He's a Greek pearl diver in Broome. Doesn't know there's a kid."

"How is it possible for a father not to know he has a kid?"

"Easy. I wanted a kid. Found a good-looking bloke, fucked him, took off, brought her up on my own. It's called living an independent life. You should try it some time."

"Shouldn't he know if you're…?"

Dom shook her head. "No way. He is not to know. Athie is mine."

"Why me? I can't look after myself, let alone a kid. No. Just no. Don't do this to me."

Dom silenced my protests by grabbing my hand with such strength and conviction it stopped the flow of words.

"Listen, you fucked this up for me and you're gonna fix it, okay?"

I shook my head again, conflicted. "How did I stuff things up?"

"I will tell you, Missy Din. Athie is three years old. When George offered me the job, I told him to fuck off. So Malachi, your dear old grand-daddy, cast a spell or whatever those fuckers do to force me into it."

"What sort of a spell?"

"Athie is trapped somewhere; I don't know where. We talk all the time through the phone. But I don't know where she is."

"Have you asked her?"

"Of course I have. She just says she's in a nice room with lots of toys and plenty to eat. Malachi said I can have her back when the job's done, but—"

"I killed him."

"Bingo."

I released myself from the painful grip.

"Don't worry. George will know how to release her. But you must give me your phone."

She took the phone from her bag and passed it to me. I pressed the *on* button and saw the same blonde girl asleep on a luxurious bed. She reminded me of an enchanted princess in a fairy tale.

"You have to get her out when I'm gone. Then I want you and your grandmother to give her the stable, loving home environment she needs. You always wanted a kid. Said so yourself."

Truer words had never been spoken. But now that it was about to become reality, I doubted I was cut out for it.

"What about your mum?" I said, desperate to wriggle out of it.

"No way. Crazy cow. She'd fuck up the kid."

"Hold on," I said, something dawning on me. "You have a kid and yet you contemplated shooting children. I find that hard to understand."

"I did it for Athie. Everything I've done since she was born has been for her. Five hundred thousand dollars, used properly, will see her through life. I'm a shit human being, but I'm leaving something good behind." Dom fixed me with the corn-blue eyes I'd once longed to fall into. "Free her."

I found myself admiring her all over again. She was barmy but totally free. Did not care about anything or anyone. I told her so and she said:

"I care about my daughter."

"What about the god you were afraid of when you were little?"

"I don't believe in him anymore, which means I'm free of the bullshit society heaps on all of us from the day we're born. I can do anything and it doesn't matter. But you don't know yourself and therefore you are more pitiable."

"Am I pitiable?"

"Yes."

"Why?"

"Because you don't know what you're capable of."

I was not sure that that was entirely true. But I did not force the subject. "Now is a good time to tell her she did not kill the kids," a voice in my head said. But I could not do it. *Let her stew in it for a while longer*, I thought.

"You're not going to die in Marree or any other place," I said, instead. "At least not just yet. We're going to find your daughter, and you will bring her up on your own. If we can change fate for Adam, we can do it for you, too."

Dom rose laboriously to her feet, stood further away from us and lit a cigarette.

"You were always a stubborn bitch," she said, smoke wafting around her head.

With all my might I resisted the temptation to tell her smoking was bad for her health. Instead, I asked Adam if he'd had enough to eat. He nodded.

"Okay, then," I said. "I'm going for a little walk."

In truth, I wanted to find a discreet place to pee. I figured the best location was on the other side of the waterhole. Plenty of cover there. I walked away, sure in the knowledge I had the upper hand now that all our secrets were in the open, and Alila was more or less out of the game.

I had never been more mistaken in my life.

CHAPTER 39

Half hour later I was still beside the waterhole, unable to get back to the mosque. Adam and Dom stood inside and watched with a mixture of horror and disbelief as my desperate efforts to rejoin them escalated.

I was staring directly at them, within easy hearing range, but no matter how many steps I took or how often I changed the speed with which I walked, I could not get near. The building remained elusively distant, floating like a mirage beyond my reach. It was like walking on a treadmill at a gym. Or a rat, making a futile dash on a wheel in a cage.

My efforts quickly spiralled from frustration and exasperation to fear and mystification.

I was close to tears when Dom said, "I'll come get you."

"No, don't," I cried. "Stay where you are. If Alila is behind this, it's safer for you in there. A djinni won't enter a mosque. Let me try something."

Out of sheer desperation, I crouched against a slender ghost gum and wrapped my right hand around my dad's magpie pendant. Closing my eyes, I said, "Dad, I'm sorry to disturb you again. But I really need your help."

I pressed my fist to my lips, kissed the warm metal, and waited for a miracle. Minutes passed. Nothing happened. No voices. No paternal apparition. "Please," I said. "I won't disturb you again. I promise." Still nothing. Disappointed, I opened my eyes and looked at the rickety structure with its two occupants waiting for me to work my magic. I gazed hopelessly at them and shrugged.

Deflated, trying to come up with another solution, I let go the pendant and noted with dismay that the black paint on the magpie's throat, breast and tail had come off on my hand. The bird was white, or rather silver. Three black smears rested in the palm of my hand, almost invisible against my own skin.

"The heat's melted the paint on my pendant," I cried.

The words were barely out of my mouth when the paint coalesced and became one black splotch.

"Oh my god," I cried, rising to my feet.

"What's going on?" Dom said.

"It's alive," I responded.

"What are you talking about? What's alive?"

I could not speak. The blob wiggled like an amoeba in my hand and dropped to the ground. It wriggled like a worm in the dirt and began, inch by strenuous inch, to climb the tree. All I could do was stare, unable to believe what I was seeing. By the time it reached my eye level on the tree's surface, it resembled a slug of approximately five or six centimetres in length. It flattened to a paper-thin consistency and then detached itself from the wood, with a quivering vibrancy, drifting away and floating in mid-air.

"Now I've seen everything," I muttered.

"What's going on?" Dom called again.

I put up a hand to stop her from speaking.

In the next instant, the shadow cast by the tree became darker on the ground. It pivoted around, from east to west, and stretched across the clearing, all the way to the mosque door. All the shadows did the same—my shadow, those of other trees and bushes around me, grasses, reeds, elongated as if they were being sucked in one pivotal direction. In seconds the ground was covered in attenuated light and dark bars that marched, like soldiers, across the land.

When this was done, the amoeba changed. The ends became narrow, tapered, while the mid-section expanded outward until it resembled a split or a fissure in space.

It looked for all the world like a pulsating vulva afloat in mid-air. The sides pulsed and vibrated. I poked it with one finger. It opened and absorbed the digit to the second knuckle. It went in but it did not come out the other side; it simply vanished. Given how warm and muggy it was in the real world, the cold in that other place was, at first, welcome. Very quickly, though, it became too cold, unbearable. I pulled out the finger and gave it a good rub, grimacing as blood flow returned.

"It's freezing in there," I said to Dom and Adam.

I held out my hand, as if they could see the fingernail covered with frost.

"I think I know what this is," I said.

"What is it?" Adam asked.

"A kind of portal," I said, thinking of the way George Green had taken my body from Nan's house to his own by sliding invisibly between time and space. "Or a wormhole that will bring me to you."

"I don't follow," Dom said.

"I'm going into it. If it works the way I think it will, I will be with you in a minute."

Dom reached into her bag and pulled out the gun. "You might need this," she said, preparing to toss the weapon to me. Then she realised there was no way for me to reach it and dropped her hand to her side. I would not have taken it anyway. Guns have no place in my world.

Standing in front of the wormhole, I placed the palms of both hands together and pushed them into the rent—all the way to the wrist. The hole grew wider as I pulled my hands apart, opening up and releasing a blast of arctic air on my face. It was pitch black inside. I turned to the others. To my surprise, Dom was grinning.

"What's funny?"

"Nothing."

"Out with it," I said, pushing first my head and then my torso into the hole and, lifting one leg after the other, stepped inside.

"Looks like you're about to stick your head into a giant—"

Thwap. A wet rubbery sound, like two lips smacking lustily together, and Dom's no doubt vulgar pronouncement was cut off.

The desert vanished. Dominique and Adam were no more. Light ceased. There was only a void, absolute and endless. It was painfully cold. After the heat, the drop in temperature cut to the marrow, raw and biting. In the next moment, I became aware of forward motion. I was moving at an accelerated rate, afloat in an embryonic state. I pulled my knees to the chest and hugged myself against the bitter cold, feeling neither fear nor apprehension. Only vague curiosity.

There was the sense of being in a pre-existent space, ancient and undying. It dawned on me that I was probably behind the scenes of the earthly plane. Back there, in the oasis, I had passed through the door I had been searching for all along. This was the backstage to the reality, or the phenomenal world, experienced by billions of people on earth. Somewhere on the other side of this curtain was the desert, with Dom and Adam. Very possibly all that separated me from them was a nanoscopic barrier.

It seemed I floated for eternity. This passive existence gave me time to think.

What had the old woman, Shahrazad, meant by quoting Percy Bysshe Shelley's *Adonais: An Elegy on the Death of John Keats*? I'd loved Shelley when I was a kid, all the high-flown drama and romance of the lyrics, the fantastical, gothic elements of his poems. They carried me away from the loneliness I felt when my parents and Dominique deserted me. Shelley had made me feel like I was the doomed heroine in my own romantic tragedy. But why would an old woman who did not look like she read *New Idea*, let alone romantic poetry, quote his lyrics, albeit in mangled form?

How did my favourite stanza in the poem go? I thought, teeth chattering as I curled in on myself.

> *Peace, peace! he is not dead, he doth not sleep —*
> *He hath awakened from the dream of life —*
> *"Tis we, who lost in stormy visions, keep*
> *With phantoms an unprofitable strife,*
> *And in mad trance, strike with our spirit's knife*
> *Invulnerable nothings.*

Who is not dead? Who doth not sleep? Did the lines refer to me or to Alila? I had survived a suicide attempt. Much as I had wanted to die, I'd been brought back to tarry with what Shelley smartly called 'the contagion of the world's slow stain.'

Alila had been roused from her sleep, too. So had Dom. She had been dead, as far as I was concerned, and she had come back into my life. So had the seven boys, for that matter. Everyone on this bizarre trip had, in one way or another, died and returned to a new life. But to what purpose?

The poem posited the notion that life was a dream from which we awaken to a greater reality. It was confusing, especially since I did not believe in an afterlife. I only believed that my body would break down and return to nature when I died. Happy to be a tree or a flower or a rock.

And what had Alila meant in the underground cave when she said, "Who is dreaming whom? Is it me or is it you?" At the time, I dismissed the question as insane ravings. Now, the pronouncement took on new meaning. Was I dreaming? Was this the dream of a suicidal madwoman?

I had no answers. All I knew was that it would explain a great deal if the last couple of days were some kind of delusion. I had felt all along, as one impossible event happened after another, that I was dreaming. No, that is not correct. More accurately, I felt as if I was caught inside someone's dream. That someone was dreaming me. It would explain why everything felt unreal, and why I felt as though I was unable to exert control on what happened.

But was Alila dreaming me, or was I dreaming her?

I shook my head to clear it, and remembered two lines towards the end of Shelley's long poem.

> *If thou wouldst be with that which thou dost seek!*
> *Follow where all is fled!*

The lines George whispered to me on Monday morning—"Follow where all is fled."—was that a reference to death?

At a loss, I continued to drift, telling myself that I knew what I must do and perhaps this was my way of taking control. The realisation built up incrementally. No sooner did I think it when, out of the depths, came a blaze of light. I put up my arm to guard my eyes and saw the entire world etched, chillingly, on my retina. Dom and Adam inside the mosque, a scattering of farms, dwellings, all of Marree from high above, the mind-boggling outreach of the red centre, stretching from coast to coast, oceans falling into terrifying depths, tectonic plates shifting, cities beyond cities, forests, mountains, people swarming over the earth's crust, all in horrendous, vivid, detail. As if I had been given new eyes with which to see.

From high above I glimpsed a little girl running. The vision was quickly replaced by another: a white room with a blazing fireplace. With it came an awareness of nullity, oblivion, coiled, like a twister, around a column of fire, bright red and incandescent. A great eye swivelled and took in my passage through its depthless realms. Alila. There was something instantly recognisable about her. Then she was gone. Or rather I felt her trailing me, like an animal follows a scent, but keeps its distance.

Darkness returned and from the vacancy erupted an eerie scream. At first I thought it was a magpie. Then I realised it was a woman. The terror in her voice was unbearable. It froze me to the core. From high above, I saw the well in Kulgera. Only this time it had a crossbeam supporting a bucket on a rope. The bucket swung back and forth, back and forth, the hideous squeak turning into a terrible lament that drilled into my head. I was about to start screaming, when a sliver of light appeared ahead.

Relieved, I tumbled towards it.

Chapter 40

I materialised behind Adam. He was standing next to Dom, staring across the clearing at the wormhole. Feeling playful, I tapped him on the shoulder.

"Miss me?"

The smile vanished from my face when the boy yelled and almost jumped out of his skin. Dom spun around, equally startled by my sudden manifestation.

"You idiot," she screamed, looking as if she was about to have a heart attack. "Scared the shit out of me."

Adam ran a finger along my left arm. "Why are you covered in frost?"

"Long story." I turned to Dom. "I think Alila is trying to separate us and take Adam."

She frowned. "What does it mean for a half-formed djinni to take a sacrifice when there's a new moon? Far as I'm aware, she can't be resurrected after the ritual period is over. It doesn't make sense. Something else is going on…"

"Yeah, but what?" I stood with hands on hips, trying to figure out what we ought to do next. My instinct was to get in the car and drive away as fast as possible. But you can't keep running forever. Comes a time when you have to stop and face your demons.

"How long does twilight last?" Adam said.

I turned to him. "About half an hour."

"Then how come it's still twilight?"

Dom and I exchanged glances. Adam was right. It was almost nine o'clock according to my watch and it was still that lovely golden hour of the day. Light poised on the edge of dark. Serene and still. But this light did not look as if it was in the mood to relinquish its hold on day.

"What fresh hell is this?" I asked.

"Shit. Fan. Marree," Dom muttered.

"For what it's worth, I think we're safe in here," I said for my benefit as much as hers. "You lie down and rest."

To my surprise, she did exactly that, stretching out on her sleeping bag and crossing her hands over her distended belly.

"I want to see my little girl before I die," she mumbled.

"She's on your phone, isn't she?"

"Not anymore."

She passed the iPhone to me. I pressed the *on* button. Behind the apps, the screen was a fuzzy blank.

"What happened?"

"Disappeared a few minutes ago."

"You will see her again. I promise."

It was a stupid thing to say, but I had to offer some comfort.

Dom flung an arm across her eyes and said, "Don't make promises you can't keep."

"I need to tell you something," I said, thinking my long-withheld news might bolster her flagging spirits.

Dom raised her head and stared at me. "Oh, god, you're not going to tell me you're a dyke, are you?"

I laughed. "Not quite."

"What, then?"

"You didn't kill the boys."

The words had an instant effect on her. She sat bolt upright and wiped the tears from her face.

"I was there, I pulled the trigger, I saw them fall. Of course I did it."

I shook my head. "You were possessed by Malachi. It wasn't you. It was him."

"How do you know?"

"George told me. You balked at killing the kids and Malachi took over, entering your body and doing the dirty work for you."

"If this is true, it might account for why I feel like he's been inside me. I feel so…dirty. No amount of showering helps." She scrubbed at her right arm as if she might rip off the skin. "When are men going to learn a woman's body is her own? They can't just take charge. Unless you want them to, of course."

Just like that, it seemed, we passed through a door, from one unhappy place in our troubled relations to a calmer realm. I looked upon her with calm detachment, fondness even. But not love and pain. I was finally ready to let go and move on. She was no longer someone I turned to for guidance and support. She was merely a woman with her own troubles: poor health and a missing child. I couldn't do anything about the former, but I could perhaps help with the latter. If we left this place and went back to Alice Springs, I was certain George Green would know what to do. Actually, when I thought about it, I didn't know why we had come to Marree to begin with. After the ritual time was over, I could just as easily have driven to Alice Springs with Adam.

I gave him an encouraging smile. Beautiful boy in a soiled uniform and a skullcap that had fallen by the wayside some time ago. I had to stop myself from thinking that one day he would make a nice boyfriend for some lucky girl or boy. How could he, given what he was? In saving him, I had condemned him to life in limbo.

"The way you felt when Dom left," said a voice in my head. "And the way George Green felt after Malachi tricked him into having a physical body. Do not repeat their mistakes."

Adam sat on the parapet, chin in hand, lost in thought. If I allowed myself to admit it, I would say there was no point in his existence now that he had no role to play in Alila's game.

"Are you okay?" I said to him.

He nodded and shifted his gaze to a point over my right shoulder, making me feel as if someone or something was standing behind me.

"What is it?" I asked, too afraid to look.

He pointed.

I turned and realised I was standing in front of the wormhole; Dom lay directly under it and although it was closed, there was an in-draught. My hair was drifting towards it. I had put it out of my mind when I stepped out of it, but now it resembled a coarse animal hair, hanging from the ceiling. Almost repulsive. I grimaced, wondering if it would eventually go away. To belie this pathetic thought, a barely perceptible vibration passed through it, top to bottom, and a thin, stringy voice emerged, more instrument than human.

"Mummy," it said, breaking up, coalescing, stretching out the vowel and then the final consonant. "Mummy."

It was a little girl.

Dom was quickly on her feet.

"What was that?"

"It came from there," I said, pointing at the wormhole.

"It's Athie. She must be in there."

I shook my head, helpless before a mother's distress. "I don't think so, somehow."

"Oh, fuck me." Dom lunged for the hole. "If that bitch has my baby…"

She did not finish the sentence. Her head, shoulders, arms vanished inside the hole. Only the lower torso and legs remained, kicking outside as she struggled to go further in. She looked like a half-formed creature, flailing at creation's mouth.

"Don't," I cried, pulling her back.

Adam rushed over to help, wrapping his sturdier arms around Dom's waist and holding on.

"I wouldn't do that if I were you, Dom," I shouted.

She popped out again, blanketed in ice crystals.

"Let go. It's my daughter. I saw her."

I relinquished my hold, but Adam continued to hold on.

"It could be a trap," I said.

"If that bitch harms a hair on my child's head," Dom said, "I'm going to kill her." She pulled the revolver out of her back pocket and brandished it menacingly in my face.

I did not believe a gun would stop a djinni. But how do you tell that to a desperate mother?

"Listen—" I said, but the words stopped in my throat as a column of black smoke shot out of the wormhole and funnelled at great speed out of the mosque. When it was outside, it turned into a human figure from the waist up and smoke from the waist down, the tail end twisting and turning like a miniature cyclone where it touched the ground. It was a little girl with golden hair.

"Athena," Dom yelled and ran out of the building.

"Don't go outside," I screamed after her.

Pointless. She was already by her daughter's side—if it was her daughter.

"Athie," she cried, flinging her arms around the girl's neck.

The girl looked directly at me over her mother's shoulder, and I knew instantly she was not Dom's kid. No child could be that glacial and cunning.

"Dom," I said. "I don't think you should be doing that."

In an instant, the apparition in Dom's arms changed from child to woman. Taller than the average human being by a couple of metres, white as milk, naked and gloriously crowned with gold dreadlocks, she was woman triumphant—a creature awakened to a new dawn and eager to test the limits of her limbs. She shoved Dom aside, stretched wide her arms, threw back her head and released a banshee yowl of tremendous volume. The noise was appalling. In its ancient song I heard the howl of wild beasts, hurricanes, earthquakes, and the collapse of glaciers.

Dom fell on her butt, gritting her teeth and covering her ears against the horrific din. I rushed to her, telling Adam to stay inside the mosque. Stepping outside was like finding yourself in a mini tornado. Nervous winds spun and rotated around Alila and Dom. The air was filled with dust, flying pebbles, twigs and leaves, forcing me to close my eyes and to put up a hand to protect my face from the stinging assault. Static electricity crackled, making my hair stand on end. Fighting against the micro-climate she seemed to be generating, I looked up and took in the amazing spectacle. I had never seen a woman like Alila—not in my wildest dreams.

Alila. I had felt her presence before, but I had not seen her. Not really. Yet seeing and feeling, in this instance, seemed to be one and the same. I had the odd sensation that I had gone blind. I felt with my eyes and saw with my feelings. That everything was fine-tuned, rubbed out, turned inside out and upside down. My all-too-human body with its limited senses struggled to make sense of what was in front of it, so alien and yet so ineffably beautiful.

Even so I could tell this was a limited creature. It was not fully formed. It flickered around the edges, broke apart and came together, like figures in a poor transmission.

I was caught in a moment, frozen between awe and terror, when Dom stood up, aimed, and fired her gun.

I screamed, "No!" but it was too late.

A bullet hit Alila in the chest. She screeched. The top half of her body reeled as a second bullet shattered her jaw. A third bullet went through the neck and came out in a gliding blue ribbon of ichor through the other side.

Dom aimed and fired a fourth time. This time the bullet passed through Alila's sternum.

"Give. Me. Back. My. Daughter," Dom shouted after each successive shot.

The djinni grabbed her ichor-spattered breasts with what appeared to be huge lion's paws, threw back her head and howled—a raving, demented, cry out of a thousand nightmares. Her jaw had been reduced to pulp, tongue lolling insanely at the lower half of her face. Amazingly, where ichor fell on the ground, flowers, wild grasses and trees sprung up from the soil. Twining plants hooped and scrolled like living things around saplings, forcing me to dance back as vines sprang out of the soil around my feet.

In the growing darkness, Alila held my eyes. The connection made me catch my breath, thinking of encounters between gods and mortals at the dawn of time. Again, I was unable to move, torn between horror and admiration; and in those unfathomably black eyes I saw a glimmer of something I recognised. I knew Alila.

"She hath awakened from the dream of life," I said.

Alila released another raving half-laugh half-gargle that chilled the marrow. I stood stock still, waiting to see what happened next and hoping she did not notice me too much. When the echo of the djinni's laughter died, she extended a slender arm towards Dom, fingers splayed like daggers. A finger touched Dom's forehead.

"*Tamam shud,*" the djinni said, in Arabic. This is the end.

Alila vanished as soon as the curse was pronounced.

I screamed and fell to my knees, shocked and horrified.

In Dom's place stood a statue of granite, pointing an impotent gun.

CHAPTER 41

I stood inside the mosque with Adam, determined to kill that thing, when my attention was drawn to a peculiar noise—a weird theremin sound, like an old sci-fi film.

"It's Dom's phone," Adam said.

"Where is it?"

"Out there." He pointed to the clearing now dominated by a statue of Dom.

I found the phone on the ground beside Dom, where she must have dropped it in her final moments. I picked it up and put the device to my ear.

"Hello?"

It was my grandmother.

"Thought I'd give you a buzz, see how things are going," she said.

At a loss for words, too shocked to speak, I did not know what to say.

"Everything hunky-dory?" Nan went on.

Her chirpy voice was unreal. The ordinariness of it belied everything that had happened in the last few minutes. I was thinking that Nan could not be more removed from my current situation when it occurred to me that it was not the case. She was directly involved. The beginning of this miserable saga could be traced to the moment Malachi forced himself on her and fathered my mother.

"I called your phone, but I wasn't getting an answer," Nan was prattling away.

"It's dead," I said. "I couldn't recharge it."

"Told you to get a new one."

"Nan. Where did Dad's people come from?"

There was an intake of breath at the other end; Nan had always discouraged me from seeking out my father's side of the family, even going so far as to forbid me from mixing with Aboriginal people in town.

The response was a tight little, "Down south."

"You ever been?"

"Once. Drove there to rescue your mum from one of her adventures."

"Where was it exactly?"

"A place called Hidden Valley."

"I've been thinking about Mum and Dad a lot lately."

"Hardly surprising. Last Monday was twenty-two years since your mum died."

"Yes, you told me."

"I had a dream about her last night."

"What was the dream about, Nan?"

"Malachi came to me. I thought he was going to hurt me again. But he told me to come with him. I got out of bed and followed him down the hospital corridor, passing doctors and nurses as if I was invisible. "Come on," Malachi kept saying. "Keep up." He opened the door to the emergency stairwell and there was a desert with a cemetery on the other side." She stopped.

"Go on."

"Malachi stood next to a crucifix with your mum's name on it. He tapped the ground with his foot, whispered some words, and a trap door appeared in the sand. 'Open it,' he said. I lifted the trapdoor and out popped your mother, wearing her favourite green dress."

My heart beat so fast in my ears I could hardly hear her. "What did she do?"

"Just said, 'See you soon, old Mum.' What do you think of that?"

I was chilled, despite the heat in the air. "Does my mother have a grave?"

"Of course."

"I thought they never found her body."

"That's true."

"Then how come there's a grave?"

"Your father did it as a tribute. It was the least he could do after ruining her life."

I wanted to argue. Tell her Dad did not ruin Mum's life. He loved her and she loved him. They were happy together. I got in the way of their happiness. And maybe, just maybe, Nan had played a part in her daughter's demise, too. She was, after all, very controlling.

"Where's the grave?"

"You know where it is. I told you many times."

"Tell me again."

"She's buried at a small indigenous cemetery outside of Kulgera."

"Hidden Valley," I mumbled, feeling sick.

"Your dad's people are from down there. The community didn't survive, but the cemetery is still there apparently. You used to visit your dad's relos there when you were little, before you came to live with me. Don't you remember?"

I remembered alright. The visits were the highlights of my young life. But I had retained no memory of the location, or rather I had gone to great lengths to block it from my mind. At one time I had even told myself that it was north of Alice Springs. But it was south, closer to the mountainous rocky areas around Kulgera, with the amazing stories I heard as a child about sacred female sites, full of caves and underground passages.

Another chill passed through me. "Nan, we camped beside that cemetery Monday night."

"Oh, how nice. I hope you put flowers on her grave."

"I didn't know…"

"Didn't know my foot. I told you a million times, but you never listen. You're a champion blocker out, my girl. It's time for some forgiveness."

"I can't, Nan."

"She's dead. It's time you let go. If I can do it, so can you."

I was not ready to forgive yet. I did not even fully understand what had happened between me and my mother all those years ago. But things were starting to shift.

"Where are you now?" Nan broke into my thoughts.

"Marree," I said. "I'm at a mosque."

"You've been on a bit of a pilgrimage. Visiting all the important sites."

"Do you know a woman called Shahrazad?"

"That cow. She still around?"

"Yep. She told me what happened between you two."

"She got what she deserved."

I was not so sure.

"It's water under the bridge now, isn't it?" Nan said.

I said, "Yes," but there was a question mark in my mind. Was it in the past or was it still going on?

"Listen, I've got to go," I said. "I'll see you soon, okay?"

My grandmother was in the middle of saying, "I thought you were coming back today," when I cut her off.

I slipped Dom's phone into my pocket and returned to Adam,

keenly aware I was deliberately avoiding looking at the statue. Adam turned to me as I approached.

"What's going on?" he said.

"I'm going in there," I replied, nodding at the wormhole.

"I'll come with you."

"No." I pushed him away. "I have unfinished business. Time to face up to some home truths."

"I'm as much a part of this as you are."

"I have to do this on my own."

"Magnolia."

"Yes?"

"Do you know how to make a talisman to bind a djinni?"

"I think so," I said, screwing up my brow. "I'm not sure."

"You must know the djinni's real name and possess something that belongs to it."

"That's right."

"And then you must bind the djinni to an object so that you can control her. Even then it can be dangerous."

"Why are you telling me this?"

He smiled. "Because we want the same results," he said, enigmatic to the last.

"I thought you were on Alila's side."

He pulled me into a tight embrace.

"I am," he said, releasing me.

"Look after Dom," I said, throwing a glance at her frozen form.

I dived headfirst into the wormhole. As it closed behind me, taking warmth and light with it, I could not have said where I was going or what I intended to do when I got there. There was only determination before the oncoming storm.

Chapter 42

A white room with a table and black chairs. Honey-coloured floor-boards reflected a blazing fire in the grate. No windows, which gave the space a claustrophobic feel, like being trapped in a prison cell. The door was closed and there was no light source. Yet I could see.

I looked around, taking in the floor, the ceiling. It was real, yet it felt like a stage, an illusion, concocted to give semblance to something that did not have physical properties. The fire emitted no warmth. That was how I knew I was almost frozen through. Rubbing my bare arms to bring life to my limbs, I noticed something odd about the fire. It kept flaring and dying down as if a pair of bellows expanded and contracted behind the chimney, emitting air to encourage the embers to blaze one moment and abate the next. I had the distinct impression the room was breathing, and the flames represented the expansion and contraction of lungs. Finding the thought disconcerting, I turned away and saw a woman sitting at the head of the table, clasping her hands before her. I recognised her immediately.

"Mum."

The long blonde hair, the round face with burgundy coloured skin, and lips like juicy berries.

"Kissable lips," Jimmy Olden used to say, taking her in his arms. "My queen. You know what your best features are."

Laila would shake her head, looking adoringly up at him.

"Your eyes…"—he looked lovingly into the blue of her eyes, then his gaze roamed down to her face, found what he was looking for—"and your lips."

He kissed her on those eyes and on those lips until she swooned—a woman adored by a man with his arms around her waist.

The magpie started to burn at my throat, warning me to back off. But I was beyond heeding its warnings, quite simply overwhelmed by the vision.

The woman rose to her feet and stepped away from the table. The pale green dress with the large red flowers was wet and plastered to her body, showing off the heavy breasts, the sensuous hips. Crystalline beads of water drifted from her, creating a shimmering nimbus around the body.

"What do you want from me?" she asked.

I shook my head. "I don't know."

The woman pulled a white envelope across the table, took out three old-fashioned razor blades, and arrayed them glitteringly on the table.

"Is this what you want?"

This time I was in no doubt. "No."

Eyes flashing, she swept the blades off the table and glared. Then she opened her arms and, with a gelid smile, invited me to step into them.

I did not think twice. I rushed into the embrace with tears in my eyes.

"Mummy, I'm so sorry."

"There now," she said, running her hands the length of my hair. "Everything will be alright."

She took my wrists in her hands and kissed my scars.

"All I ever wanted was for you to love me," I said.

"The question is, do you love me?"

"Of course I do."

"How much?"

"More than anything in the world."

"Prove it."

The words were barely out of her mouth when she pushed me away and delivered a vicious blow to my face. Shocked but not surprised, I reeled back, crying out with outraged pain. I closed my eyes, hand flying up to my right cheek as I pushed back the fury welling up in my gut. I was used to this treatment. It was expected. Hugs, kisses, and then a slap, a savage pinch, gritted teeth, burning eyes.

But I was a big girl now. I would not put up with it anymore. It was intolerable, unacceptable.

"No!" I shouted, opening my eyes.

The woman was gone.

My diary sat on the table. I bought it when I was nine or ten years old, wrote in it once and set it aside, never to be opened again. Picking it up now, I used the tiny gold key to unlock it, remembering its peculiar quirk and turning it in an anti-clockwise direction.

The lock snapped open.

The covers parted with a slight crackle of the dry spine.

I sat in the chair recently vacated by my mother and flicked through it. There was only one entry, written in a barely legible scrawl. The rest was blank pages, waiting to be filled. Taking a deep breath, I proceeded to read…

CHAPTER 43

The Tale of the Woman in the Well

Magnolia was afraid. The six-year-old huddled against the stone wall, eyes closed, hands clamped over her ears, begging the screams to stop.

"Please go away."

She opened her eyes, but dared not take her hands from her ears. The awful sounds might come back.

Across the clearing she saw a dozen houses surrounded by small, fenced-off yards. Behind the houses, hills flowed in smooth undulations against a cloudless sky. It was one-fifteen in the afternoon and the sun was high in the sky, blazing down so that all of the earth's creatures were in hiding.

"Make it stop."

Hoping her prayers had worked, Magnolia removed hands from ears.

"Mags, help me. For the love of God, help."

Magnolia made the sound stop by clamping her hands over her ears again. She scrunched up on the ground, bringing her knees to her chest, and told herself it was best not to listen. "The woman in the well will go away soon," she told herself. "It will not be long now." The thrashing in the water had grown feeble over time. She was making wet, bubbling sounds. The voice sounded tired, distant and afraid.

At first Magnolia had been defiant. She might even have taken pleasure in what was going on. Treated it like a game from which she could withdraw any time. When the screams had grown far-off and vague, the wails intermittent, the splashing less voluble, she had become a little scared. Even someone as young as she could see that there was a world of consequences ahead. Repercussions that spread like the rings of Saturn she'd admired in picture books. She knew that she had been bad and she was bound to be punished.

Even so, she wished there was something she could do to make the woman stop yelling. It crossed her mind to throw down a large rock, a heavy one, and crush her skull like a tiny bird. Or put the cover on the well to stop the terrible sounds from coming out. But the lid was too big and heavy for her to lift by herself; she had watched her mother struggle with it earlier.

"Mags, find a rope."

"Go away," Magnolia chanted. "Go away."

"Mags, are you there? Answer me."

The voice came out of a mouth full of water. If there was anyone nearby, they would be sure to hear and come. But there was no one. Everyone had left. Every single man, woman and child had gone away. They were on a trip, leaving the white woman and her white daughter alone.

"Mags, listen to Mummy. I promise you're not in trouble. Just go find a rope." And when that did not work, the voice gave way to helpless shrieks that broke like wild, desperate birds out of the ground.

Time being meaningless to a child, there was no telling how long Magnolia sat in the boiling sun, holding her hands over her ears. Nor did she know when her father was due to return. There was only intense heat, crying, and the sun moving across the sky. In due course, the woman ceased to exist. There was only the disembodied voice, rising and falling, like hideous music. One minute it came out of the earth and the next it fell from the sky, haunting the little girl's dreams.

"Peace, peace, he is not dead," she sang, remembering a hymn her father sang. "Peace, peace."

Or was it a poem?

She must have fallen asleep because the next thing she knew a skinny dog with a wet, pointy nose sniffed at her face. It scampered away on rapier legs when she flailed her arms, its shadow longer and skinnier on the ground because the sun was being sucked into the western horizon. A magpie let off a series of raucous calls, opened its wings and hopped onto a hot tin roof.

Startled, Magnolia realised what had changed.

The voice had stopped. There was silence as far as the ear could hear.

"Peace, peace," she sang under her breath.

Pressing her hands in the dirt, she pushed herself to a standing position. She was holding something in her right hand. It was a clump of gold hair. She stuffed it in her pocket and approached the well.

The stone wall came up to her shoulders. She put her hands on the topmost section, raised herself on tiptoes, and peered over the edge, expecting her mother to leap up and drag her into the depths.

Nothing happened. There was only darkness and quiet. Not even a ripple on the water's surface, way down below. Only a reflection of herself, peering over the edge. Even the rose perfume her mother wore had dissipated. The air smelled only of the honey grevillea that grew in the area and from which the black women made sweet drinks. Magnolia wished she had some now.

The magpie called a second time and flew off to tell her father what had happened. When Magnolia turned, the dog was in front of a pale-yellow house with a small verandah. It was only when she crossed the bare patch of ground and sat in a white plastic chair and looked towards the well that she realised what had happened.

Events played in front of her, like the cinema screen the young men set up to watch movies under the stars.

It was the third day after her father and his kin had departed, leaving Magnolia and her mother alone. Before leaving, Jimmy Olden assured his wife Laila there was plenty of food in the house. She was not fussed. It was not the first time she had been left behind with the child. Nor was it likely to be the last for the white woman whose kid was too white to be black and too black to be white. Everyone said so. Black and white. They said the same about the woman herself. But she was not bothered. She could handle herself. She was tough. Had to be, growing up in Alice Springs without a father, and a mother who wanted to control her life.

On this particular day, there was no water in the house. The three bottles and three plastic containers with the black screw-on lids were empty. Laila had to draw water from the well.

This well had been in older times a spring whose waters flowed with stories. They bubbled to the surface for the people to drink and to make a part of themselves. So that they too, in time, would become the source and sustenance of stories. After a toddler's accidental drowning, council workers sank a shaft in the water basin, lined it with concrete and built a wall around the perimeter. A concrete cover and a hand pump became the jewels in the crown. When the hand pump broke and no one came to fix it, a resourceful youth smashed the covering with a sledgehammer and installed an old-fashioned crossbeam with a bucket on a rope. A wooden lid was installed as a concession to safety.

Laila had struggled to remove this lid. The cumbersome object made a heavy grating sound as it subsided across the worn stone. The hole in the ground was very wide, breathing out cool, moist air, like a ghost.

"Don't get too close," she had said to her little girl. "A djinni might pop up and drag you in." Because everyone knew djinns lived in wells, toilets and ruins.

A long stick with a hook at the end was needed to draw in the bucket. When the lid fell on the ground, Laila lowered the bucket and pulled it up, sloshing with water, so cold and clear you could smell the underworld. Desperate to please her mother, Magnolia held the funnel in the plastic container while her mother filled it to the brim. Then she pushed away the full container and replaced it with an empty one.

It was during the third attempt at drawing in the bucket when the stick slipped out of Laila's hand and plummeted, hook first, into the depths. She swore. Kicked the wall. Then she plonked her backside on it, held onto a rotting wood post, and leaned dangerously across the gaping hole, reaching with wriggling fingers for the fraying rope.

She reached out, strained, grunted, swore some more. Fingers wiggled in air, inches from the rope. Could not quite make it.

In the end, she told Magnolia to hold her around the waist while she leaned further out over the precipice.

Magnolia stood behind her mother, reached out a small hand and pulled it back.

Uncertain, she hesitated for an instant.

"Mags, do as I tell you."

The little girl snapped out of her reverie. There was perhaps no thought of the sly beatings she had endured over the years. The slaps. The elbow to the temple. Yet they must have been there, in the back of her mind, because she was aware only of a need to punish her mother the way she imagined teachers punished children at school when they are bad in class.

Make her see the error of her ways and she will not do it again.

Magnolia extended the index finger of her tiny right hand, hesitated, pulled it back, put it out again…

The sun beat down. Birds cried from high above: "Don't do it, Magnolia."

"Do as I tell you, you little shit."

The mother kicked out with her right leg and hit the little girl in the stomach. Magnolia fell to the ground, but there was no time for tears.

"Hurry up. Hold on to me."

Magnolia stood up, went to her mother, and prodded her with one finger in the lower back. Gentle as it was, almost a tickle, the gesture startled Laila. She let out a yelp, jumped, tilted over, lost her balance and, with a surprised cry, she tipped over and fell into the well.

The flailing arms grabbed hold of the bucket and held on for dear life. The flushed face turned on a corded neck and looked with fear-filled eyes.

"Mummy."

Magnolia reached out. Her fist closed on her mother's hair.

Laila's lips parted and before she could utter a sound, the rope snapped. A sharp crack and the woman dropped out of sight, leaving the child with a wad of golden hair in her hand.

Not a word was uttered as she fell. Only when she hit the water with a tremendous sound did the screams begin.

"Mags, get me out. Call someone."

When Jimmy Olden returned days later he found his daughter inside the yellow house. There was no sign of his wife.

"Where's Mummy?"

"A djinni came and took her away," Magnolia told him.

CHAPTER 44

I closed the diary and thought about the things I had read, hands pressed gently to the cover. I had killed my mother. That was the black hole I had walked around all my life. I had murdered the woman who gave birth to me, and spent the years since trying to come to terms with it, hoping to atone. But how do you make peace with the fact that your mother no longer exists because of your actions? Having gone so far, how do you come back?

"Do you love me?" Laila had said.

Of course I loved my mother. That went without saying, despite the malicious way she had treated me. Every child loves its parents, doesn't it? But obviously I did not love my mother enough. Why? Because I was intrinsically bad, having come into this earthly plane from the womb of a woman whose father was a diabolical ifrit. Evil begets evil. I could face that now. There was more bad in me than good. Or perhaps the two were at war in me, trying to gain the upper hand.

Of course there was always the possibility that the woman I had seen was not my mother, Laila, at all. It could have been one of Alila's tricks, an illusion to confuse and destabilise. Djinns were known for deception.

I was contemplating all of this when the door opened and a monumental creature stepped through. Her stupendous nakedness was accentuated by an emerald cape with puffed sleeves that billowed behind her like mist caught in a whirlpool, bringing to life the intricate floral pattern. The feet were adorned in high Ottoman bath clogs secured with studded leather straps. The base and stilts were decorated with lapis lazuli and mother of pearl; and the entire sable body, head to toe, was covered in intricately painted designs and patters of henna. Every orifice bristled with silver piercings, causing her to sparkle and shimmer as she moved. Elaborate tribal earrings adorned a head that was finished off with dreadlocks fashioned out of gold hair, whipping around the face as if they were living tentacles.

Alila came into the room with the assurance of one who believes she is welcome anywhere, any time.

Knowing myself to be studied, despite the fact that the djinni did not look directly at me, I pushed back my chair and rose to my feet, heart thumping. I wanted to be ready to run, should I need to.

"Troublesome," Alila said in a voice that was glass on glass. "The mouse has teeth."

I remained silent. Alila's next words took me by surprise.

"I love you, Magnolia."

That, at least, gave me something to which I could respond.

"You love yourself."

"I am you and you are me."

"Sure we are."

Alila stopped pacing. "We both are and are not."

We stood near each other. For me it was like finding myself uncomfortably close to a cobra, my worst fears come to life. Even though I was trembling, I found the voice to say, "You're not making any sense."

Alila turned to me. The fire in her eyes froze my will to live. My determination to fight collapsed. Even so, I stood my ground and waited.

"Change is constant," Alila said. "Everything is always partway between being what it was and what it will be, in a process of regeneration and dissolution." And it seemed to me that in the next instant Alila took charge of my throat and larynx, and put in the words that flowed unbidden out of my own mouth: "We are what we are now and are not what we were a second ago or will be in a second from now…" Like a singer in an operatic duet, Alila plucked the next words from me and said, "And in the transformation, there is a point at which we are nothing and all three."

I stepped away; the nearness was too much, the heat, the smell of roses too thick and rich. I could not think or breathe.

"What do you want from me?"

"The question is what do you want? You called me. I didn't call you."

Another step back. "No."

"Yes."

"This is crazy."

Hoping to put distance between myself and Alila, I took another step back. But Alila was too quick for me. She reached out and held me in place by hooking a long fingernail around the leather thong that secured the magpie pendant to my throat.

"Going so soon?"

"What do you want?" I repeated, turning away from her pressing face.

"You."

"Why?"

"I already told you. I am you and you are me."

"No."

In my haste to step back, the leather cord around my neck snapped. It dangled momentarily at the end of Alila's finger, before she flung it over her shoulder, straight into the fireplace.

"You have no choice," the djinni said.

A talon nestled beneath my chin, the sharp nail digging into the skin. I tilted back my head, but Alila continued to press, a smile on her lips. Her eyes swirled like black ink in water.

The nail pierced the skin directly beneath my chin. There was a momentary sharp pain and then I felt ichor enter my system and spread rapidly through the body. The effect manifested first in the hands. The skin turned white, then blue. It calcified. The veins rose to the surface, turning purple. I felt my body ossify, from the inside out. Tissue hardened until I was rigid, imprisoned in my body, unable to move, yet fully conscious. The scream that built inside me, by degrees, turned to floating detachment. I was outside my body, pushing out, secreting…

The grin vanished from Alila's face as the process reversed. My body went back to normal, blue ichor coming out of the pores, like sweat dripping to the floor. I was still trying to understand what had happened when the magpie sat up in the fireplace. It shook itself, fluffing out the feathers in the fully grown body. Firelight licked the now white plumage as the bird fixed a gleaming eye on the djinni.

"There's more than one way to skin a cat," Alila said.

Two beats of the wings raised the bird, like a phoenix out of the flames, and made it soar through the air behind Alila. With an ear-splitting cry it pierced her with its beak through the back and emerged with a terrific burst of ichor through the chest. In a silent ballet, the djinni opened her mouth, arched her spine and bent over backwards. Her head touched the floor moments before she disappeared.

Triumphant and now covered in blue, the magpie took on the form of Jimmy Olden. There was time enough for me to note the rangy body, the eyes covered with dark hair, the thin moustache.

"You are on your own now, daughter," he said and vanished.

The room evaporated and I found myself floating high above a glassy surface. It went on as far as the eye could see. Darkness above, seething, glasslike cauldron below. Going on instinct, I allowed my body to drift. The further I penetrated into this stifling, vaporous, world, the more I realised that I was travelling at speed over molten lava. Far below, glowing magma spurted, forming giant bubbles that burst as they released trapped gasses from inside the earth. After a while, the lustrous sleekness was replaced by a rubbly drift with higher viscosity, arching its back and producing a thicker though no less heated flow. The cold was forgotten. It was now so hot I was sure to melt if I dropped lower than my current position.

This knowledge came with further understanding. I knew where I was and where I was headed. I had read about this realm in the Quran and in *The Arabian Nights*. I was headed for Mount Qaf, the legendary land of the djinn, over the eternal sea that surrounds the world. The great mountain awaited at the point where one world ends and the other begins.

At first it was a distant impression, a deeper darkness against black. Then it gained form, height, substance, volume. I did not see the mighty cities of jade and glass and of shiny emerald legend had led me to expect.

Instead, I saw millions of windows. On the other side of each pane of glass was a world of possibility. One window presented a bedroom in which a girl committed suicide by razor blade. Another window showed a room in which the same girl sat on her bed, crying, feeling sorry for herself, knowing she did not want to die. She just wanted the pain to end. She got up, went to the kitchen and wolfed down the birthday cake her grandmother had left in the fridge for later that day. And when her grandmother came home, they went out for dinner at a Chinese restaurant in town. Yet another window showed a woman sitting on the edge of a well as she drew in a bucket of water. "Don't fall in, Mummy." She did not fall in and the father came home to find his wife and daughter alive and well. He did not hang himself in prison. And nine years later his daughter did not kill herself to atone for her sins. In yet another window, Dom and I lived in a small brick house and raised a daughter with blonde hair.

On and on it went, each vista playing an endless possibility and variance. I was presented with a dizzying vision, a universe of universes, some drifting so close to each other that their edges touched, causing titanic explosions of confluence and effect.

Overwhelmed, I closed my eyes and wished they would go away.

When I opened them, a full moon floated high above. The buoyancy, the drifting, made me realise that I was underwater, hair afloat around my head.

Alarmed, I saw that I was at the bottom of a well. That was not a moon. It was the mouth of the well, distantly lodged against the sky.

This was the background against which Alila appeared, a prize beyond all searching. Here in Mount Qaf, the djinni was restored to her full glory, a colossus that soared above and below, so that her feet and her head were barely visible. She was a stupendous creation. Painted blue-black from head to toe, she possessed four arms and wore at her waist a girdle of human limbs and heads.

Horrified, I realised the heads belonged to my boys: Harun, Salih, Zaman, Rashid, Musa and Hasan. Still alive, they looked at me out of despondent black holes.

The djinni leaned forward from a great height and I saw that her eyebrows were painted red. Elaborate earrings of precious stones and gems adorned the lobes and two enormous fangs protruded from her upper lip, making her a stunning, fearsome idol. At first her radiance overwhelmed, intimidated. But Alila was also seductive, alluring, drawing everything to her.

"Come to me, my darling."

Seeing what hung from her belt, I shook my head, and that brief hesitation broke the spell. I knew how to fight this leviathan. I had to control and contain, bring everything I saw down to a manageable level.

I focused with all the power of my mind in creating a smaller, more contained space, and a room of almost human proportions began to take shape around me. It was, in essence, a giant air bubble, a high-vaulted chamber on whose gleaming floor I was but an ant.

When it was fully formed, Alila lowered her awesome bulk into a throne made of millions of dancing, flashing silver fish.

"You and I," she repeated, "are the same."

"We're not the same. I wouldn't do that to children." I gestured at the gruesome girdle.

"Really?" A peel of laughter. "The boys are food for the gods."

"You're no god. You're a psychotic bitch."

I never swore. Never used foul language. To do so was low and common, ugly and aggressive. Yet uttering the word 'bitch', as it burst from my lips, felt good. Beyond good. It was stupendous. It liberated the poisonous snake I had bottled up inside, allowing it to leap forward, to spit and bare its fangs.

"Need I remind you what you did to your beloved Dominique?" Alila went on.

"I only wished her dead. You did the rest."

"Be careful what you wish for." Alila shook her head, the dreadlocks flying around her face.

"You're not Alila, posing as my mother. You are my mother, posing as Alila."

The djinni smiled. Instantly, my mother stood in front of me, while Alila remained seated regally in the throne. My mother was naked, the width of the sensuous hips, the beautiful breasts presented without shame or embarrassment.

She opened her arms. "Come to me. All is forgiven."

I rushed to her. And it was only as the arms closed around me that I realised my mistake. I was not in my mother's arms. I was held high above the ground in the palm of Alila's hand. Colossal fingers closed around me, like steel bars on a cage.

I wailed, grabbing hold of the fingers and looking up at the djinni, knowing I could not hope to win against this colossus. I was alone. I blinked away tears and saw Adam's face etched on the back of my eyelids.

"Don't call him," I said to myself.

I tried to block the image, but it was too late.

There was a wobble in the air and the boy floated down to the floor. As soon as his feet touched the ground, he ran across the parquetry and stared up at Alila.

"What have we here?" she said, staring at him. "Boy juice." She smacked her lips and drooled obscenely.

"Let her go," Adam shouted, extending his right arm. "It's me you want."

He held the bronze medallion I had seen in the car, a scorpion with raised tail at the centre of a hexagram.

"In the name of King Solomon," Adam shouted, "I command you to put her down."

Alila froze. The seal was too strong for her. Tendons creaked in her arms as she lowered me. Sweat broke on her brow as she fought against the spell. By the time I stepped out of her hand onto solid ground, I knew the resistance had cost the djinni a great deal. The towering figure trembled as she sat up straight.

"What are you doing here?" I hissed, standing between Adam and the djinni.

"You called," he stated, tucking Solomon's seal under his tunic.

Alila grabbed the moment. At her command, an enormous black eel darted out from under the throne and, with lightning speed, surrounded Adam, tearing the medallion from his neck with razor-sharp teeth.

Unperturbed, Adam watched as the monster disappeared.

"Now," Alila said, "where were we?"

That was when I remembered the salt in my pocket. It would be soggy, but it would still have some effect on the djinni.

Alila performed a tortuous, slithery calisthenic that removed her from the throne and placed her squarely on the floor before us.

"What a troublesome larder you turned out to be," she said in an infuriatingly calm voice.

She advanced towards me and Adam, causing us to step back. As we moved away, I kept my eyes glued on the djinni and slipped my left hand in my pocket. My fingers brushed first the granules of hardened salt and then the filaments of my mother's golden hair. I blinked, remembering I had stuffed the pouch that contained them in my pocked when I left Alice Springs.

I closed my fist around salt and hair. As I did so, Adam's earlier words came to mind. He had told me how to make a talisman to entrap the djinni. You must know the djinni's name, he said, and you must have something that belongs to it.

Now that I could see clearly, the beginning of the tale to the end, I knew that Alila was an anagram of Laila. My mother's name.

"I have everything I needed at my disposal," I thought.

"Let's put an end to this," Alila said.

The smile on her lips was elusive, ambiguous, halfway between amusement and regret. Or perhaps it was acceptance. Watching her, I thought the smile could mean anything and nothing. Which just about summed up my mother. Eyes only for her husband, never for her daughter. The little girl might as well have not existed. I was insignificant. Even Alila had eyes only for Adam, looking on him with shameless hunger and exultation.

A towering, uncontrollable rage rose up inside. I wanted to scream, "I am here. Look at me. I matter, too." Momentarily, I was blinded by the desire to be seen and to be acknowledged. I wanted to hurt, to cause pain. Because that is what impotent people do. That is when people saw me. When I hurt them. When I caused injury. Arrayed before me were the boys and girls I had attacked over the years. Pulverised and bleeding as I stood over them, teeth gritted, fists clenched. I caught a glimpse of the imam in the mosque, blood seeping between his fingers. And I turned all that fury on Alila.

"No," I said.

Alila saw and she was pleased. Her eyes sparked. A vulpine smile broke on her face.

At that moment, Adam pushed me aside and rushed Alila.

"Adam, no!" I screamed, reaching out to stop him.

Too late. Adam did not get far.

Alila merged her insubstantial form with Adam's right arm so that two separate arms became one, while remaining firmly in the djinni's control.

"Let him go," I pleaded.

I might as well not have spoken for all the attention she paid me.

"You don't want him. You want me."

"What do you have to give?"

I hesitated.

Adam looked over his shoulder. "It's fine, Mags. This is how it was meant to be."

He smiled as a long talon shot out of Alila's right pointer finger and sliced open his throat. Skin and cartilage parted with an audible pop, slicing through his head and coming out the top of his cranium. Blood squirted all over the place, covering me so that I stood, gasping and holding up my hands in horror and disbelief.

Who would have thought a boy had so much blood in him?

Covered in gore, I dug into my pocket and grabbed the salt and hair.

"Enough," I yelled.

"You defy Alila?" the djinni said.

"You're not Alila. You're my mother. Your real name is Laila," I shouted, thrusting the salt and hair in her face.

Startled, Alila leaped back.

"Your name is Laila," I repeated. "In King Solomon's name I revoke your power over me."

The effect was swift.

Alila turned into Laila. She froze. Gasped. The eyes glazed. A shadow fell across the magnificent face and a great—boundless—perplexing sadness took hold as life drained from her. The uncomprehending eyes grew misty, distant, still and lifeless; as the skin turned white, hardened to the consistency of porcelain, I wondered what I had done. Having tried to kill Alila for so long, I wondered if I had the right to take the life of such a majestic creature?

I was still pondering the question, seeing nothing more than the calcified form of my mother in front of me, when the bubble I had created burst. Water rushed into the sanctuary from all sides, taking oxygen with it.

I came to my senses. The chamber was crumbling. Only not in the expected manner. The throne did not collapse with a mighty roar. The floor did not crack in noisy profusion. The high cathedral windows did not shatter with an almighty crash. Distant doorways did not crumble with a volley of sound. Instead, the chamber fell apart in silent slow-motion. No noise. It was a lament of dissolution. Not a triumphal song of destruction.

I turned to my mother.

In front of me stood a porcelain replica of the woman who gave birth to me, arms clutching her breast in grotesque parody of tragedian posture, head thrown back, mouth agape in a silent scream.

The statue teetered on the unstable floor and toppled on its back. Again, there was no sound. Only a silent pantomime.

A plume of smoke formed, like mist, above Laila's parted lips and hovered.

An obscure instinct compelled me to fall to my knees and seal my lips to hers. As I took the full force of the djinni's vapour into my body, allowing it to fill my being, I knew that the priestess Ninsar was acting through me. But I did not know if I was breathing life into Laila or if Laila was breathing life into me. When the essence ceased to flow, I fell back and breathed a deep sigh of relief.

By absorbing my mother, I became the living talisman, the prison, that will contain her for so long as I lived.

But I did not have time to revel in my triumph. I was underwater, deep inside the well in which she had drowned, and I was running out of air. My lungs were at bursting point. I had to get out or die.

When a silver disk appeared high above me, I thrust arms and legs and I shot up towards the beckoning light.

CHAPTER 45

I popped out in George Green's basement. Or was it? Momentarily, I was confused, not sure where or when I was. Maybe this was not George's cellar after all? Perhaps I was in the basement of the abandoned train station on the Oodnadatta Track? And when was I? For all I knew it was thirteen years ago, when I awoke after the suicide attempt. But that could not be right; I was wearing Dominique's clothes—the tight blue jeans and the emerald shirt. Soaking wet. Wherever or whenever I was, I told myself, the surrounds were at least familiar. The stone ceiling, the eerie wall paintings that came to life in the flickering light of an oil lamp, and the brooding shadows.

It was only when I crossed the cramped space to the base of the stairs that I realised I had been standing in what amounted to a shallow grave. With a shudder, I noted that there were seven other such graves next to it, gestating bodies in rounded bellies. My gorgeous boys, I thought. What stories you must have to tell. Silently acknowledging them, I wondered if they were destined to awaken in the future, like the other legendary seven sleepers in the cave. Was I then the dog assigned to watch over them, as stated by the holy Quran?

I ascended the stairs, emerged through a hole in the floor, and found myself inside a walk-in pantry. Peering through the partially open door, I saw George seated at the head of a wooden table in a kitchen.

"Welcome back," he said, looking up. "Warm drink?"

It looked like he had been expecting me. I nodded and took a seat opposite him.

George busied himself at the sink. I waited impatiently for him to return. More confused than ever, I was keen for him to tell me what was going on. I had been in Marree. Now I was in Alice Springs. How was that possible? George took his time, rattling cups, pouring hot water over tea leaves. If anything, he appeared to be enjoying himself. Watching him, I was struck by how young he looked. He was rejuvenated, light on his feet, compared to the man I had seen in the desert…was it two days ago? As I follow him with my eyes around the room, I saw the difference. The shoulders were relaxed, allowing the long, slender neck to hold up the bony head without tension. The face muscles were loosened, too, so that the remarkable eyes sparked.

"Here you go."

He placed a white cup and saucer on the table.

He returned to his seat and turned those amazing eyes on me. Unable to hold his gaze, I looked out the window behind him. When the rectangle of darkness became too much for me, I shifted my gaze to the clock above the kitchen sink. 1.16 a.m.

"Time has started to move again," I said. "Not stuck on 1.15 anymore."

George smiled.

It was odd sitting in that house, knowing Nan was a few minutes across town, in a hospital bed, unaware I was back. Odder still to think of Dom still petrified outside a mosque in Marree. What will the old woman, Shahrazad, think when she goes there in the morning?

"Where's Alila?" George said. "I lost track of her."

"She's not Alila. She's my mother, Laila. I should have known."

He nodded, clutching his own teacup with both hands, relishing the warmth.

"All in good time," he said, lips puckering in another smile.

"You knew."

"Of course."

"I killed her."

"Feels good, doesn't it?"

"Killing a parent does not feel good."

"I meant it feels good to face it. To accept facts."

I shrugged, pulled a face, picked my nails. "I didn't say I faced up to it. Maybe one day…"

"Small steps."

I was exhausted, tired to the core. I sipped tea and looked across at him.

"She was not a good mother, but she didn't deserve to die."

"You were a child. You were not responsible. Besides, you can't take it back. All you can do is decide how to deal with it from now on."

"She terrified me. The sound of her voice made me break into a cold sweat. I'd pee myself with fear. I hated being alone with her. I was so afraid. All the time. So afraid that, in the end, I turned her into a monster."

"She can't harm you now."

"No."

"You have your own life to live."

Trees moved in the window behind George. One or two stars glittered between tossing branches.

"The hardest part was coming to terms with what happened to Dad afterwards," I went on.

George's silence encouraged me to continue.

"He went downhill after Mum died. Nan blamed him, of course. Even after the facts came out. Dad started to drink. Got into trouble, ended up in jail, and hanged himself."

"How does that make you feel?"

"How do you think it makes me feel? I killed my parents. They are not around because of me."

George laughed. Aside from taking me by surprise, the laughter humanised him. I thought he was handsome when I met him. At that moment I saw that he was also very much a boy, no more than about twenty-three, and maybe that was why he could laugh at inappropriate things.

"Not funny," I said.

"You'd laugh if you saw what I see."

"What do you mean?"

"Your mother is not dead; she lives on in you." He stood up and pushed his chair neatly under the table. "Come with me."

I followed him along the corridors to the bathroom. Turning on the overhead light, he guided me to a mirror in a thin silver frame.

"What do you see?"

At first I saw only the face I had lived with all of my life. The wide mouth with the full lips, the skin stretched over olive cheeks, the long, slightly kinky hair falling over slender shoulders. I was very much my father's daughter, or so I liked to think.

Then I saw something else. My mother looking out of my eyes. There was no feeling, no sensation, no sudden realisation. Only an impression of another being using my eyes to examine a world she left long ago and was keen to know again.

The Water Mother turned over and adjusted herself within the limits of my flesh.

"Parents don't die," George said. "They live on in their children and in their grandchildren, and in successive generations."

"I'm their carriage to the world," I said, linking eyes with him in the mirror. "Just like Mum was my carriage to the world."

George nodded.

"What will happen now that she is in me?"

"That's up to you."

I examined myself in the mirror again. The Water Mother retreated to the optic nerve, seeking refuge in my cornea. Seconds before she faded, I was presented with two sets of teeth in my mouth, one superimposed over the other. One assemblage was small, slightly yellowed and chipped, the other white and bigger, sharper at the edges. Moments before they clamped down, cutting off access in or out of the mouth, an eye swivelled at the back of my throat, regarding the world with open curiosity. Then the teeth snapped shut, the lips closed, cutting off access.

George took me back to the kitchen and sat me at the table. He took his place opposite.

"Why is life so hard?" I said, overwhelmed by the prospect of going on.

"Life is not meant to be easy," he said, "but it can be delightful."

I rolled my eyes, made a disgusted noise. "If you're going to quote George Bernard Shaw, do it properly. 'Life is not meant to be easy, my child; but take courage: it can be delightful.'"

George smiled. "Delightful, yes, delightful."

"To which I say," I continued. "Life is not meant to be queasy. I can't forgive you for what you put me through."

George shrugged as if it did not matter to him one way or the other. "I told you that the ends justify the means."

"I mythologised my own pain, grief, anger…"

"The better to understand it."

"Was it one big, cosmic therapy session for selfish old me?"

"Isn't that the case with every story?"

"Was it real?"

He waggled an elegant right hand. "It was as real as anything can be in life."

A night bird cried outside. Starlight touched the upper reaches of the window. I covered a yawn and perhaps it was because I rubbed my eyes or perhaps because the moon's first beams chose that moment to come through the glass, but it seemed to me that George's head was transparent, so that he seemed insubstantial.

"You're going away, aren't you?"

He nodded, and perhaps there was an element of sadness in the gesture.

"My time is up," he said.

"Tell me something before you go."

"Of course."

"Where's Dom's daughter?"

"The answer lies with you."

"Don't start that again."

"But it's true."

I rolled my eyes. "I'm too tired for this."

"Where was she the last time you saw her?"

"In Dom's phone."

"What happened after that?"

"Alila turned Dom into a statue."

"O Magnolia, daughter of Laila, grand-daughter of Malachi and Kiraz," he said, using my grandmother Cherry's Arabic name, "collect thy thoughts and do whatsoever I bid thee to the minutest detail, nor fail in aught thereof—"

"I haven't got all night."

George smiled and said, "People were more patient in the past."

"Blame fast food and TV."

"Close your eyes and tell me what you see."

I did as told. My vision flooded with one object: Dominique's statue. Starlight touched the right shoulder as she pivoted, pointing a gun at a non-existent threat. She seemed terribly alone, all by herself in the desert.

"Dom," I said, opening my eyes. "You have to bring the statue here."

George sighed. In it I heard all the disappointment he felt for me. He might as well have yelled in my face, "You still don't get it, do you?" But yelling was not his style. Gentle intimation was. He stood and pushed the chair under the table, fastidious to the last.

"Sleep on it," he said.

"I don't want to sleep," I said, shooting to my feet. "We need to bring that statue here before something happens to it."

He gripped my shoulders and said, "Sleep."

A terrible lassitude swept through me. Too weary to contemplate walking to my home, let alone rescue Dom, I made my way to the nearest room and collapsed on the bed.

I awoke several hours later. Outside. Sun on my hands and face. A rock dug into my back. I sat up, spat the dust out of my mouth. Despite the early hour, it was very warm. At first, I thought I must have dreamed everything. That I was still in Marree, with Dom and the boys. Then I spotted the fences and the backs of suburban homes. I recognised the start of Rubina Street.

This was Alice Springs. The scrubland between Larapinta and the new residential development further out. But where was George's house? How did I end up outside? I stood up and brushed down my clothes. Or rather Dom's clothes—the clothes I will not give back because Dom does not need them anymore. Besides, they suited me. I was very comfortable in them.

After a futile search for George's house, I went back to Rubina Street. Far as I was concerned, the disappearing house was part and parcel of what had been happening to me the last few days. Djinns and ifrits prowling the hinterlands of my mind, resurrected children, and a mysterious man who could be in two places at the same time. Hadn't Nan's friend, Leah Unger, said the house wasn't there when she looked for it?

As my feet touched the concrete walkways of my suburb, I looked back at where George's house had stood and heard, as if coming on the wind, the words George had whispered the day I set out on this mad adventure.

"If thou wouldst be with that which thou dost seek, follow where all is fled."

The pronouncement made no sense then, but it made sense now. For the longest time, Dominique Device was the love of my life. All I wanted was to be with her and to recreate the way we had been when we were girls, going to school and coming home to steal kisses in her room. She abandoned me. But when fate sent her back, I willingly followed her out of my comfort zone, into the wilds. Anything to be with her again, even though her heart was cold as stone towards me. She had love only for her daughter, Athena. Alila turned Dom to a lifeless statue. Yet George Green intimated that life still ran in her veins. Could it be that there was still a chance for me? That I could have my cake and eat it, too?

"This should be interesting," said the djinni inside me.

I told her to be quiet. It was not time for her yet. She would have her moment in the sun soon enough.

"If I'm to be kept down," she answered, "you must keep me diverted. I demand a story."

And so I told…

<h1 style="text-align:center">CHAPTER 46</h1>

The Tale of the Woman With Raven Hair and the Girl With Flaxen Hair

It is related, oh fearsome djinni, that a woman with raven tresses lived in a town in a great desert, and she was a puzzle even unto herself. Magnolia by name, she was neither man nor woman and she stood between worlds, crossing boundaries, living and dead, black and white, and belonging neither to one nor the other.

One morning, Magnolia stood behind a tree, looking at the house in which she had lived with her maternal grandmother the greater part of her life. There was nothing remarkable about the dwelling. Hundreds like it had sprung up in Alice Springs, except that this house had an inviting porch covered with wisteria and pink clematis. Magnolia's grandmother had nurtured the garden, desiring to create a cosy, shady nook to absorb the heat of the day. She had succeeded. It was certainly the greenest garden in the street.

Even at this early hour of the morning, the air was muggy and still. As though it was holding its breath, waiting for something to happen. Clouds pressed on the suburb, promising rain.

From where Magnolia stood, she could see her battered car parked on the street. A newer, cleaner car was parked in front of it. How small and remote her own vehicle seemed after the distances she had travelled and the spectacular things she had seen. Thinking about all of it made her smile. She could not imagine going back to a normal life after such tremendous adventures.

Yet she must. This house, and one of the rooms in it, was where the story began. And this was where it must end.

Magnolia crossed the street and passed through the gate, intending to walk up to the front door and unlock it with the key in her pocket, change into clean clothes and then drive to Marree. She had to bring back Dominique's statue and find her lost daughter, Athena.

At the last minute, she was alerted by a sound coming from inside the house. Startled, not wanting to be seen, she shot across the yard, past her bedroom window, and hid down the side of the house.

Back pressed to the wall, heart racing, she peered around the corner and saw her grandmother's friend, Leah Unger, come out with a small bag. The door slammed shut behind the woman as she raced to the blue car. Leah drove off, presumably with a few necessities for Cherry's stay in hospital.

Magnolia had been standing with her back to the wall, feeling bricks and mortar beneath her fingers. Now she realised that she was touching wood. Puzzled, she turned to find a door—a door that had not been there seconds earlier.

She recalled, as if from another life, what Adam had said.

"You must open the door to myriad worlds."

With the boy's words echoing in her mind, Magnolia reached out with a trembling hand and clutched the round brass knob. She pulled open the door and gazed over the threshold into a realm that seemed to her both real and fantastical. Existing, as it did, between spheres.

To her left, teenage Magnolia bled to death in her bed. Across the other side of the room, an older version of Magnolia descended a flight of stairs cut into a wall streaming with water. The mature facsimile was covered in mud.

Astounded, recalling her own descent into the gorge when Malachi kidnapped Musa, Magnolia stepped into the room as the woman and the steps evaporated, leaving behind a blank wall.

She stood at the foot of the bed.

"Have the clocks started yet?" young Magnolia said, looking up from the bed.

Magnolia nodded.

"About time," said the girl.

She threw back the duvet and, swinging her legs over the side of the bed, stood up. Her wrists were cut and bleeding.

"Can you do something for me?" the girl said.

"If I can."

"Set me free."

"How?"

"Get me out of this room. I'm sick of being stuck here. It's no fun."

"I think we can manage that," Magnolia said, thinking of all the times she'd circled the suicide room in her mind, unable to break free. "Come with me."

Holding hands, they walked to the mysterious door in the wall and passed through it.

Innumerable paths opened before them, veering in different directions, branching, forking, going off every which way. They walked together, hand in hand, for a long time. Eventually, they came to a fork in the road.

One path led to a wide, open plain. The other to an ochre desert.

"I want to go this way," the girl said, pointing to the plain.

"I need to go this way," Magnolia said, pointing to the desert.

They embraced and parted, promising to keep in touch, even though they knew they would never see each other again. Each had her own destiny to fulfil.

Some time later, Magnolia stood in a clearing surrounded by trees that struggled out of loamy soil. Frogs chirruped in the waterhole, hidden by reeds. The shambly mosque stood to one side. In front of her was the Fiat. It seemed suddenly very dear to her, the repository of dreams and high adventure. To the right was the statue. Dominique twisted and coiled, in her final moments, with life and energy as she pointed an impotent gun at the impervious sky.

Magnolia placed a hand on the small of Dominique's back and ran it up the spine to the base of the neck. Then down again. She was as gentle and unobtrusive as possible, even though it was an intimate gesture. She had longed to do precisely this during the trip, remembering the times she had done so when she and Dominique were lovers. Running a hand up and down Dominique's spine as Dominique purred like a cat. A prelude to fumbling, giggly and often times intense lovemaking. They did it almost every day after the first kiss, as if they could not get enough.

"I know you're in there," she said now in Dominique's conch-like ear, and imagined her voice diving into the labyrinth inside to reach the still-beating heart. "I will get you out."

Magnolia stood in front of Dominique, and even thought the latter had a ferocious expression on her face, Magnolia kissed the statue on the lips, gently and with tenderness, warm lips to cold. No passion. Only love for times gone by and the kind of forgiveness that owed much of its power to plain old acceptance of a situation that had changed from one thing to another. Magnolia wanted to say, "I forgive," but she could not. Tears streamed down her face and her throat was blocked. Her heart ached.

As she stepped back, she heard a terrible sound, like the earth splitting apart. The statue's heart glowed red. A large crack ran from sternum to belly button. The interior, Magnolia saw, was pitch black, immeasurable and empty, falling back into an infinitesimal universe. Even so, Magnolia could swear she heard, over and above the birdsong and frogs of the world around her, a small, frightened sound, like a sob, or the cry of a dreamer.

Magnolia put her eye to the crack and looked inside. What she thought she saw made her catch her breath and pull away. Startled. And then with slow realisation, she approached the statue and, using both hands, pried open the bronze chest as though it was made of soft cheese.

Out popped a little girl with flaxen hair, coiled in on herself and asleep. She was three years old and wore a simple turquoise dress with short, puffy sleeves. Her bare feet showed the delicate toes of a young child.

She fell on the ground and stayed there, eyes closed. She did not even appear to be breathing.

No matter what Magnolia did, the child did not awaken from her slumber. Then she noticed the tiny hand clutching a mobile phone. Reaching into her own—or rather Dominique's—back pocket, Magnolia took out Dominique's phone and looked at the screen. Not wishing to alarm the child, she retreated inside the mosque, selected a phone number labelled *Athena* from the contact list and dialled the number. Immediately, the phone played a happy tune in the child's hand.

Athena opened her eyes, sat up, and put the device to her ear.

"Mummy," she said, "is that you?"

"Yes, baby, it's me," Magnolia lied. "Listen very carefully. I have something to tell you."

"Perfidious to the last," said the djinni inside her.

"Like mother, like daughter," Magnolia replied.

"Don't blame me. Take responsibility for your actions."

"You can talk. But I haven't finished yet."

"Go on then. What are you waiting for?"

Not long after, Magnolia strode determinedly along the hospital corridor, hand-in-hand with a little girl. They entered Cherry's ward.

"Lovely," Cherry cried. "You're back." She squirmed up in the bed and opened her arms. Magnolia fell into the embrace, closing her eyes and giving thanks for her Nan's presence in her life. When they parted, Cherry cast an eye over the little girl standing beside the bed. "And who's this gorgeous creature?"

Magnolia brought the girl forward and placed a possessive hand on her shoulder.

"This is Athena."

Cherry took in the blue eyes, the flaxen hair and the creamy complexion, and she knew immediately who and what she was looking at.

"My, my," she said in an undertone, "wherever did you find her?"

"She's Dominique's daughter."

"No doubt about that..."

Cherry's eyes flitted to Magnolia. Grandmother and granddaughter remained thus connected for several moments, the heaviness of unspoken words passing from one to the other, as Athena stood between them, luminous as an angel.

"If I can't have Dominique," Magnolia plainly stated, "I will have her daughter."

"Have it your way," Cherry said.

Both women turned on the child the full warmth of their womanly smiles, Magnolia looking on her from above, and Cherry from across the expanse of her sick bed. If a doctor or a nurse or a patient chanced to look at them at that moment, they might have seen that each woman's smile contained its own secret purpose—one ordained from the giver of the smile. And since there is only a finger's difference between a fool and a wise man, Magnolia's grin contained within its expression the naive, hopeful love of a first-time mother. While Cherry's twinkle contained a mix of pity and concern for the child's future.

"I hope you know what you're getting yourself into," Cherry said.

"I'll find out soon enough, won't I?" Magnolia said.

And so endeth, O mighty djinni, the tale of the woman with the raven hair and the girl with flaxen hair, till there came to them the Destroyer of Delights and Severer of Societies, the Plunderer of Palaces and the Garnerer of Graves.

"By the keen-eyed Kalandar," quoth the djinni great, "I have not seen, nor have I heard, the like of such perfidy."

"The apple doesn't fall far from the tree," her daughter said.

"Not so fast," the djinni cried. "Which Magnolia was that? The one who went to the right or the one who went to the left?"

"Does it matter?"

"It does."

"How so?"

"Maybe the other Magnolia does not have the nature of a hyena. Tell me what happened to the other one, for I shall not rest until I have heard it all."

`Whereupon Magnolia began the tale of…

AFTERWORD

G iven the times in which we live it was deemed necessary to include an adjunct to the novel, explaining why I wrote about an Afghan-Aboriginal woman—a sex and ethnicities to which I do not belong.

In the first place, I did not choose to write about Magnolia Din-Olden. She came to me almost fully formed and asked me—no, demanded—I tell her story. It was only when I could no longer ignore her persistence that I began to write about her fantastic adventure as she told it to me. She was of Afghan-Aboriginal descent when she appeared in my head; I did not make her thus out of political or aesthetic necessity. Furthermore, I did not know she was lesbian until five chapters into the first draft; I was as surprised as the reader might have been. So much for writerly esoterica.

Second, and perhaps this is more important, I believe that as a writer it is my duty to represent all facets of Australian life. Otherwise I would be doing writing a disservice. I cannot in all conscience write only about what I know—this being possibly the worst advice to give a writer. If that were the case, I would only write about Greek-Turkish gay men and that would hardly be worth the effort. Writing is, after all, fifty per cent empathy. Or learning to walk in someone else's shoes. If writers do not do that, they write autobiography.

As some readers know, I am of Anatolian Greek heritage and I have lived in Australia most of my life. I grew up in Turkey, an Orthodox Christian in a predominantly Muslim land. A heady combination of Greek myth and Islamic folklore were the touchstones of my early imaginative landscape, as was the knowledge that I descended from the once mighty Byzantine and Ottoman empires that stretched from eastern Europe to Afghanistan.

My family migrated to Australia when I was ten years old. We were, in essence, political and economic refugees. As a boy, I struggled to fit in and I did not relate to the largely hostile, resentful Anglos encountered in

Melbourne streets. At no time did I feel at home here, yearning to go back to Turkey. Surprising allies were found in destitute black men who lived in cardboard boxes and in well-hidden caves in the dense bush along Merri Creek in Northcote. They were funny and, given they were usually drunk, oddly welcoming of the migrant who, like them, was looked upon with suspicion by society.

Imagine my surprise when I discovered these were Australia's original inhabitants. "Interesting," I thought. "They are second-class citizens in their own country. That's how nationalist Turks treated us too."

I began to read Aboriginal histories at the school library. To my surprise I found I could relate to their belief systems, creation stories and spiritual connection to land; I felt the same way about my birthplace and many Anatolian Greeks claim their traditional land sings to them when they step on it.

As an adult, I travelled to Central Australia. Aside from falling in love with the astonishing landscape, I experienced Indigenous people and cultures up close. It was on hearing up to four different Indigenous languages spoken at various points that I had an inkling of the richness and variety that exists here.

"This is the real Australia." I thought. "Not the pseudo-European outposts that cling to the coast. This is something I can embrace and call my own."

From then on I was happy to call Australia home, synthesising the Greek-Turk with Anglo and Aboriginal Australia.

This is a long-winded way of saying every writer draws from a personal wellspring of life and experience to create literature. I cannot write a novel and ignore the pluralism that exists in my country. Pared back to the bone, *The Woman in the Well* is a metaphor for the different layers of Australian history, from Indigenous to European, all the way to Islam, which probably first came to this continent from Indonesia and later via the Afghan and Pakistani cameleers brought over by British explorers.

It is often said writers write to discover what they think about a topic. While writing this book, I realised that I have more in common with Indigenous people than differences. It is commonalities that bring people together. Besides, I will not be a party to further making Australia's original inhabitants invisible by excluding them from my stories. It is only by incorporating them that I can understand my place in this country, in relation to them. And, hopefully, vice versa.

Dmetri Kakmi, 1 August 2023

Acknowledgements

This book was written with the support of Natalija Grgorinic and Ognjen Raden at Zvona i Nari Writers' Residency in Croatia, where the second draft was completed. Thanks also to Zoltan Danyi, Dr Philip Batty, Yolande Kerridge and Angela Slatter.

www.ingramcontent.com/pod-product-compliance
Lightning Source LLC
Chambersburg PA
CBHW030612170726
48283CB00002B/570